Praise for *The Woman From Saint Germain*

'This book is a dream. Eleanor Gorton Clarke is a character
whose presence lingers long after the last page is turned.
Brave yet vulnerable, intelligent yet fiercely moral, she's a woman
of her time and ours, a heroine rarer than a first edition of
Finnegans Wake. I'd follow her anywhere.'
Lauren Chater, bestselling author of *The Lace Weaver*

'Between liberty and death you can find a fellow traveller. A
necessary murder, a race to freedom, James Joyce and a bookshop
set the stage for a tautly paced and thrilling chase that hurls
you towards a revelatory finish.' **Marta Dusseldorp**

'A thrilling game of cat and mouse and an unlikely alliance drive
a desperate race across Nazi-occupied France.'
**Tania Blanchard, bestselling author of
*The Girl from Munich***

The
WOMAN FROM
SAINT GERMAIN

J.R. LONIE

**SIMON &
SCHUSTER**

London · New York · Sydney · Toronto · New Delhi

A CBS COMPANY

THE WOMAN FROM SAINT GERMAIN
First published in Australia in 2019 by
Simon & Schuster (Australia) Pty Limited
Suite 19A, Level 1, Building C, 450 Miller Street, Cammeray, NSW 2062

10 9 8 7 6 5 4 3 2 1

A CBS Company
Sydney New York London Toronto New Delhi
Visit our website at www.simonandschuster.com.au

A catalogue record for this
book is available from the
National Library of Australia

Cover design: Christabella Designs
Cover image: Everett Collection Inc/Alamy Stock Photo
Typeset by Midland Typesetters, Australia
Printed and bound in Australia by Griffin Press

The paper this book is printed on is certified
against the Forest Stewardship Council®
Standards. Griffin Press holds FSC chain
of custody certification SGS-COC-005088.
FSC promotes environmentally responsible,
socially beneficial and economically viable
management of the world's forests.

To Alex, with love

Morning, Friday, 5th December 1941

'Well that's dead on arrival,' Eleanor growled after reading the sentence her frozen fingers had just typed out. The almost empty page winding through the spool of her typewriter, it wasn't a page at all but a naked pink tongue poking out at her, mocking and spiteful. She could have railed against the cold too, but what was the point when coal for heating wasn't to be had, even on the black market. Everyone was in the same boat and everyone said the same thing. On her feet, she wore two pairs of ugly woollen socks, although not everyone was also sheltering in a mink coat. 'A vulgar thing,' her mother had written to dissuade her from buying it. Eleanor had refused to be intimidated by such stiff New England morality. It was her money, after all, and the times had been good. Now, during the second terrible winter in a row, she was glad of it. She caught a glimpse of herself in the mirror. The contrast with the Delaunay portrait of her on the wall, painted only four years earlier, was mortifying. The tall, statuesque auburn-haired beauty in the painting gazed loftily down from that happier time to her present self, a cross between Minnie Mouse and a grizzly bear. She certainly felt as vexed as a grizzly.

She reached for a cigarette but resisted. She'd already had her morning ration of nicotine with her morning ration of coffee. She could have another before bed. Two cigarettes a day wasn't proving as difficult as she'd feared. When she'd imported them, the French customs duty had been eye-watering, but how glad she was now, because the Germans had struck only days later. Her stash would see her through this dreadful winter at least, and with luck, into the summer. After that, she'd have to smoke straw like everyone else, but that day that problem. She rubbed a smudge off the shiny red skin of the little Olivetti that Claude had bought her before the war. It was yet to produce a novel or, the way she was going, any semblance of one.

On the shelves behind her, mocking her present incoherence, were her published works in their original editions with their French, Spanish, Italian, and even Polish and Czech translations. *Walevska and Napoleon,* her first to achieve success, followed by *The Italian Serenade of Emma Michaelis,* then *The Lovers of the Île-de-France, Love in the Afternoon* and *The American Woman.* Quite a haul, if she said so herself, especially once she had begun to sell back home in America. No one could say she had been after Claude's money. She had plenty, and all her own work. Her physician father and mother had given their children as fine an education as was to be had in their neck of the woods, which was very fine indeed. But apart from a loving if narrow home life, that was it, because after raising six children even a Providence physician could afford little else.

For the first time, a man was her central character. But the real Claude, the self-made businessman, the man of action, infantry colonel and military innovator at a time of stagnation, one of de Gaulle's pals, who, had he survived, would have gone over to London too, this real Claude crowded out Eleanor's imagination. Everywhere she looked in her apartment, there he was: his tall spare frame along the sofa, his pipe still on the stand, his nightshirts in the closet with the clothes he kept for the mornings after, his hairbrush, his razor in the other bathroom, his laughter. Even the Delaunay painting, which he had commissioned, the dress she'd worn and the way she had her hair done for the sitting. They'd had such fun; their senses of humour were in harmony as much as their bodies. Best was how he had loved her. The worst, now, was the bedroom, where her ache for his touch was a torture.

She considered making more coffee – it would warm her up and might stimulate her brain – but she remained firm. The alternative was chicory and roast grain of uncertain provenance, but while she had the cash, was frugal and the black market was still providing, if at great cost, this was another problem for that day of reckoning. Work was the only way out of this slough, and she was a Rhode Islander who had the ethic in spades. So she persevered and began again, but halfway across the page she noticed that while her fingers were working the keys, no words appeared on the page. She inspected the ribbon, which disintegrated between her fingers.

'That's just dandy!' she exploded. She'd known it was on its last legs; she had been typing in hope. Like paper, typewriter ribbons were in short supply. But she was enjoying being annoyed. It provided an outlet for her many discontents and frustrations. She pushed back her chair, grabbed a fresh pack of Chesterfields, replaced the ugly socks with boots that needed repair and pulled on the fur hat that went with her coat. Then she stopped. It was one thing to wear a fur inside her apartment to keep warm, but going out in one, a mink of all things, on a mean day like today? You just didn't do that, not unless you wanted to attract envious glances and resentment – or worse, for people to suspect you might be slinging yourself around one of those blond Fritzes who had even taken over the Café de Flore and the Deux Magots. While drawing a line at the mink, she refused to go out looking like a tramp, Germans or no Germans, so put on her cashmere coat and a matching toque hat. After a quick dusting of her face in the mirror and a spray of Schiaparelli, she set out.

Eleanor lived across from the local market, on the top floor of a building at the corner of Rue de Montfaucon. Facing south on one side, its high ceiling and large windows let in the light and she never tired of its joys, even now when the light was pale and unfriendly, the sun far away and her discontents many. She owned the lease on the place, having bought it after her second success. With rugs from Constantinople, paintings from New York, sculptures and glassware from the racier galleries in London, the apartment was a log of Claude's business trips. His own home was much less exotic, he told her. His wife's taste was for the French, and high bourgeois at that.

The cold outside was all the worse for being damp. The sky was grey and low but thin, so she doubted it would snow. She hiked along Rue du Four to the shop she figured might be her best bet. The woman was, rumour had it, pally with the Germans, so it would either overflow with typewriter ribbons or be empty because they'd taken the lot.

She entered and found the place unusually gloomy and thought the woman must be saving on electricity. All the lights were off except one over the counter. Maybe the Germans weren't so pally after all. As Eleanor found out later, it turned out to be quite the opposite, which was why it was taking an age for the electrician to turn up to fix a faulty connection. Serve the treasonous bitch right.

The woman knew who Eleanor was but insisted on behaving as if they had never met.

'Typewriter ribbons? Not for love or money, madame.'

'Don't give me that,' Eleanor replied. Her French was Paris-pure, unless she was worked up, like now. At such times, she sounded a bit like the pre-war racy set of American literary tourists who if they spoke French at all, it was the French of Paris, Texas. She thrust her hand into her bag and drew out the pack of Chesterfields, which she plonked onto the counter.

'That should be worth at least ten typewriter ribbons,' she said, and damn it all, she was right.

'Alas, the Germans,' the woman said, which was the excuse for everything these days, and while it was usually accurate, Eleanor's dander was up. This woman was a liar, even when she said 'and' and 'the'.

'If you don't believe me,' her tormentor sniffed, 'you're at liberty to go to the *Kommandantur.*'

Eleanor scooped back the proffered pack of cigarettes. 'I might just do that,' she said. 'And whom should I ask for?'

The woman was furious. 'Go back to America before you run into real trouble,' she spat as Eleanor stalked out. It was ages since anyone in Paris had said that to her and never, ever anyone French – always American or English, and always male.

Eleanor strode up to the boulevard but headed towards the Odéon rather than the Saint Germain des Prés metro, not for the exercise but as a test to see if her anger would last long enough for her to go through with this escapade. And it did, lasting even as the train failed to stop at Sébastapol to allow passengers to change to the other line. No explanation, but no explanation was needed. The Boches did this all the time, suddenly closing this metro station or that. On she rode. The carriages were dimly lit and full. No one spoke, but people seemed cheerful, mostly because packed in together they were at least warm. Because the Boches travelled free and always crowded out the first-class car in the middle, they at least had a break from the occupier.

Eleanor's defiance, not so much against the Germans as against the woman at the stationery shop on the Rue du Four, began to run out of puff at Place de l'Opéra. But now she was here, she was determined to go through with it, although what she was exactly planning to go through with wasn't clear, least of all to her. Fury and resentment were enough to propel her forward. At the top of the steps out of the metro, the cold embraced her like death, and there in front of her at number 2 was Death Central itself, the *Kommandantur,* the German commandant's office. This was where all Parisians had to go for any permit or allowance, even to breathe. Hanging limp on this mean day under a mean sky, the red-and-black swastika flags in their ordered ranks looked especially sinister and intimidating. At the entrance were the occupiers in their grey steel helmets, their shiny boots and their rifles, like turds on a gold plate to Eleanor's eyes.

They were just the sight to boost her courage, or her foolishness. She seemed not at all mindful of the possible consequences of her haughty demand to see General von Stülpnagel himself. To her astonishment, this got her inside.

SHAKESPEARE AND COMPANY, 12 RUE DE L'ODÉON, PARIS VI

Afternoon, Friday, 5th December 1941

'Some major agreed to see me,' Eleanor said as she parcelled up *The Grapes of Wrath* for a Shakespeare and Company subscriber. Steinbeck was allowed by the Germans but not Hemingway, although only in English. 'I demanded he give me a permit to buy typewriter ribbons so that I could continue my work as a writer, whereupon he took out a large book, opened it presumably at the page for T or whatever the German is for typewriter ribbons and said, "No, not permitted," whereupon – ' Eleanor stopped. 'You sure you want to hear this?' she asked.

'Are you kidding?' Sylvia said.

'Whereupon,' Eleanor continued, 'I told him they were all thieves, they'd stolen not only the food from our mouths but every type-writer ribbon this side of the Rhine. He had me physically thrown out and threatened to arrest me if I ever came back, American passport or no.'

'You can be very you sometimes,' her friend Sylvia said, laughing.

'A fool?' Eleanor replied.

'No, you goose, pig-headed.'

'I've forgotten how to be me,' Eleanor muttered. 'Does anyone still borrow my books?' she asked.

'Stop being pathetic.'

These days, Sylvia's hair was streaked with grey and she admitted exhaustion from the strain of keeping the bookshop going, especially since the war began, but her face was still like a pretty bird's and her eyes remained bright and intensely curious. Eleanor kicked herself now and then for having let her fears get the better of her.

Sylvia wasn't at all intimidating. Her girlfriend was – Adrienne, whose dress and plumpness made her look like a stern abbess.

Since late '39, just after the war began, Eleanor had been coming in a couple of afternoons a week to help. The English and the Canadians were all gone, and most of the Americans. Many of the French subscribers had dropped away, although some were now returning, a token act of resistance against the invader. Germans came in, always in pairs or threes, never alone. They were like schoolboys doing something illicit, as if the shop sold dirty postcards. Few purchased anything, and they always asked if Sylvia or anyone minding the shop was a Jew. The Gestapo came regularly with the same question. Until the invasion, Sylvia had employed a Jewish girl, a Canadian, which was a black mark against her. 'We'll come for you one day,' said the Gestapo. This obsession with Jews went beyond the prejudice most French imbibed with their mother's Catholic milk. Everyone knew it was the Germans who'd set off bombs in all those synagogues two months before. The Fritzes thought the Parisians would cheer, when all it did was gain the Jews sympathy, including Eleanor's.

Sylvia wanted to put up a sign, No GERMANS ALLOWED, but with the company she kept, she was already on thin ice, and Adrienne, with her outspoken views on the Nazis and what they were doing to the Jews, even more so.

*

When Shakespeare and Company, Sylvia's English-language bookshop on the Rue de l'Odéon, opened after the first war, Eleanor had been a shy, gawping American girl with ambitions but no achievements apart from driving an ambulance for the American forces during the last year of the war. This had been her excuse to get to France. Patriotism was permitted; wanting to be a writer was not, not when you were only eighteen.

After war's end, she'd gone home to Bryn Mawr. The moment she graduated, she married a young American who also had literary dreams of Paris, and back they came on the SS *George Washington* to the City of Light, where they mixed in those heady circles that became famous. While he broadcast his dreams to whomever he met, she kept hers to herself and suffered the patronising smiles of Miss Gertrude Stein and her arty pals in silence. Eleanor had been too intimidated by them to admit her aspirations. Their haughty disdain would have driven her back to the States, and that was the last thing she wanted.

With its higgledy-piggledy shelves stashed with books, photographs of authors squashed in where there was space on the walls, chairs and large pillows, and a stove to keep the place warm in winter, Shakespeare and Company was both shrine and refuge for Eleanor, whose visits were always shy and solitary. Meantime, she wrote in secret while her lovely husband talked but never wrote a word, until she was published and he, unsurprisingly, wasn't. That was that. She'd betrayed him, so he claimed. She wouldn't go that far but still, when push had come to shove, in a choice between being married to Fred or writing, writing had won. No contest.

How she'd hurt him, he complained, how she'd broken his heart. He really had loved her. Yet, as Eleanor had countered, his love hadn't stretched to allowing her to be a writer when he had failed. Young as she was, she'd recognised that as ego. At least she got a book out of it, eventually, her most recent, *The American Woman*, and her best. It was also her most successful, helped by its brush with the Lord Chamberlain in Britain and being banned in every state south of the Mason-Dixon Line and then some, as well as causing a United States senator to call for her passport to be taken away. Even her mother had defended her against that outrage; she'd first taken the precaution of having the book explained to her by Eleanor's sister Muriel, rather than having to read it herself.

The novel's main character, Selina, had been inspired by the young American woman in Mary Cassatt's painting 'Woman with a Pearl Necklace in a Loge', which Eleanor had seen many times in a collection of one of Claude's friends. Selina is a talented artist who moves to Paris with her young artist husband, inspired by Fred, and their young child. Like Cassatt, she ignores the prejudices against women and is taken up by Degas and his circle. While her husband fails, she succeeds. Given his ultimatum, she chooses art, so he throws her out. Worse, she then scandalises Degas and his weekend bohemians by her passionate love for a young artist from Brittany, whose miraculous talent is divided in equal parts between sculpture and trouble. She finds him in La Santé prison, where he has briefly landed himself after killing a rival in love. That's the last she sees of her child.

What a dream it had been to write, in great contrast to her present creative stew. But that was before the invasion, before Claude's death.

*

Eleanor had contributed anonymously to the Friends of Shakespeare and Company, which was set up to keep the shop open during the tough times after the Depression. She'd taken another couple of years to own up to her contributions. She knew what jolly old Gertrude and Miss Toklas, with her moustache and pickled mouth, said about her books, although they'd never read them, and of the opinions of the other literary and artistic Americans who moved excitedly around the Left Bank like raptors from the future. They dismissed her as a mere woman's writer, which meant not a real writer at all.

When *The American Woman* was published, oh how they and their critic pals had erupted. 'Karenina gets away with it,' bellowed literary headlines filled with the rage of these standard-bearers for the rights of women. 'Karenina lives happily ever after!' How dare Selina choose artistic calling over husband and child; how dare she run off with a killer? How dare they love and live and make beautiful art? Just as infuriating, how dare Eleanor make so much money out of it? They, her critics, refused even to grace her with her name. She was just 'that woman from Saint Germain', with all its inferences, cheap and trashy being among them.

Their sneers hurt, as sneers always do.

But hang it all, she was, along with the great Gide, a supporter of Shakespeare and Company, and, like Gide, with money she'd earnt herself, not from some trust fund. Eventually, she owned up to her contributions, only to discover that Sylvia had known but respected her evident desire for anonymity. She also discovered that Sylvia was blessing her endeavours by stocking and lending her books. 'You're popular,' she explained. This wasn't meant in a back-handed way. 'My customers are intelligent, they know good writing. And darling,' she added, 'I make money out of you.'

*

'I'd write in blood on the walls if I had anything to say,' Eleanor groaned that afternoon.

'Now you really are being pathetic,' Sylvia scolded.

'Maybe it's time I went back to the States.'

'Scandalous-writer-turns-prodigal-spinster,' said Sylvia. 'I can see the gloating headlines in Providence now.'

'Come now,' Eleanor laughed. 'Wayward, perhaps.'

'You were a married man's mistress,' Sylvia reminded her. 'Twice divorced before that.'

'Once, strictly speaking,' Eleanor corrected. One divorce was enough of a scandal in her family's circle back home, even though she hadn't asked for it nor done anything to deserve it, other than put her head above the literary ramparts. Becoming a married man's mistress, common enough in Paris, only confirmed her status as the Gorton black sheep.

'You should have an affair,' Sylvia enthused. 'Twelve months of mourning is too long. Eighteen months is egotistical. Affairs revive the creative juices.'

'I've thought of that,' Eleanor drawled, 'but the current opportunities are all dishonourable. It's the only way I really would become a black sheep.'

The bell tinkled as the door opened. Sylvia and Eleanor, who had gone to the tiny kitchen to make tea, were startled because they had been their own company since the shop opened at two.

'Oh no,' Sylvia muttered as she looked at the mirror placed strategically to show the door.

A mangy ankle-length fur had entered, out of which poked a face that looked like a malevolent pear with two bulbous studs for eyes and wearing a toque hat. This was Hester Rosen, a cast-iron leftist of indeterminate age, originally from New York, who, with a family fortune behind her, bought rather than borrowed books from Shakespeare and Company. For her causes, she bought big. She didn't believe in make-up and it wasn't so much that she disbelieved in manners as had no patience for them. She banged the bell on the side shelf imperiously.

Eleanor still had just enough of her dander up to spare Sylvia the encounter. She pasted on a smile and emerged from the tiny kitchen.

'Why, Miss Rosen, what a pleasant surprise,' she said with gay insincerity.

'Where's Miss Beach?' Hester Rosen demanded.

'She's busy at the moment. May I help you?'

'I want Miss Beach to order in ten copies of *Native Son*.'

Eleanor could scarcely believe it. Talk of being in denial about what was going on around her. Was it senility? 'Shakespeare and Company hasn't been able to get American books in since the German occupation, Miss Rosen,' she replied.

'Well, where am I to get them?' Miss Rosen snorted. 'This is very annoying.'

'Maybe the library at the Russian embassy has had better luck with our occupiers,' Eleanor said with sweet venom, and she imagined she could feel the draught from Sylvia's gasp of breath behind the kitchen curtain.

'If you mean the Soviet embassy,' Hester Rosen replied haughtily, 'the Union of Soviet Socialist Republics has broken off relations with the collaborator regime in Vichy, unlike the government of the United States.'

'Oh, that's right,' said Eleanor. 'And the Soviets used to be such pals with the Nazis until the recent unpleasantness.'

Miss Rosen looked Eleanor up and down, as if preparing her for the firing squad. 'You're still working here, Miss Clarke,' she said, momentarily disarming Eleanor by remembering she had a name, even if it was only the latter half. Eleanor replied that she liked to help Miss Beach now things were so precarious, which they were.

'Isn't that just peachy of you?' Miss Rosen began her retaliation, her eyes bulging with malice and mischief. 'I suppose you have nothing better to do. How long is it since you had a book out?'

It was early 1939 but Eleanor kept quiet so as not to give Hettie any ammunition.

'Oh well,' continued Miss Rosen, undeterred, 'you shouldn't be surprised. Art does imitate life, and the well of bourgeois fantasy you rely on has long dried up. Still, I can't think the masses or American literature will be the poorer. Such a pity all those marriages of yours didn't work out. There was a child, wasn't there?'

'Miscarriage, and only one marriage,' Eleanor growled, hoping common decency might shut Miss Rosen up.

It didn't. 'What a pity,' she continued. 'You would have had lots of children to look after by now instead of sitting around watching history pass you by. A good day to you.'

Sylvia appeared as the bell tinkled and Miss Rosen's mothy fur exited the front door.

'How about that,' Eleanor said, tears welling. 'I thought I wasn't able to write because of the German occupation, but now I realise Hettie Rosen and her coven of reds have put a curse on me.'

She felt something in her hand. Looking down, she saw a fresh typewriter ribbon that Sylvia had curled her fingers around.

'On one condition,' Sylvia said and made a typing motion with both hands. 'I don't believe in writer's block or covens or curses or having babies.'

Eleanor did weep, but briefly; this wasn't the sort of place a writer should cry, even in these bad times. She dabbed her eyes and kissed Sylvia on the cheek and again regretted those years before she'd been brave enough to open her mouth.

'Blow the tea,' she said, 'we need a whisky.' She fossicked in her bag for the small flask she carried to ward off the cold. 'Just a swig. My supply has to outlast the Nazis.'

Neither really believed it would, but you said this sort of thing because you wanted to believe it. They looked at each other with an empty-handed gesture bordering on despair.

Before Eleanor could retrieve her flask, the bell announced another arrival. A sleek middle-aged German officer in grey uniform nodded, smiled and wished them a good afternoon. He removed his cap, which he tucked under his arm, and announced himself with a slight, debonair bow as 'Gunther Krolow at your service' – not Herr Major Krolow and none of the heel-clicking they usually went in for. He clasped his hands and looked around the bookshelves with a sense of pleasure such that out of the uniform of the conqueror, he might have been one of those fresh-faced, blue-eyed Americans stepping for the first time into their longed-for literary Mecca. But each of the women saw only that uniform, you could hardly ignore it, and wondered if this wasn't the promised visit to take Sylvia away, with a postscript for Eleanor that her morning's foolishness at the *Kommandantur* might have landed her in hot water.

'You have a copy of *Finnegans Wake* in your window, madame,' he said in excellent French. 'I wish to buy it.'

'I'm afraid not,' Sylvia replied briskly. 'It's not for sale.'

'May I ask why not?' he said politely, although you could tell he was not only surprised but hurt.

'It's my only copy,' Sylvia explained.

'But you have it in your window,' Krolow said, toning back his sense of pained entitlement.

'Yes, as a sign of what we stand for,' she said. 'In any case, I doubt you would understand it.'

'But we admire James Joyce very much in Germany,' said Krolow, ignoring the provocation and adding a pleasant we're-all-literary-people-here smile. He was going to argue his case. From his leather satchel, he produced a copy of *Ulysses*.

Sylvia and Eleanor could see it was a first edition.

'Published by you, madame,' he said proudly, offering his treasure as his credentials. Sylvia didn't even look as if she would take it, so he handed it to Eleanor. 'I like to think of myself as quite an expert on your Mr Joyce. I have collected first editions of all his books except *Finnegans Wake*. I would be willing to pay any amount.'

'It's not for sale,' Sylvia persisted, unmoved.

'I am so very disappointed,' he said. 'Are you quite sure?'

'I am,' said Sylvia obdurately and he sighed. He took back his copy of *Ulysses* from Eleanor and said, switching into perfect English, 'Is this not Miss Gorton Clarke?'

Eleanor was mute with astonishment.

'My wife is a great admirer of your work,' he said. 'She of course must read you in English or French. Your work is still a little risqué to appear in German.'

'What on earth would your Doctor Goebbels make of *Finnegans Wake*, then?' Sylvia blurted out. It was the obvious question. Eleanor held her breath.

'He personally would approve,' said Krolow, continuing in quite mellifluous English, 'but for the larger good at the moment, he cannot make exceptions until we bring this dreadful war to a conclusion.'

He saw the look of incredulity on Sylvia's face. 'You misunderstand him, madame,' he said, reverting to French. 'Like me, he is an educated man. He understands Joyce's literary quest, which of course is metaphysical. And after all, the character Bloom is the quintessential Jew, at the end of his line of evolution, is he not? Replaced by Boylan, the lusty, stronger Aryan?'

He was giving what he thought was his best shot. Sylvia, used to bizarre commentaries about *Ulysses* – though, as she would say later, this was possibly the most bizarre – wished him a curt good afternoon and even held the door open for him to leave, which he did and without any of the courtesies he'd used on arrival.

Once he was gone, Eleanor quickly poured a generous drop of whisky into each of their cups. They deserved it. They deserved a cigarette too, and to hell with her self-imposed rationing.

'His copy of *Ulysses* is freshly procured,' Eleanor said. She'd noticed the Rothschild ex libris on the inside cover. It was probably from the library of Baron Maurice, who had racier tastes than his cousin, Baron Édouard, and whose collections had been found recently, hidden near Lourdes. They'd been immediately purloined by Vichy only to be plundered by the Nazis.

'No wonder he wants your copy of that book,' she said.

'I guess I should be relieved he asked and took no for an answer,' Sylvia said.

'You're lucky I saw he'd filched his *Ulysses*,' said Eleanor. 'If I'd been here by myself, I would have sold your precious last copy of *Finnegans Wake* for a sou, even to a Nazi.'

Sylvia laughed and made a long sound that began with *baba* and was followed by an unbroken disjunction of consonants. On the page, the word, allegedly the longest in English – if it was English, which Eleanor disputed – was *bababadalgharaghtakamminarronnkonnbronntonner-ronntuonnthunntrovarrhounawnskawntoohoohoordenenthurnuk!*

'That's what God said when he discovered Adam and Eve had eaten the apple. Page one,' Sylvia had told Eleanor in one of her attempts to persuade her to read *Finnegans Wake*. 'You go to church every Sunday, that should appeal to you.'

'I'm an Episcopalian, darling. Going to church every Sunday is a civic duty,' Eleanor countered, flippantly disguising her stubborn adherence to her childhood faith. James Joyce was a rebellious Irish Catholic as far as she was concerned, which accounted for everything – his creativity, which she acknowledged, although on advice, and his crackpottery.

Since the war began, saying the word was now Sylvia's little joke with Eleanor when things were going wrong, a way to lighten prospects that seemed forever dim. She was the only person in the entire world who knew how to pronounce it and, Eleanor was sure, the only one who commonly did.

'How does he know who we are?' Sylvia asked.

'He's a major in the security service,' replied Eleanor, for whom this was obvious. She wasn't a writer for nothing. She'd noticed the

Sicherheitsdienst SD diamond patch on the sleeve of his well-tailored grey uniform, and through the window, she'd seen his car parked out front, stolen from its French owner, probably a Jew. She thought everyone in Paris knew those markers by now.

'Actually, dear,' she said, 'I doubt he will take no for an answer.' She had seen the anger in Krolow's eyes as he'd left, his jaw like concrete.

Morning, Sunday, 7th December 1941

Since the arrival of the Germans and the departure of the dean, services at the American cathedral had been held in the adjoining tiny parish hall, led by the cathedral organist, Mr Whipp. The congregation, smaller of course, didn't look as diminished in the hall, which also had the advantage of a fireplace. Each Sunday, Eleanor kept noticing one or two fewer parishioners – no warning, gone, just another empty chair. This caused the stayers to question their own wisdom but at the same time allowed them to feel morally superior in sticking it out. They were, they said to one another, like one of Paul's congregations surrounded by hostile pagans of every variety. They did what they could, raising money for those among them who were in trouble financially; making a separate fund for foreign Jews in the city, who really were in greater trouble than any of them would ever be; looking in on the elderly and the sick and raising money for the American Hospital.

When the war started, the raptors from the future, the literary set with their moral certainties at sea because of the Soviet–Nazi pact, fled abruptly, as if the Black Death had arrived, though it didn't really arrive until June 1940. Only then did the American colony begin to shrink to those like Eleanor and Sylvia, whose loyalties were of heart, family and moral obligation; or like Mrs Gould and her set, who, with their husbands' money, had the Germans to dine; or like Hettie Rosen and her gang, who, since Hitler had turned on their hero Stalin, were, in Eleanor's opinion, proving how insane they were. Like Eleanor, they were protected only by their American passports and the red seals the US embassy had affixed to their front doors.

Eleanor was hardly naïve. Sure, at the time of Munich, she'd felt immense relief. She'd seen with her own eyes in 1918 what happened in war, and if giving Hitler the Sudetenland kept the peace, give it to him. It was full of Germans, after all, and if they were stupid enough to want to live under Hitler, good luck to them. When finally war came and Claude was called to his regiment, she'd tried to join the ambulance corps, but this time around there wasn't room for smart girls from America with driver's licences and their own ambulances, especially those like Eleanor, who was no longer a girl. She didn't feel at all American, she felt French. They'd sung the 'Marseillaise' at the bar in the Pigalle where she and Claude had gone the night before he left for his duty. Going back to the States then would have been a betrayal and dishonourable. Her mother and father had constantly pressed her to return. During her last trip back, in the summer of '39, when she knew what was likely to happen, the thought of staying hadn't crossed her mind – even when her parents tried emotional blackmail about each having one foot in the grave, which they most decidedly did not. She'd always enjoyed their visits, and hers to them, but she also enjoyed having the Atlantic between them. Now, she couldn't even write to them or receive letters, a loss she felt quite keenly. They, she was realising with some dismay – her parents, her two sisters and three brothers – had been the rock to which she'd kept her allegedly bohemian self firmly tethered.

If you were a stayer, what you thought would happen if or when the United States entered the war depended on whether you were an 'if' or a 'when'. The 'ifs' said it would never happen again, and even though wicked FDR clearly wanted it, Congress would stop him. Eleanor started the war as an 'if'. But Claude was killed and France occupied, which bound her even more strongly to stay. The Nazis had placed terrible restrictions on the Jews, and only the other day they'd shot Jews as hostages. She knew evil when she saw it. She'd always voted Republican but now she was a 'when'. The Germans had interned all the British and Canadian women, so she knew the fate that awaited her. But truth to tell, she was like so many others, becalmed – hoping for the best, expecting the worst.

If cutting and running in September 1939 or June 1940 would have been a betrayal, now it was difficult because the Germans had recently forbidden all foreigners in occupied France from going to the Vichy zone at all. Short of joining the missing in a daring escape across the Vichy demarcation line, she was trapped and she knew it.

During the homily that morning, Eleanor drifted back to Sylvia calling her a scandal. If she was a scandal, she was a pretty poor example of one in a congregation that before the war had included the Duchess of Windsor. The characters in her novels were much more scandalous and adventurous than she had ever been. Each had risked everything for love – their happiness, their reputations, even their lives. Looking around the hall that morning, it also dawned on her that she was now the congregation's chief plutocrat as well, when before the war they'd had real ones. This really was a joke.

At the end of the service, Mr Whipp played a Bach cantata on the piano, which kept everyone in their seats with the joy of it and Eleanor's forebodings at bay. The visit of that SD officer to Shakespeare and Company on Friday had rattled her more than she at first admitted. She, who didn't have a superstitious bone in her body, thought his intrusion a bad omen.

Afterwards, Eleanor walked down to the metro on the Place de l'Alma, carefully avoiding the patches of ice lurking across the footpaths. Remains of the light snow that had fallen during the night still dusted windowsills and architraves. The morning was so quiet she could hear her footsteps through the still air. No traffic at all; not even the Germans were about. Along the riverbank, fishermen were out in such numbers she wondered the Seine had any fish left.

She'd certainly eaten none of it. What did hearten her, though, was seeing a small group of students over on the quay painting at their easels, a sight that had charmed her when she'd first come to Paris and still did. On closer inspection, she was dismayed to find they were in the grey-green uniforms and caps of the Wehrmacht, soldiers having their *einmal in Paris* experience.

Curious, she got close enough to see if any talent was on display. To her great surprise, one of the boys – and they were boys – whose face was quite sensitive and startlingly handsome, was making something light and dreamlike of the wintry grey quay with the Eiffel in the background outlined in snow, not as subject but as a signature in the form of Chinese calligraphy. He caught her in momentary admiration of his work and he blushed. Eleanor apologised for intruding. In reasonably fluent French, he replied he was not much good but hoped one day he might be. Against every instinct, she immediately recognised him no longer as an occupier but a human being, a fellow artist at that.

She had steeled herself against such encounters: no eye contact, no discussion. They were there, she couldn't avoid them, but she'd have nothing to do with the army that had killed Claude and taken over the city she loved, her home. But here it was, she couldn't help it. She also couldn't help discovering they could be human. She wished him all the best with his work, excusing her lapse on Christian charity. As she walked away, she looked back, not at the painting but at him. Christian charity, my fat aunt, she scolded herself the instant she realised what she was doing. She'd admit to desire for the male lovers in her novels, and Claude, whom she desired most of all. But they were imagined or dead, like Claude, while here she was lusting after one in the flesh – and worse, a mere youth, and even worse than that, a Boche. She hurried towards the metro, almost forgetting to buy the flowers she needed.

The choice was limited – delicate snowdrops, some flowering quince, winterberry and Christmas roses – but given the early winter, any colour was welcome. Besides, flowers seemed to be the only things in relatively good supply.

Eleanor remarked on this to the flower seller.

'The Boches don't go for flowers,' the woman replied, matter-of-fact, which nicely fed Eleanor's attempt at working up a temper against the Germans. Really, she was seeking an antidote to her addling urges.

AUVERS-SUR-OISE, VAL D'OISE

Late morning, Sunday, 7th December 1941

Eleanor's journey out to the little village beyond the north-western edge of the city took twice as long as usual, for no apparent reason. As she walked through the narrow streets to the Church of Our Lady, the clouds dissolved and the sun appeared, thin and pale. Usually, the graveyard was busy with the curious and the reverential visiting the famous artist buried here but today the place was strangely empty, except for two small children, a boy and a girl, about three and four years old, playing among the headstones. Their laughter was infectious and Eleanor smiled as she watched them for a moment or two before she continued along the path to Claude's grave.

As she approached, she came to a sudden stop. In a vase on his grave was a generous bunch of fresh cyclamen. Eleanor was surprised. Claude's family usually came in the afternoons. She did not relish a possible encounter. Then she saw a woman standing in contemplation nearby, not one of the family but vaguely familiar. She looked to be in her mid-thirties, was hatless, her hair brown and lustrous, and she had a simple face, not pretty but kind, and now a study in sadness. The children ran up to her – 'Maman, maman,' a race to be in her embrace – and the woman's sadness fled. She laughed and held them, and they laughed.

Eleanor caught her breath as she realised who this woman was. She looked away, as if intent on a grave in another direction. When she looked back, she saw the girl slip from her mother's grasp and kiss Claude's headstone and the boy did that too, if awkwardly. He had to stand on his toes to reach the spot where his sister had kissed.

*

In June of the previous year, the whole country had been grief-stricken for the soldiers who had fallen beneath the Nazi blitzkrieg. Thousands and thousands of them. It infuriated her that the British still thought the French forces hadn't put up a fight. To those old enough to remember, it had been as bad as 1915, when the church bells never stopped tolling. Claude was killed at the battle on the river Aisne, where the French had outfought the German panzer divisions, a victory now forgotten in the awful malaise of defeat and occupation. His had been a heroic death, a shining light, although hardly so to the three women in his life, especially when two of the three had believed that she was unique.

A widow inviting her husband's mistress to his funeral wasn't unusual, but to encounter another mistress, known to the widow but not to each other, was highly charged, even for France.

Until the burial in the graveyard of the family church, Claude Fournier's wife and his mistresses all played their roles with dignity. As did his three children, the eldest now eighteen, none of whom Eleanor had met or had ever given much thought to. She couldn't help seeing Claude in each of them – eyes on the girl, mouth on the eldest boy, ears and nose on the middle child, another boy – enough to upset her composure as each brushed their cheek to hers.

The widow, who was older than Eleanor, had not gone that far, just the touch of gloved fingers passing for a handshake. Eleanor had been determined not to avert her gaze; it was time they looked each other in the eye, wife and mistress. If not now, never. The widow had looked right back at her. Their veiled eyes met and glistened. Shared grief or resentment or even triumph on the part of the widow, Eleanor hadn't been able to tell – and really, did it matter? Madame Fournier was the widow and had Claude's children. Eleanor had no title or children, just memories. What mattered more to Eleanor was the other woman, but her determination to see the face of this surprising presence, let alone her eyes, was thwarted by the woman's hasty departure before Claude was even lowered into his grave. Had she quailed at being received by the widow? Or was it the shock of discovering she had been but one in a *ménage à quatre*? Whatever the answer, in fleeing, this third woman had left a gap in a circle of reconciliation, superficial as it may be, and never to be joined.

*

In the graveyard, Eleanor retreated, winded. She was the intruder, she felt. She realised who was unique and who was not – at least, in her misery that's the way she was thinking. The reasons she conjured up for the difference were unflattering to her. No wonder this woman had left Claude's funeral. She'd had his two babes at home awaiting her embrace.

'Oh God,' Eleanor said out loud. How this stabbed at her. Yes, Claude had asked her more than once if she'd wanted a child, but it had never occurred to her that he had been asking for himself. He had three children already. Yes, before Claude, she'd had that miscarriage to a French louse and that had been painful and sad, but then her second book had catapulted her into the ranks of real popularity, and soon after she'd met Claude. What more had she wanted? Her brothers and sisters had produced grandchildren enough for her parents, and she delighted in each of them when visiting or when they visited her, but she'd not felt the call of motherhood herself. She and Claude dined regularly, he made love to her, sometimes luncheon on Saturdays, the theatre and the opera now and then because his wife didn't go for it, and after she'd become a pal of Sylvia, he came with her to the soirées. Had he offered her a gift, the gift of motherhood, which she had rejected? Now here they were, these two children that might have been hers.

Did she really mean that? She didn't know what she thought.

She fled the church and went straight back to the railway station, just managing to catch the train as it returned to the Gare du Nord. She would be on time for lunch at the apartment of her pal Madeleine. At least she might get drunk.

'Well, dear,' said Madeleine, once Eleanor explained her mood, 'you've been well and truly out-mistressed, haven't you? No wonder you're angry.'

'I'm not angry,' Eleanor protested. 'I'm heartbroken.'

'Of course you're angry,' Madeleine said. 'You've been angry since the funeral.'

Eleanor thought she'd been in grief, but like a djinn's curse, once out, what Madeleine had said couldn't be unsaid.

'I'm surprised you of all people hadn't wondered,' she continued. 'I mean, if a man can have one mistress, why not two? One with children, one without.'

The answer to that was simple. Writers never placed their real lives under the microscope reserved for their fictional characters. They thought they did, but what they looked at and what they saw was rather like the wicked witch with her 'mirror, mirror on the wall'. And Eleanor was nothing if not vain, a quality she shared not only with Madeleine but with Aphrodite, whose symbol, after all, was the looking glass. Eleanor felt no shame in her goddess, even if it did lead to some blind spots.

Madeleine, whom she'd known since their days driving Red Cross ambulances at the battle of Saint-Mihiel during the Great War, ran an irregular sort of salon with her mouse of a husband, a librarian. He was a royalist, which was of little consequence compared to the fact that he was rich and a count of the pre-Napoleonic kind, giving Madeleine a certain cachet when shopping. Eleanor always enjoyed these Sunday gatherings because she was Madeleine's only real writer and her opinions, in the manner of the French, were listened to with respect.

Political representation, though, had fallen off: the Catholic right had decamped to Vichy and the Free French to London, leaving only a couple of royalist pals of the mouse, who despised the reactionaries that were now infesting the soirées hosted by the German ambassador. As for the left, since Hitler had turned on their chief sponsor, the Soviets, they were carrying on their intellectual and literary pursuits as if the unpleasantness around them was merely a change in the weather. Eleanor, as an American, officially a neutral, felt she was hardly different, another flame to the fire of her current discontents.

Sunday luncheons were a rare pleasure now. You could only do it if your guests shared some of their ration tickets, though Madeleine's mouse had close family connections in Bordeaux. Even then, Madeleine's cassoulet wasn't able to run to any duck, not even a stringy chicken. She'd made do with beans, some root vegetables and some sausage, but since Madeleine could make stones taste delicious, Eleanor had no trouble asking for seconds. The supply of good Bordeaux helped, which was just what she needed to dull the pain in her heart and the fury in her blood. The talk was all about what one could or couldn't buy, and where one might buy it on the black market, and how disgusting black marketeers were, and how one should as a principle boycott them.

'Not while I've got a face and my last franc,' Eleanor muttered, her only contribution to this conversation she was finding tedious.

Then someone said, 'But my, aren't some of the Boches incredibly handsome?' This caused a great philosophical quarrel that animated even the mouse, whose patriotism was offended. Eleanor stayed out of it. Had she not had a civilised encounter with one of the handsome occupiers that morning, exposing her desire all too clearly, the more unsettling because he was so young? She took another glass of wine and sank back into the sofa to indulge her grievances. At least she forgot about the Nazi security officer.

RUE DE MONTFAUCON,
SAINT GERMAIN DES PRÉS, PARIS VI

4.30am, Monday, 8th December 1941

Eleanor slept fitfully. At some time during the night, she thought she heard a baby crying. In those mysterious moments between sleep and waking, she was sure of it, yet the instant she was awake, she heard only silence. It was not the sort of dark silence that would frighten a child, for while she heard no echo of what had drawn her out of the depths of sleep, this silence was so sharp and intensely bright, her skin tingled and her mind buzzed with curiosity. She lay in wonder, but as the dark quickly became cold and unfriendly, wonder was overwhelmed by remembering what had happened at Claude's grave, clearly the cruel genesis of this vivid and unsettling dream.

In the distance, she heard what sounded like a shot. You could hear the footfall of an ant it was so quiet at night since the Germans came, but better an ant than gunfire. If it was someone taking a pot-shot at a German, they would take hostages and murder them. She switched on the lamp and read until she dozed, but she didn't really sleep properly so was easily disturbed by the loud knocking on her door.

She could hear the urgent voice of her concierge through the racket, 'Madame, madame.'

When she opened the door, he and his wife both fell through as if fleeing a visit from the police, or worse, the Gestapo.

'Have you heard the news?' Mr Teixeira said in his Portuguese-accented French.

'I heard it first,' his wife interrupted and pushed him aside. 'You were asleep. Let me tell her.'

As they bickered, Eleanor noticed the clock. Four-thirty am.

'Japan has attacked America at Pearl Harbor,' Mrs Teixeira reported. 'A big attack – the American fleet is destroyed.'

'At last!' Eleanor cried out in English. This wasn't how she'd thought it might start, except she'd hoped it would – how else could the Nazis be defeated? Then she remembered her youngest brother, Will, the family pet. He was an officer in the army, stationed where she did not know. Her nephew Tom had gone into the marines last year, and she thought of all the mothers and their sons, and she was ashamed by her elation. But elated she was. She'd been as if in the grip of a boa constrictor that was just taking its time to squeeze the life out of her and now, suddenly, it had released her.

12 RUE DE L'ODÉON, PARIS VI

Around 5am, Monday, 8th December 1941

'I'm getting out,' Eleanor said to Sylvia after abruptly waking her. Daylight was still hours away, although the clocks, on Berlin time thanks to the occupiers, didn't think so.

'The curfew,' Sylvia murmured sleepily.

Before the curfew was lifted, Eleanor had left home with the Teixeiras, who were going to early Mass at Saint Germain de Prés for the Feast of the Immaculate Conception, and if the occupiers along the boulevard objected to them breaking the curfew, Mrs Teixeira was quite prepared to direct them to the Blessed Virgin herself. Eleanor had au-revoired them downstairs and then slipped around the deserted back streets, encountering only the carts going to and from the market, the horses' droppings steaming on the cold stones behind them like tiny exploding bombs. The market had just opened, though God knows why, she thought – they only had rutabaga to sell.

Ever since she'd seen how swiftly and without warning the Germans had swooped on the Canadian and British women, Eleanor had kept a valise packed with cosmetics, underwear, socks and woollens. She did not want to be caught unprepared. Now that the unoccupied zone rather than an internment camp was her immediate destination, she really only needed to get money, lots of it, and a *passeur* who would take her across the demarcation line for a fee. She'd heard figures from 50 francs a head to 500. Some even did it for free. Her anger and sadness had lifted, as had the listless apathy about her life, which showed all too clearly the self-indulgent rut she'd been in. She felt young again and excited by the prospect of flight.

'But the United States isn't at war with Germany,' Sylvia said to her.

In Eleanor's opinion that was a matter of days. She had no time to lose and neither did Sylvia. The Germans hadn't been handing out passes to foreigners to cross into Vichy since October. They certainly wouldn't be handing out any now, especially to Americans. She bubbled to Sylvia about having received the names of two possible *passeurs* from her concierge, behaving as if they would be leaving before the day was out.

'I can't go,' Sylvia said, bringing Eleanor down to earth. 'You know that.'

'You'll be interned in a camp!' Eleanor exclaimed. 'What good can you do there? We can do war work at home.' She had no idea what war work she'd do; she imagined it would be useful, whatever it was. 'We speak French like a native, after all,' she said. 'Soldiers and sailors need books. Besides,' she added with flourish, but really she was babbling, 'growing up with three brothers, I can shoot a rifle and a pistol.' Yet none of this mattered. The pull of country and family at war was all that mattered. What was keeping her here? While she wasn't ready to admit it, her upsetting discovery at Claude's grave had loosened what she'd thought was the tie that bound her to stay for the duration. Before, it seemed dishonourable for her to leave. Now it was her path of honour.

Sylvia said she'd talk to Adrienne, so they arranged to meet again at one o'clock.

'Pack a bag,' Eleanor cautioned and added a checklist of essentials.

'In one suitcase?' Sylvia said, incredulous, but Eleanor said firmly, 'Darling, if I can, you can.'

MONTPARNASSE, PARIS XIV AND XV

Around 8.30am, Monday, 8th December 1941

Eleanor walked up to the Saint Germain metro and caught a train to Montparnasse. She found the place, an electrician's shop near the railway station. To the enquiry from a red-faced woman at the counter, she replied that no, she didn't have anything to repair, she wanted to get into Vichy as soon as possible, which was clearly the wrong answer, because the red-faced woman said the shop was closed.

'The door's open. The sign says "Open",' Eleanor countered.

'You shouldn't blurt out what you just asked,' the woman relented. 'It's dangerous.'

Eleanor apologised for not sticking to the niceties, but she didn't have time; if she didn't get cracking, she might end up in a German internment camp.

The red-faced woman sniffed. 'Couldn't be worse than the one we're in now,' she said. 'But things are too hot at the moment.' Everyone already knew about Pearl Harbor, and if this wasn't making the Boches nervous, too many Jews were trying to get out, and what with the Wehrmacht canteen having been shot up, the shits were shooting first, no questions asked, and they were everywhere.

'Come back next week,' she suggested. 'Things might have cooled down.'

Eleanor saw she was wasting her time when she had none to spare. Her second chance was a café in the fifteenth arrondissement, along Garibaldi, only a couple of stops from Montparnasse. 'Ask one of the waiters,' Mr Teixeira had told her. She debated walking or taking the metro. What decided her was hearing hobnailed boots suddenly start running in her direction, that grating unmistakeable tocsin of the occupier up to no good. The next moment, as she turned to descend into the metro, she saw them, helmeted and armed, running onto the station's main concourse from a line of trucks that had just pulled up. She wondered if the US and Germany were already at war and these troops were about to pick off fleeing Americans.

The tension suited Eleanor. It made her think more clearly. She found the café without any trouble.

'It's right next to a brothel,' Mrs Teixeira had gleefully told her.

That was obvious enough because Eleanor saw German soldiers coming out of a nondescript double-storeyed building right next door. She went into the café, as much to avoid the Germans as the morning cold on yet another grey, mean day, but then if there weren't three Germans in uniform at a table by the window. She had no choice. She sat. A young waiter came over, just another kid; the Germans were still hanging on to most of the French soldiers they'd interned.

Eleanor had been so agitated by the news that morning and so determined to get herself organised that she had left her apartment forgetting to eat, and worse, to drink her morning coffee and smoke her morning cigarette. She was now giddy. She decided to try her luck and ordered the coffee she would have asked for in normal times. This café was patronised by the occupier, so they probably had a good supply of the real thing, as well as fresh milk. By the look on the boy's face as she spoke her order, she expected to be told it was *succédané de café*, the bilge made from chicory and roast grain, or nothing, bad luck. But that wasn't the problem at all. She'd said just two words, 'café léger'. She may as well have stood on the table posed as the Statue of Liberty and sung 'My Country, 'Tis of Thee'. The kid's face blanched, his eyes darted to the three German soldiers by the window and he scuttled in panic into the kitchen before Eleanor, exasperated, could ask for something to eat.

While she awaited his return, she picked up the menu but nearly dropped it in shock. Sure, they had plenty to eat but at black-market prices only the occupier could afford, which she supposed was the point. She admitted to herself she could afford it too, but if she wanted to consort with the occupier, she could do so in greater comfort along Boulevard Saint Germain. Since she was still sitting there, unattended, all these musings were hypothetical. Then a large man appeared from the same door and came to her table.

'Would madame care to come into the kitchen to look at what we have?' he asked.

'Madame would indeed,' said Eleanor, her pure accent restored. But it was too late, her cover had been blown.

'This place is crawling with Boches,' the man hissed at her.

Eleanor said she could see that for herself. 'The United States isn't at war with Germany,' she added smartly. The man gave her a look he'd give to a stupid child, which Eleanor thought she deserved, but then they got down to business. Sure, he could arrange a passage but it would cost 3,000 francs.

'What's that?' Eleanor protested, aghast. 'The American price? I'm not a tourist. I live here.'

She was American, the man said with at least one version of logic on his side, but worse, she was a woman. The risks were much higher. Three thousand was rock bottom, others would charge seven; and when 'les Amis' did declare war on the fuckers, it would be double, triple for a woman.

'Take it or leave it,' he added. He had better things to do than argue.

Despite the large bowl of fresh eggs sitting by one of the stoves – there must have been two dozen waiting to be cooked for the 'fuckers' as he had so crudely put it – and despite the aroma of recently made real coffee, Eleanor decided she would leave it. He was on thin ice as it was, she told him with a viperous glance at the eggs, so how dare he use her present distress to extort money, and what had being a woman got to do with it? The man couldn't have cared less. She'd come to him after all. The door was that way. Goodbye.

As she scuttled along the sidewalk to the metro and began to calm down, she wondered why she was fussing about pennies when the alternative was worse. She nearly turned around to eat humble pie, impelled by her brush with what might have been a ravishing breakfast, but stubborn pride stopped her. She'd find a cheaper, more honourable alternative near the American Cathedral, where she was now headed. 'Even if I starve to death on the way,' she muttered to herself. Of course she wouldn't, but that wasn't the point.

Approaching the station main hall, Eleanor smelt fresh bread on the air. The pavements and shops had lost their usual charms as life sagged along, heaving every now and then for breath. The senses had become dull, except hearing and smell, which had grown acute, the former because of the instinct to survive and the latter because people, while not starving, were constantly hungry. Noses could now sniff out fresh coffee or bread a block away, the coffee inducing resentment because it was probably going down a German gullet. But Germans or no Germans on the station concourse, she would faint if she didn't eat something, and this bread, even if it was half sawdust, was irresistible.

Inside, she saw a queue into the only boulangerie that was open, accounting for the crowd, not that it had something worth queuing for. She joined the silent line, which was moving fast enough for her impatient frame of mind. She looked around for evidence of the German troops she'd seen enter the station earlier but the place seemed occupier-free.

A girl appeared, so small and thin it made her eyes seem larger and sadder than they were. She hovered rather than join the queue, eyes moving from person to person to see who would look back, the weak link in a chain of hard-heartedness. Eleanor refused to engage with the child's moral blackmail, her own hunger making her obdurate, but of course she felt guilty. She said to herself that she'd wait and see if the girl was still there when she came out. The queue slowed, then stopped. She tried to look over the people in front of her to see what the hold-up was. When she looked back, standing immediately behind her was an elderly woman in a shawl who had not been there before.

Eleanor, hard-hearted against the girl, gave way without a second thought to the woman. And so did they all. The woman, with a face from the Pale to which Parisians had become familiar, was a foreign Jew. But since the round-ups of foreign Jews in May and August, their precariousness made them even more obvious, when that was the last thing they needed. The woman went straight to the front, where she bought her ration of fresh bread. The baker threw in an extra loaf. She secured her purchases in a hand-sewn cloth bag, turned and left with her head down, her eyes avoiding any contact with her benefactors, not a word to them, nor to the baker.

'See?' someone muttered. 'Typical Jews. No thanks. Just take, take.'

But Eleanor understood. She had seen it on the woman's face: her humiliation at her current predicament. She'd seen the same thing on black faces in the American South, and it cut into her Christian sense of justice in a way the girl's attempt at moral blackmail could never do.

Only her hunger kept her glued to the queue, and once she had her bread and was out the door, she pulled away a large chunk to eat. If it was partly sawdust, it still tasted delicious and only later would she feel it heavy on her stomach. In mid-chew, there was the large-eyed girl staring at her, and with bad grace, Eleanor slapped a piece of bread into the child's hand. 'That's it, girlie,' she said. The kid wasn't a Jew and she didn't look malnourished, Eleanor told her annoying conscience.

Later that morning, Monday, 8th December 1941

The parish hall and the dean's garden were abuzz with Episcopalian purpose although Eleanor could feel the panicky edge to the chatter amid the coming and going. In all the talk of who had sons in the navy or the army and if anyone knew anyone in Hawaii, which may as well have been on the moon it was so far away, only one topic of conversation really preoccupied them.

Flight.

Some had been over to the *Kommandantur*, which was besieged by refugees desperate for an *Ausweis*, a permit, to get into Vichy, but the Germans had closed the border even to French with permits. So the talk was about how to cross the demarcation line illegally and who knew such and such, who might know such and such, who might take them across and how much. Eleanor told them of her experience. The 3,000 she'd been quoted seemed stiff to the others, which made her feel justified until she discovered they were talking from no experience at all. But at least, under the topsy-turvy nonsense of rules and regulations, even though crossing into Vichy would be illegal, Americans with their Paris residency permits would be legal once they got there. Another arrived to report that the American bank branches were still open and operating normally. Yet another reported they'd been told on excellent authority that the Spanish and Portuguese consuls in Lyon and Toulouse were still issuing visas to people with valid passports plus the requisite visas for entry into third countries. This news was golden for Eleanor. She, who had foreseen the need to keep a packed valise in case of internment, had not seen any need to maintain current Spanish and Portuguese visas in her passport, showing her just how skewed her thinking, or lack of it, had been.

Someone wondered if they shouldn't be careful talking so openly, mightn't the Germans be listening so they could nab Americans as they fled? But who among those coming and going that morning were not parishioners? 'Wallis is the only one who'd blab,' said one caustic tongue. For a brief moment, they were able to laugh, if ruefully, because Wallis Simpson and her king were now basking in the Bahamian sun, although, as another said, they were probably no longer going on about how Hitler and the Nazis were the ant's pants.

Then if Eleanor didn't see coming through the door, of all people, Hettie Rosen.

'Miss Rosen!' she exclaimed in surprise.

'Ah, Miss Clarke. Miss Beach said I might find you here. You have to give me some money, Miss Clarke,' said Hettie, and although it was in Hettie's usual peremptory manner, as she might command 'Fire!' when directing an execution squad, Eleanor could see the fear behind her lack of charm.

Hettie had been to her Swiss bank that morning to discover her accounts suddenly barred to her.

'They can't do that,' Eleanor said. 'You're an American.'

'I told them that,' Hettie said. 'But they said I wasn't.'

And that, as it turned out, was the truth. Hettie hadn't been an American citizen since 1920, when she married a Frenchman she'd met on a trip to the newly minted socialist paradise in Russia. The travel she'd done since had been on a French passport. She, the great internationalist, had thought nothing of it; a passport was just a matter of convenience and if you were born in America, you were American.

Eleanor was flabbergasted, not about the passport; she had escaped the pitfalls of marrying foreigners overseas only by what at the time she thought was a great misfortune but which was a skin-of-the-teeth blessing in disguise. What amazed her was that Hettie had been married at all. Who, dear God, even a communist, could have put up with her? It turned out, as Hettie explained, he hadn't, because they parted soon enough but had never divorced. The German and Vichy *Ordnungs* against Jews, particularly natural-ised French Jews, which she was, did thus apply to her. Since June, as her bank now realised, what had been hers was now under the control of the Nazis. Unless she could be an American again, she could lose the lot.

'Wait here,' said Eleanor, who knew better than Hettie what was really at stake. She found Mr Epherson, a lawyer who was a stayer because he was married to a Frenchwoman. Indeed, he did know something. Hettie could have her citizenship returned in the United States in person by a simple declaration of allegiance, although Mr Epherson said he wasn't up on the latest changes about whether her husband had to have been continually in the States too.

'What? "Continually", meaning "since the marriage"?' Eleanor asked, incredulous. Mr Epherson said that had been the case but he wasn't sure now.

'But she can also do it in Vichy at the embassy,' he added help-fully. He thought in that case, the whereabouts of the husband wasn't important.

'That's some comfort,' said Eleanor. But getting from Paris to the US was no longer a matter of slipping over to the Cunard Line office, so it was a cold sort of comfort.

'So,' she said, trying to make it clear to herself, 'in order to regain her birthright, Miss Rosen, Madame Whoever-she-is, has to escape across the demarcation line to the American embassy at Vichy and declare herself a citizen of the country she was born in so she's no longer a French Jew but a neutral one.'

'Yes,' Mr Epherson said. 'An American, thus free of the restrictions.'

'Indeed,' said Eleanor. 'And once she's done that, she can return to Nazi-occupied Paris, where she can reclaim access to her own money. Is that the situation, Mr Epherson?'

'It seems so,' said Mr Epherson but added that as a French Jew, Miss Rosen had not needed a residency permit for Paris, unlike other Americans, so the moment she became an American again, she'd be in occupied France illegally and when she came back to Paris, she would need to apply for one. 'Which the Nazis won't approve,' he added helplessly, 'especially as she's Jewish.' Eleanor looked out to the garden where Hettie was smoking impatiently and looking for her. There was only one thing for it and no time to waste. She hurried outside.

'Miss Rosen, you simply cannot stay here,' she said. Hettie thought she meant the cathedral, jumping to the wrong conclusion, which, Eleanor thought, was at least in character. Once they sorted out that confusion, she told Hettie to forget about her bank account, worry only about getting out alive. Her legal situation was ridiculously complicated. She had to get her passport back in Vichy, get the hell out of France via Spain, and then she could deal with those damnable Swiss back in New York.

Eleanor gave Hettie the cash she had on her, which was way more than she usually carried, because she was expecting to pay for a passage to the unoccupied zone. She told Hettie to come to Shakespeare and Company around two o'clock, when she and Sylvia might have the names of possible *passeurs* and when she would be able to give her more money. Hettie nodded, got up and left, but without a word, and although Eleanor called out to remind her to meet her at the bookshop, Hettie kept on without a backward glance or any acknowledgment. Oh God, Eleanor suddenly thought, I'm going to have to take her with me. A journey with Hettie even on the metro between two stops was one journey too much. Her heart sank.

Having given away her money and heard Hettie's scarifying tale of what had awaited her at her bank, Eleanor went as fast as she could to her own, which at least was French, and there she armed herself with a letter of credit. She took from her safety deposit box all her American dollars, some of which she would need to give to Hettie, and withdrew enough francs to see her through to the Spanish border, this at her bank manager's suggestion.

SHAKESPEARE AND COMPANY, 12 RUE DE L'ODÉON, PARIS VI

Early afternoon, Monday, 8th December 1941

'All the crossings are hot, lady,' explained Maxim, a twenty-year-old student and acquaintance of Adrienne's through her doctor. At least Eleanor's escape was no longer an 'if' but a 'when'. Maxim's contact didn't mind taking women across the demarcation line and his price, 1,000 francs, was reasonable given the number of people, including Germans, it would pay to look the other way. If she wanted a guide to take her to the Spanish frontier, that would be double. Across the frontier, triple.

Eleanor replied she could make her own way south from Lyon and make an entirely legal and above-board crossing at Cerbère, on the Mediterranean.

'Lucky you,' said Maxim, though where she crossed into Spain wasn't his concern. Was it one passage or two?

'Two,' she replied, bowing to the inevitable, if with a heavy heart. She glanced at her watch. Two-thirty exactly. Hettie was half an hour late.

'Show me the route,' Eleanor asked, but Maxim said the less she knew the better.

'Just buy a return ticket for Nevers on the line to Clermont-Ferrand,' Maxim instructed.

'But if I'm going via Perpignan, isn't Lyon better?' Eleanor asked, though France outside Paris was only a vague set of names on an even vaguer map.

'Yes, but you're not going by one of the legal crossing points,' Maxim replied patiently. 'It doesn't matter where you cross.'

'I think he knows what he's doing, dear,' Sylvia said sweetly in English.

'From there you take a bus to this village,' he continued, pointing to a village on his little map. There she was to wait in a café called the Excelsior. Someone would come for her around nine that evening. They would bring her in a party across the line and lead them to Lyon.

'Do not carry a valise,' Maxim cautioned. She could send that on ahead of her. Luggage didn't need a permit to travel across the demarcation line. She should at most carry a rucksack. The less American she looked, the better.

'How will your guide know it's me in this café?' Eleanor said, her excitement advertising her origins all too clearly.

'I'm sure he won't have any trouble identifying you, dear,' said Sylvia, 'but neither will the Germans if you don't stay calm.'

The bell over the door tinkled as it opened.

'I hope that's Hettie,' Eleanor said. They had left the door unlocked for her. But it wasn't.

'Where is that copy of *Finnegans Wake* you had in the window, Miss Beach?'

It was the German. He now spoke in English, and by the peremptory tone of his voice, this time he was Herr Major Krolow of the Security Service, not Gunther Krolow the civilised bibliophile.

Maxim snapped his notepad with the map shut. 'Thank you,' he said, casually picking up a novel on top of a small pile of returned books on the table and putting it into his coat. 'I'll get it back in time, don't worry.'

'M'sieur,' he said as he slipped past Krolow for the door, which tinkled his exit from danger out onto Odéon.

'I put it away,' Sylvia replied to Krolow, gasping momentarily because she'd been holding her breath.

'For whom?' Krolow demanded.

'For me,' Sylvia said easily, her courage recovered.

'You would be wise to sell it to me,' Krolow said. 'I would give you a very good price.'

'I told you,' said Sylvia. 'It's not for sale.'

'Then permit me to inform you that if you do not sell this book to me, I shall return and confiscate every book you have in this shop,' said Krolow. 'Now what do you say?'

'You can't,' Eleanor said. 'This is American property.'

'I think your president has more immediate problems on his hands at the moment, Miss Clarke,' he replied.

'I'm sure you can confiscate me too if you want,' Sylvia said coolly, 'just like you confiscated that nice French car you get driven around in, but that still won't get you my copy of *Finnegans Wake*.'

'So be it,' the German said crisply and he went to the door. 'It would be very unwise to abscond,' he added and then left.

Sylvia ran to the window and watched Krolow drive away. 'Quick, run after Maxim,' she said urgently. 'You'll find him at his house above his father's surgery, you know, up on the boulevard. If Hettie turns up, I'll send her up there too. On your way, get Adrienne to come down straightaway with boxes.'

She had already begun to stack books on the table.

'I'll help you,' said Eleanor, but Sylvia said she could help once she'd organised her departure with Maxim.

'If we're still here,' she added.

'You're staying,' said Eleanor flatly. She was hardly surprised.

'I'm staying,' Sylvia confirmed.

GARE DE LYON, PARIS XII

6.15am, Tuesday, 9th December 1941

German soldiers, rifles over their shoulders, walked in pairs past Eleanor. Ridiculous, absurd, she thought, always in pairs, like love-birds in steel helmets and boots. But was it not also ridiculous and absurd that here she was, standing in one of the long queues for a train ticket at such an early hour, frightened and in shock?

*

Merely securing a scarce ticket on the train wasn't the only reason for her early departure. Yesterday, after organising passages with Maxim for herself and, not without a sense of gloom, for Hettie, she returned to the bookshop, where she joined a small group of Sylvia and Adrienne's friends to finish packing the books they were storing upstairs in a vacant apartment. Sylvia had even got someone to paint out the Shakespeare and Company sign. The move had taken them only two hours, with each minute, each second spurring them on lest the Nazi book thief return any moment to carry out his threat.

Krolow would have been back within the hour had he been able to organise transport and the necessary squad of troops to take the books, but short of doing it himself, that had not been possible. It wasn't Krolow's demand to close down a mere bookshop that was out of the ordinary in the circumstances, far from it. Shakespeare and Company had been on a Gestapo list of undesirable places even before German arms allowed them into the city. Of all the literary bookshops in that city, it was one of the most infamous, and that it had survived was due entirely to the nationality of its owner and the red American embassy seal on its front door.

But Krolow had more pressing concerns yesterday afternoon, yet further demands from higher-ups in Berlin, *die da oben* as they said in German, for artistic loot, two paintings by van Dyck. The Jews who owned them had been forced to hand them over. Organising the crating and shipping had taken Krolow all afternoon, and only after four pm was he able to devote his attention to his own looting. The bookshop wouldn't go away, after all.

But when he arrived, it had.

Eleanor had watched with Sylvia and the others from behind the curtains of Adrienne's apartment across the street as Krolow discovered neither bookshop, nor any sign one had ever been at 12 Rue de l'Odéon. The back door of Adrienne's apartment was unlocked in case Krolow came searching, so they might escape into the stairwell and out through the back laneway. He wouldn't find any books there.

But he was interested in only one book.

Sylvia handed it to Eleanor.

'Take it with you,' she said, and her eyes beckoned Eleanor to the back door and escape. 'Now, while he's making up his mind.'

Eleanor pushed it into the bottom of her coat pocket.

'While you've got it,' Sylvia added, 'he never will.'

Eleanor had an inkling that this was a curse she was putting into her pocket, she who'd have sold the wretched thing for a dime, given it away as a doorstop.

'Your Mr Joyce is even more trouble dead than alive,' she said drily.

'*Bababadalgharaghtakamminarronnkonnbronntonnerronntuonnthunn*,' said Sylvia. She didn't have the energy to complete God's cussing according to the Book of St James Joyce, but everyone got the general idea.

'Amen to that,' Eleanor said, and they all laughed. A sad laugh, but they laughed. And that was Eleanor's last sight of Sylvia and Shakespeare and Company as she hurried to the back door and down the stairwell, which led to the courtyard and a passage through to the back laneway and away.

After leaving, she'd decided it was not a good idea to go straight home. In any case, having committed herself to taking Hettie with her, she had to find her. Where was she? Why hadn't she come to the bookshop as arranged? Eleanor had the address.

The building, along a street not far from the Luxembourg Gardens, was of bare and shabby stone, four or five storeys high. In happier days, its shabbiness would have been even more marked, but now the façades of its grander neighbours were soot-blackened and just as run-down. Still, Eleanor thought tartly, the Luxembourg neighbourhood was hardly a statement of socialist solidarity.

The entrance was behind a forbidding grille of ancient iron bars, but the gate was open and she went to the door and rang. No one answered. Nor did she see any light as she peered through the smeared glass of a small window. She wondered if Hettie had already skedaddled. She persisted with the doorbell and when that still brought no answer, she went back to the sidewalk and to the door of what looked to be an empty shop that occupied the other half of the ground floor. Behind a curtain covering the glass in the door, she was sure she detected a faint light. She rapped as hard as she could and eventually a voice from behind the veiled door rasped a 'Go away'. It sounded like Hettie but she couldn't be sure, so she decided to pester the old bat until she got her attention.

'Open the door, Miss Rosen,' she called out in English. 'It's me, Eleanor Clarke.'

Her persistence won and the door opened, if only by an inch.

'What do you want?' the old lady asked. It was not Hettie.

'Miss Rosen,' said Eleanor with some urgency, 'I need to see Miss Rosen. Do you know where she is?'

'Ask at the morgue,' the old lady snapped and Eleanor thought at first this was a sick joke, but it wasn't a joke. 'The old bitch topped herself this afternoon. Good riddance.'

Eleanor gasped; she thought she'd faint. She grabbed the wall.

'You're American. You better not stick around,' the old woman advised. 'The Gestapo came. They're coming back.'

The woman shut the door. Eleanor tried to light a cigarette but her hand shook so much it took ages. Her fury at the Germans boiled up, which at least stopped her shaking and propelled her all the way back to Sylvia's. But Sylvia was no longer at home, nor over at Adrienne's, which, absent her misery and fury about Hettie, would have worried her. She scribbled a note with the terrible news and a plea to call her the moment she got in, then pushed it into Sylvia's letter box.

She dragged herself home to discover that the Herr Major, after searching Sylvia's and Adrienne's apartments, had come to hers, terrifying the Teixeiras. It was proof the Germans had tabs on all Americans. But for some reason, he had not pushed past the red US embassy seal on her door, instead leaving a calling card that requested her to report the next morning at eleven sharp to his office on the avenue Foch. Everyone in Paris knew that address. Avenue Boche, they called it.

Sylvia hadn't rung and Eleanor wondered if Major Krolow hadn't taken her in. Frantic with worry and frustrated by her inability to do anything, she distracted herself by writing letters to her bank manager and to her agent, who would have to look after her affairs now she was leaving. But she couldn't sleep. At midnight, ear pressed to the radio, she'd listened to the BBC from London reporting that FDR had signed Congress's declaration of war against Japan. She'd tried to read in bed but kept hearing unsettling sounds through the terrible silence of the night, imagined or real. At two o'clock, she got up for the news from London, which reported diplomatic activity in Berlin. Would Hitler declare war on the United States tomorrow? She hadn't really concentrated – she was too overwhelmed by what had happened to Hettie. She wrote a long note for Sylvia, which she would get Mrs Teixeira to drop over in the morning. Only movement helped, so she took the risk of farewelling the Teixeiras before the curfew was raised. She could then catch the first train as soon as the metro opened at five. She needed to be early to secure a ticket for her getaway. Before she left, she rang Sylvia. Too bad if the SD minions of Herr Major Krolow were listening in. But she got no answer. Of her friends apart from Sylvia, she'd told only Madeleine. Next Sunday at the cathedral's parish hall, her seat would be another of the empty ones.

*

The clock over the station concourse was on 5.35. She was still in the queue, which had been long even when she arrived. The sun was far from up, and even if it had been light, the vast glass canopy and its intricate beauty was grimy and neglected in defeat, with some panes gone or cracked, leaving the place open to the rain. Early-morning workers, vastly more women than men, arrived from the overground trains, their wooden-soled shoes clacking over the tiles through the strange and dense hush. From the moment the occupier had arrived, Parisians seemed to stop talking, at least in public. Yes, you could hear the locomotives and their hissing steam and the squeal of brakes and the slamming of carriage doors and the whistles for departure and the calls from the conductors, but all the starker for the silence they failed to fill.

Another pair of helmeted Germans passed her, their suspicious eyes looking her up and down. Jew? American? Or so it seemed to Eleanor.

She forced herself to stare vacantly right through them and willed the queue to move quicker, but it didn't. She had been able to send her valise through to Lyon without any difficulty, a slightly larger one than she'd prepared for internment in order to cram in extra warm clothes, her large cosmetics bag and three cartons of Chesterfields. Around her neck, over her thick woollen pullover, she wore the crucifix that Mrs Teixeira had given her as protection that morning. This was ironic to an Episcopalian, who would never cross the Tiber to save her life. Faking it as an ordinary Catholic Parisian, off to visit a sick sister in the country, should be easy. Not many Parisian women these days would be wearing a perfume by Schiaparelli but Eleanor comforted herself with a current prejudice that if it wasn't sauerkraut, no German would have a clue.

The queue inched forward. The German pairs kept returning, although not the same ones each time. Eleanor was dying for her morning's cigarette but smoking a Chesterfield right now might be asking for it. The bottom part of her rucksack was full of cigarettes. She was damned if she was going to leave them behind to get stale – or worse, fall into German hands. At one point last night when finishing her packing, she'd faced a choice: one of her own novels was tucked into her valise, but for her rucksack, it was either her Bible or *Finnegans Wake*, which was why that pest of a book was now stuffed tight into the left breast pocket of her coat like a brick. In the other was her travelling cosmetics bag with its far more precious contents. She'd kill any German who tried to take her cosmetics, but if he wanted the book, he was welcome to it.

She was wearing Claude's old woollen coat, a brilliant stroke, she thought. His was thicker than her own and more generously pocketed, a decided advantage given the load she was carrying. She'd noticed plenty of women wearing the shirts and pullovers and coats of their husbands, either killed or in German POW camp. Slightly outsize as it was, it helped her to fit in rather than stand out.

As instructed, Eleanor bought a return ticket to Nevers. She asked for a seat on the express. The woman behind the ticket counter threw her a weary look. Seat? Express? She'd be lucky to find a place to stand and it was all-stops. Take it or leave it.

'Delayed half an hour,' the woman added for good measure.

Eleanor had hoped she and the wretched book would be well away in a couple of hours' time, when she was expected in the Herr Major's office, but she could do nothing about that. As long as there was a train, she was content.

She did not relish hovering for forty minutes around the entrance to the platforms, so she hastened to the famous buffet, which would be warm and where she could secrete herself. She had not been there since the arrival of the occupier.

The gold leaf on the walls and ceiling of the Salle Dorée was so vivid in contrast to the grime outside that she gasped like some peasant arriving from last century. Really, she was stepping back only eighteen months or so, before the conqueror had burst across his foggy borders. It seemed a lifetime. She sought a table in the more discreet Tunisian Salon but found it full. The Algerian Salon was closed off for German officers and had a posse of guards at the door, so she sat in the Grande Salle. It looked, she thought, as one imagined the palaces of Saint Petersburg after the Bolsheviks had taken over: baroque cavernous rooms with painted ceilings and gilded mirrors and caryatids around the walls but now infested by tribes of peasants and their fleas, and she in her oversize coat, hat and boots was one of them. Foie gras? Steak tartare? She could have beans with sausage. 'What a surprise,' she said. And *succédané de café*, although there was something in the voice of the waiter that hinted at what might be possible if madame were more imaginative with her cash, something this madame was decidedly not in the mood to oblige.

Walking down the steps from the buffet afterwards, she observed the helmeted guards stationed at the entrance to the platforms. But it was their officers who were looking at tickets and checking identity cards, although not those of everyone who passed. They were looking for fleeing Jews. Approaching the destination board, she kept reminding herself this was no game. Not only must she look

French, she had to be French. American women in Paris, even the meekest, walked differently from their British and European sisters, as if they owned the world. Since most Americans who made it to Paris had ambitions they at least believed they could fulfil, they had that grab-the-world gait in spades. This morning, though, as she shuffled along with stooped shoulders, her gait was the only part of her that didn't feel fake.

At the entrance, she encountered a crush of people being held up by the French ticket inspectors and the German officers who were checking this one or that one. Who got checked seemed random, and it probably was, apart from those who looked like Jews. But most Parisians looked Jewish to the Germans, hence the crush. With her rucksack half full of cigarettes and that wretched book in her coat pocket, Eleanor felt obvious. German soldiers returning to their units or going for a day's outing were being waved past the cordon to the trains, their uniforms their tickets. Was there anywhere they weren't going to? she wondered and joined the queue that was being checked by a French policeman.

Directly in front of her, one young man in a coat, a local by his dark hair and beret, showed a pass. 'Where's your ticket?' the policeman demanded. He wasn't travelling, she heard the young man say in excellent French, he was only seeing his men off. She didn't understand. His men? Then, to her dismay, the policeman called over the uniformed German officer. It was too late for her to join another queue. The major scowled as he looked at the man's pass then barked at him in German before waving him irritably onto the platform. She hadn't for a moment suspected the young man as a Boche but she couldn't dwell on that. It was her turn.

She already had her ticket and her unopened Paris residency card on display. If the German looked at it closely, he would see she was American. He waved her onto the platform without even a cursory glance. As she slipped past him, she saw the SD patch on his sleeve.

TRAIN TO CLERMONT-FERRAND

After 9am, Tuesday, 9th December 1941

Once on board, Eleanor realised that buying a second-class ticket had been justified. The press of human flesh in the corridors alone guaranteed her anonymity. She pushed her way along the side corridor but found no seat free in any of the compartments, nor any man willing to give his up for her. She would be standing all the way. Even the superficially civilised manners of the station buffet were far behind and she wasn't about to display her cash just to get a seat. The only space was in the vestibule near the toilet. The loud-speakers began calling remaining passengers to board. She looked at her watch. Just after nine. The door of the toilet opened slightly and a grey German uniform squeezed out, quickly shutting the door behind. It had insignia for rank on its shoulders and sleeves, a lance corporal. She was determined to think of 'him' as an 'it'. But then 'it' slipped on a cap, which brought into focus a face as suave and darkly handsome as the young artist's on the previous Sunday morning had been fair. 'It' thus became a 'he', a human being, despite the sinister black leather glove on each hand.

'*Bitte*,' he demanded. Eleanor knew the word meant 'please', as much German as she cared to know, but the tone said, 'Get out of my way. Now!' The German was again an 'it'. Consumed by the nuances of her response – she really had become French – she hadn't noticed she was still blocking his way.

She stood back. He stepped past her without a nod or word of thanks. Instead of moving up the corridor, as she expected, he slipped out the door onto the platform and away. She thought she might quickly use the lavatory, because it would be impossible before long. As she opened the door, it was pulled back hard against her. The Occupied sign clicked on, alarming her. Someone was still in there. Why and more to the point, who? Gestapo? The Sicherheitsdienst? More rationally, she realised that someone must have slipped inside while she was dealing with the German soldier. Still, with her nerves so taut, she pushed away up the corridor towards the far end of the carriage. Whistles blew. The train lurched into motion. People cursed as they were thrown against one another and grabbed at handles and pushed and shoved and shuffled until some decorum was restored, however ill-tempered.

The train heaved its exhausted way out of the station. Eleanor tried to settle herself and forget about the lance corporal and his Bocheness. She found not even a ledge to lean against, just the door to one of the compartments, which was full. Then the train ground to a juddering halt, shoving the sardines against one another with cursing and swearing and no sorries or I-beg-your-pardons to soften the irritation. Were they to be stuck here, not yet halfway out of the station? The locomotive whistle blew again, at least preparing the crowd for the jerking resumption of their journey. This time the train managed to pick up speed, if gradually, and they really were away. Eleanor had no time to settle, because a new crush of people came from both directions looking for seats that did not exist. A black-eyed young man, impatient and rude, swung her about as he barged through.

'Damnation,' Eleanor snapped in English and she grabbed at the handle of the compartment door to stop herself from falling. No one helped her but in the brief turmoil that the young man's rough passage had caused, she saw a vacant spot on the ledge against the window. She grabbed it so fast and with such determination that none of the men dared try dislodge her. She reached for her cigarette case but it wasn't in her side coat pocket. She checked the other side pocket. Gone. She knew it wasn't in either of the breast pockets. She realised when and she realised who.

'*Ce malfrat maudit*,' she spat coarsely – that dirty thug – and went after him along the corridor, ignoring the curses and the swearing as she pushed people aside. She hauled open the door to the next carriage. It was as crowded as the one she'd just exited but this did not deter her. Eventually she spotted him up the corridor three cars along, as far as he could go, and what if the little shit wasn't smoking one of her cigarettes. He hadn't seen her enter, so she slid her way between the crush of bodies like a shiver bathed in oil, not even upsetting the fleas infesting the clothes of her fellow travellers.

When she reached him, she grabbed his wrist. 'You stole my cigarette case, you damn thief,' she accused him in very loud French. He pushed her away, calling her a *putain*, a whore. The people she fell against swore at her and pushed her back so she collided violently with the young man, knocking him hard against the window, which cracked although it did not give way. No one seemed at all inclined to help her. She saw the emergency stop cord, high on the corridor wall, and reached up to pull it, but her neighbour wasn't having any of that. 'For fuck's sake,' he growled as he grabbed her hand. Then he turned and with his right fist, he hit the thief in the stomach. 'Give it back so we can get some peace here,' he snarled inches from the face of the young man, who now gulped for breath. He wrenched open the young man's coat. Instead of Eleanor's cigarettes, he found a frightened black kitten.

'No!' the young man cried out and pushed Eleanor's rescuer away, closing his coat protectively over the kitten. He reached into his outside pocket, withdrew Eleanor's cigarette case and slapped it petulantly into her hand. '*Va te faire foutre*,' he muttered. Fuck off.

'You want a smack in the mouth, punk?' the man said, holding his fist at the ready.

Eleanor told her saviour that wasn't necessary, she had her property back, she was grateful for his help. She opened the case and offered him a cigarette as token of her thanks.

'Christ,' the man exclaimed, 'American.' He took one, then on second thoughts, added two more to his haul. He chuckled. 'I'd be heading home too if I was you.' Eleanor was comforted that at least her French hadn't slipped in the encounter, that she'd been outed only by her Chesterfields. It was disconcerting, though, to hear her story moving along the corridor from lip to ear. 'She's a Yank. Getting out while she can. Did you see the cigarettes?'

'Next time,' she snapped at her thief, 'ask.'

He ignored her. Worse, she realised, he didn't do it actively or ostentatiously. To him, she'd become invisible. She removed her compact and, while dusting her face, she cast an already critical eye over him in the mirror. Since *The American Woman*, she'd considered herself – and was considered, at least in literary circles – something of an expert on his type. This was ridiculous, of course; unlike most of her characters, she'd conjured Yann up entirely from her imagination. If she'd based him on a real one, like this little creep, she wouldn't have written a word.

His French, the little she'd heard, had been vulgar, and accented at that, although she couldn't place it. He had the face of an elf, with elfish, slightly pointed ears, spawn indeed of Cain. Under the beret, stolen doubtless, his sandy hair was coarse and unruly and ill-cut, probably using sheep-shears. His eyes, though, they weren't black at all but dark blue, like sapphires, somewhat spoiling her demonic image of him. His cloth knapsack was so small and meagrely packed, it could have belonged to his cat. She knew she was indulging her furies rather than exercising cool judgment. Apart from her cigarette, it was her only remaining pleasure.

Then the kitten poked its head out from his coat. His hard face softened as he stroked the little creature. That failed to wash with

Eleanor, who didn't much go for cats. Who did he think he was? Dick Whittington? Suddenly he caught himself in the mirror of her compact. In the blink of an eye, the smiling face went, he was an elf again, his sapphire eyes glinting a curse at her so fierce that she snapped her compact shut as her ears and face burned in embarrassment. Even then, she had to use willpower not to look over at him again. To distract herself, she focused intently on the cigarette case in her hand.

Apart from her memories and photographs tucked away in some album she'd long interred, it was all she had from her only legal marriage. Oh, there was her name – well, part of it, he was a Clarke, she was a Gorton, and there they were, engraved on the silver lid, her EG woven around his FC, making her Eleanor Gorton Clarke. Suddenly Fred's face came vividly to her as he had been, young and so beautiful, lovely brown eyes, that strong chin, oh, and his dark, spiky moustache that prickled deliciously as he transported her with his tongue into delights that growing up in staid Providence had lamentably not prepared her for. He, who'd grown up as staidly as she, had learnt well from Parisian whores during the last eighteen months of the war. Better late than never, she thought and smiled inwardly. That particular talent, transferred to Yann in *The American Woman*, had helped earn the book its shady reputation, however poetically she'd disguised it from the censors. No wonder Fred hadn't spoken to her, but she'd rarely given him much thought in the years since. She wondered where he was. Too old now for this war. She suspected he was probably trying to get back into it. He had a talent for adventure and none to write about it, a would-be-Hemingway. Mind you, she didn't feel sorry for poor Fred. Fred came from plenty of money.

She cast a furtive look at the elf again but he was gone, leaving her unsettled by this brush with something she didn't like and that she had let get the better of her.

Through the window, the last of Paris was passing by. She was able to see out by manoeuvring her head around; she dared not move her body or she'd lose even her standing room. What she saw was drab, hardly a streetscape to evoke deep feelings, but it tore at her heart and she fought tears. The enormity of what she was doing hit her hard. She was leaving her home. Would she ever be able to return? Would she even make it back to Providence? Visiting her family was one thing, living with them would be quite another. If she made it.

A VILLAGE NEAR NEVERS, BURGUNDY, GERMAN-OCCUPIED FRANCE, 260 KILOMETRES SOUTH-EAST OF PARIS

6.30pm, Tuesday, 9th December 1941

The bus groaned as it turned every corner, yet its passengers were mutely compliant when once the driver would never have heard the end of it – too slow, too bumpy, too crowded. Eleanor had been instructed by Maxim to take a bus from Nevers, south of Paris on the Loire, to a village, which, she had worked out, was well away from the demarcation line. Why not closer? she wondered, but too late, and anyway, what was the point? She was doing as instructed. Maxim had not informed her the only bus came into Nevers in the morning and went back in the afternoon, so until the time to depart she had moved from café to café, as much to escape the sleet and rain as to blunt her desolation over Hettie with the remains of her whisky. By then, two hours after the bus was supposed to leave, the skies began to clear.

Eleanor managed to find a seat. With her fellow passengers crammed so close to one another, you couldn't have added a mouse. Despite the enforced physical familiarity, she'd sensed an invisible circle form around her, in which conversation was entirely absent. She was the outsider here. Everyone knew everyone. She could barely see through the smudgy window. Now and then she could see shapes against the pale waning moon, a church steeple, the top of a chateau, a village – never a light, not a one. It was as if they were driving through a dead landscape.

Some way into the journey, she remarked to her immediate neighbour that at least it was warm inside the bus.

'You're American!' the woman exclaimed and, as in the train, news of her nationality spread from lip to ear, and while Eleanor felt the whole bus relax, she was again discomfited by having her cover so quickly blown. She really would have to be careful about her French. Now that she was going home, was her American self beginning to reassert itself? They knew exactly what she was up to. Lucky her for being able to get out. But you couldn't be too careful these days, her neighbour said quietly. The Germans were planting people in buses and trains and in cafés, not only to pick off any fleeing Jews, but to eavesdrop. Unless you knew the person well, you kept your mouth shut. Even then you had to be careful they were a true friend, because someone might denounce you in revenge for some slight years ago. She offered advice about the German patrols, which were lazy because they didn't like the cold. The colder the night, the less chance they'd be out and about causing trouble.

'If only the war had started in winter,' she opined as a corollary, 'then we would have beaten the bastards. You're our only hope,' she said, patting Eleanor's arm.

The weary passengers around her suddenly came to life, because the last gasping turn of the bus was onto the road into the village. She looked at her watch. Really, it had not taken as long as she'd thought.

For all the sudden if late conviviality inside the bus, the moment the vehicle stopped and the door opened, it emptied swiftly.

'This is it,' said the bus driver to Eleanor, who was the last to alight.

By then, her fellow passengers were shapes departing as quickly as they could through the shadows to the safety and warmth of their homes. The bus left with its lights out. She was alone. The silence folded in over her. With no streetlights, she could barely make out the houses ahead, though she figured the church steeple might indicate the square or centre of the village. She had to find the café called Excelsior, which seemed a rather grand name for what looked like a depot stop in the middle of the Canadian prairie. She hefted her rucksack and set out in the direction taken by most of her fellow passengers. Underfoot, the ground was wet and sloshy. She heard a car approaching, an unnerving experience because by now a car usually meant Germans. She stepped away from the roadway before the car's lights could pick her out. It passed without revealing its identity. She watched its receding tail light. Soon it stopped. Its doors opened and shut. She heard voices, another door open and shut, then silence.

Closer, she saw the car had stopped in the village square, which was more triangle than square. Along one side were stone houses behind little gardens, on another the church with its small bell tower, and on the other were darkened shops. But there was the Café Excelsior, the exception, as bright as Christmas under a simple pitched roof. The car, carrying no identification, was parked right outside. Inside, through the curved bay window, Eleanor saw a tall, elderly man removing his civilian coat, helped by a young officer and a soldier, both in the grey uniforms of the occupier. Her heart sank. No military marking on the car? They had to be Gestapo. Confirmation came immediately. The few locals who had been inside started to leave by the main door, which was in a recess by the side. If she went in, she'd be the Gestapo's only company, not to mention a lone woman and an American. What to do now was perplexing. She looked at her watch. Over two hours until the nine o'clock rendezvous. She hoped they would have decamped by then, though by the look of things, that might be hope of the pious kind. She'd freeze waiting. She looked around. Her first impressions were confirmed. Everything was shut.

She noticed, though, that she was being observed from the little garden of one of the houses. The figure beckoned her over. Nothing to lose, Eleanor went closer.

'Madame,' the voice whispered through the dark.

Eleanor needed no encouraging. Her companion from the bus ushered her quickly inside and shut the door. 'You can stay here until your guide comes,' she said. 'If you sit back here, that chair by the wall, those Boches won't see you, but you'll be able to see the café.'

Eleanor took the woman's hand in both of hers, saying she was grateful beyond words, and that was the truth. 'Oh, your hands,' said the woman. 'Come,' she said and led her to a room with a sink and a large wooden tub and a boiler, which was still warm. She filled a pail with water and handed it to Eleanor. 'The toilet is through there,' she added and left.

Refreshed, Eleanor returned to find the woman had left her a cup of steaming soup. She thought of offering some money but had the good sense to offer cigarettes instead. 'For your husband,' she said. The woman looked at them and said blow her husband, she was keeping these for herself. She liked a cigarette every now and then and hadn't had one now for weeks, and certainly not an American one.

She wished Eleanor good luck and said to let herself out when she needed to go. She went to the next room to attend to her family, who were curious about their visitor in the front parlour but were told to mind their own business and leave her alone. Eleanor sipped her soup and wondered how she would occupy herself until nine. The doorway into the parlour was curtained off, though the light from inside seeped through, just enough for her to read. She had packed her last book as proof of the life she was leaving in case she ever forgot or never came back. That was in her valise, which God, the French national railways or even the Nazis willing, was on its way to Lyon. She had her small King James Bible but was not in the mood for the comforts of her religion. That left *Finnegans Wake* in her coat pocket. 'All right then,' she said, prising it out.

riverrun, past Eve and Adam's, from swerve of shore to bend of bay, brings
us by a commodius vicus of recirculation back to Howth Castle and Environs.

That was as far as she'd ever been bothered to venture. Now she persisted, telling herself not to worry that it didn't make any sense word by word, or even sentence by sentence. 'It's not supposed to,' Sylvia had said, 'but a wonderful story emerges, of life and death and resurrection. Fin agains wake. Just let it happen.' Yes, yes, Eleanor thought, we'll see.

Sir Tristram, violer d'amores, fr'over the short sea, had passen-core rearrived
from North Armorica.

Eleanor concentrated – quite an effort and quite absurd. An absurd book for an absurd situation, better at least than the alternative of internment or the despair of Hettie Rosen in the face of the Nazis.

Then she came to it. God's response to the Fall.

Bababadalgharaghtakamminarronnkonnbronntonnerronntuonnthunntrovar-
rhounawnskawntoohoohoordenenthurnuk.

She heard Sylvia and she smiled. She missed her pal so much, she thought she might weep. To save herself, she pushed on.

of a once wallstrait oldparr is retaled early in bed and later on life down
through all christian minstrelsy.

'What?' she said aloud. 'What?' And in the next paragraph, *pftjschute* and *humptyhillhead* and *tumptytumtoes*? She kept on for a couple more pages, but this wonderful story of a dream that Sylvia had promised was making even less sense than those Old Testament tales like Lot and his travails in Sodom with his wife and incestuous daughters. On that thought, however, she wondered if she'd uncovered some clue, if only in an abstract sense. The laughter of a child in the next room was decisive. 'Only a child could read this,' she said and set the book aside. She closed her eyes but did not go to sleep.

At five to nine, she got up to leave. The light in the parlour was out, the family presumably gone to bed. She let herself out as quietly as she could. The sight of the German car still parked outside the café kept the biting cold at bay only briefly. She hovered in the shadows. Would her guide or guides risk entering with the Germans there? If they did, and she was not there, that would be that.

From where she hovered across the street, she peered inside the café and saw no Germans. They must be further inside, she thought. This was her only chance. As she walked briskly across the road, she looked inside the car to see the driver snoozing in the driver's seat under his greatcoat. If he awoke, he'd see her, so, heart in mouth, she gently nudged open the café door, desperate to soften the tinkle of the bell.

To Eleanor's ears, it rang loudly enough to waken the dead. The elderly German in civilian clothes and his young uniformed offsider were sitting by the fireplace deeper inside the café, drunk and too intent on singing a maudlin song. Her eyes met those of the proprietor, and he beckoned sharply for her to sit at an alcove at the front. Comforted that she was expected, she did as she was told, making herself as small and insignificant as she could. The proprietor slipped a not-too-bad brandy in front of her. She was so cold and tense that she swallowed it in one gulp. Before she could ask for another, he retreated to the back of the café to the Germans. Their singing ceased. The proprietor offered them more wine. She heard one of them reply in French, as fluently as a bottle of wine might allow, that they had to leave, it was late.

As Eleanor felt for her cigarettes in the side pocket of her coat – if now wasn't time for an extra cigarette, she may as well give them all away – she sensed something was missing from the breast pocket, and of course she'd left Sylvia's copy of *Finnegans Wake* in the house of her protector. In other circumstances, she might have said, well, isn't that a crying shame, too bad. Now she had no choice but to go back for it, though not immediately, because the uniformed officer was leaving the café. Her heart missed more than a beat as he passed her on his way to the front door. He looked exactly like the dark, doe-eyed and thoroughly Nazi soldier she'd seen exit the toilet on the train at the Gare de Lyon. That is absurd, she said to herself, this German is a lieutenant, an officer. The soldier in Paris had been an ordinary army lance corporal. She noticed that sort of detail. Really, she thought as he went outside, they did all look the same; this was just her rattled imagination at work.

In moments, the officer returned with the driver to help the old fellow to the car. Now it was the driver who looked to Eleanor to be the very image of the lance corporal on the train at the Gare de Lyon. He had the single stripe to prove it. She was seeing shadows, she realised. She had to get a grip on herself. This was her chance. She slid out of the alcove and through the side door into the night, like a thief, and walked quickly across the road to the house behind the garden where she'd found refuge. She could hardly knock on the front door, so slipped down the side, hoping to find a door at the back. Her thoughts about that book as she stumbled over something on the muddy path were un-Christian. A talisman? It was a curse and here was proof. Come what may, she had to get it back. The next moment, a hand was across her mouth and she was pressed up against the back wall of the house, a knife shoved at her terrified face.

'It's her, it's her,' said an urgent voice and it was her rescuer, called again to save her, though this time from something potentially much worse.

'What the hell do you think you're doing?' demanded the man holding her fast. His hand was huge and fleshy and strong and he was big. His French was rough and difficult to comprehend. 'You want to stay alive, lady?' he threatened as he released his hand a little from her mouth.

'My book,' Eleanor gasped. 'I left my book inside.'

'It is her,' the woman repeated in a French that was Loire-pure, in contrast to the man's. He swore in whatever was his native tongue. Catalan? Eleanor couldn't place it. Out on the street, the Gestapo boss was humming as his underlings bundled him into the back seat of the staff car. In moments, they drove away. The man released Eleanor.

The woman led her inside and through the house to the front room. The man followed close behind, his knife still in his hand. *Finnegans Wake* was sitting on the table where Eleanor had left it. She grabbed it and squeezed the pest of a thing back inside her pocket. 'And that's where it can stay,' she said to herself.

'Jesus,' he muttered. 'You're lucky, lady.' The Germans were beginning to slip their own agents into the escape lines, he told her. He could easily have cut her throat.

'Do I look like a German agent?' Eleanor retorted.

'You'd pass very nicely with your accent,' he said, which Eleanor thought a bit rich coming from him whose accent she was now able to place as Provençal. 'There was supposed to be two people,' he added. 'Where's the other one?'

Hettie.

Eleanor had wondered if they'd notice. 'She couldn't make it,' she said, trying to avoid complicating fuss or explanation. In the next instant, she rebelled at such chilling callousness and bellowed it out in rage, for all the world to hear: 'She killed herself!'

'A yid,' the man said; explanation, not question.

Eleanor nodded.

'You a yid too?' he asked, his tone aggressive.

'Does it matter?' Eleanor snapped.

'No,' replied the man, in retreat.

'No,' she said and left it at that.

'Let's move,' he said gruffly.

Thus, Eleanor met her guide, Silvan. She understood this was not his real name but Provençal enough to account for his accent. He had watched her go into the café but then, to his consternation, watched as she had then decamped only minutes later, back to this house.

A FARMSTEAD NEAR THE RIVER ALLIER, SOUTH OF NEVERS, BURGUNDY, GERMAN-OCCUPIED FRANCE

9.15pm, Tuesday, 9th December 1941

Silvan ordered Eleanor to follow closely. The path was uneven and wet and now that the moon had set and the starlight was so faint, it was difficult to see in the shadows. She wondered if she was expected to walk the whole way to the demarcation line, which, she had worked out, was miles away. Silvan gave her no hint as they walked beyond the village, along a stone wall that skirted an open field, and in through a copse of leafless trees. She had to trust him and keep on, hoping her boots would keep her feet dry as she made her way through the watery mush of mud and decayed leaves. They came to a gate onto a narrow roadway lined with winter-bare trees. Silvan stopped and gestured her to wait, not a sound. He cocked his ear to the wind. Eleanor, with her recently developed canine hearing, was convinced she could detect the tinkle of ice crystals on the air, blown about by the wind coming down from the north. Silvan had less romantic concerns as he made an owl call with his hands around his mouth. He waited, eyes on his watch. Any immediate response was signal to turn tail immediately. The right response was silence for exactly half a minute, and then, precisely on the thirtieth second, he heard the return call. He signalled to her and they crossed the roadway and went through the gate. On the other side of a derelict wooden barn was a car whose familiar silhouette looked ominous and made her nervous. She was wondering how it had escaped the light fingers of the Nazis when the passenger door sprung open too suddenly. She recoiled, her hand to her mouth. The man who emerged stank of alcohol.

'Hiya babe,' he said cheerfully in Hollywood English as he opened the back door for her and swayed to the rhythms of Bacchus. She was barely settled into the back seat, which already had an occupant, when Silvan, now in the driver's seat, roared the engine to life and put his foot down, almost leaving behind his pickled colleague, who was only halfway into the front passenger seat.

'You are one classy broad,' he said, turning around in disorder and mirth to look at her properly.

One match, Eleanor thought, reeling from his breath, and they'd go up like Vesuvius.

'That's Al,' said Silvan, 'your guide to Lyon.'

'How do you do, Al?' she replied in English, though wondered if he might be disappointed she didn't speak like some movie gangster's moll. He was still probably only in his early thirties; his unshaven face had once been handsome, but in his left hand was his downfall, the bottle.

'I do very well, babe,' said Al. 'That FDR, he's a number one swell guy.' He took a swig from his bottle and handed it over the seat to Eleanor.

'I'm a Republican,' she responded, but really, who cared anymore? She felt foolish, took the bottle for a demure sip to be friendly, and gasped. This wasn't the hooch she expected, this was fine cognac. She looked at the label. My God, how did he get it? She took another, healthier draught before handing it back. 'Keep it,' said Al. 'I got plenty.' He produced another, which he opened and drank as if it were water.

'FDR!' he exulted.

She wasn't about to go that far. 'The United States,' she replied, and drank generously. In the spirit of the moment, she passed the bottle to her anonymous fellow passenger in the back seat, but as she did, the car swerved and some of the precious brandy spilled over him. He cursed in what sounded to Eleanor like Polish, pushed the bottle back at her in irritation, and started trying to dab the liquid from his gabardine coat and a brown paper parcel he was holding close to his chest for dear life.

'Shoulda drunk it, pal,' Al said in a French that carried the same Hollywood flavour as his English and sounded just as ridiculous. Eleanor couldn't help laughing when really they were travelling at such a breakneck speed she should be reciting the 23rd Psalm as fervently as she could. At least Al wasn't at the wheel. As they sped along back roadways, with no headlights, she comforted herself with the cognac. Silvan must know where he's going. Her fellow escapee huddled in the far corner of the seat as if she were carrying the plague. Too bad for him, she thought and sipped the nectar that chance had placed in her hands. How long they drove, she didn't notice. She felt free of any responsibility for anything and only came back to ground as the car turned a corner through some gates and came to a startling stop. Immediately, the door opened. She was bundled out of the seat by two men and brusquely pushed away. She held on to the bottle for dear life.

As the two men took over the car and drove off, Al and Silvan beckoned Eleanor and her fussy companion in through the door of a large barn. Inside, she smelt a rich fug of warm cows and their ripe ordure. Their large friendly eyes shone in the dim light from a lantern attached to a rafter, where they fed in stalls at the other end, domestic and reassuring. Silvan gestured for her and the thin Pole to wait. He and Al disappeared into the darker recesses of the building.

Through the mulled light, other people began to manifest. Wrapped in shabby clothes, silent, solitary and pensive, they leant against the stalls. The scene, Eleanor thought, was timeless, like a painting. Nearest her was a willowy, shaven-headed young man in rough dungarees, hands in his pockets to keep them warm. He smiled at her, saying nothing, keeping his purpose and identity to himself.

Another car pulled up outside. In through the door came two elderly ladies who looked as old as the pyramids, and God knows, what on earth were they doing here? Eleanor said good evening to them. They confided in hushed voices that they were sisters returning home after visiting another sister in Paris, such were the minor travails of the times. She opened her cigarettes to them but each declined. As she herself resisted the urge to smoke and closed the case, a generously proportioned gentleman, who had arrived before her, slid over to her as if he were a skater on ice. He had a gleaming face that spoke of living well at the expense of others.

'Madame,' he said with barely restrained extravagance and brushed hay and dust from a wooden box so that she might sit, his eyes fixed on her cigarette case.

Eleanor thanked him but said she was happy to stand and possibly he might keep his voice down.

He was 'Szegedy Tibor from Budapest,' he said in quite good English. He'd jumped to the right conclusion about Eleanor's nationality and purpose. Amused by his performance, she flipped open her cigarettes. He gathered one up with as much reverence as a priest the host at Mass – or, more like, an actor playing a priest with the host at Mass. She lit it for him.

'Ah,' he purred and savoured the pleasure as if it were the finest hashish to be had this side of the Levant. Eleanor wondered if this charming rogue's nom de guerre was the only Hungarian he could speak.

Her face stiffened. The maybe-Hungarian was aghast. Had he offended her? He begged forgiveness.

'I didn't know we'd be travelling steerage,' Eleanor snapped.

Her attention was not on the poor Hungarian but on the latest arrival, who came through the door like a dark cloud on a sunny day, the very same *malfrat maudit* elf who had stolen her cigarettes on the train.

He saw her, stared a moment in puzzlement. Then he realised. Of all the bad luck. He gave her an aggressive clenched fist and a sullen look to go with it. He didn't like the rich on principle. The first chance he got, he'd steal from her again. Successfully this time.

In other circumstances, Eleanor would have slapped his insolent face. She was about to retreat to the cow stalls and their more cordial company when Al appeared.

'The Boches are after an American dame with a book,' he said to her. Eleanor could hardly believe her ears. He saw her face of dismay.

'You gotta lie with your face better, lady,' he said with a chuckle. Even funnier was the Germans wasting time over a stupid book.

'How do you know?' she asked, flabbergasted.

He shook his head. Stupid question. Of course they'd know, just as they knew what time the patrols set out, which parts of the line were to be hit harder that night than others, why they moved from barn to house to church, whom to pay off, which German-lovers to keep away from.

'If it's that important, hide it better and keep your mouth shut' is all he said.

'But it's not important,' she replied, as if she was making an excuse. That was the truth, though it was too difficult to explain and, really, she couldn't be bothered. She would toss it into the nearest river if it caused any more trouble. But Al was keen to see a book that was fussing the Germans so much. Reluctantly, she produced it. He opened the first page and read aloud the first line, which in his eccentric English made her laugh. That was quite something given her snappish mood.

'Hah,' he said, handing it back. 'It's in secret code, that's why.' He made a motion to button his lip and he winked.

'That's the best explanation I've heard,' said Eleanor, resisting the urge to plant Mr James Joyce into the nearest cow pat.

Silvan appeared and led her into a makeshift photography studio, one of the cow stalls, whose walls were covered in burlap. Inside was the only bright light she'd seen since June 1940. She had to hold a hand up to her eyes until they adjusted.

'Your documents for the other side,' explained Silvan, who stood at the other end of the camera. 'Al will give them to you tomorrow morning.'

'I don't need new documents for Vichy,' she said. 'I've got my passport and my Paris identity card.'

'What's it to be, lady, an American middle-aged woman on the run with a book the Nazis want or Madame Eugenie de Lisle, a widow, going home to Toulouse?' he said irritably.

Vanity rebelled against both choices, at least as Silvan described them. She admitted the logic of his argument, however. 'Real still, doll,' said Al so close that she almost gagged on his alcoholic breath. Silvan took her photograph. She saw her fellow escapee in his gabardine coat was next, so got out of the way. Al had to tell him to let go of the parcel but he didn't understand a word of French, and when Al came over and forcibly pulled it away, the man held on to it and wouldn't budge.

'Another secret code, eh, pal?' said Al, losing his humour. He showed him where to hold it so it wasn't in the photograph. Then she saw it was the turn of the young thief, and if he didn't look as innocent as a child as he looked at the camera. Of all the cheek!

The cat's head was poking out below the kid's collar. 'Ditch the kitty,' said Al in French. But Stalin did nothing so Al pushed it back inside his coat.

'What's his name going to be?' Eleanor asked Silvan. 'Al Capone?'

'Stalin,' the boy answered. 'Joseph Stalin.'

'Hah,' Eleanor exclaimed because she'd hit the bullseye. Hadn't she placed him as some insurrectionist? Like face, like nature.

'Stop fooling around and look at the camera, kid,' said Silvan.

'What?' asked Stalin in exact French. 'I do not understand.'

'Look at the camera, Joe,' Eleanor said, thinking his question was because of Silvan's thick accent. 'Think of it as a firing squad,' she added. He got the drift of her French and muttered under his breath. Something about this young man, she thought, was not right. His French was sparse, accented and rehearsed.

Once the photographs were taken, Silvan stripped away the burlap; another man removed the light and the camera. Al led in a cow, although he stumbled as he threw in the hay, which he fell into and laughed like a kid having fun. His clothes and hair had straw sticking out of them but he was unbothered. He took another draught from his bottle of cognac and shooed Eleanor and her companions of the road like a gaggle of geese towards a smaller room, which housed the barn's machinery and smelt of oil and gasoline. Outside, through the grimy window, pale light from the stars bathed the landscape. Inside were two young queens, earlier arrivals, who were bored and in need of entertainment. One whistled saucily when he saw Eleanor's young thief.

'Shut up, Darlene,' Al said as if this were regular behaviour, which it was. 'They're just bumming a lift to the other side,' he explained to Stalin. 'Don't take no notice of them.' Stalin's French wasn't up to punk talk, which Eleanor thought was surprising in a punk. He retreated into a permanent scowl. The little cat's head poked through the top of his coat.

'Hey, Mac,' said Darlene, 'what's the kitty's name?' Stalin took not the slightest notice.

'Jesus,' said Darlene's companion, whose name was Luc, 'why ask the cat's name? Ask *his* name.'

'I like cats,' Darlene protested. Like the tired half of an equally tired comedy routine, Al said, 'You can say that again,' which made the two saucy pals laugh, but no one else. They were just keeping up their spirits. Too bad if no one else could be bothered.

'Come on, handsome,' Luc asked, 'what's your name?'

'Try Joe Stalin,' Eleanor said for the heck of it. He might not understand every word, but he knew what she was about. It took all his self-control not to lash out at her.

'A red,' Darlene purred, 'how exciting.'

'I am Jew from Amsterdam,' Stalin muttered darkly in poor French. A warning. Keep away.

'A yid?' Luc exclaimed. 'You don't look like no yid, you're too handsome.'

He couldn't understand French at all, Eleanor realised.

'English?' she asked. 'Do you speak English?'

'Perfectly,' he replied in a surprisingly un-punk manner.

'Kid,' said the Hungarian wearily in English, 'take my advice. Don't be a yid, just be a Dutchman.'

'I am not ashamed,' said Joe Stalin.

'Then you're a crazy yid,' said the Hungarian, washing his hands of him. He was certainly no punk, Eleanor figured, he was just a frightened Dutch kid putting on an act, even the glare he shot at her when he saw her looking at him. She laughed.

'You needn't look at me like that, sonny,' she said. 'The only one of your identities I'm concerned about is "thief".'

'He's one of your kind, Darlene,' Al reported.

'I'm in love,' cried Darlene, and Al said, 'Yeah, a thief,' and Luc laughed and laughed.

'Everyone's a thief these days,' said Darlene. 'It ain't so special no more.' He was bored with these people.

Stalin withdrew. He hated being the object of any attention – lust, pity, anger or otherwise.

Silvan entered. Soon they would leave. Al would lead the way, he instructed, while he would bring up the rear. They were to stick no more than three metres from the person in front of them. The river was one kilometre away; this side was the German side, the other was Vichy. They had to be careful because the German army patrols went across regularly to chase escapees.

'How do we cross the river?' Eleanor asked. Silvan's reply confirmed her foreboding.

'Rocks.'

'Don't worry, doll, the river's real low this time of year,' said Al in French. 'But don't scream, whatever you do.'

'I'll fish you out,' said Silvan. That was not reassuring, nor the end of the dangers. 'When you cross, you crouch as low as you can,' he added. 'If the Germans see you, they shoot you.'

Then came a sound most of them were all too familiar with, unmistakeable and unwelcome, as German army trucks came out of the night, getting louder and ever closer. Through the grimy window they could see headlights stab the dark as the trucks slowed. Silvan and Al cautioned silence. Darlene began to giggle. Al snapped at him to shut the fuck up. He couldn't help it, he said, and fuck the Germans and fuck all this trouble, when suddenly a knife was at his throat with Joe Stalin at the other end of it. He'd had enough of this stupid damn queen. He kept his knife pressed into Darlene's neck as the windows began to rattle. Eleanor, expecting the terrible sound of hobnailed boots across the hard ground and ugly guttural shouts, said a silent prayer for their safety, the sort of instinctual prayer any Christian in her situation might offer. Apart from the Lord's Prayer, which she said every night before she went to sleep, prayer was something Eleanor found difficult, like reading out a shopping list to an empty house, so best left to the clergy. Whatever the power of her prayer, the German purpose that night was elsewhere. The trucks kept on after making a turn on the roadway nearby, the engines revved, the gears changed and soon they were gone. Joe Stalin backed away from Darlene but kept his knife out just in case.

'You ask for it, Darlene,' Al muttered. Darlene, for once, had nothing to say.

Now they could leave, said Silvan. The next patrol would be in about twenty-five minutes. They still had to be careful, because they didn't know if the Germans might stop and start a sweep back towards them.

'If you fall behind,' he told them, 'you're on your own. We can't stop for anyone and we won't go back for anyone. Understand?'

He waited a moment to make sure they took this in.

'But,' he added, and stopped so he was sure he had their attention, if any got separated and made it to the other side, they were to go five hundred metres south through the woods to a stone fence, which would lead them to a road, then go in a westerly direction up the hill to the village.

'Remember the first house on the left. You ask a young woman there, "Is this the boulangerie?" She will answer no, but she has nice apples. She'll direct you.'

With that reassurance, Silvan opened the door. Al took a draught of his cognac and was the first out into the night. Eleanor wrapped her scarf around her head, then found herself behind Stalin, who at least allowed the two sisters to go out before him. He wasn't entirely without manners, even if they did not extend to her.

Around midnight, Tuesday, 9th December 1941

Silvan led his party at a cracking pace along a rutted cow path beside a stone fence, which gave them some cover, and then through a gate into an open field, where mist was gathering in the hollows. Though they kept to the side where it was unploughed, the wet soil was clayed, so it stuck to the bottom of their shoes, making the going harder. The closer they approached the river, the thicker the mist. Eleanor could see the silhouette of Joe Stalin in front of her. She glanced behind but the mist was too dense to see who was following, even more reason not to let the little shit out of her sight. He seemed to be going faster, which made it more difficult for her to keep up. She had to stop to catch her breath, just for a moment, but seeing him fade into the mist, she pushed herself forward in case she lost him. At least she could see his footsteps on the muddy ground, and these she followed. Then she walked straight into a stone fence, hurting her knee. She cursed silently, found the imprints of his boots again and, although she saw no one, trudged on, hoping to God she was going the right direction.

She kept at this for another couple of minutes, suppressing her fear that she might be lost and no one would be rescuing her. She could feel the river not far away: the air had become colder, a good sign, and the mist if anything was even heavier. It had to be nearby. She stopped in the hope she might hear someone from the party, but if she had developed canine hearing, it brought her no help now. All she heard was that vague soughing given off by the earth itself, its own murmur of life. Then an owl called. Was that Al or a real owl? When she heard no response, she knew she was lost.

'You idiot, Eleanor,' she muttered. The cold, which her determination and concentration had kept at bay, now chilled her skin. What she felt was fear. She dragged herself on, hoping to find a fence or another stone wall, then walked into one. She needed to rest. She certainly needed a cigarette and crouched to light it. Her head swam with relief. She stood back up, right into the barrel of a rifle.

'*Hände hoch*,' said the German soldier. He then made an owl call, which was returned from some distance away. Eleanor dropped the cigarette. She was too terrified to gasp, even to breathe. The soldier pushed the barrel of his rifle into her chest.

'*Hände hoch oder ich schieße*,' he snarled. She could see the whites of his eyes. His face was smeared with grease. She raised her hands.

In the next instant, his eyes bulged, he gulped and he dropped as if he were lead. It was so fast that Eleanor didn't immediately understand what had happened. Had she conjured him and his rifle up out of her fears? She cried out as the shock burst from her, a stifled cry, because a hand covered her mouth and she found herself looking into the wild eyes of Joe Stalin inches away. He released his grip slowly, brought a finger to his lips and then he wiped the blood from his knife. Eleanor had no time to respond, because something or someone was approaching and it made an unconvincing owl call. Had she her wits about her, she could hardly have been surprised. This was the other half of a pair of armed lovebirds.

Stalin wrenched off the dead soldier's helmet, pulled it on and gave the return call.

'Nitschke?' called the voice close by.

'*Hier*,' said Stalin convincingly in a loud whisper and he stood. The other soldier, seeing the familiar silhouette, relaxed and came closer, closer. '*Ich hab' einen gefangen*,' Stalin added. I've caught one.

'*Wer, Mensch*?' the other called over-excitedly as if this were a game. '*Ein Jude*?'

Eleanor saw the knife poised in Stalin's hand. As he lunged his body at the German, she cried out, giving the German a split-second warning to fall back. The German fell to the ground, but Stalin kicked his rifle out of his hand before he could fire. Then the German brought him down with his foot, and there on the muddy earth, they grappled with each other in a death scrabble. Eleanor, pressed up against the wall in terror, couldn't see who was who, could hear only the grunts of desperation, and even then, what could she do? The soldier's boot hit her leg as he sought something to push against. Instinctively, she pushed him back. This gave him the heft he needed to launch himself back at Stalin. In moments, a horrible rasping gasp reached out to Eleanor through the cold air and expired as if right in front of her. She didn't need canine ears to hear the heavy breathing of only one man.

The victor raised himself from the ground as if he were made of the earth itself. Dread consumed her. Both men wore the same awful helmet.

Insanity or the last gasp of an instinct for self-preservation, Eleanor hurled herself at what she assumed was the German.

'Stupid woman,' Stalin snapped, pushing her back. He reached desperately inside his coat to take out his cat, which he held to his face, comforting it with soothing words, his tenderness in shocking contrast to what he had just done. He gave it a tit-bit, then set it down by the water's edge, where he held it while it drank.

Eleanor festered in impotent fury by the fence.

When he had calmed the kitten and returned it to his coat pocket, he turned to the bodies. He felt inside the pockets of the soldier he'd only just managed to kill, removed some money, which he pocketed, and then cigarettes, although only two. Better than nothing.

'Quickly,' he said in English and hooked his arms under the dead man's shoulders.

'What?' she cried. He couldn't be serious.

'Do it,' he ordered. She was numb by now and took up the man's booted feet. They were so heavy she dropped them. Lifting them up again, she thought she heard a moan.

'He's alive,' she said, horrified.

'Dead,' said Stalin blankly as they struggled the limp body to the river's edge hardly ten feet away. But when he rolled the body into the icy water, the man did come alive. He grabbed Stalin's leg with both hands in a deathly vice grip. His eyes were wide open and full of hate and fury. Stalin looked down at the man, the one who'd asked if the other had caught a Jew. He leant in close enough to bite the fellow's ear off. '*Ich bin Jud', du Nazi Schwein*,' he said and coolly thrust the knife into his chest, not once but three times. He kicked the body out into the stream so the current would carry it off some way before it sank. Eleanor gasped, appalled.

'Come,' Stalin ordered as he went to the first soldier, whose body was still lying a little way off. He felt through the soldier's pockets, removing some coins and only one cigarette.

'That's a mighty haul,' Eleanor said.

'For you, not so much,' he said, putting her and her sarcasm in their place. He saw the man's knife and took it. Then he lifted the man's shoulders. 'How are you so easily lost?' he demanded as she reluctantly helped him carry the body to the water.

'I was following you,' she answered in the same aggressive tone. If that was how he talked, so could she. 'What were you doing here, then?' she continued in the same vein. 'Certainly not looking out for my welfare.'

They tumbled the dead soldier out into the river so that he too was taken up by the current. 'You were lost too,' she said.

Stalin hurried back to find the rifles and the other helmet. Eleanor watched hopelessly as the second body drifted away on its back. As it slowly turned over, she saw the soldier's face. Under the grease he'd smeared on, as if they'd been playing cowboys and Indians, he was just another boy. Eleanor felt her stomach heave and she threw up into the water.

He returned with the rifles and hurled them out into the river as far as he could. 'I am not lost,' he said.

'No, you were just going the wrong way,' she retorted.

He filled both helmets from the river and splashed the water where he had felled the two Germans, repeating the action until he had washed away any blood and their tracks. Then, he sat on the ground, quickly unlaced his boots, removing them and his socks. His bare feet were marble white. He stood up, dropping not only his trousers but his long underwear, turning away from her for modesty's sake.

'What are you doing?' she demanded.

'We cannot stay here,' he replied, matter-of-fact. He wrapped trousers, underwear and boots around his neck, hoisted up the lower part of his coat, leaving himself completely naked from the waist down. From the back, she saw he was tough but so thin and spare, almost gaunt with it.

'You can't just leave me here,' she said.

'It is shallower up here,' he said, moving upstream a few yards to where the water rippled and eddied over rocks just below the surface. He kept his back to her all the time. In each hand, he carried a German helmet. With tender words to his cat, he waded into the dark water, which was bitterly cold. His curse might have been silent as he recoiled his foot so fast he nearly fell. He gritted his teeth and just got on with it. It wasn't the first time. What she did, he couldn't care less. She had warned the Nazi. His escape had almost been thwarted right here on a freezing French riverbank, where he was as far from the destination of his dream as hell was from heaven.

Eleanor ripped off her boots and woollen socks, hitched up her dress and coat as best she could, and followed. She couldn't remove her long underwear – she wouldn't, damn it – so had to suffer them getting wet. She waded in after him. The water was awful. After the wrenching shock she'd had already, another had little effect. All her energy and concentration went on staying upright as the current eddied around her legs. Underfoot, the riverbed was covered with tiny pebbles but these helped her keep her footing, and though the water became deeper, reaching her thighs and wetting her dress as well, she was able to make it to the other side.

Towards 1am, Wednesday, 10th December 1941

Stalin was already hitching up his trousers. Eleanor's feet and legs were numb, her clothing from her thighs down wet. She needed a cigarette badly and hoped beyond hope the water hadn't seeped inside the case.

'Thank God,' she said. Before she could even remove a cigarette, he snatched the case from her hand.

'You escape the Nazis, now you tell the gendarmes where you are,' he snapped. 'They will give you to the Germans. Tomorrow, this place is very hot. We must get away.' At least he returned the case to her.

'What about Al?' Eleanor said, as she dressed. 'What about our papers?'

'What papers? What about them?' he demanded as he laced up his boots. Of course, Eleanor realised, his French was limited to what was his name, 'whore', 'no' and 'fuck off'. No wonder he'd got lost and she, the fool following him, was now in this predicament. It was all his fault.

'If you're caught without papers, they'll hand you back.'

He seemed to accept the logic of her argument. 'We both need new papers,' he said.

'I don't,' she said, not in a friendly manner. 'I have an American passport and a Paris identity card.'

She was felled by the look he shot back at her. Envy? Disgust? Terrible fear? Desperation? It was all these. Really it was the look of one who was doomed, gazing at one who was saved. Worse, she realised, it was the look Hettie had given her at the American

Cathedral as she comprehended her fate, surrounded by Christians with their US passports.

He dismissed her and her smug comfort, turned and walked off. But he was going in the wrong direction. She knew it. His sense of direction was unerringly bad. Besides, he had no idea where he was supposed to go.

'That's not south,' she said. 'Silvan said walk in a southerly direction to find the road, then west to the village.'

'Thank you,' he said, although she could tell he did not mean it in the slightest.

'One good turn deserves another,' Eleanor responded. Even now he was heading off-course. And why was he still carrying the helmets of the men he'd killed? Souvenirs? She hurried after him. 'This way,' she said. The bottom of her dress and coat hung heavy and wet; her feet and legs were still numb. She led him through the woods to the stone fence. Beyond was the road, which was unsealed, wet and muddy. No car, truck, horse or human had been along it since the rain. If this was the right road, Eleanor thought, she should be able to see the tracks of others from their party. Given the lack of an alternative, she kept her concerns to herself and her feet in motion. If she stopped, she might never get going again.

She led the way, cautious through the darkness, which was inky and unrelenting. Only the fence was a reliable guide. The ground was wet and rank with rotting vegetation and cow manure.

'Stop,' he said. He used a flat stone from the top of the fence to dig out a shallow hole, which wasn't difficult as the soil was loose and wet. He filled each helmet with the manure and placed them in the hole.

'Give me two stones,' he ordered. Eleanor took them from the top of the fence. He put them on top of the helmets and covered them with soil, which he tamped flat with his boots. He drew a stick across the surface to cover his tracks, washed his hands in a puddle and stood up.

'Helmets float,' he explained.

They set off and soon began to go up a rise. A dog barked not far away as it sensed the arrival of strangers. They came to the first house on the left, set back from the roadway behind a small garden.

Around 2am, Wednesday, 10th December 1941

'At last,' Eleanor muttered impatiently. She went to the door. Her knocking seemed to echo through the village. If that didn't waken their contact, she thought, it would certainly waken the dead in the church graveyard. The door opened, and framed by the entrance was a woman, just as Silvan had promised. She was young, with pretty bobbed hair. Eleanor noticed that the smile she flashed was directed not at her but at Stalin.

'Is this the boulangerie?' Eleanor asked, as instructed. The young woman said no, but she had nice sweet apples.

'You are the first tonight,' the young woman added. Given what had befallen them, this surprised Eleanor, and in the next moment worried her. Had the Germans caught the others? 'It's dark,' said the young woman. 'The Boches are everywhere on the other side, so they must wait until they're gone.'

'We need to get our papers,' said Stalin to Eleanor, who in turn asked the young woman.

'Tomorrow,' said the young woman. That much he understood.

'We need to get them now,' he pressed, seemingly immune to the young woman's charms.

'They are not ready,' she replied in broken and heavily accented English.

'Where are we to spend the rest of the night?' Eleanor asked.

'In the barn behind the blacksmith,' she explained. Eleanor wasn't having any of that. She said she would pay to sleep in a bed if one was available. Without a moment's reflection, the young woman agreed and mentioned a price, which Eleanor was happy to pay. She'd have paid a king's ransom if asked, and she handed over the money.

'We cannot stay,' said Stalin. 'We must get away.'

'Go then,' said Eleanor. 'I'm staying.' How could the Germans possibly find them? They didn't even know what had happened. Anyway, she didn't care if the Gestapo burst in on her, she had to get herself dry; she couldn't continue right now, murders or no murders. Where on earth would they go? She had no energy left to argue with him.

The young woman saw the little cat poke its head out of Stalin's coat. She lost any interest in showing Eleanor to her room.

'Oh,' she said, charmed, and if being kind to his cat was the way to make Stalin into a human being, it worked. She offered milk, which he accepted with 'Merci, merci' and, Eleanor noticed, with the nearest she had seen to a smile.

The young woman ushered them both inside, shut the door and quickly lit a small lamp that gave off enough light to show the way.

'Toilet,' said Stalin but he meant for the cat. How ridiculously fastidious, Eleanor thought. Had it whispered to him? 'Of course,' said the young woman. She handed the lamp to Eleanor and bade her go up the stairs to the room on the left at the top while she attended to the cat.

'I too need to use the toilet,' Eleanor growled. Be damned if she was going to play second fiddle to a cat or to the flirting of the young. The young woman pointed absently to a door at the far end of the house and guided Stalin, with cat, outside. Eleanor was furious. Where he was going to sleep, she did not care.

The room upstairs was tiny, the ceiling steeply slanted; you could stand only in the middle. Two narrow beds were against opposite walls, separated by a single bedside table at one end; a narrow wardrobe partly blocked the door at the other. Eleanor quickly took off her clothes, hung the wet things to dry in the wardrobe, found clean underwear and, after sprinkling the bed with some of her perfume, slipped under the heavy blanket. It might have been rough, but dear God, it was warm and she was alone at last. Except she became acutely conscious of her unwashed face, which felt as if it were smeared in pig fat with a top layer of grit. Sleep was almost impossible but she was damned if she was going to ask that minx where the bathroom was. Yes, she knew she was cutting off her nose to spite her unwashed face, but it was enjoyable in the perverse mood she was in. She got up, retrieved Al's bottle of cognac and true to her perversity, *Finnegans Wake*, then crawled back into bed. She took a generous slug of the cognac, opened the book and tried unsuccessfully to find where she'd left off. It didn't seem to matter.

The door opened. Stalin entered, followed by the young woman. 'You are comfortable?' she asked pleasantly.

'Yes,' said Eleanor. 'What's he doing here?'

'Two beds,' replied the young woman as if it was obvious, 'two people.'

'In separate rooms,' Eleanor insisted as she realised she had paid for him as well.

'There is no separate room' was the reply.

What about yours? Eleanor was about to suggest, an agreeable solution given the way the young woman had taken such a shine to Stalin. Or was it just the cat? In any case, he was inside now.

'Do not open the curtains or the window,' the young woman instructed. She would wake them in time in the morning, she said, closed the door and left.

Stalin said nothing to her. With no by your leave or may I, he sat on the other bed, dropped his rucksack, took off his boots and his socks, which Eleanor noticed were quite new and of good quality.

Stolen, she had already concluded. He put the cat on the bed as he removed his outer garments.

He was here only because he couldn't think of an alternative. At least this was the Vichy side, though that made him feel only marginally less insecure. The Nazis would be searching for their soldiers by now. How long before someone found them? Who might find them? These sorts of killings made the Wehrmacht insane with fury, and he didn't trust any frontier created by them. He'd been worried because the bodies had floated off in the wrong direction, back up into Occupied France, not down into Vichy as he had expected. He was no good at north and south, and Miss Rich American had already caught him out. She was glaring at him, too lousy to offer him a cigarette. Sure, he'd taken – what was it, two, three lousy German army ration cigarettes? Big deal. Then he saw the open cognac on the bedside table. He had a good mind just to help himself.

She read his thoughts and handed him the bottle, and, as an afterthought, her cigarettes.

'I'm Eleanor,' she said. 'At least we should know each other's name.'

He took a draught of the cognac and handed it back. 'You know my name,' he replied and lit one of her cigarettes.

'Your real name,' she said.

'There is no point,' he said. After he finished the cigarette, he slipped under the blanket and drew in his little cat so it was warm and safe.

He can please himself, she thought. She'd tried. When next she looked, the little cat was sitting outside the cover cleaning itself. Stalin was either asleep or feigning sleep. At least the cat loved him, she conceded, and he loved it. She noticed something around his neck, a locket of plain silver on a cheap silver chain. What was in it? A hair from the bald head of Lenin? Given what had happened earlier, she now considered it a travesty to read the meandering fantasies of

James Joyce. The cognac wasn't working. She'd be sick if she drank much more. Her heart felt empty. She was angry. Hettie's suicide weighed on her. She reached for her rucksack and drew out her King James and went to the Psalms, to the 23rd. 'The Lord is my shepherd; I shall not want. He maketh me to lie down in green pastures . . .' As she read, she began to feel some comfort; she no longer felt alone.

5am, Wednesday, 10th December 1941

On waking, Eleanor noticed her companion sleeping as peacefully as his cat. He woke with a start and saw her staring resentfully at him.

'You're just a boy,' she said, not meant as a compliment.

'I was never a boy,' he replied. 'What is the time?' He didn't wait for an answer, reached for her wristwatch on the bedside table to see for himself. 'We must leave.' He lifted the cat, got up and started to put on his clothes. 'My name is Henk,' he said.

'That's an improvement on Stalin,' she replied.

He nodded as he sat to do up his boots. He indicated *Finnegans Wake* sitting on the bedside table.

'Why do the Nazis want this book?' he asked.

'How do you know that?' she asked suspiciously. 'I thought you didn't understand French.'

'Your friend Al speaks it in English,' he said. She was still suspicious.

'Greed,' she replied. 'It's a rare first edition with an extremely fine provenance. The author will be rolling in his grave.'

'You are an intellectual,' he sneered.

Eleanor smiled at his rush to judgment on such thin evidence. 'That's not what my fellow writers say about me and they're right. I don't understand a word of it.'

'Why do you carry it?' he demanded.

'You sound like a certain Boche major of my unwilling acquaintance,' she replied coolly. Disappointingly, he did not bite.

'I'm American,' she said. 'I'm duty-bound to defend Mr Joyce's right to scribble gibberish and get away with it, not to mention to stop it from falling into the hands of a voracious Nazi.'

Her attempt at levity got nowhere. He picked up her Bible. She snatched it back.

'You believe in Stalin,' she snapped. 'That's what I believe in.'

He shook his head. 'You are a fool,' he said.

'An intellectual and a fool as well!' Eleanor replied. 'My, what a poor wretch.'

She wasn't going to engage with him any longer, a waste of time and breath. She mightn't be a good Christian but when she read the Gospels, she knew the writers had been trying to make sense of what they had seen and experienced, something mysterious and life changing. The stories were too vivid for fiction – their differences and contradictions were proof of that. She had known it so as a child, the alpha and omega of her faith, her present distemper notwithstanding. Private, not for the likes of him to trample over with his ignorance, disdain and contempt. He was just like the literary raptors with their leftist certainties and moral vanity. But what did the Bible say about loving thy neighbour if he was a murderer? Why on earth was she caught up with such a pest? She was mindful of the irony of this Henk in her life. He was as far as could be from Yann, the young killer who captures the heart of her alter ego Selina in *The American Woman*. The contrast between art and life couldn't have been greater.

She got up and felt her clothes. They were still damp. She was desperate for the bathroom. Her hair was a mess, her face a catastrophe.

The sharp rap on the door startled them. The young woman pushed in, wide-eyed and nervous.

'You must leave now,' she said. 'There is trouble.'

Both knew much more about the trouble than did the young woman. Eleanor only had time to put back on her damp clothes. The young woman hurried them down the stairs and out through a back gate to a path, then led them to the barn at the back of the blacksmith's. As they hurried away through the dark, Eleanor took out her cognac, drank a generous drop to fortify herself and handed it to Henk, who did the same. Without a hint of thanks, she noted.

The blacksmith's forge was already firing up. They could hear the curses of the blacksmith and the bellows he was trying to coax into action – to him it was a day like yesterday, the day before, any day. The young woman tapped on the door and it opened to Al, who was sober and sour for it. He beckoned them in and shut the door behind them.

'What happened to you?' he demanded.

'The mist was so thick,' Eleanor answered as lightly as she could, 'but we made it across safely.' She assumed he knew where they'd stayed the night.

'You never saw nothing? No Boches?'

'Nothing,' Eleanor replied, leaving it at that. She could see plainly enough that Al had wind of what happened. Enquiry might lead to complications. She didn't think Al would be best pleased to hear they were the cause.

'Your papers,' said Al, handing them over. Eleanor glanced at hers.

'Madame Helene Rouget?' she exclaimed. 'I thought I was to be the widow de Lisle.'

'You are still the widow,' explained Al, 'but because of your accent, you are the mama born in America. He is your French son, Anton. You are from Toulouse. Neat, huh?' Explaining his ingenuity was improving his mood. 'You're going to Toulouse, kid,' he said to Henk.

'He barely speaks a word of French,' Eleanor said.

'Shit,' said Al in French. This was news. 'But you do,' he said, as if this fixed everything. 'Don't forget the accent. Look,' he added, pointing proudly to her new identity, 'born in Hollywood, Calif.'

'Toulouse?' Henk said. 'No. I pay to go to Pau. Not Toulouse. Pau. I pay for that.'

'Yeah, Mac, we heard you,' Al said in his faux gangster English.

Eleanor switched to French. 'I don't need these,' she said. 'America's not at war with France. I have my American passport; I can make my own way now.'

'You're in the middle of nowhere, babe,' said Al. 'Help the yid out till Lyon, then you can be whoever you want to be.'

What does it matter? she said to herself, resigned. Could things get any worse? She consented she owed her present freedom to him. But Pau?

'Are you insane?' she said to Henk. 'You can't cross into Spain over the Pyrénées. It's coming winter, unless you haven't noticed.'

'I have paid for a passage to Spain through Pau,' he replied stubbornly.

'More fool you,' she muttered. She thought she'd erased the wretched place from her memory but there it was, like a scab waiting to be picked.

Al returned. 'Let's move out,' he said in French, then to Eleanor in his Hollywood best, 'The Indians are on the warpath, babe. Two of their braves was scalped last night.'

Eleanor feared she was like General Custer at the wrong end of the Battle of Little Bighorn. Outside, the rest of the party were boarding a small truck. Everyone else had made it across without incident. Henk clambered in. Al helped Eleanor up, whacked the back of the truck and scrambled himself in as the motor revved and they were away.

ORTSKOMMANDANTUR 891, NEVERS, BURGUNDY, GERMAN-OCCUPIED FRANCE

5.15am, Wednesday, 10th December 1941

Missing? Two? How?

Through the early-morning hours, each level of the German army responded in exactly the same way as they reported higher up the chain of command. The details did not change.

Two men, a private and a one-striper, were in a ten-man section patrolling the German-occupied side along a stretch of the Allier River in Section A. The mist was thick, so the section broke into pairs for the rest of the patrol, agreeing to regroup at a point two kilometres downstream. When they did, Private Schelling and Lance Corporal Jentsch, eighteen and twenty-one respectively, were missing. The section waited fifteen minutes beyond the appointed time of 0130 and radioed the lieutenant, who brought up the rest of the platoon, and they searched in a line upriver for five kilometres. This had taken them to the beginning of Section B, by which time it was after four am. In the process, they captured three Jews and apprehended six French citizens who were trying to cross the river into the *Zone Süd*, the South Zone, as they called the unoccupied part of France. There was neither sign of their two missing comrades nor any indication that they might have come to grief. It was as if they'd been lifted off the earth without a trace.

The theory was they had encountered escapees or those who were helping them and had been either murdered or captured. Whatever the case, this was intolerable. Now a more complete search was to start using army dogs. The French police on both sides of the demarcation line had been ordered to help, although it was clear that the Vichy police would help in their own good time. Posters were being prepared with photographs of the two soldiers and a reward had been offered for information. The French as well as the Jews taken last night were being held as hostages.

The *Geheime Feldpolizei*, the army's secret field police, were being brought in as a matter of urgency, but no Gestapo – not yet, if anyone could help it, unless the GFP got nowhere.

Around 7am, Wednesday, 10th December 1941

The young man yelled '*Vive la liberté*' but didn't get past the '*vive*'. The shots cut short his cry as they cut short his life. The lieutenant of the squad went quickly to confirm the prisoner was dead. Then he marched up and saluted Geheime Feldpolizei Kommissar Anton Bauer, who was standing at the back. Bauer followed him to the young man's body, sagging forward from the wooden post to which he had been bound.

'That's him,' muttered Bauer, who had tracked him down and arrested him. There was no doubt, but they had to stick to the legalities. The young man's age on the death certificate was wrong. Eighteen years old?

'That's not right,' he said to the lieutenant. 'He was twenty-four.'

The form, however, was correct. He was just a kid, bravura and all.

Stupid, stupid, Bauer said to himself. These kids, they're easily led. He'd like to get his hands on the ones who had poisoned this one's mind to shoot a German officer in the back. *And* had given him the gun. They'll die in their own beds at ninety, while this boy was for the worms before he'd had a chance to feel a girl's caress. The old copper in Bauer could still be incensed. He hated those old lags who corrupted the young into crime. He took no pleasure in executions except when it was one of those grey-bearded devils. He'd pull the lever himself to drop one of them to the bottom of the rope. Never was allowed to, wasn't his job. His job was to nail them. That at least was a satisfaction. Not like this, though. He countersigned the death certificate and left.

On the drive back to his office at the Hôtel Bradford on Rue Phillipe du Roule, he had his driver stop for a little while in the Bois de Boulougne, to clear his head and lighten his sour mood.

Bauer was fifty-one, average height, with thinning grey hair and a face you could see in one of those seventeenth-century Dutch paintings of peasants at a country fair. He had big peasant's hands with thick, clumsy-looking fingers. Too old for this war, he had served on the Eastern Front during the last. He knew what war was like. Every single day since this one erupted was another day off his own life because of his worries for his two sons on active service. He'd volunteered when the GFP was set up in 1939, not because he was sick of the Nazis intruding on even the most mundane detective work in Frankfurt, although he most decidedly was. It was because, inside the army, he could keep an eye on his kids through the army's First World War old-boys' network. This was how he knew his nineteen-year-old, Karl, was alive and well in a Panzer brigade outside Tobruk with the brilliant Rommel, and that the other, twenty-four-year-old Georg, an infantry lieutenant in Army Group Centre, had reached the gates of Moscow.

Though the German public knew nothing of it, he was also aware that a week or so before, the Soviets had launched a savage counter-attack on the Moscow front that had taken General Guderian by surprise. Hardly a coincidence, it came at precisely the same moment as the arrival of the equally savage Russian winter, to which both sides gave the honorary rank of general. Having served on the Eastern Front himself in the last war, he understood all too well about Russia's 'General Winter'. At least Georg was alive and unwounded. As for himself, what could he do except make sure his wife sent the boy the warm clothes the army hadn't provided, and extra food to both Karl and Georg, as well as the Pervitin all German soldiers were using to stay awake. Each week, he sent encouraging messages and letters, mostly about his cases or funny stories about the ways of the French. Silly old papa, they probably thought. Still, he was sure they appreciated knowing he was always thinking of them.

Lost in his reverie, Bauer was startled by the sudden bark from the car's wireless. His office. Urgent.

Around 9.30am, Wednesday, 10th December 1941

The body was discovered west of Nevers on the river's bank, not far from its junction with the Loire. The river's flow, before the winter rains and snows, was just a trickle.

'Who found it?' asked Bauer, who had left Paris not long after returning to his office from the execution. He'd grabbed this case with both hands. It got him out into the field again. There was also the advantage of access to French country food, which he would send home to his wife and to his two boys, and which was a steal at the compulsory exchange rate.

The Wehrmacht major who had collected him from Nevers indicated an elderly fisherman standing nearby who was smoking nervously. He had informed the local gendarmes but now wished he hadn't. He'd figured it was some poor unfortunate trying to cross the demarcation line. How was he to know he'd found a Boche soldier? 'They're all in it,' said the major in disgust, 'making money helping the Jews. You can't trust any of them.'

'He did tell us, major,' Bauer, whose nominal army rank was captain, reminded his superior officer. He loosened his heavy tweed coat so he could examine the body. Yet another boy. He could tell at a glance roughly how long the kid had been in the water, how long it had been since he was killed. And the most likely murder weapon.

'The kid put up a struggle,' he said, pointing to the bruising on the boy's face and the cuts on his hands where he had tried to stop the knife. The boy's tunic was still stained with blood, despite having been in the water. Bauer undid the buttons and saw three knife wounds in the chest and then, on further investigation, another in the kid's stomach, probably the first wound, from which he'd lost a lot of blood. He checked the boy's pockets. Money and cigarettes gone; he could see faint nicotine stains still on the fingers of the right hand. The boy's wounds had him wondering about the murder weapon, because their size and shape – clean cut at the bottom, a tear at the top – indicated a knife of similar size and shape to a Wehrmacht combat knife. Could have been the French army's version. They were everywhere since the French defeat. He checked the dead boy's knife. It was still in its sheath on his belt.

'You have the dog squad in action?' he asked. The answer was affirmative. Not ten minutes later, the major was radioed that the second body had been found and a possible crime site.

'Good old dogs,' said Bauer with genuine affection. 'Ours or the froggies'?' he asked.

'Ours, of course,' the major replied, as if this had to be obvious. 'Wait for any help from them, we'll be here until kingdom come.' The army was furious, the local commander in particular. He was threatening to have one hostage shot each day unless the killers were turned in, starting with the foreign Jews.

'You can shoot all the hostages you want, major,' said Bauer, 'but until proven otherwise' – which was his modus operandi – 'whoever did this is well over the line and headed for Spain without a backward glance.'

'We have to discourage this sort of thing,' the major replied.

True enough, Bauer thought, but shooting hostages would only poke a stick into a hornet's nest; and as a Catholic, even a bad one, he didn't like punishing the innocent. Even in wartime.

The second body had been found upstream a few kilometres, caught on the bottom of the river, the boy's booted foot wedged between rocks. When Bauer arrived, it had been brought to shore. 'Another kid,' he muttered to himself. Stabbed in the back. He didn't like that at all. A coward's strike. He looked at the wound. Same knife as the other. Coward the killer might be, but he knew where and how to stick in a knife.

He checked the boy's pockets. Money and cigarettes gone. His combat knife was also gone. Why would you risk being found with one? Or was that now two?

A call came from the boat searching the river. A carbine had been found. Moments later, the other carbine. No helmets. They could be floating downstream anywhere between here and the Bay of Biscay.

'This boy's knife's missing,' he called out to the searchers. He doubted they'd find it but had to make sure.

Bauer went over to a stone fence that ended at the riverbank, where the dogs had tracked the last movements of the two soldiers. Their lumbering handlers had tramped around the spot and the dogs had not been able to find any other scent trails. The rain during the night had not helped. By the water's edge was a small branch recently broken off. This, he figured, the killer or killers used to cover up any tracks. You could see the marks across the muddy soil. He easily found the tree where the branch had come from, right by the stone fence.

He didn't need the dogs to tell him this was where the murders had happened – for murders they were – and that whoever committed them was no fool. Then he saw, at the bottom of the fence, a fresh chip in the sandstone where something, the sole of a boot most probably, had hit against it, evidence of the fight. It was a German boot most likely, from the hobnail on the sole. Whoever did it had crossed the river here on foot; it was shallow enough. On the other side was freedom. It would be an illusory freedom if he had anything to do with it.

These two soldiers could have been his own two boys. Putting the killers before a firing squad, no matter how young they might be, would not only be his duty but a grim pleasure.

He saw a soggy cigarette on the ground. He looked closely. Unlit. He took out his magnifying glass.

'Chesterfield,' he said. 'American.' Does that muddy the waters? he wondered. Black marketeers still got hold of American cigarettes. Would a black marketeer try to light a cigarette when he was trying not to be seen by us? Bauer would think on this.

He removed a cellophane packet from his deep pockets and tweezered the prize in, handing it for safekeeping to his young one-armed assistant.

Originally from the Berlin police, Gunther Kopitcke had lost his left arm in a training accident in the army. Now a sergeant in the army's field police, he was as close as he would get to any action, much to his regret. To compensate, he behaved as if he were on the front line, always ready with a '*Jawohl, Herr Kommissar*' and a heel-clicking salute.

'No need for all that,' Bauer would say. Kopitcke felt he had to look like he was doing his bit as well as doing it. Which is why he chose to wear the Wehrmacht uniform, optional in the field police. Experience had taught Bauer that a uniform was a barrier in his line of work. It put people on edge. Mind you, these days, the Gestapo was turning that argument on its head, what with their big fedoras and heavy leather coats. He thought they looked ridiculous, like extras on a film set.

'I'm going across,' he declared to the major. 'Call the boat in. Come along, Kopitcke.'

'You'll have to inform the French first,' said the major with distaste. Bauer said he'd do just that and not to worry about the protocols, they didn't have any time to waste. His French, courtesy of his maternal grandparents and mother, who were Alsatian, was fluent, the reason he'd been sent to Paris.

The boat arrived.

'What have we got so far?' he asked as they were rowed across the river. Kopitcke knew not to answer. 'We have the locals who know the lie of the land,' Bauer began his surmising, 'who probably know how and when our patrols operate.'

He saw this bothered Kopitcke, who would demand the spies be caught and shot. Bauer told him to calm down; this was France, after all, not Germany. They were the occupiers, the fish swimming in a French sea. It was impossible to operate in any significant way without being watched all the time.

'Where was I?' he continued. 'Yes, that's right, the French who are running these escape lines. They're mostly doing it for the money but also to get up our noses for defeating them. Half the escapees are Jews who are a soft touch. But they're careful, Kopitcke, they're not going to run into one of our patrols if they can help it. They see any of our boys, what are they going to do? They're going to lie low. What's the point of being banged up by us or worse for the sake of a few francs and a few Jews? And if on the rare occasion they do run into a patrol, they'll cut and run, leaving the yids and whoever else to their fate. Makes me think it wasn't one of them smoking that American cigarette.'

'You're saying, Herr Kommissar, it's not the *passeurs* themselves who killed our soldiers, but escapees?' Kopitcke said, feeling he was now allowed to say something, as long as it was the right something and said as a question.

'Precisely.'

'Herr Kommissar,' Kopitcke returned as politely as he was able, 'surely Jews could not have killed our men?'

'*If* they're Jews. Why not?' Bauer said.

'Our men are well-trained soldiers,' Kopitcke said. 'Jews don't have it in them to fight. They try to destroy us by insidious infiltration, pretending to be like us, and that's how they take us over, not by confronting us physically. They don't have the physical strength or the physical will.'

Bauer sighed. 'If you're French and you're crossing back and forth, smuggling or just visiting a girl, you don't go out of your way to kill a couple of German soldiers unless you're a red or you've been ambushed. They know the Wehrmacht will take French hostages, they're not stupid. One of our boys was stabbed in the back. You do that because you have to. Say you've been captured by one of our boys. What's the only quick and effective way to get yourself out of that hole?' Bauer made a sudden stabbing motion. 'Escapees are our suspects, until proven otherwise – a minimum of two.'

Kopitcke nodded and said, 'Yes, Herr Kommissar,' because when the Herr Kommissar outlined it like this, well, it was so obvious.

'Don't think all yids are soft-skinned patsies,' said Bauer. 'I've met some tough yids in my time, don't you worry, especially the red variety. We've made a hell of a lot of enemies, don't forget.' He might have added 'unnecessarily' but Kopitcke already doubted his ideological credentials.

'The cigarette, Herr Kommissar?' Kopitcke asked. That had slipped Bauer's mind. Nothing slipped Kopitcke's mind, which was why Bauer kept him close.

'Until otherwise proven,' said Bauer, 'stolen.'

A little later, morning, Wednesday, 10th December 1941

The boat approached the shore. Bauer was the first out and gave a hand to Kopitcke, whose lack of an arm affected his balance.

'Wait here for us,' he ordered the rower, who was French.

The sun was up but distant and cold through the thin layer of clouds that hung low over the land. Above the riverbank, a chateau sat atop a hill, laid bare by the winter trees that in summer would keep it secluded. Bauer's eyes were for evidence, not beauty. The chateaux of the Loire and the rivers and the landscape were lost on him. Besides, the Rhine and the Main had castles aplenty if you liked that sort of thing.

He led Kopitcke along the river's edge, hoping the rain during the night might have spared possible tracks. Kopitcke found them first. 'Herr Kommissar, Herr Kommissar,' he called excitedly. And there they were; they might have been blurred by the rain on the muddy ground, but these were footprints. They'd crossed barefoot and here they'd put their shoes back on.

'Hah,' Bauer said, pointing to the ochre smears on the grass and mud. 'Clay from the other side. How many, do you think?'

'At least two, Herr Kommissar. We should get the dogs over,' said Kopitcke with relish. 'We'll have them quick smart.'

Bauer said they didn't need the dogs; there wasn't time and it would create complications with the French. He and Kopitcke would do just as well on their own, but they mustn't waste a moment. The tracks from the river's edge across the grass with their tell-tale smears of clay gave out. It didn't take a genius to see where they'd headed. The roadway was marked by a stone wall and lines of bare trees either side. The question was, which direction? Again, genius was hardly needed. They could see the village on the rise ahead, about a kilometre and a half away.

'Keep your eyes on the ground in front of you, Kopitcke, not on the village,' Bauer said when he saw his assistant hellbent on getting to the village before the murderers got away. 'They'll be gone by now.'

'See there,' he said not a hundred metres along. He pointed to the top of the stone fence, where three flagstones had been removed in the last few days. The newly exposed stones below showed no weathering at all. 'What's that all about?' he asked. It didn't take him long to find the helmets, because further rain during the night had exposed one of the stones used to cover them. They dug them up quickly. Bauer made Kopitcke hold the helmets and stay behind while he went into the village. His uniform would not help.

'They see you in that, son, they clam up. You go back to the river and wait for me by the boat.'

Bauer knocked on the door of the first house and introduced himself to the middle-aged woman who answered. To counter her fear when she learnt he was not only a cop but a Boche cop, he used his fluent French and a charm that seemed naïve; he had refined it to an art like an accomplished actor. No, she'd heard or seen nothing, naturally. Then, on his further enquiry, she knew all these Jews were flooding through, not that she herself had seen any – but, and she lowered her voice, 'You should ask across the street.' Ah, Bauer thought and smiled, if only people knew what their neighbours really thought about them. It was the same in Germany, even before the Nazis.

Bauer went to the house opposite and knocked. The young woman he found a little too cool and calm. She too had neither seen nor heard anything. He asked if he might have a glass of water, he was parched. There was a chance she might let him inside, and it worked. She drew him water from a faucet in the kitchen. On the floor was a small china bowl with milk in it, as placed out for a cat. What struck him about this bowl was that it was from a set he could see in the dresser. This family cat drank from the family crockery.

'Ah, you have a cat,' he said as a genuine cat-lover. He'd always had a cat, he said as he looked around for it.

'She's out,' said the woman crisply, which was an altogether odd thing to say.

'Oh? At the market? Visiting friends?' Bauer quipped, and eureka, the look she gave him, something wasn't right here. He had hit a nerve. She most probably was part of one of these illegal crossing businesses. Back on the other side of the river, where German Occupation rules applied, he'd have taken her in. On this side, he was supposed to work though the French police, but what did the rules say when there weren't any French police to work through? He had his pistol. 'Hands up' is all it would take to have her on the other side in half an hour.

'What colour's yours?' he asked.

'Black,' she replied immediately, 'with a white tip on its tail.'

'Ah,' he smiled. 'Mine's black too. No white tip.'

He drank his water. She watched. He smiled.

'What's its name?' he asked, surprising her with his suddenness, as he had intended. She faltered before landing on 'Felix'.

As one would, Bauer said to himself, gave her another smile, thanked her for the water and left.

He supposed if he'd been a Nazi, he would have taken her in and dismissed any consequences with the French. Instead, he would play by the rules and have the French police investigate her.

He returned to Kopitcke waiting by the river's edge.

'Where's the boat?' he complained.

Kopitcke protested that he had recalled it, and pointed to the middle of the river, where the boat was heading their way, if slowly. 'The French,' Kopitcke muttered as explanation.

'Whoever it was passed this way,' Bauer reported as they waited. If they had time and the manpower, they'd search the whole town and find evidence for sure. Would they find who murdered those two boys? No. The killers were now on their way south – Lyon if they were headed for Perpignan, or Clermont-Ferrand and on to Toulouse if, say, they were headed for Latour-de-Carol, the easiest gateway into Spain by train.

'Lyon's my hunch,' he said. 'Especially if you've knocked two German soldiers off. I'd be wanting to get out quick smart.'

Absent a definite lead, Bauer admitted to himself that 'young and male' was hardly a useful description. He'd attract derision if he ordered the French police to check the trains arriving in Lyon or Clermont-Ferrand for 'young males'. He wondered about the cat, black with a white tip on its tail. He couldn't quite credit anyone except a sentimental old lady carting a cat across the demarcation line. The combat knife, French or German, was something else. Young, male, armed with combat knives, at least one of them belonging to a Landser, an ordinary Wehrmacht soldier. That would be a start.

The boat arrived. Bauer and Kopitcke boarded, Bauer ordering the rower to get a move on. They would get a car to Lyon, where he'd organise more French help and tap into their intelligence. Speaking fluent French opened all sorts of doors.

'And Kopitcke,' he added, 'you get yourself into civvies before we go. This is a murder case and you're a cop, not a field marshal; and we're in France, not Germany.'

BACK ROADS EN ROUTE TO LYON THROUGH THE AUVERGNE, VICHY FRANCE

Late morning, Wednesday, 10th December 1941

The truck Silvan drove was his own and he kept it on the Vichy side of the line. He'd initially thought it too old to interest the Boches but it was American, which meant it was not only sturdy but simple and easy to maintain. The Wehrmacht didn't seem fussed about national provenance. These Fords, they'd run forever with only the slightest attention. He'd hidden it on a pal's farm and now it was handy for ferrying his passengers once they'd arrived in what was laughingly called the *zone libre*, the free zone. Petrol was expensive, but you could get it. The quicker you got your passengers out of your hair, the quicker you could go back for more, and the more money you made. And sure, it was a way to cock a snoot at the bastards.

In the back on one side were the two sisters, the Hungarian and the silent Jew clutching his parcel to his chest. On the other were Darlene and Luc, Eleanor and Henk. The young, taciturn man Eleanor had first encountered when she arrived at their departure point sat with Al on the floor with their backs to the cabin. Along these back roads, the ride was uncomfortable. The protection they had from the cold was no protection at all: a tarpaulin with flaps over the rear, which were tied together with twine to stop anyone seeing in. You also couldn't see out, so there they were, squashed like sardines into a claustrophobic box with the wind whistling in through gaps in the tarpaulin. The revving motor and the gearing were the only way they could tell if they were climbing or cruising downhill, turning this way or that way across the undulating landscape of bare fields and trees. Better than any alternative any could think of, and that was it.

Henk's cat seemed their only collective interest as he let it attack his hands and fingers, a game both seemed to enjoy. Al asked Henk how come he got lost so easily.

Eleanor had to remind him again that Henk didn't speak French. She also doubted that Al's interest was innocent. Attention returned to the kitten, whose tail swished and whose pupils were wide with excitement as it coiled itself and leapt at Henk's fingers.

'Where'd you cross, pal?' Al asked in English.

'The fog was thick and it was dark,' said Henk. 'How do I know?'

'Rocks? A weir?' Al persisted.

'I take off my clothes and walk through the water,' Henk replied, his attention on the game with his cat. 'It is not deep.'

'That's right,' said Eleanor. 'I was with him.'

Al nodded. 'You never saw no Boches?' he asked her in French.

'We thought we did, so we hid behind a wall until they went away,' she replied, 'but the fog was so thick, it was hard to see.'

'Yeah, a real pea-souper,' said Al flatly.

Did he believe them? Eleanor sensed he did not. It was natural he'd be suspicious. Who, after all, had a knife and seemed to know how to use it? She wondered what Al might do if he knew for sure, a thought that left her uneasy. She caught Henk's eyes and could tell he didn't trust Al.

He didn't trust anybody he didn't know intimately. Yet he couldn't afford not to trust this rich American and that put him on edge. He let the cat maul his finger until it hurt.

SAINT POURÇAIN SUR SOUILE, AUVERGNE, VICHY FRANCE

Midday, Wednesday, 10th December 1941

They seemed to have been driving for longer than their watches told them – so many turns this way and that way, enough to disorient even Eleanor's acute sense of direction. They knew they were headed for Lyon, so when the truck stopped and the motor was turned off, there was a sense that the journey was over. Nothing happened. Al didn't move. They heard no movement from the front cabin. Trouble? No one said a word as they waited. Suddenly, Silvan drew back the flaps, startling everyone. The sun, bright and chilly, poured in from just above the roofline of a small, deserted courtyard. This was not Lyon. Ridiculous. Lyon was miles away.

'Lunch,' said Al without much enthusiasm.

Silvan helped Eleanor and the two sisters down.

They were to eat at a restaurant on the corner of the square and had to pay for themselves. It was all arranged. They were to enter down a narrow alley off the courtyard, which he pointed out. Since it was not a market day and there would be few outsiders in town, they were to enter in ones and twos, not as a group. The town might be quiet, but given what had happened, the Germans would have their eyes out and about. 'Trust no stranger,' he said, 'and no flapping your mouths.'

Eleanor, ever-practical, walked quickly down the alley and in through the back door where Silvan indicated. Starving would hardly help her situation. She needed to eat. First she needed a bathroom. One glance in the mirror at her face and hair confirmed the horror. Yes, in the present scheme of things, she well understood the judgment others might make as she repaired the damage, but if she didn't, she wouldn't be able to think straight and that was that. Besides, judgment, as with vengeance, was the Lord's. When she emerged, she at least felt as if she looked like a human being. The waiter, an elderly man, gestured with a nod of his head where Eleanor should sit. The others followed in dribs and drabs.

'All this is available?' she asked in surprise when given the menu, forgetting Al's order not to flap her mouth. The Polish Jew looked alarmed. She was too engrossed in the menu. She couldn't believe it, and of course it was too good to be true. She could have beef stew, and if that was it, she would not complain. Beef. It was enough to make her dizzy, and even dizzier when her meal arrived in moments from the stove, where it had been cooking for hours. Her taste buds, made acute by shortage, detected the merest hint of butter in the mashed potatoes. The bread was made with flour and not sawdust. She drank greedily from the glass of wine like a thirsty peasant. Memory was true: this was how it used to be. Her entire being focused on her stomach as she savoured every mouthful. Until she noticed Henk at a table by himself, feeding his cat from a crust of bread. He was not eating.

'It's on me. Order what you want,' said Eleanor, remembering now at least to keep her voice down.

'I am not hungry,' he said.

'Don't be ridiculous,' she replied. 'You haven't eaten anything since we left.'

'I said I am not hungry,' he repeated, and she thought, well, please yourself.

'Why do you not eat the lady's food?' said the thin Polish Jew in soft English. Eating the same beef stew doubtless accounted for the improvement in his demeanour as much as it caused him to let down his guard. Even his parcel was no longer held to his chest but sat casually on his lap. Eleanor was startled he could speak at all, let alone English.

'Only the rich eat,' said Henk. Be damned if he was going to have to rely on her again. He'd rather starve.

The thin man laughed, shook his head, spooned a large portion of his own meal onto a plate and pushed it over towards Henk. 'Be rich, my friend,' he said, 'on a poor Jew from Warsaw.'

'Thank you, comrade,' said Henk and shared the food with his cat, which ate as greedily as he. Eleanor watched, part bemused, part exasperated. He was a poseur and the sooner she was rid of him, the better. He irritated her beyond reason. It was like being in the company of a petulant child. She ignored him and contented herself with enjoying her meal. Even now, the writer in her couldn't help mulling on what was happening to her and how she might tell this story. For a moment, she had to remind herself it was actually happening, not something she was conjuring up.

She sipped her wine and gazed through the windows to the square. Opposite was a hipped-roof building, another restaurant whose windows and doors were shuttered. Beyond was a church and an ancient round stone tower whose clock could have been on 1938 time. Here she was in *la France profonde*, seemingly unchanged by defeat and the occupiers sitting on the other side of the river Loire not so far away.

'Madame,' came a voice, and she looked up to see a large man with a round face, red from the heat of the kitchen, the owner of the restaurant and its chef. He was honoured to serve a dear American lady. Eleanor wondered if her itinerary hadn't been sent on in advance. She supposed Al or Silvan had said something, but then it came. 'I heard you speaking English,' he said, 'and wanted to meet you. You are our great hope, madame.'

Eleanor let pass the fact that, as far as she knew, the United States was at war only with Japan, but thanked him. Mostly she thanked him for the food. They became momentarily a mutual enthusiasm brigade as they beamed at each other, until the waiter came over to him and whispered quickly into his ear.

'Gendarmes, madame,' the owner said quietly to her. They were coming through the back entrance, the same way Eleanor and her fellow travellers had come. She saw how surprised he was. He'd probably paid them off, which was why Silvan brought the escapee business to him. But something had gone wrong and she knew what that might be.

'Have your papers ready,' said one of the gendarmes.

Conversation stopped. Henk retrieved his kitten. The Polish Jew began to sweat. Eleanor could smell his fear and it frightened her. The Hungarian, charming in his accentless French, handed over his papers first. Slowly the gendarmes worked their way around the tables, where steaming food was being left to cool and curdle. Eleanor handed over her fake identification papers. She realised that she had forgotten who she was supposed to be and where she was supposed to be from. She remembered only that she was originally Madame de Lisle, but now?

'Madame is American?' the gendarme asked.

'Originally,' she said as lightly as she could, trying to be aware whether she was sounding too American or not American enough. 'But married to a Frenchman for twenty-three years.'

The gendarme's colleague pushed over to peer at Eleanor's papers before handing them back to her. 'Born in Hollywood,' he said approvingly, as if she were royalty.

'It was smaller then,' Eleanor replied with remarkable élan.

Henk handed over his papers, which both gendarmes studied.

'Same name,' one pointed out to the other. 'You are with this lady?' he asked.

Henk, with hardly any French, stared out the window. If it was insolence, the boy was a good actor, Eleanor thought, but this was not the time for insolence or causing any damn trouble. The little shit just sat there. The gendarme repeated his question.

'He's my son,' Eleanor told them. 'We quarrelled. He won't speak to me. He refuses to speak to anyone.'

The gendarme smiled, handed Henk his papers. 'A good son should obey his mother,' he said. He tickled the cat's neck.

The other gendarme studied the papers of the Polish Jew, clutching his precious parcel back to his chest. Eleanor could see the sweat dripping off the poor man.

'What's your name?' asked the gendarme.

'Marcel,' replied the Pole.

'Marcel what?'

'Marcel Tua . . .' he faltered.

'Says here your Christian name is Armand,' said the gendarme. Eleanor realised the poor man hadn't bothered to learn his new name. She could hardly blame him for that.

'Marcel,' said the Pole, trying to smile.

'Where are you going, Marcel?' the gendarme asked, toying with him because already they knew they had him. Why not a little bit of fun?

'Off to Spain for a holiday, are you?' the other gendarme asked.

'Marcel,' said the Pole, though with a rising inflection, as if this were now a question. Even he sensed he was done for.

'You're just another yid on the run, aren't you?' said the gendarme, lifting him from his chair.

Eleanor felt the weight of the owner's hands pressing down on her shoulders to keep her still and calm, which she most decidedly was not. The Polish Jew burst into tears as they led him out the front door, still holding his parcel tight. No one said a word. When he was gone, Eleanor gesticulated but no words came, only tears.

'There's nothing you can do,' explained the owner. He didn't know what had gone wrong. Sometimes, it didn't work. At least the gendarmes had taken only the foreign Jew; they were always fair game.

Eleanor sat in mute despair. 'You gotta eat, babe,' said Al, pointing to her half-eaten lunch.

'I'm not hungry,' she snapped in French, sick of Al and his gangsterisms. Henk reached over and took her plate for himself, and he began to finish it. He was famished, even after polishing off the food the Polish Jew had shared with him and his cat. Disgusted, Eleanor pushed back her chair and stalked out into the square, only to see the back of the police car taking away the Polish Jew. She and everyone she knew had heard stories about Gurs, the concentration camp on the Spanish border, where Vichy let its undesirables rot and die. The fumes from the exhaust of the departed car hovered around her like the stench from a corpse. Leaning against the fountain, which had been emptied for winter, she was too immobilised even to smoke.

Henk appeared with his cat. 'You did not pay,' he said.

'I barely touched it,' she responded, which was not entirely true.

'But I eat,' he said.

'Then you pay for it.'

'You said you would pay.'

'I've changed my mind.'

'You do not think you owe me one miserable meal?' he demanded, ratcheting up their mutual anger.

'I didn't ask you to kill those two men.'

'They are soldiers. Nazis.'

'How do you know they were Nazis?'

He couldn't believe this. Was she stupid or just obtuse?

'You know better, do you?' he launched into her. 'Same uniform, same army, but no, he is not Nazi, he is a good German. That one over there, he is the real Nazi, he has Nazi eyes and Nazi hair. You stupid woman, all Germans are Nazis now, and you think you have no responsibility, you can sit to the side and enjoy your precious life. How annoying it must be to you that I save it.'

'Don't you lecture me, sonny,' she snapped. 'I wish I'd been caught now. At least my conscience would be clear.'

'Your conscience,' Henk taunted, his finger pointed barely an inch from her face. 'What does your conscience say to Nazis killing Jews? Huh? Our job is to survive and so far we survive very good.'

'At the cost of three lives.'

'Forget the Polish Jew. His time is finished long ago.'

'Really? How do you know that?'

'Because I am here and he is not.' His finger hooked the crucifix Madame Teixeira had given her, and pulled her towards him. 'And so, Madame Rich Christian American, are you. Please,' he gestured to a bench nearby, 'sit out this war, let others fight it for you.'

She pushed him away in fury, but then his face froze. She turned instinctively to see what he was looking at.

'Oh God,' she muttered as her heart and stomach sank to her shoes. They were staring across the square at the *mairie*, the town hall, where an elderly man, doubtless a bureaucrat in his high collar and vest, hurriedly closed the door where, drawn by their eruption, he must have heard them. She had to assume the worst, that he had understood them perfectly. They both grasped the weight of their stupidity and ran inside to find Al.

'We must leave,' said Eleanor. She plonked down enough money to cover the meal. 'Now,' she added. Her tone and demeanour didn't require an explanation for Al. He bustled everyone out, had a quick conversation with Silvan, and in minutes they were on their way, silent and grim. The arrest of the Polish Jew was reason enough. As they fled the town, Henk and Eleanor sat as far from each other as was possible in the squeeze.

SAINT GERMAIN DES FOSSÉS, AUVERGNE, VICHY FRANCE

Afternoon into evening, Wednesday, 10th December 1941

A short while later, the truck slowed and, after some turns, stopped. Silvan opened the flaps and beckoned them out. They had arrived outside a railway station, which was all they could see as they alighted. There wasn't much to it. Circumstances had changed, said Silvan. They would continue to Lyon by train from here. The French among them took the news with some relief: at least a train would be more comfortable. Al, who was to be their guide to Lyon, hopped into the front passenger seat.

'The contacts in Lyon!' exclaimed the Hungarian, who realised before Eleanor and Henk that they were being dumped. 'You were paid to take us there.'

'It's too dangerous,' said Silvan. He slammed the door, not having switched off the motor. 'You're all safer getting there separately.' He found the gear, released the clutch and drove away as quickly as the old crate would go. Henk raced after them, his fist raised as he cursed them in what Eleanor took to be his reddest Dutch. It certainly sounded so, though to what avail? As useful as a dog chasing cars. He stopped and walked back, his fury unabated. The French, resigned to things, had already started to enter the station building. Who knew when or even if a train was due.

'If only you shouted louder,' Eleanor muttered at him, 'the Germans in Paris could hear you.'

'Sons of bitches,' he said, ignoring her sarcasm. Then they saw Silvan and Al driving back towards them. Henk ran onto the road to stop them. Silvan slowed, avoided Henk, pulled up by Eleanor and the Hungarian. Al leant out of the window.

'The Café du Levant,' he called out quickly, 'in the Croix Rousse.' With that, Silvan sped away.

'What?' Henk said and Eleanor repeated it.

'Where the hell is that?' he asked.

'Lyon, presumably,' Eleanor said, pleased at least that in winter this village was in a state of summery midday torpor. No one was about to witness this latest public declaration of their plight.

Where exactly were they? She saw the sign but that was hardly useful. She'd never heard of the place. She went inside. Was the ticket office open? It was. She saw her fellow passengers crowding the window. Were there trains? When and where to? They could go to Vichy, or to Clermont-Ferrand and, yes, to Lyon, but the next train heading for Lyon would not be until the evening. Some bought tickets for Vichy, anything to keep moving. The Hungarian and Eleanor bought for Lyon. The man at the counter, who easily figured out what was going on, cautioned them not to sit together. He suggested the two sisters and Eleanor might sit inside, not only to get out of the cold but because this was not a busy station and the gendarmes might think it odd to see a group of people so many hours before a train was due. 'They are nervous,' he added. 'More than usual.' He didn't know why.

The two sisters did as he suggested. Before Eleanor followed them, she noticed Henk. He had not yet bought a ticket.

'Why not?' she asked.

'I already pay to be taken to Pau,' he said. 'Why must I pay now to go to Lyon when I do not have enough money?'

For once she agreed with him. She bought him a ticket.

'Thank you,' he said and sat quietly with his cat away from everyone else under the platform canopy, which was just a tin shed. If gendarmes paid another visit, he wanted to be able to get away easily.

Eleanor came out after fifteen minutes to have a cigarette, her rationing rule forgotten. She couldn't in conscience not offer him one.

'Why do you still insist on going to Pau?' she asked.

'If you have no visa for Spain, it is the best place to cross.'

'I keep telling you,' she said, exasperated, 'the Pyrénées are in the way and it's winter. Cèrbère is much easier and closer, not to mention a whole lot nicer.'

'The Nazis do not expect you to cross there now, so it is better,' he said, not without some logic, she conceded. He took out the knife he'd stolen from the German soldier and began to pare his fingernails.

'Would you mind putting that thing away?' she said.

'You do not like being a criminal?' he taunted, resting the knife in his hand.

'What I don't like is being a sitting duck,' she said. 'I'm not a criminal.'

'You travel on forged identity papers,' he countered. 'Is this not criminal, "Mama"?'

'Well, "Sonny",' she said, 'I'm doing you a big favour. I'm not, as you so put it, sitting out this war. I'm duty-bound as an American to break a bad law, and by definition, any Nazi law is bad.'

'This is a point of view morally flexible, is it not?' he said.

'On the contrary, the principle couldn't be clearer,' she replied.

'You just decide yourself what is a bad law. How is that a principle?'

'A bad law,' she said, enjoying defending herself and the American constitution, 'is one that oppresses individual liberty.'

'And how do you defeat these tyrants? With nice words in book?' He ostentatiously sheathed the knife back inside his sock. 'Is it not a bad law that the few have all the wealth while the many have nothing?'

'That's got nothing to do with law. That's human nature,' she countered. 'In the United States of America, if you have money, it's your duty to help the less fortunate, just as I paid for your lunch. And your train ticket.'

Get yourself out of that, she said to herself. She might not have convinced him, but she'd argued him into a corner and it pleased her that he frowned and could say nothing.

A pair of pigeons flapped above them in the canopy, the only signs of life. Outside, the place was deathly still. Not a breath of wind, just the damp cold.

'Tell me, why did you save me back there?' she asked. Henk turned away from her. 'You needn't have,' Eleanor persisted. 'You could have stayed hidden.'

Henk ignored her. He could see where she was going, the trap.

'I'll tell you why,' Eleanor said, not allowing him to escape. 'Because underneath all this left-wingery, you're a human being with compassion. You can run all you like, but you can't escape your condition.'

'You see things differently when suddenly you are on the bottom,' he said.

'Oh?' she said. What was this?

Too late he realised he had let slip something about himself. A truth. He must be more careful with his anger in future and use it to save, not endanger, his own neck.

Trains passed by in both directions but only one stopped, taking some of their number to Vichy. Eleanor tried reading James Joyce, which she found was still a perfect sedative. She dozed the rest of the afternoon away. When, much later than advertised, well into the evening, still unseen, a locomotive whistled its approach up the railway track, they ignored it. Presciently, the locomotive kept announcing its arrival, although it took quite a while before it rattled into the tiny station and stopped, exhausted. None minded it was already overcrowded, as long as it moved, which it did.

GARE DE LYON-PERRACHE, LYON II

Towards 6am, Thursday, 11th December 1941

Lulled by the rhythm of the train or merely stupefied by the exertions of her journey, Eleanor dozed most of the way to Lyon. Only when the rhythm was interrupted – crossing points or a short stop – did she open her eyes. Each time, there was Henk, awake, gimlet eyes on her, fiddling with the locket on a chain around his neck, petting his cat. He was the chain around her neck, she thought, looking forward to Lyon and freedom. That was a long time coming, a night of anxiety. Something was up, though all she had to go on was her imagination, fed by the anxieties of those crowded in around her. The train stopped many times and, when it did move, one could frequently have walked as fast.

When at last they came out of the tunnel onto the bridge over the Saône, with the Perrache station just on the other side, it was around 6am. Then the wretched train stopped yet again. Tempers flared. They'd all had enough. Soon the chatter reached their carriage. Another train was ahead of them and the station was in uproar because of a disturbance.

A riot? Communists? Yes, the reds were at it again.

Eleanor saw Henk come alive when he heard the only word in any language that excited him. He looked to her for explanation.

'Your pals are causing trouble,' Eleanor stated the obvious.

'What about?' Henk demanded, trying to look out the window.

It was about prices, although as everyone, including Eleanor, knew, it was really about helping the Soviet Union.

'Pity they weren't so helpful in May last year,' Eleanor said, although she wondered how this disturbance might help the gallant ally under threat so far away. She tried to look out the window. This train was going nowhere. Passengers began opening the doors and soon were pouring down the sides and along the rail line like a swarm of invading ants. They crossed the bridge in front of the train and headed towards the station, or they went back to the mouth of the tunnel so they could climb down to the road on this side of the river. Henk stood to join them.

'Where are you going?' Eleanor asked.

'It is better than staying here,' he replied, which she conceded. She clambered down after him. On the track, Henk turned to cross the bridge leading to the station on the other side of the river, where the riot was still happening. A red moth to a redder flame, she thought, a bad idea at the moment, and she said so.

Did she know better? he demanded. Did she know of the café?

Eleanor had no idea. She wanted merely to put distance between them and the railway station. Truth to tell, she wanted to put as much distance between herself and him, and soon she would do just that.

'I'll take you to the café, then you're on your own, buster.'

*

Kommissar Bauer stood with his assistant, Kopitcke, at a window looking down over the melee on the concourse of the Perrache station, part amused, part astonished. The gendarmes were being led a chase by what seemed to him to be very few troublemakers. Like rats, they darted out from holes and then ran back into other holes, leaving the gendarmes confused. This was causing trouble just for trouble's sake. His French counterpart, Sub-Inspector Girard, told him the real purpose was to clog the railway in order to interrupt shipments of goods north into the occupied zone.

Thence to the Germans, he might have added.

A good snarl would take ages to fix, connections would be missed, schedules interrupted. The reds, it was always the reds, were getting good at these sorts of seemingly random actions, Girard added.

'They know they're invulnerable,' suggested Bauer. 'Hang a few.'

'Gladly,' said Girard, 'if I were in charge.'

Where Bauer was shambolic and comfortable, Girard in his neat uniform was stiff and correct. His sympathies were entirely with the marshal in Vichy; he was one hundred percent *travail, famille, patrie*, and these reds were the enemy who had helped France to defeat. He was a detective, here to help Bauer, a German colleague, with his investigation, a murder, a criminal matter. Bauer, he had found so far, was correct and deferential. A professional. His French was perfect, with the hint of an Alsatian accent. He had even noticed the way Bauer tried to limit the grating effect of his unfortunate underling.

Bauer was trying very hard. Kopitcke had changed into civilian clothes, as ordered. Looking at him, though, Bauer had no doubt that any half-blind Frenchman would see Kopitcke exactly for what he was. The new fedora was enough, but even without the hat, his hair, which was fair, was bristle-short on the sides with a severe part in the middle; his blue eyes were not friendly; his suit was suspiciously classy, while no other part of him was; and he still clicked his heels all the time. Bauer expected him to 'Heil Hitler' too, because that was what he had been taught. So far, it had come out only once. The heel clicking, though. 'Kopitcke, please don't do that,' he said. 'The French don't go for it.' He apologised to Girard about Kopitcke when first they met. 'Don't mind him,' he said. It was more often that Kopitcke forgot to speak French to his boss. '*Français*, Kopitcke, *français*,' Bauer kept having to remind him. '*Ici nous sommes invités.*'

They had come to the station so that Bauer and Kopitcke could look over people picked off the trains by the police. If in doubt, nab them. Young or male or Jewish – that description accounted for most of the detainees. Bauer was most interested in the foreigners. They were all Jews, it turned out, mostly female, mostly older, defeated and demoralised, not the sort who'd knife two Wehrmacht soldiers to death. Besides, if any had possessed a knife, they'd since gotten rid of it. Then the riot had erupted, so Bauer, Kopitcke and Girard returned to police headquarters.

Girard knew hostages had been taken on the other side because of the murder of the two soldiers. He knew the Germans were angry enough to start shooting if suspects weren't produced. He was of a mind to produce a someone, no matter who it was. In Bauer he discovered a curious, old-fashioned morality.

'No, inspector,' Bauer said. 'I want the real killer.'

'But you have French hostages,' Girard said.

'All the more reason we get on with it,' said Bauer in his charming French, although he did admit that his stomach was growling, so Girard's offer of breakfast was timely.

LA CROIX ROUSSE, LYON IV

Around 7am, Thursday, 11th December 1941

Eleanor had only a name, Café du Levant, and, she presumed, the area, La Croix Rousse, of which she had never heard, in a city that she, the Parisian, had visited only once. She asked a passer-by. Her elegant French was not lost after all. Her respondent, an elderly gentleman rugged up against the morning chill, told her it wasn't a nice place for a lady. In as firm but ladylike a manner as possible, she said she had no choice. He led her to the quayside by the Saône.

'Up there,' he said, pointing ominously to the top of the hill on the other side of the river. 'La Croix Rousse.' Through the smoke and grime from the chimneys of the city, she could see tenements rising from its steep slopes. Her confidence that she would come to no harm in a place like that was, she admitted to herself, because of Henk and his knife, although, on reflection, her confidence didn't take into account his ability and willingness to use it.

After thanking her helper, she and Henk crossed the river from the old city and took a tram north, as directed. On further direction, they took a dubious-looking funicular up the sharp incline to La Croix Rousse, sparking Eleanor's writerly imagination. She was hardly da Gama rounding the Cape, but she did feel the shiver of excitement that came from venturing into uncharted and possibly dangerous waters. Her imagination, at least, was not disappointed. The air was foul and she had to cover her face with her scarf against the grime. The laneways and alleys had names that spoke of the old silk-weaving industry, which still partially survived. On their way to work, *Canuts*, weavers in smocks and wooden clogs, slipped past like ghosts from another time, although the clogs were due more to the lack of leather, all taken by the Germans for the boots that stood on the French neck, than to any romantic attachment to the past.

'There,' she said in triumph when the Café du Levant appeared through the murk on a rare part of a street that was level, just where the man who had given her the directions said it would be. The large dirty window, the faces of the men and women inside, fogged in cigarette smoke – it perfectly fitted her imagination, still under the spell of writerly fancy.

'What are you doing?' she asked as Henk went to go inside.

'The contact,' he replied. 'I shall ask. They owe me.'

'You can't be serious,' she objected.

'You are a rich bourgeois,' he said with contempt. 'Here that is not good.'

'Better than being a Jew who doesn't speak French,' she snapped. She was at the end of her patience. She saw him smile, more a triumphant sneer. Immediately she regretted her words. Handing him the merest hint of moral superiority was intolerable. 'I didn't mean it like that,' she said. She had, and he knew she had.

'It is best we are honest,' he said, handing her his wretched kitten.

'Oh, no you don't,' she said, handing it back. 'We'll both go in. You sit at a separate table and leave things to me.'

Once they were inside, eyes that ignored him picked her out like searchlights would an enemy bomber. The little shit might be right, she conceded with bad grace. This was no set for *La Bohème*; the cast could not leave after the curtain went down. Here conversation grumbled rather than hummed, fed on discontent and poverty. The smell of sour beer and the food, even in her hunger, made her gag. The faces lost their romantic halos.

She lit a cigarette to settle her stomach. The searchlights picked out the packet. She could feel them. No imagination necessary.

She glanced at her watch. Once she had found his contact, she would leave as if she really were just an extra in *La Bohème*. She would find herself a comfortable hotel in the main part of the city and fetch her suitcase from the railway station. Surely the riot would be over. Later, after lunch, she would go to the Spanish and Portuguese consulates, where they would stamp her American passport with the necessary visas. Soon she would be on her way home to Providence via Madrid and Lisbon, and this would be as a passing nightmare.

She had beckoned a waiter twice. Eventually, he appeared at her table, sour-faced and surly.

'Beer,' said Eleanor. '*Et un passage*,' she added, as if asking for a bowl of soup. The waiter nodded and left. Henk was owed his escape through to Spain, but what was the point of asking for a contact whose name she did not know when, worse, doing so might require her to explain something that was better left unexplained? The witness to their argument back in Saint Pourçain hadn't looked as if he'd keep his mouth shut or for long. She and Henk, she figured, were on borrowed time.

Henk sat one table away. He knew how to ask for a beer. She'd given him a cigarette and saw him lean over to a man among a small group at the table between them to get a light. And if he then didn't take out that blasted cat. In moments, a piece of bread landed on his table from the same small group. Faces that Eleanor had found sinister and unfriendly under matted hair and worker's caps now smiled at Henk and the cat through unshaven rutted cheeks and broken teeth. They wore rough dungarees and in their huge hands were bottles of beer, which they drank from the spout.

'*Pour le chat*,' said one. Henk smiled, nodded his thanks.

'What's his name?' another asked.

'Stalin,' he replied, having foreseen the question.

If Eleanor had been in a better frame of mind, she would have laughed. Like cat, like owner, poor thing. She saw these workers' faces react in surprise and then they broke into broad grins. Henk's zealous blue eyes glowed in response.

A tiny piece of meat, more fat than meat, landed on the table. The cat flew from Henk's hands to snap it up.

'Stalin,' said one of the men and clenched his fist discreetly close to his chest.

'Stalin,' Henk encored, looked over at Eleanor to gloat and displayed his defiant fist more openly.

She watched as another poured milk from a small jug into a cup and handed it to Henk.

'Thank you, comrade,' he said, dipping into his sparse French.

Dismayed, Eleanor watched the cat drink. Only a few days ago, she'd have paid a king's ransom for so much milk. Clearly the working classes of Lyon were not as oppressed as they made out.

At a doorway into the back of the café, she noticed the waiter pointing her out to another man, younger, with lustrous dark hair, clear, dark eyes and fine skin on a tight, closed face. In his dark leather jacket over an open-necked shirt, he was a handsome bour- geois among all this proletariat. The younger man slipped back out of sight. The waiter came to her table. He indicated that she follow him.

Passing through the kitchen, Eleanor came face to face with a lump of pork that looked green and smelt as it looked. She gagged and drew her scarf across her fastidious Parisian nose. The cook laughed. His assistant laughed.

She hurried down the hallway after the waiter.

He opened a door to a room and indicated she wait inside. Someone would come soon. She told him she wasn't alone, they were two. 'The young man with the cat,' she said. The waiter left.

The room hadn't seen paint since Napoleon. It had a couple of iron beds with bare, stained mattresses, which looked recently slept on, a couple of old chairs, a cupboard with a battered suitcase and a serge jacket hanging on a hook. A window, presumably giving out onto the back lane, was shut and covered by a blind and a dirty curtain. After the warmth of the café, she had returned to winter.

The door opened. Henk entered, with cat and the cup of milk, which he set down on the floor. 'You have made the contact?'

'Possibly,' she replied.

He turned on the tap in the dirty basin. The pipe groaned and squealed but soon water came out. He took off his coat, his top, his shirt, his undershirt, hung them neatly on one of the chairs and lowered his trousers.

'Do you mind?' Eleanor said.

'I must wash. Do not look,' he said. 'Then I will not look at you.'

Eleanor sat in the other chair, facing away from him. She dared to lift the cup of milk from the cat, thinking she might use it for her face. It wasn't milk at all but a watery soup with a rancid fishy flavour. Disappointed, she returned it to the cat, tempted as she was to throw it all over Henk.

'You have been to Pau before,' he said, as he sluiced the freezing water over his genitals.

'None of your business,' she muttered. Her attention was on his undershirt, draped over the chair in front of her. It looked new and of good-quality cotton.

'Yes, you have,' he persisted. 'I could tell. You do not want to go there.'

'I keep telling you,' she said, as she felt the fabric behind his back, 'it's the stupidest place to cross into Spain this time of year.'

'That is not your reason,' he said.

The little shit. Was he psychic?

Emboldened by his meeting with the French workers, he seemed to be enjoying her discomfort.

'There is another reason,' he needled.

'A honeymoon,' she replied. 'Years ago.' If she hardly ever thought of Fred, she never thought of this would-be husband, whose name she had to dredge up from a vault labelled 'Forgotten'. She remembered his nickname though. Roméo. That alone should have warned her but there was nothing like a woman hitting thirty and being alone – a *femme seule*, as the French so harshly put it – to frighten her. She found it hard even to conjure up his face.

'You do not have this husband anymore,' he said, fact not question.

'I didn't have him then. He was married already,' she said. 'I was pregnant.'

'To him?'

'Yes. His instinct was honourable. Then I miscarried and so did he, so to speak.' She chuckled.

'Why do you laugh?' Henk demanded with a severity that would have done a Providence Presbyterian proud.

'He was one of your lot.'

'A Jew?'

'Yes, though they'd converted a couple of generations before,' she said. 'I meant a socialist. Not that he would ever have fronted a barricade. A bar more like.' What on earth had she seen in him, even as a ticket out of her solitary status?

'A bourgeois socialist,' Henk sneered.

'Until I met you, I didn't know there was any other sort,' she replied airily. Her attention was on the faint imprint on his undershirt. She picked it up for closer inspection. What she saw chilled her, an eagle with a swastika and underneath that, 'Deutsche Wehrmacht'.

Henk turned, drying his hair on the dirty pillow case he'd taken from the bed.

'We shoot such people,' he said.

'I would have shot him too but I didn't have a gun,' she said.

'Hah?' he said, on the precipice of a mocking smile. 'The only real difference between you and me is you are born in rich America and I am born in – '

He stopped. The precipice had turned into a real one.

'Warsaw?' Eleanor fished through the hole he'd opened up for her. 'Minsk?' She pointed to the Wehrmacht imprint on his undershirt. 'Or might that be Berlin?' He snatched it from her and pulled it over his head.

'Vienna,' he conceded.

'Stolen?' she said, pointing to the undershirt.

'No,' he said, 'legal. But illegal if we agree that no Nazi law can be obeyed.'

It was easier to tell her now rather than have her needle him the whole time. The minimum to shut her up.

His father, a Catholic, he began, had been a records clerk in an insurance office in Vienna, his mother a worker in a cigarette factory. They'd hovered on the insecure margins of the respectability his father craved. He, the last child, the bright one, went to the gymnasium, the only one of his four brothers and sisters to get an education. But his father's attempt to sling him up into the bourgeoisie was thwarted; he was kicked out before he could take his matriculation.

'Too much Comrade Stalin,' she said.

'It doesn't matter why,' he said, weary of her sarcasm. 'It happened and I got sent to a camp.'

This shut Eleanor up.

'A labour camp,' he said. He could see she had misunderstood; they rubbed each other up the wrong way, he and she. 'Austria didn't get Nazi concentration camps until after the German invasion. Twelfth of March, nineteen thirty-eight.' He paused, although not for dramatic effect. He was sick of it all. 'My nineteenth birthday,' he added grimly.

She'd had him at only nineteen, yet here he was, nearly twenty-three.

In the turmoil of the Nazi takeover, he had been able to escape the labour camp because plenty of the inmates had been young Nazi toughs who were suddenly top dogs. He made it back to Vienna past the checkpoints by pretending to be one of them. He found his father had not only joined the Nazis but had started divorce proceedings against his mother. She, he now discovered, was a Catholic convert; her parents and she had been Galician Jews.

'Now, suddenly, I am half-Jewish,' he said, a fifty percent *Mischling* under the Nazi race laws, which the Germans applied immediately. His mother killed herself; he tried to enter Switzerland but the border was clogged with desperates like him. The Austrian border police, who were all Nazis, refused exit passes if you didn't have the money to pay the bribe. He tried to cross illegally. 'Nearly got caught.'

'I went to the Jewish charity in Vienna, who tell me to get lost. Hitler said I was a Jew, my mother was a Jew. According to them, I wasn't. So I joined the Wehrmacht.'

'The German army?' exclaimed Eleanor in disbelief.

'The only place you are safe from the Gestapo is in the army, where they have no power,' he said. 'You know better, do you?'

She shut up. His rebuke was deserved.

'I take a chance and say nothing about being a *Mischling* Jew,' he continued. 'My father wanted to get rid of me so signed the papers.'

He decided, he told her, that he would be the best soldier he could. He would fit in. He would survive. He had managed it in the youth labour camp infested by young Nazis.

'Some were human beings,' he said, forgetting his current black–white view of his ex-compatriots, 'but only in secret. Same in the army.'

In the Polish campaign, he unfurled his story further, he won an Iron Cross for bravery and was made a lance corporal. Then, in April

1940, a personal order from Hitler forced the army to weed out the half-Jews like him, just at the very moment, with terrible German precision, his mother's conversion documents met his army file. This was news to him, he had said, defending himself, and if they didn't believe him, he'd drop his pants to prove he was no snipcock Jew. This didn't wash. Ignorance and not being circumcised might be an excuse for getting into the army, not for staying.

'Fifty percent Jew was fifty percent too much Jew.'

He was saved only by the start of the military campaigns of May 1940 and the connivance of his platoon, his lieutenant and his CO, all Austrian. To them he was no Jew – a backhanded compliment, he understood. He joined the invasion of Norway, his unit along with the other Austrians being detailed to rescue the Wehrmacht's Third Mountain Division at Narvik, which they had done. This was a joke. They were all city boys from Vienna. Then they were sent to Lapland, of all places, for the invasion of Russia, although after only one month, he was finally forced out of the army. He'd thought of trying to get to Sweden from there, but German soldiers had been told: do that and the Swedes will send you back, and you will be executed. And they did. He had no choice but to go to Vienna, where his father gave him money to disappear. He tried again to get into Switzerland, succeeded this time, was caught by the Swiss, who kindly posted him back to the Gestapo, who sent him to a camp near Linz. Had he not been discharged formally from the Wehrmacht, he'd have had that bullet.

'This camp, its name is Mauthausen,' he said. 'The "bone mill" they call it. Hard labour, digging out granite rocks. But I was strong and I was tough.' Better than a ghetto in Poland, where the rest of the Jews went, the Gestapo told him. 'Mauthausen was really a reward for earning an Iron Cross,' he said with grim humour. 'Another reward was a red triangle the right way up on my sleeve instead of an upside-down yellow triangle. Even though I was kicked out of the army, I wore the mark of a Wehrmacht deserter instead of the mark of a Jew. That saved my life. The Jews got worked the hardest. If you couldn't work anymore, if you were sick, they just shot you.'

He sighed.

'You have no idea how people who are skin and bone struggle to stay alive when they are finally trapped by death.' He stopped. The telling of this was draining him. He wanted to lie down, to sleep and wake up in Palestine. Or in heaven. Really, he wanted to forget.

With an insight into the darkness of individual members of humanity from her experiences in the Great War, she appreciated acutely that what he was telling her now was more than just another rung on the ladder of war and its miseries.

'No one knows this,' she said.

'In Germany they do,' Henk replied, without emotion. 'My father knew. They all know. They choose not to know the gory details. Every soldier in Russia knew the SS commandos were killing off the Jews. They saw them doing it. You think they don't tell anyone?' He paused. 'Now I tell you so you know too.'

He sat silent for a few moments. She didn't say a word; the look on his face was too distant, too lost. But he was not finished.

'One damp, freezing morning,' he continued, 'the beginning of last month – November, end of October, you lose track of time in the camp – I am with Russian prisoners of war who they give the hardest rocks to crack and treat like Jews. My name is called out. I think: this is it, I am to be shot. But no. Things are not going so well in Russia.'

He was being recalled to the army, to a probation unit on the Eastern Front, where, if he did well and survived, he would earn the right to return to his old unit.

'That is a joke, no?' he said. 'The only way a half-Jew like me can get out alive from the bone mill is to die fighting Jewish Bolshevism in Russia. This is more reward for earning the Iron Cross. You think the Nazis do not have a sense of humour?' He paused. 'Once I come out through those gates with my *Wehrpass* and my back-pay, I do not oblige them.' He saw the look of astonishment on her face. 'Yes, even funnier they give me my back-pay since I was kicked out,' he explained. 'So this,' he said, fingering his Wehrmacht undershirt. '*In der Not, frisst der Teufel Fliegen*,' he said. 'In need, even the devil will eat flies.'

Eleanor noticed her reflection in the dirty mirror, an observer of life from the silk sheets and gowns of privilege to which she'd return as soon as she had organised his passage to Spain. The divide between their experiences was unbridgeable. Her face burnt with shame.

'Presuming you get into Spain,' she said, 'and presuming General Franco doesn't lock you up, where will you go after that?'

'Since I am now a Jew, to Palestine,' he said.

'Oh God,' she said in a mix of despair and sudden fondness, 'with your sense of direction, how will you ever find it?'

'Someone always show me the way,' he said. His cat meowed and he picked it up.

'And Henk?' she questioned his name.

'Is better than Heinrich,' he replied. 'The French cannot tell Dutch from German.'

Towards 8am, Thursday, 11th December 1941

In the canteen, Bauer and Girard ate a hearty Lyonnaise breakfast whose quality Bauer couldn't quite believe. Clearly not all the French were being starved to feed Germany and even if they were, most of it was going to the armed forces. Frankfurt detectives and their families had eaten none of it. Kopitcke, who complained constantly about French cooking, picked at the food on his plate.

While he ate, Bauer read through the autopsy report on the two murdered soldiers, delivered by Girard himself. The boy with the single stab wound in his back had been alive when thrown into the river, where he'd drowned. The poor kid, Bauer thought. That's not something the parents should learn. The report confirmed his initial hunch about the murder weapon. Most probably a combat knife, possibly French or German, although the British version had a similar blade, shape and width. The doctor offered his opinion in a notation in the margin of the official document that it was a German infantry knife because of the shape of the wound. This raised more questions than it answered, though they were questions that got Bauer thinking about the how and the who.

He had never seen a current army combat knife in Frankfurt criminal circles – First World War knives, yes, but not from the Wehrmacht. After breakfast, he'd use his old-boys' network and official lines to get information in case the doctor's opinion was spot-on. Bauer had his doubts. A Landser who lost his knife would have gotten into great strife, even before the war. Now, especially on the Eastern Front, he'd end up in a punishment battalion. Another argument against the doctor's opinion was that after the French collapse last year, discarded French weapons had been everywhere, including infantry knives, which were good quality and popular. It would be hard to pick the difference between a wound made by one or the other. Still, Bauer was not about to discard the doctor's view.

Then came an urgent message from a police informant. Girard hurried to his office.

'One of the *passeur* groups has your killer, Kommissar,' Girard loftily informed Bauer after he had been summoned.

Bauer didn't follow. A *passeur* group? What was going on?

'They're offering us a deal,' Girard explained. 'Your killer for two of their fellows we've got on remand.'

'This will release the French hostages in Nevers,' Bauer said as encouragement.

Girard didn't need Bauer to spell that out. The sooner Bauer was out of his hair, the better.

'There's a catch. The *passeurs* won't personally hand the killer over,' he explained. 'They've got him holed up somewhere.'

'Let's go then,' Bauer interrupted.

'Slow down, Kommissar,' Girard said. He hadn't finished. They would only get the address once the two on remand had been released. Did they think he was stupid? He was bringing them up to the front door of the commissariat where their pals could see them. Once they had the address, and only then, he'd release the two.

'I'm doing you a big favour,' he added. 'These two are crooks who'd sell their grandmothers.'

A policeman knocked and entered. The two were now at the front door, visible from the street.

'Now we wait,' said Girard.

Hardly a minute passed before his telephone rang. It was the informant.

'The Café du Levant in La Croix Rousse,' Girard repeated the address given him. He was up and on the way. 'Wait till we're gone, then let the bastards go,' he ordered as he hurried downstairs to the waiting car with Bauer on his heels.

'The killer's in the backroom with an older woman,' Girard said. 'An American.'

'That might explain the Chesterfield cigarette,' Bauer mused, intrigued as much as he was excited. 'I wonder what else?'

Just before 8am, Thursday, 11th December 1941

The door opened. The waiter urgently beckoned Eleanor.

'Wait here,' she said to Henk, handing him her cigarettes and lighter.

The waiter led her to the kitchen, where the young man with the fine skin and tight face was standing in a corner.

'You are American?' he asked. Only later, in hindsight, was this question significant. Now it merely unsettled her. Had her mouth again betrayed her? She let it pass, neither confirming nor denying.

'I personally don't need a passage into Spain,' she explained. 'The young man I'm with, he paid for a passage through to Pau. Before the *passeurs* dumped him, dumped us all, they gave us this address.'

'You are the ones in the party of Silvan?' the fellow interrupted her.

'Thank God,' Eleanor said. 'You must be the guide to take him on from here. If there are any further charges, I'll pay.'

'Why do you pay for him?' the suave young man demanded.

'It's my Christian duty to help a fellow human being in need,' she replied. 'He needs to get away from the Nazis and he has no money. I don't particularly like him. Come to think of it, I don't like you, either. Why is it any of your business?'

'I suggest you leave Lyon,' said the young man. 'Immediately, if you know what's good for you. Alone.'

Eleanor's blood went cold, stilling any protest she could have made about how they owed Henk. This fellow already knew who they were, and she understood how he knew; her cigarettes, her mouth, not to forget his infernal cat. Yes, it's us, the killers and she the fool, had just confirmed it. At least their eavesdropper in Saint Pourçain had not informed the Germans. She sensed, however, that the result might be the same.

As casually as she could, she turned to go back to the room.

'Where are you going?' the young man demanded.

'I'm taking your advice,' she said, calmly. 'I must get my rucksack.' She kept on. The waiter followed her.

'Hurry up,' he said as she went inside. Immediately, she slammed her hand over Henk's mouth to stop any question he was about to ask. She ran to the window, pulled aside the blind and the curtain and tried to lift it open but it would not move. Desperately, she beckoned to him. She did not have to explain. He pushed her away and hauled the window up. He grabbed his cat; she grabbed her rucksack. He scrambled out, then helped her.

They were on a back lane. The suddenness of their need to escape, her surprise that they had escaped, caused her to shake so much she faltered. Which way? Where were they to go? And how?

'I must go to Pau,' said Henk.

'Let's get away from here first,' she replied, regathering her wits. They bolted down the laneway.

'Someone betray us?' Henk asked, once they were on the street and disguised among people coming and going from work.

'We betrayed ourselves,' she replied. 'We can't trust anybody. We're on our own.'

They came to a crossroad. I go this way, she thought, he goes that. She knew she could not – but, really, she didn't know what to do.

'Wait here,' said Henk. 'I will get help.' She was horrified to see him run back in the direction they'd come.

'You can't go back there,' she cried, but he was gone. She tucked herself into the entrance of a shop that had not yet opened. She felt for her cigarettes and lighter but he had them. In moments, although it felt like a century, Henk returned with two of the workers he had befriended over his cat and the joys of Comrade Stalin. Seeing Eleanor, their friendly faces soured.

'Who the hell's she?' one asked. Henk did not understand, although it was clear his comrades were not happy.

'Why are they angry?' He was mystified.

'Who cares,' Eleanor snapped.

'Ask them,' he demanded.

'Who are you?' they asked, saving her the trouble.

'His moneybags,' she growled, her French veering towards the Texan variety. 'Rockefeller,' she added, spitting out the word with angry pleasure. 'Are you going to get him to Spain before the Germans catch him? If so, please do. I'm fed up with him.'

'What are you saying?' Henk demanded again. 'They're comrades. Do not talk to them like that.' He turned to the two men. 'Comrades, please,' he managed in French. 'We – '

'You want to go with them?' she said to him. 'Go. Feel free. If you want to come with me, I'm going now. Make up your mind. But if you stay here, those treacherous shits inside will hand you over to the police and they'll give you to the Germans.' She'd had enough. She had no idea where this street went, but she was determined to go now. Bugger him.

Henk looked at Eleanor hurrying away, looked at the comrades. 'Sorry, comrades,' he said, then chased after her.

Whatever the two comrades said to each other, Eleanor had no idea. Nor did she care. One of the men was quickly on their tail. 'Wait,' he called out. 'I will show you. I am Michel.' Eleanor ignored him, just kept going. Henk shook the fellow's hand. Only when Eleanor came to the end of the street did she stop. Which way?

'This way,' said Michel, leading them into a stinking lane. At the end, they reached a slippery clay track that zig-zagged down through the steep bushy slope between La Croix Rousse and the city that spread out below them on the finger of land between the river Saône on the right and the Rhône on the left. Eventually, they emerged from the bare thickets onto a street. Michel pointed to the tram passing only a block away.

'Spain?' he asked.

Eleanor nodded. 'First, I need to find a hotel for us to hide in so I can look for new *passeurs* south,' she said. 'Can you recommend one?'

'You'll need one that doesn't talk,' Michel replied. 'They'll take you to the cleaners, and even then, they'll drop you in the gendarmes' pocket quick as look at you. The concierges, they're all on the payroll. Lady, you'll be safer paying me and the wife to put you up. Won't be what you're used to, but sounds like you don't have much choice.'

Eleanor translated the offer.

'Thank you, comrade,' said Henk in French, ignoring any need for a discussion, shook his hand and said in English, 'We accept.'

'How much?' Eleanor asked the obvious.

'What would you pay for a hotel?' Michel asked and when she replied, halving the amount, he laughed. Even this was so high a figure as to be ridiculous. 'You gotta be a yid,' he said. 'That why you're on the run from the Boches?'

'It's as good a reason as any,' she replied, too on edge to see the funny side.

'Come on,' Michel said cheerfully, his early suspicion forgotten. What Eleanor and Henk's exact relationship was, he really didn't care. He led them to the Saône side of the city and into the old city, over the same bridge she and Henk had crossed earlier. He was heading for work in that direction in any case.

Each side felt they had a bargain.

*

When Girard, Bauer and a detachment of police arrived ten minutes later, the Café du Levant was as the *Mary Celeste*. Cigarettes still smouldered in ashtrays, drinks were half finished, a pot of hot stew sat on the stove. But there were no smokers, no drinkers, no flame from the gas burner and no cook. The backroom was empty.

'The window,' said Bauer, who pulled the blind back and saw it had been forced open from the inside.

'He was here and he smelled the rat,' Bauer said. He saw a cup on the floor.

'What do you make of that?' he mused. 'There is a table but you put the cup on the floor.' He sniffed it. A fishy, thin soup.

Girard was not interested in the cup or what was in it. His indigestion, bad at the best of times, was killing him. Missing their quarry, so close, he would never be free of this Bauer. Worse, he had released two crims in return for nothing.

'Let's go,' he said curtly. What happened to Bauer's killer, he no longer cared.

Bauer, lost in consideration of the cup and its contents on the floor, ignored the summons. He was adding to his computations the fine saucer of milk provided by the young woman in the village for her non-existent cat called Felix. Until proven otherwise, the evidence now suggested that either the young killer or the American woman with him might be carrying a cat. It would seem a ridiculous thing to lug a cat on your escape across France, but he understood people who liked cats. Wouldn't he do the same? Rather than automatically assume it was the woman, he left the cat's ownership open. At this point, calling for Girard to start looking for a young man or an American woman with a cat would still be foolish. They'd think him ridiculous. He'd keep it to himself, until proven otherwise.

'Inspector,' Girard snapped. He was at the end of his tether with this whole business.

'Tell me,' Bauer said as Girard shepherded him to the car, 'if you know your so-called helpers want to trade you in for their pals in jail, you'd want to get out of town quick smart under your own steam, wouldn't you?'

'Train, to the frontier at Cerbère on the line to Barcelona,' answered Girard. Yes, he then agreed with a sigh, he would put on extra men to check departures south immediately. Yes. Yes.

'How about alternatives?' Bauer asked.

'Latour-de-Carol's the only other one this time of year, on the Toulouse to Barcelona line.'

'What about a freight train?' Bauer asked.

Girard frowned. 'Why, when the passenger trains are running and much quicker?' Besides, searching the freight yards would require the help of the gendarmes, the military police, who considered themselves above dealing with mere criminals.

'This is a matter of state,' Bauer said, 'not just another homicide.'

A request would be better coming from Bauer, Girard said. For this, he would need to see the general of the gendarmerie in person. When they arrived at the building, they were told he was indisposed but would be available later in the day. Girard managed a sneer. Still in bed with his mistress.

'What do you make of this American woman?' Bauer asked as they drove towards the Perrache station.

Girard smiled. 'Why not?' This was the only interesting twist in the whole affair.

Bauer laughed. What do they call them in Hollywood films? 'We say "*Gangsterbraut*". Gangster bride.'

'A moll,' replied Girard drily.

'That's it,' Bauer said, impressed. He needed the evidence, and that room hadn't provided any. 'Your contacts?' he asked. 'Concierges, waiters?'

'Of course,' Girard agreed airily, without the slightest intention of passing their details on. Whoever this man and woman were, they were gone, and so too, sooner than later, would be this Bauer.

*

Bauer joined Kopitcke in the police office above the station concourse for a while. The action by the communists was well over. Rail operations were slowly getting back to normal. Once the whistle was sounded for departure, the next train going south moved a few hundred metres, was locked then searched. Although the French encountered some truculent young men, none had a Wehrmacht combat knife; nor was one reported with a cat. Bauer wondered if this was just too absurd, that he was being played for a fool or, worse, playing himself for a fool. He did not share this doubt with Kopitcke, whom he detailed to go off and read through all the police and gendarme reports in the hours since the killings. He was wasting precious time here. Something wasn't right, and he didn't know what.

OLD TOWN, LYON V

Towards 9am, Thursday, 11th December 1941

Eleanor and Henk followed their host into the old town with its narrow, dirty streets and dank laneways that out-stank the gritty air. South, Eleanor figured, at least they were heading south. South, eventually, was Spain. Babies screamed, mothers yelled and children squabbled in houses that sprouted like untidy mushrooms either side of the laneways. She smelt something foul and saw human excrement in the gutter.

Michel turned out to be a cheerful fellow who chattered away to Eleanor as they walked along. Now he was more human, she saw he was handsome, with dark features and dark, flashing eyes. He was a machinist in one of the modern silk-weaving factories; he'd been up in La Croix Rousse visiting old pals he used to work with. His wife was a cleaner on the railways; his two soldier sons were being held by the Germans. This surprised Eleanor. He didn't look old enough to have two sons in the army.

'At least they're alive,' he said. He didn't blame the Germans, he blamed the defeatists in the government and the army. 'They preferred defeat by the Germans to an alliance with the Soviet Union. Comrade Stalin offered. Now look where we are.'

Once this would have been a red flag to the Republican bull. Now Eleanor bit her tongue. Michel led them in from a back laneway through a silent workshop of dusty, rusting machinery and up two flights of stairs into an ancient tenement. Locomotives shunted freight cars not far away. Coal dust was in the air, on every surface and, by the sound of hawking and coughing, in every chest.

'You'll be safe here,' he said. 'No one sees nothing, no one asks questions.'

'How far is the station?' she asked and learnt they were across the river from it; the main line from Paris came out of the tunnel not far away.

Michel opened his front door. Inside, he lit a paraffin lamp that gave off a golden light but also acrid black smoke. They were welcome, he said. The room had a couch, an armchair, a table and chairs and a stove. The bedroom was through a doorway draped with a curtain.

'Half now,' said Eleanor handing over the francs, 'half when we go?'

He took the money.

His wife came out of the bedroom. She was a petite woman with a face whose lines were a map of her hard life, yet the echo of youthful prettiness was still there in her eyes. She pushed her straggling hair back from her face as her husband told her they had guests for the day at least. She was late for work. Despite having two guests imposed on her, she was welcoming in a French she spoke with a strong Spanish accent. The money her husband showed her helped. She also seemed to Eleanor to be too young to have two boys in the army.

'Excuse me – ' Eleanor said. She'd almost said 'madame'; it had been on her tongue. 'Comrade' was a step too far. 'Where is the toilet?' On the way, they'd stopped for that wretched kitten, not for her.

The toilet was downstairs, where they'd come in; they all used the washrooms of the old workshop, the wife replied. 'Do not go now,' she added. 'The men from the night shifts are there. You can use the commode.' Eleanor's Parisian nose had already smelt that possibility and rejected it.

'Thank you,' she said to the woman. 'You are very kind.'

The woman excused herself. The man bade them a good morning. He too was going to work.

'Why don't you ask him for bread,' Henk said irritably.

Suppressing her annoyance at being called out for something so obvious, Eleanor managed to ask before Michel disappeared through the door. 'Add it to our bill,' she said. Michel laughed. There was only bread and potatoes. They were welcome to the bread.

'On the house,' he said, gaily pointing to a bread box on the dresser.

There they found the meagre end of a loaf which, Eleanor thought, looked like a brick. It certainly felt like one as she failed to break off even a crumb. Henk produced his knife and hacked the brick in two. 'You soak it in water first,' he said exasperated as she tried to chew on her lump, risking her teeth.

'So, comrade,' said Henk after they had eaten, 'who saves whom now?'

Eleanor laughed. The little shit. 'We're not saved yet, sonny,' she replied. 'I certainly must look like one of the comrades,' she grumbled, looking unsuccessfully for a mirror. 'That's telling, isn't it? No mirror.'

'Not necessary,' said Henk. 'No vanity.'

'Yet another reason why communism will never work,' she said.

He had already shut his eyes. His little cat jumped up onto him and began to wash itself.

'What a cosy little scene,' Eleanor muttered.

Secure in his light snoring, she felt she could accommodate herself even to the stinking commode, a torture to take her mind off her discontents, which were many. The cure was remarkable. She sat in the armchair, put a cushion over a protruding spring, covered herself with her coat and halfway through the Our Father, she was asleep.

OLD TOWN, LYON V

Mid-afternoon, Thursday, 11th December 1941

A baby's cries woke Eleanor. She was stiff and she was cold and it was dark, but she had slept soundly. Fleetingly, she thought it was the same dream-child that had so disturbed her sleep after her upsetting discovery of Claude's other family in the churchyard at Auvers-sur-Oise. The cries, however, were coming from next door. There was no getting away from them, and try as she might, there was no getting away from the memory of that day. She had been so distracted by the events of the past few days, she had pushed her anger and confusion aside. Now those children returned to inhabit her every fibre. She felt as heavy as lead so stayed where she was, letting fester whatever poisons were being released in her. Didn't those children mean she was still the mistress, the only mistress, and blow what Church and state might say about that? She had the wit to realise that if this was her only comforting thought, it was a pretty dismal one. She had never questioned her life with Claude. As his mistress, she had felt, she admitted it, superior. Hers was a love above the everyday and the mundane, a love between two free spirits, the sort of love her readers took delight in because they were bound by children and husbands and housework and jobs, which she, the writer, was not.

'Twaddle,' she muttered. What she didn't like admitting was that she was jealous, but she was. And angry.

She hurled herself out of the chair. Her watch told her it was three, although she wasn't sure if this was morning or afternoon. She pulled back the rough curtain covering the window. Outside, the day had little light to share. She lit the paraffin lamp. In hope, she ventured down to the washroom. The boilers stood unlit and empty; the faucets delivered only lukewarm water and with a grinding sound that put her teeth on edge. She managed to wash the minimum and refresh her complexion and lipstick.

'I have to get my suitcase from the luggage bureau,' she said when she came back up. Henk had woken and was playing with the cat.

'I would not go. The police will be there,' he said and yawned. The cat meowed. It was hungry.

'I don't care,' she said. 'I need fresh clothes.'

'What about getting away?'

'I'll make enquiries,' she said.

'How can we trust them?'

'We can't,' she said. 'What else are we going to do?' Thrusting 20 dollars into his hand, she told him if she wasn't back in an hour and a half, he would have the dubious pleasure of being right. There were enough cigarettes in her rucksack to bribe his way to Jerusalem, even past Rommel and his Afrika Korps.

She walked down the dark stairwell. Was it wise to leave him with such temptation? She fought her prejudices. He hadn't tried to steal again. When push had come to shove that morning, he had chosen to follow her rather than the comrades. If her help was given with bad grace, which it had been so far, she admitted, what sort of Christian was she? She knew the answer to that, alas. She had to trust him. She would trust him.

A little later, afternoon, Thursday, 11th December 1941

Out in the open, she could barely see the other side of the street. The sky seemed lower. The world had closed in around her. From not far away, she heard the soughing and chuffing of the locomotives that were clogging the air with coal dust. She found the quay and saw a tram labouring past full of passengers. She bet on its destination and followed, remembering to shuffle along at the same pace as the others rather than stride like some flashy, confident American. She certainly did not feel like one. For all that, as she came to the bridge across the river upstream from the railway bridge and tunnel, she was cool-headed and determined. Traffic was sparse: no cars, with only a couple of motor lorries among the horse-drawn carts, whose horses snuffled and nickered as they shook their heads against the bits and harnesses. Their droppings steamed on the cold roadway, adding a top note to the air's already pungent aroma.

On the other side of the river, she came into the square that opened out before the railway station. More people were about, which was comforting. She had not seen any police or gendarmes, another comfort.

She stopped, caught by a wonderful sight.

Appearing like a mirage through the gritty gloom across the square was an El Dorado of golden lights and shining brass doors, an imposing beaux-arts hotel of many floors, under a grand mansard roof. It was beckoning her with open arms. A simple 'Open sesame' and she would be folded up anonymously into its comforts. Henk had her rucksack, the cigarettes, the money; he could make his own way. She had her passport and her bank accounts, and soon she would have her valise.

The struggle against Satan was not difficult. He had appeared only a few hours too soon. On her way here, she had seen cafés at each of which she would try on her way back to secure Henk's passage to Spain. Why, possibly even this night, she would say the magic words, enter this hotel with a clear conscience and let the devil take the hindmost.

First, her valise.

She sensed them even before she'd entered the main concourse of the railway station: gendarmes or police, she couldn't tell the difference. They were at the entrance to all the platforms, where passengers were being held up, where tempers were frayed and voices vented in frustration and annoyance. Eleanor was not innocent of the danger. If the *passeur* in La Croix Rousse had been willing to trade Henk, it was possible even the Germans might now know who he was. She, his accomplice in their escape from the café, could be implicated as well.

She skirted the concourse and found the *consigne à bagages* in a far corner. She slipped under the arch and in through the door. No other passengers were there; luck was with her. She saw no attendant either but was used to French ways and soon an ancient kepi'd gentleman appeared at a shuffle and greeted her. She returned his greeting and handed him her receipt. He put on the lorgnette he wore around his neck and peered at the scrap of paper in his hand. With neither word nor any change in his demeanour, he shuffled away. She glanced at her watch.

Another five long minutes, and the attendant returned with her valise.

'Identification card, madame?' he asked when eventually he came to the counter.

'But you have the receipt,' she said.

'Rules, madame,' he said, and waited.

She handed him her *carte d'identité*.

'Madame is American?' said the old man in some surprise. She had the comfort at least of knowing that her French had not betrayed her.

'Resident in France for many years,' she replied.

'Ah,' said the old man and handed over her valise but did not let go as she went to take it. He leant close.

'Do not try to board a train now,' he whispered. 'They' – his eyes shot in the direction of the concourse with its police and gendarmes – 'they are looking for an American woman and a young man.'

'Really?' she said, as blithely as she could. 'For what reason, do you know?'

He did not know, he said with a weary shrug. They were always looking for someone or other these days.

She thanked him and offered a generous tip.

'Oh no, madame,' he said. 'You will need it more than I.' They exchanged generous smiles and she left as casually as her panic allowed.

Outside, her El Dorado hotel beckoned her, but it was a fool's gold. She was shaking so much, she had to stop. Instead of tempting her, Satan was bent on making a meal of her. She set down her valise and went to light a cigarette. She remembered she had left them with Henk. It crossed her mind to liberate one of the packs she'd stowed in her suitcase, but she could hardly do that in the middle of the square. She tried to gather her wits, missing a flurry of excitement whose epicentre was the news kiosk, where a lone van had just delivered a swathe of those thin sheets that gave out the news approved by the regime in Vichy. Normally, these newspapers were useful only for rolling cigarettes. Now they drew a crowd actually wanting to read its tidings.

Eleanor heard the voices across the gritty air. 'Hitler's declared war on the Americans,' they were saying. 'The Yanks are in at last!'

Her blood quickened. Gone her fear, gone the shakes. Her vanity allowed her a brief moment of vainglory at suddenly finding herself on the front line of this new war, a representative of the United States of America, even if no one else had the faintest idea who she was. Energised and excited, she picked up her valise and headed away into the fading light. Sylvia came to mind and the vainglory that had briefly shone a halo above her vanished into the gritty air.

Meanwhile, same time, mid-afternoon, Thursday, 11th December

At this same moment, at a table inside Eleanor's El Dorado, under warm, golden wooden panels bordered by gentle Nouveau curves, with friezes that could have been painted by Degas himself, sat Kommissar Bauer. The day's searches had produced plenty of Jews on the run but no young man with an American woman, with or without a cat. Nor had Girard's informants given him anything that was useful. Hadn't Bauer known in his gut since that morning that the birds were flown? He was frustrated, he was tired and he was cold. He sipped a cognac. Kopitcke, who had spent the day poring over police and gendarme reports since the murder, entered the room. Meticulous fellow, he did have something to report.

Gendarmes had arrested an illegal Polish Jew in the village of Saint Pourçain at lunchtime yesterday. They'd encountered a whole party of people who'd come illegally across the line the night before, the night of the killings, but once they had the Jew, they ignored the rest because they were French. Kopitcke had spoken to the two gendarmes who had arrested the Polish Jew. And yes, they reported, a young man had been in that party. They remembered him and his mother because she was an American, married to a Frenchman. The son wouldn't talk to them; he wouldn't talk to anyone, because he and Mama had been in an argument.

'Hah, he can't speak French!' Bauer said with triumphant glee.

'That's what I said. The idiots!' exclaimed Kopitcke, in German. He saw the pain on Bauer's face. 'Sorry, boss,' he said in French. 'Sorry.'

'That's all right,' said Bauer. 'You get a good description from them?'

That was further cause for complaint from Kopitcke. The answer was no, nothing beyond the generic, nothing distinctive. Her hair was brown, his hair was short; he looked about eighteen, she about fifty. Up to Kopitcke, these two gendarmes would have been cashiered.

'No point in gnashing one's teeth about that,' said his boss.

'Oh,' Kopitcke suddenly remembered, 'they said the young man had a little cat.'

Bauer smiled. Eureka. This was the best description he could have. And it was the young man, not the woman. Proven – amazing, but proven.

'If you'd been in charge, Kopitcke,' he asked, 'how would you have known the boy was the murderer?'

'I wouldn't but I would have made him talk and we'd have known immediately that he didn't speak French,' Kopitcke replied. 'That would have been enough to arrest him and we'd have him in the clink on our side, like we've got the Polish yid. Then we'd make him confess.'

'Exactly,' said Bauer. Kopitcke glowed. 'The French are still too soft,' he added. 'Now what?' If their quarry wasn't French, what was he?

His enquiries among his Wehrmacht contacts hadn't yet produced any results. 'Who does the evidence point to so far, Kopitcke?'

Kopitcke knew by the tone of Bauer's voice to answer the question with his own question. 'What do you think, Herr Kommissar?'

'Unable to speak French, a military combat knife, the ability and willingness to use it against two trained Wehrmacht soldiers,' said Bauer. 'We're looking at one tough customer who has no love for us.'

'He has a cat,' Kopitcke protested.

Bauer smiled. 'I like cats, young man,' he said. 'I'd do the same in his shoes.'

'But you're not a killer, sir,' Kopitcke rejoined. Liking cats proved it and thus his doubts that the young man in question could possibly be a murderer.

'Keep the cat in,' Bauer said. 'I've killed in my time, young man, don't forget. Legally, but plenty.'

'He's an American?' Kopitcke replied. 'The gendarmes said the woman really was an American; they could tell by her accent.'

'Possibly,' Bauer allowed. The papers were forged to cover the kid's lack of French.

Kopitcke had it. 'Mother and son,' he said, convinced. 'Getting away together to Spain and back to America, taking their cat with them. Our boy bails them up, the kid knifes our boy in the back, lies in wait for the second, knifes him after a struggle. Look at their gangsters. Everyone carries knives and guns. It's a wild west.'

'Not bad,' Bauer offered and nodded approvingly. 'If he'd gotten a combat knife. I've asked for tests to be done using our own and the French combat knife. If it's definitely French, you might be on to something. If, as the doctor surmises, it turns out to be German, that takes us in quite another direction.'

Still, all speculation. Where were their quarries now?

'Ah,' said Bauer. It was obvious. 'On a freight train or trying to find one.' Why would you go on a passenger train with a cat? You couldn't keep it hidden.

Sub-Inspector Girard arrived to see that Bauer was settled and to report that the gendarmes were at last covering the marshalling yards.

'Better late than never,' Bauer said agreeably. 'Kopitcke has discovered our killer is travelling posing as a French son with an American-born mother and that they're carting a cat along with them.'

'If so, that makes them both enemies of the Reich,' said Girard.

'The cat as well?' Bauer posed lightly.

Girard saw that Bauer hadn't picked up on the import of what he'd just said. 'Haven't you heard? Your leader's declared war on the United States,' he said, slipping the news in like a stiletto between the ribs.

Bauer felt the blade strike his heart.

'Kommissar?' Girard said, genuinely concerned.

'It's nothing,' Bauer responded. This was untrue. He felt dreadful. He had a pain in his chest, his stomach ached, his head ached. He hurriedly drank some cognac.

Girard said he was going to call a doctor.

'No, thank you, inspector,' Bauer said. He saw Kopitcke staring mutely at him aghast or astonished, as if he, Bauer, might have had a stroke. But Bauer's mind was working its way through this most terrible news. He took another more generous draught of his cognac and ignored the pains in his body.

'Your news, inspector, I admit it has taken me by surprise,' he said.

'It's wonderful, sir, isn't it?' Kopitcke exclaimed with his Hitler Youth enthusiasm.

Wonderful? Bauer couldn't begin to respond to such idiocy. His thoughts were consumed by his boys. The odds of them surviving this war had just worsened considerably. All along, he'd had his doubts about Hitler, though who could argue against success after success? But he knew first-hand what it was like after he and his men had been transferred to France following the Russian withdrawal from the war in 1918. They were exhausted and there in front of them were a million fresh American troops with the promise of more. Now the Soviets, supposedly on their last legs, were counterattacking outside Moscow. He was convinced that Germany was led by a fool and they were done for.

'Will you join us for dinner, inspector?' he asked Girard in the fervent hope he would decline.

Girard, relieved his well-aimed blow had struck but not killed his German colleague, declined with gracious thanks and left.

Bauer was floundering. He'd kept defeatist thoughts and fears at bay. Now they were eating him up. Worse, wouldn't they help condemn his sons to certain death?

Then, the oddest thing happened, especially for a man who was so methodical and evidence-based in his thinking. In a flash of quite profound comprehension, he saw a clear and strong link of causality: that by pursuing and catching this bastard who'd killed those two Landsers, he'd be keeping his sons alive. It wasn't rational and couldn't be explained, but he knew it was true. Then a dread realisation: this is what happens when you've had a stroke. But he saw himself in one of the mirrors, lifted his eyebrows and scratched his head. He was sound of mind and, now he noticed the pains gone, sound of body. Indeed, he felt reinvigorated.

This morning, he had come tantalisingly close to catching the killer, but so what? The bird and his companion were hiding or flown and the trail cold. He had no high hope that Girard or his police would catch them; they were more interested in cornering communists.

'We head south to the frontier and lay an ambush,' he told Kopitcke. 'We'll eat and then we'll go. Immediately.'

'Here?' Kopitcke asked, quailing at the thought.

'Here,' Bauer confirmed. 'Truly, Kopitcke, there's more to eating than filling yourself with pig's stomach and beets.'

OLD TOWN, LYON V

After 4.30pm, Thursday, 11th December

Eleanor checked her watch as she came in off the street. She was late. She had her suitcase and its precious cargo of cigarettes and her cosmetics but no passage for Henk. The waiters in each of the cafés she'd tried on her way back from the railway station had either been unable or unwilling to help. One was simply a crook; she had seen it in his eyes the instant she produced cash as her credentials. She got herself out of there in a hurry. With reasonable fear she might be followed, she doubled back to the quay, where she felt safe, then found her way back to their lodgings. She would ask their protector where she might go. She should have asked him before.

The building was back to life as she climbed the stairs, with children playing in the courtyard and up the stairs and along the balconies. The corridors stank of paraffin from the lamps. She arrived on their floor and pushed open the door.

He was gone. Knapsack, cat and attitude. The lamp had gone out.

'Damnation!' she erupted with anger, and she paced back and forth for a few moments before a torrent of words in French and English poured out to describe what she thought of him: cheat, liar, thief, but really, ingrate fitted the bill. Rank ingrate. She'd said an hour and a half. She hadn't been all that much longer. Mere minutes. Then she realised: the silver lining. She was absolved of any further responsibility for him. She relit the lamp to get some light in the room.

There on the floor was her rucksack with its stash of cigarettes and dollars, right where she had left it.

This did little to lighten her mood. She hoisted her rucksack. Now she herself was probably on a wanted list, she would find another café well away from here, up in La Croix Rousse. She would buy herself a passage out of Lyon, past the police, and into Spain, past the Germans. If she met the little shit on the way south, she could ignore him with a clear conscience. She picked up her valise and went towards the door, when it opened and there he was.

'Where are you going?' he demanded, pushing past her to get inside.

'Where have you been?' she countered. He was freshly shaved. He must have been in the washroom. She couldn't back down now.

'You were leaving,' he replied.

'You left.'

'You have no trust.'

'Not of you, no,' she said. 'I said I'd be back.'

'You said if you weren't back in an hour and a half,' he corrected her.

He produced a loaf of bread, a sausage and some milk from his cloth knapsack. 'Good worker's food,' he said, tearing off a piece of bread and sausage for himself. 'I have enough for the journey too.'

'How did you get it?' she demanded. The milk was particularly galling.

'Hah, you think I steal it,' he said. 'I pay. My money.'

'You told me you don't have any money.'

'I said I could not afford something, not I did not have any money,' he said. 'You bought me food. Now I buy you food.'

'You can't speak a word of French. You don't have any ration cards.'

'Fine,' he said, sitting down to help himself. 'Go. Do not eat.'

She was furious. The contribution of this or that specific complaint or hurt was immaterial. He drove her insane and now it was made worse because she was completely in the wrong. She wanted to drop her valise on his head.

'The police in the railway station,' she said accusingly, 'they're looking for a young man and an American woman.'

He shrugged his shoulders. 'You must be surprised I did not steal it,' he said, pointing at her rucksack as she slipped it from her back.

She set her valise down. 'Did you hear what I said? They're looking for us.'

'Why are you surprised? I am not surprised.' He sliced more sausage and bread off with the knife he'd taken from the German soldier. 'Now you are a criminal, you need to behave like one,' he said, handing her the food, which she ate, slaking her hunger instead of her resentments.

'Good?' he said.

'Good,' she conceded with bad grace.

'They look for an American woman, but you must act as if it is not you but some other American woman.'

'And you must act as if the police are looking for another young man?'

He picked up his kitten. 'But I am a young man with a cat,' he said. He then handed it to her. 'You are a woman with a cat. Who in their right mind would escape carrying a cat?'

'Now you mention that,' she said sourly, holding the poor creature as she might a hand grenade. He poured the milk into a glass, retrieved the kitten before she did it harm and set it down before the glass.

'The whole glass?' she said, dismayed.

'Be patient,' he said quietly as he watched the cat sip delicately from the top. When it had finished its portion, he handed the glass to her. She hesitated.

'Drink,' he said. 'Milk is good for you.'

She, whose normal use for milk was to keep her skin young and supple, drank, cat saliva and all. Then, having consumed half the cat's leavings, she handed the glass to him.

'There,' she said, feeling she'd triumphed over humiliation whether he drank or not, but of course he drank. Only now did she wonder why on earth she had not bought any food. Yes, the station had been crawling with police. Yes, they were looking for her. But the thought had not crossed her mind, even though she was hungry and had been in three cafés. She was obtuse to the point of stupidity, she realised. If she continued like this, she wouldn't reach Providence. She wouldn't even get to the Spanish border.

'People are kind,' he said. 'I do not need ration cards.'

'You pay double without ration cards,' she said. 'Triple.' True, but really, he was right, yet again. Without their Good Samaritans, where would they be?

'We will go on a freight train,' he said when she'd reported her failure at the cafés.

Eleanor noticed the 'we' as much as the conveyance. Both dismayed her. She knew what this was. Freight hopping. Hobos did it. But they were hobos, were they not? The bites she had felt after sleeping in that lumpy chair were proof.

'The wife,' she said, 'she works as a cleaner on the railways.'

They awaited her return. The woman wanted nothing to do with their idea. The money Eleanor offered changed her mind.

'You Jews, you know how money talks, eh?' she said as a matter of fact.

'I suppose we do,' said Eleanor. If only the little shit understood French.

CONFLUENCE, LYON II

After 8pm, Thursday, 11th December 1941

Their hostess led them on foot across the city between the two rivers, then down the Rhône quay. She went ahead with Eleanor, not saying much beyond 'This way' or 'We go here' or 'That way'. Henk followed some way behind. They were just three among the many railway workers leaving or heading for their shifts who traipsed along the same footpaths through the foul night air, shoulders hunched against the chill. The excitement of the previous day's actions – 'Red Riots' the Vichy propaganda sheets had called them – was gone, although the gendarmes were still about, harassing people at random with identification checks. After leaving the Rhône quay, they walked past the abattoir and its deadly smells and along a street with the marshalling yards around the Gare des Marchandises on the other side. Shunters shouted as they assembled boxcars like boys with a train set. Comrade though she was, the woman was helping them for cash, so Eleanor felt able to make some demands. They wanted to go to Pau, she said.

'Why there?' she asked. 'It's winter.'

Eleanor agreed but could hardly say so. 'My son says it's safer from the Germans.'

'Your son?' said the woman sceptically and with a smirk. Eleanor couldn't remember what lie she'd told about why they were together or if she'd said anything at all. Too bad. She didn't care and let it pass. So did the woman, who advised they'd be better going to Perpinyà and then over the demarcation line.

'Demarcation line?' Eleanor asked. What demarcation line? She thought she'd only recently crossed it. And Perpinyà? Where was that?

'The French call it Perpignan,' replied the woman with some heat. 'My country is Catalunya, divided between fascist France and fascist Spain.'

Eleanor fell silent. In her ignorance, she'd stepped into a minefield of history. The woman was seething so much that Eleanor wondered if she might leave them to their own devices, or worse. But she kept walking, and Eleanor stuck as close as she could. The woman leant over to her, as if to share a confidence. 'In Barcelona, there's an American Jewish organisation,' she whispered. 'They'll help you.'

'What about the Francoists?' Eleanor asked with studied innocence. She thought it ironic that so many Jews were desperate to enter a country that had expelled all its Jews hundreds of years ago and whose government was in power thanks to Hitler.

'Scum,' spat the woman, clearly from hard experience. 'All Francoists are scum. Money talks with them.' She rubbed her fingers in contempt.

Eleanor, under different circumstances, would have smiled. This was the pot calling the kettle if not black, then grey.

'At least they're cheap,' the woman added. 'In Portugal, the fascist scum, they're even cheaper. You should go there as soon as you can.'

'Papers!'

The word most feared, especially from the mouth of a surly gendarme.

Two stood athwart the footpath, flashlights in hand. With her valise, which Eleanor figured advertised her journey, and her *carte d'identité*, which showed she was from Paris, not to mention an American, she was in trouble. Yet her anxiety was for Henk behind them. Cross the damn street, she said to him in her mind as if it were a transmitter. She produced her papers. I'm not that American woman, she said to herself, over and over.

'Paris?'

'Hurry up,' the woman snarled at the gendarme's surly question, thrusting her own ID into his hands over the top of Eleanor's. 'I got to get my sister-in-law to the Paris train and then I got to get to work. Ain't you got nothing better to do? We're just ordinary people, you know.'

A gamble. Eleanor was aghast. The woman's accent was strong. The gendarmes didn't differentiate. The Spanish in France were all Republicans. Reds. What if they met truculence with truculence? You want to make trouble for yourself, sister?

'Calm yourself, lady,' he said. 'We're just carrying out orders.' He handed back both sets of papers. She and Eleanor continued, Eleanor fighting the urge to look behind.

Henk had thought of slipping across the street but this would have done for him, even in the dark. He approached the gendarmes. 'No insolence,' Eleanor had warned him in case of such an event. This had infuriated him. She had nothing to tell him about surviving and the memory of her saying that, it got him worked up in an instant.

'Papers, have your papers ready.'

He produced them. Did they say his mother was American? He'd never bothered to ask. He thought not, but too late now. The gendarme shone his flashlight on them, then on Henk's face. The kitten moved inside his coat. He shifted his beret, which he'd removed so they could see his face, and held it across his chest, all the time wondering if his beating heart was comforting or alarming his cat. She moved again. The gendarme handed back his papers. He took them. 'Don't say a damn thing,' she of all people had cautioned him.

'Merci,' he muttered in a good attempt at resignation and moved on as he slipped his beret back onto his head. Out of the corner of his eye, across the street in the shadows, he noticed two more gendarmes into whose arms he would have fallen. He'd known it, he'd sensed it. Isn't that what his platoon, his lieutenant, would have done? What they did in Norway to catch the resistance?

Once out of sight of the gendarmes, the woman left Eleanor with Henk in the shadow of a stone wall by a small copse of leafless trees clinging to life in this desert of coal dust. They watched as she walked across the tracks towards the signal box.

'They're comrades,' she explained before she left. As soon as she was out of hearing, Eleanor berated Henk for not having crossed the road to avoid the gendarmes. He forced himself to put her right so he could call her an idiot, which she was.

'I will decide what is safe,' he said, 'not you.'

She bristled but mostly because he was right. She didn't like being chastised and certainly not by him.

Soon the woman returned. The gendarmes had made a sweep of the yards some twenty minutes before but were now withdrawn except for those on the streets. As far as her comrades had heard, it was just intimidation; they were not really searching for anyone in particular, though they had caught a few Jews trying to hop the freight trains. Half the time, they found them squirrelled in laden boxcars that were headed north, into German hands.

'Dumb yids,' she said with a laugh. 'You want to escape, you travel in the empty trains. They're the ones headed south.' This barb, Eleanor thought, was probably for her benefit but she translated it all for Henk with great pleasure.

'You cross where I did,' the woman pointed. 'Go past the signal box. Count one, two, three trains. The fourth is all the way to Pau. You'll know it's the right one because it'll be empty. The ones heading north are full of our wheat, our wine, our labour.'

She was working herself up again. Eleanor wondered if this was the right time and place for a propaganda speech.

'Find yourself a boxcar,' the woman said. 'They're kept unlocked.'

'What about the guard?' Eleanor asked.

'They're human,' said the woman, 'got families to feed.' She said they had twenty minutes before the train departed, so they better get going.

Henk thanked her. Eleanor decided she'd handed over enough money already and while, yes, the woman had saved her trouble with the gendarmes, there was no need to tip above the amount she'd agreed with her husband. She could see the woman's expectation. Eleanor turned away. The woman gave her a cynical look when she saw she wasn't getting any more. 'Jews,' she muttered and left.

'Nice to see your comrades are so supportive,' Eleanor said.

'Come,' he said. He knew she was goading him again. This was still just an adventure for her, he thought with contempt.

They went through the gateway onto the tracks. Henk didn't like what he saw. The moon was on the wane and barely visible through the sooty air, but the dust itself reflected the light – people didn't understand this – and they would be silhouetted like wooden figures at target practice.

'I go first,' he said. 'Once I am at the signal box, you follow.'

She watched him walk at a steady pace across the tracks, though lost sight of him quickly, which made her anxious. She waited a few moments, then followed, also at a steady pace. Part of her was terrified; part of her, the writer, observed her own self, wondering if this were merely just a story she was making up from the safety of Rue de Montfaucon. She was snapped out of her reverie by Henk hissing at her to follow and to avoid the light thrown from the signal box. He went ahead to the first freight train. She followed. 'Keep going,' he told her. 'Don't crouch, don't look like you're trying to escape. Look like you're doing a job, you're supposed to be there.'

'My valise,' she said in a moment of panic.

'You do not listen,' he replied, irritated. 'It does not matter, being a woman either, just act as if you're meant to be here with your valise.'

He slipped between two boxcars of the first train, peeked out to make sure no gendarmes were in front of them, then went to the second train, the third and then the fourth. There, he went over to the space between two cars on the side of the train facing away from the signal box. She followed. He cautioned her to wait as he walked purposefully alongside the train, away from the guard's van. She kept him in sight and when he waved, she joined him. By then, he'd hauled back the door of one of the cars. He clambered up, put out his hand for Eleanor. I'll never get up, she thought. He told her where to place her feet, and though it was an effort, she made it. He pulled the door across. Although some slats were loose, the light outside wasn't strong enough to make any difference. She handed him the flashlight she'd kept in the valise as part of her survival kit in case of the German round-up.

'And a supply of fresh batteries,' she said in an effort to regain some of the considerable face she had already lost. 'Use sparingly.'

Henk flashed the light around their accommodation but immediately turned it off when he saw loosened slats along one side at the top. He cursed. Too late to change now. Eleanor saw bare wooden floors, no windows; if it had been cleaned in a year, she'd have been surprised. But really, she kicked herself mentally, what was she expecting? A Pullman?

'How will we sleep?' she asked plaintively.

'Use your rucksack for your head,' Henk told her, 'and lie on your back.' Then she remembered the cognac Al had given her, still in her rucksack, still over half full. She brought it out.

'This might help,' she said and handed it to him. When he drank, she noticed, it wasn't a slug, it was barely a sip.

'You can have more than that,' she said, wondering if inside all that truculence was a gentler soul. His next sip was healthier.

Outside, the crunch of footsteps along the gravel. Voices. They were hushed and they were German. Henk went to lean his weight against the door to stop it being opened but was a second too late and he nearly fell through the opening as whoever it was outside hauled the door back.

'*Scheiße*,' said one of the voices in great surprise to see a figure in the open doorway staring down at them.

'*Hau ab, Arschloch*,' Henk snapped in Wehrmacht German – piss off, arsehole – and they scattered in terror, crying to each other to run. Watching them flee, he realised that even in swearing, their German had been High and pure; they were probably Germans who hadn't been Jewish until the Nazis made them so. Nuremberg Jews, just like him. He had no room for sentiment. They had to look out for themselves, as he was. He saw Eleanor's face in the fleeting light as he pushed the door closed.

'You have complaint?' he asked.

'No,' she replied.

'Good,' he said.

A whistle screeched into the night and before they could steady themselves, the locomotive heaved itself forward, sending a ricochet of movement back through the cars as each lurched and then stopped and then lurched again. Eleanor fell forward. The cat jumped. He picked it up to comfort it.

'You'll get used to it,' Henk said wearily.

Late night, Thursday, 11th December 1941

The cognac contented Eleanor for a little while and she dozed to the easy rhythm of the wheels clack-clacking over the joints in the track. Soon, however, Dr Morpheus deserted her and she found herself wide awake. The judder of the wheels along the track was prising apart every joint in her body, as if she were on a medieval torture rack. She'd have sung like a canary if there'd been anyone to sing to and if the song opened a pathway to the paradise of a seat, even a wooden one. She sat with her rucksack against the wall. This improved nothing. Then sitting on top of her valise, leaning against the wall. The valise kept falling over. It was all she could do not to haul back the door and escape – frying pan into a possible fire, to be sure, but unknown perils were more alluring than known discomforts. Henk was fast asleep on his back. Naturally, she noted resentfully. His cat slept a while, visited her once and twice; she felt its nose inspecting her nose and ears at one stage when she was prone. Then she could tell it was relieving itself in a corner. It crossed her mind to strangle the little pest, but he would strangle her if she did that.

Now and then, the train stopped and she, who thought she'd been wide awake, woke. A glance at her watch confirmed she'd slept through some three hours of the torture, but really, she had dreamt it. Her body ached. Henk woke. He hauled open the door and pissed out into the night.

Right, she thought. She stopped him closing the door, slipped her feet over the edge and jumped down before he could stop her.

'Hurry,' he said. Of course she would damn well hurry. She didn't need him to tell her. She squatted by the tracks, modesty and dignity forgotten. After she returned, she asked him to remove the cat's contribution to their insanitary conditions before he shut the door. When he came back, they kept the door open and sat at the lip, dangling their legs out as though they were children. Their only company was the soughing of the locomotive at the front of the train.

'Where are we?' she wondered.

'Nowhere,' he said. 'It is good to be nowhere.'

On the fresh night air, she could smell the invigorating scent of pine trees. He stopped her lighting up.

'You don't learn,' he said to her.

'We're in the middle of nowhere,' she protested.

'Until you light a cigarette,' he replied. 'Then we might be somewhere.'

He said he hoped Palestine didn't have any trains. Once he was free of Europe, he never wanted to be on a train ever again. She said she couldn't agree more but wondered how he'd still managed to sleep.

'At least there is only you and me,' he said lightly, but there was a sting in his tone, she noted. Experience, and not a good one.

The night was clear. But the moon, little that it was, had set, and the light from the stars was faint. They could hardly see the winter-bare woods running alongside the track. Henk stiffened. A light had swung out from behind their boxcar and was coming towards them. The guard, who had been checking his train along the other side, had chosen to cross the track between their car and the next. Too late to push the door shut. Henk coiled, a snake ready to strike. Eleanor didn't breathe. Her instinct to cry out was now bottled as firmly as if someone had put a stopper in her mouth. But the guard turned around and walked back to the end of the train. Neither Henk nor Eleanor said a word. What if he'd knifed the guard, she wondered? Another death but this time a Frenchman's.

'You treat everyone as an enemy,' she said, once they were moving again. 'We're in France. They're on our side.'

'You know this?' he replied.

'Yes,' she said.

The train rolled on during the night, stopping frequently. In the early hours, they trundled through Narbonne, then headed west towards Toulouse, stopping briefly in the marshalling yards to take on water and coal. Both were awake. In case gendarmes were about, each kept watch through gaps in a couple of loose slats on either side, but they might have been in a cemetery for all the movement they saw. Soon, the train lurched back into its journey. Light from the signal box shone in through the gaps, briefly painting the inside of their car and their faces with stripes of light, making them look as if they were in convict uniforms.

She had planned to cross into Spain from Perpignan, which was south of here, on the Mediterranean coast – an easy journey in a Wagons-Lits car after a comfortable night in her El Dorado hotel, and with Spanish and Portuguese visas affixed to her US passport. She wondered why she wasn't steaming with resentment at her predicament, at the change in her circumstances from well-known author returning home in first-class comfort to criminal on the run from the Nazis. She thought of Hettie. She thought of the two German soldiers Henk killed, saving her from a German prison, probably saving her life. Yes, she was alive. She even allowed herself the heretical thought that she had never felt so alive.

CERBÈRE, PYRÉNÉES-ORIENTALES

Around 8am, Friday, 12th December 1941

Bauer stood, his head in a fog of cigarette smoke, seemingly far away. Kopitcke, worried, asked him whether he was feeling well.

'Sir?' Kopitcke asked again.

Yet another French railway station, if on the frontier. Yet another French police interlocutor, pretending to be polite and collegial.

Passenger and freight trains had been checked. Yes, the French had discovered people with dodgy papers and plenty of people who couldn't speak a word of French, but Bauer and Kopitcke could tell as plain as the noses on their faces that the French felt they had better things to do. What were they to do with all the people they rounded up except to lock them away in Gurs? A problem for another day but still a problem. Better to let them slip across the border for the Spanish to deal with.

'If you want to catch Jews, Kommissar,' the local inspector had said, 'just throw out a lasso.' This was a frontier post after all, and the easiest to cross.

Bauer cared only about the killer of those two boys whose facial features had faded in his mind, replaced, to his horror, by the faces of his own two boys.

Bauer had heard Kopitcke, even the concern in his voice, but still he did not reply. He drew on his cigarette. He'd made a mistake coming here. He'd too easily accepted Girard's logic that this was the chosen route of the killer. Why? Because it was the most direct and quickest from Lyon. But they hadn't been apprehended, not here nor at Latour-de-Carol, the other rail crossing this end of the Pyrénées, also suggested by Girard. He hadn't thought it through himself.

None of this mattered right now. Bauer had received a coded telegram not half an hour before from Georg's colonel, who'd served with Bauer at Lake Naroch on the Russian front in 1916. Georg's whole platoon had been missing for more than twenty-four hours. This could just mean they'd been cut off or had lost radio contact in the chaos of the Soviet counterattacks. He hoped that is what it meant, although he knew that 'hope' was not a word you could safely use for what was happening outside Moscow. Russia's General Winter was snipping off the toes and fingers and ears of the German boys, even freezing the grease in their machine guns and the engines in their tanks. And what if that incompetent barbarian General Stalin hadn't chosen right now to send in even more waves of fresh troops, whose feet and hands and faces were protected and warm, whose machine guns spat fire and whose tanks raced across the snow firing destruction. Seeing his boys' faces on the murdered soldiers was an ill omen. Georg was strong, however, and knew to look after his men and himself. What if the worst was that he'd been captured? At least he'd be alive.

'We're fools, Kopitcke,' said Bauer, trying to force himself out of his terrible fear. 'Our ambush has been in the wrong place,' he said. 'Get the car ready.'

Relieved, Kopitcke clicked his heels and gave a salute, although, thank God, not the Hitler salute. Bauer was back in control of his fears. They had wasted too much precious time. He turned to the French inspector. Could he get the schedule for freight and passenger trains from Lyon to Pau? A quick call to the national railways, the SNCF, produced four current possibilities. Bauer thanked him. 'We're leaving,' he informed the Frenchman, who was delighted to be seeing the back of these Germans. Bauer curdled his delight by reminding him that the Wehrmacht's fury at the murders hadn't abated one iota. Did he want the French hostages in Nevers to be shot?

Innocents? Bauer's conscience asked.

There were no innocents anymore, it replied. Not now. What would he say to Georg?

His threat about the French hostages worked, conjuring a way to get to Pau well before those trains were scheduled to arrive there. The nearest airfield belonged to the French air force, although apart from the tricolour and the khaki-coloured huts and hangars, one would never have known that. They were empty, while a biplane stood alone outside the old operations hut. Bauer expected its provenance to be uncertain, its airworthiness dubious. Otherwise it would now have *Luftwaffe* markings on its side and be flying some military VIP somewhere between north of the Vichy demarcation line and the front outside Moscow. It looked like it wouldn't fly high enough to top a church steeple, but their route would have them skirt the highest peaks of the Pyrénées. Even this would be faster than a car, which would have to manage the winding, narrow roadway from Perpignan to Pau. The train would have taken them back up the coast and inland to Toulouse. Even longer.

The pilot came out as their car approached. He saluted Bauer. It was evident that he had been led to expect someone more impressive.

'What's the point of a damn ambush if you set it up after the enemy has passed?' Bauer muttered to Kopitcke as they strapped themselves in. His stomach was playing up, and serve him right. While he'd been eating like a king, his Georg was lost on a battlefield deep in snow and enemy soldiers.

'Take us to Pau,' Bauer ordered in French. Pau had the only other direct rail link into Spain that was not under German control. Pau also had the German Armistice Commission, the only official German presence in Vichy France apart from the embassy in Vichy itself. It would be a potentially useful source of support if the French played hard to get.

To Bauer's considerable surprise, this piece of aviation history, an English De Havilland, flew well. The sky was clear and looked like a glacier upside down, blue and glistening with ice crystals. He saw with startling clarity the mountains to the south and the pine-clad French valleys that wound up into them through the rising hills now dusted in snow. They branched out into smaller, steeper valleys and reached the higher peaks to become passes, which eventually led to the other side. The ways into Spain were myriad and would be impossible to stem during summer. Even now, early winter, some might still be navigable. He wondered about his two quarries. If they were sticking together, they might even chance their luck by staying on the train down to the frontier and across. Who would expect them, a woman especially, to use this route to escape at this time of year?

Bauer had a hunch about this. He preferred facts to hunches but this one was particularly strong.

TRAIN SOUTH FROM TOULOUSE

Early morning, Friday, 12th December 1941

The train rattled south through the valley of the Garonne, slowly ascending all the time against the flow of the river, whose waters, bound for the Atlantic, they crossed and re-crossed many times. How much quicker it would be if only they had a boat. Eleanor was allowing herself to daydream of peaceful days, of no Germans on the French Atlantic coast, as if Providence were but a short hop away. It was further than the moon. They passed small villages clinging to the higher slopes, sheep here and there, as peaceful as heaven. Their food was lasting, not their water. At the next stop, Henk hoped, they would still be close enough to the river for him to fill their canteens.

When the train did stop, it was in a siding carved into the woods that fell away down a short slope to the river. The day was clear, the sun hung golden, without warmth, just over the line of hills, as high as it would get today. Henk scrambled down. The grass was damp, but there were enough stones protruding to stop any precipitous fall, and besides, he was wearing good Wehrmacht boots. He quickly filled the canteens then watched carefully over the cat while it relieved itself. It was a funny little thing, fussy about getting dirty, happy always to climb inside his coat because it didn't like the cold, oblivious to the danger its master was in.

Eleanor went to another part of the riverbank, to bear her aches in private. Squatting was torture, although the cold was invigorating after being cooped up for so long. She finished and then, to her great satisfaction, found a small stream trickling down to the river from higher up. She washed her face and her hands and applied some crème. She got up and turned back, and there was the guard at the open boxcar looking down at her. He was older, squat and overweight, and he threw her the filthiest look, then spitefully hauled the door to their car shut.

'You think I didn't know you were there,' he snapped. 'Freeloaders. You speak French?'

'But of course,' Eleanor said as demurely as her fear allowed. This quite stopped the guard, who had expected another load of foreign Jews. He was sick of them. They were dirty; they left the cars filthy, unfit for reloading. The guards, who were always being urged to help the refugees, got the blame.

'I'm willing to pay you for all your troubles,' Eleanor said and produced the handful of francs she kept in her coat pocket, offering them to him.

'You're from Paris?' he asked, suspicion still in his voice.

'Paris,' she confirmed and didn't have to pretend to be wistful. 'I could not stay there anymore, you understand.'

'A lady like you,' he said, 'what's to stop you going on a passenger train?'

'My son,' Eleanor replied, heart moving towards her mouth at each question from the guard. 'He got himself into trouble with the occupier.'

'I knew you had someone with you. Where is he?'

'Down there, filling our canteens,' she said and pointed to the river. 'Please,' she added, and pushed the money towards him. 'We all have families in these hard times.'

He took the money. 'You're lucky,' he said. 'They were watching the trains through Toulouse today and yesterday. They'll be watching in Pau.'

'Why do we stop all the time?' Eleanor asked.

'The Germans take all the best coal, leaving us the rubbish,' he explained. 'The locomotives can't go very fast and have to stop more often to load up, so everyone behind gets held up. We were supposed to reach Pau around midday, but at this rate, I don't know.' He sighed. 'I'm sorry, madame, for snapping at you. Times are difficult. You understand.'

She felt sorry for him. 'Do you smoke?' she asked. He nodded. She took out her cigarettes and he took one. 'Take a couple,' she said. 'But hide them. The Americans are the enemy now. We have to be careful.'

He tipped his cap to her with a smile and went back to his van, his boots crunching more lightly along the gravel, his shoulders less stooped. How quickly his mood had changed, she saw, and how small the reason, just some American cigarettes. Eleanor waited until he was gone. A cold wind began to sweep down from the mountains and kicked up eddies of dust around her.

'You can come out now,' she said.

Henk had slipped under the wagons to the other side and was waiting between their boxcar and the next, ready to spring at the guard. She'd seen him there the whole time; she'd also seen the knife in his hand.

'Not all people are your enemy,' she took pleasure in reminding him.

The wind was too cold to stay outside. They ate sparingly and drank the fresh water, though it was meltwater and freezing. She held his hand back as he started to lift the canteen to drink more.

'Enough,' she cautioned. 'Wait till it warms up. The American Girl Scouts winter survival list, point two, if I remember.'

'And what's point one?' he asked with a hint of sarcasm.

'No sneering,' she replied tartly. She wondered if Hettie would have been as difficult a travelling companion. She probably wouldn't have killed anyone. But she was dead, and the thought sank Eleanor into a gloom that crowded out her aches and pains.

The coal-loader was now silent, yet the train remained stationary, as if stranded and forgotten. Henk took out his knife and began to hurl it at the wooden wall, a particular slat his target. Thwack after thwack. His cat didn't like it.

'You're frightening your cat,' she said.

He threw it again, this time right by Eleanor. Thwack. She jumped. 'Put it away,' she told him.

'No,' he said. 'Come. I'll show you.'

'Show me what?'

'How to defend yourself.' He grinned. The look on her face. 'What? You let me save your life every time?'

It was a good knife, he told her, a Wehrmacht infantry knife.

'I'd rather not,' she said.

'This knife saved your life,' he said.

'I'm all too aware of that,' she replied.

'Then this is the knife you should learn from.' He slipped the knife into his pocket. 'Watch.'

'If someone comes at you,' he said, 'you step right foot back, keep left foot forward while you take your knife out, like so.' And he showed her the way to hold it, diagonally across the palm. 'Don't grasp it. You squeeze it, is a waste of energy. Again.' And he repeated the action, stepping back as he took out his knife. 'They come for you, you step forward, they step into your knife as you thrust your arm – not your hand, your arm. Now you do it.'

He put the knife into the pocket of her coat and made her take it out three times before she held it properly.

'This is ridiculous,' she said. 'I feel ridiculous.'

'Ridiculous is better than dead,' he said and made her go through each movement, counting them out, one, two, three, four.

'Now, I attack you. Step back, knife out, I keep coming, step forward, your arm for thrust, knife in my stomach.' He grunted, grabbed his stomach, staggered back. His eyes back in his head, he fell. She really did think she'd hurt him and cried out. From the floor, he laughed. The kitten thought it a game and jumped on him.

'It is easy,' he said, cuddling the cat and setting it back down.

This was the first time she'd seen him really laugh, and what a difference it made to his face. The zealot was suddenly human. 'You should consider a career on the Palestine stage, if there is one,' she said drily, handing him back the knife. He hopped up but did not take the knife.

'Again,' he said. 'Liberty is better when you are alive.'

He made her do it six or seven times. Then she said, without considering the consequences, 'What is the use? I don't have a knife.' Thereupon, he offered her the knife he'd taken from the German soldier.

More standard Wehrmacht issue, she noted. She could hardly complain.

Before handing it over, he demanded she promise to keep it in her coat pocket. Always. She said she would. He said he did not believe her, that she was just saying that to shut him up. He wasn't going to waste a good knife on someone unprepared to use it.

'You still do not understand,' he said. 'You still think this is a holiday, soon you will be home again, back to normal. This is not a holiday. I have killed two German soldiers. If the gendarmes catch us, they will hand us to the Germans, who will cut off our heads with a guillotine.' He slapped his hands together.

He gave her the knife. Chastened, especially as he had said 'we', she placed it in her right-hand coat pocket, and thereafter, every now and then, she put her hand in to test her ability to take it up without cutting her own wrist. Which she almost did when the train lurched unexpectedly into life and she lost her balance. But they were moving and the grind of the wheels on the rails that had driven them out of their minds was suddenly as sweet a sound as they could hear. Only minutes passed before they and their every cell were being juddered again.

TRAIN EN ROUTE TO TARBES
AND LOURDES

Around 9am, Friday, 12th December 1941

From the Garonne, the railway twisted and turned as they headed in a northerly direction towards Tarbes. For some distance, the train went so slowly, they might have reached Pau faster had they walked. Both tried to sleep but the anticipation of arrival, even at a rate that would have them there some time in the next year, kept them alert and on edge. The bleak beauty of the hilly countryside below the snowline was quite lost on them. When the train's wheels ground to yet another halt, both cursed. Henk pulled back the door. They were on a siding, which curved around a gentle slope. From the rumble of a loader up ahead, the locomotive was taking on yet more coal and water. But here they were out of the wind, and when the sun appeared from behind a cloud, it brought some warmth into the car.

Henk removed his coat and under-jacket and then removed his boots and socks to expose his skin to the sun's rays. He thought of the Lobau, the Social Democratic nature heaven outside Vienna, on the other side of the Danube, lying naked under the sun by the river as free as he could remember, before he was a Jew. It was a place where even Jews and their fat wives could wander naked without comment. The police kept away, unless they were there as good party members in the uniform they were born with, like everyone else. If she wasn't here, he'd strip down right now.

'You should do this,' he said to Eleanor, stretching his feet and toes. 'Put fresh air and sun on your feet.' She, who preferred looking at nature while comfortably and fashionably clad rather than being part of it and naked, declined. His kitten joined him in the sun and began washing itself.

'Is it a he or a she?' she asked, not having cared less before. Really, she didn't care now and was just passing the time.

'I did not know when I get it but now I know he is a she.'

'It seems a damn strange thing to carry with you in your situation,' she said.

'She does not like to live under the Nazis either,' Henk said. 'I find her hidden and frightened in Wien Westbahnhof when I start this journey, so tiny, she fits on my hand.' He smiled, then closed his eyes. 'She trust me immediately.'

Eleanor picked up his socks, able at last to satisfy her curiosity about the quality of his clothes. Woollen and thick, certainly not standard Wehrmacht issue. Even more interesting, each carried a name tag, an *H* and a *K* joined by a *V* for an aristocratic *von*. *H* for Heinrich, yes, but the rest? He with his peasant features? His cat looked more the aristocrat than he. Normally, her curiosity would feed her imagination, for that is what fed the pages of her novels. Now her curiosity had a more prosaic motivation. Forget whom she might conjure up to be HvK. Who the hell was he really? Until she realised with an uncreative thud.

Stolen.

She took the opportunity to reorganise the contents of her rucksack and her valise, swapping worn clothes for fresh, and moving one of the cartons of Chesterfields into her rucksack.

'What is this?' Henk said, picking up the copy of *The American Woman* that she was carrying in her valise to take back home.

He sounded to her like a Puritan preacher in colonial Boston before one of their book burnings. 'What the title says it is,' she replied.

'This is your book,' he continued in the same manner. 'Is this not vanity?'

'Not to read it,' she said. His impertinence was intolerable.

'I will read this and tell you if it's any good,' he said.

'I hardly think reading *The Communist Manifesto* or tales of hero workers qualifies you to judge,' she said. 'If you can read at all, that is.'

For the most part, since they'd been forced together, he'd been able to hold his temper. But now?

'Before all this, the war, everything,' he said defiantly, springing up and inadvertently dislodging his kitten, 'I am first in my family to go in the gymnasium. I read Heine and Goethe and Shakespeare, real love stories, *Romeo and Juliet*, *Tristan and Isolde*. Are your stories so good? I do not think so. You and your safe life, what would you know about love?'

He was close enough so the whack she gave his face was loud and hard enough to knock him back. 'How dare you,' she said, her anger as cold as the icy wind whistling through the trees outside.

His kitten took fright and leapt out the open door, down onto the track and into the undergrowth. He cried out, pushed Eleanor away and jumped down after it.

'*Katze*,' he called desperately, '*Katze. Komm, kein Angst, bitte, Katze.*'

Eleanor, in her fury, was unmoved. It's a wonder this hadn't happened before. It would come back. Even if he was no longer calling it Stalin.

He couldn't see the cat, but then he heard it calling and saw it under a large bush. Frightened and bewildered, it mewed, and he struggled his hand through to reach it, all the time calling to it, soothing it. He did not hear the locomotive's whistle, or if he did, he ignored it.

'We're leaving,' Eleanor called out to him from the open door. 'For God's sake.'

He ignored her; he kept trying to reach the mewing cat.

The whistle went again, and Eleanor could feel the strain on the boxcar as the locomotive heaved with a tremendous effort to pull the cars forward.

'Leave it, for God's sake,' Eleanor cried as the train lurched forward with the familiar concertina of banging.

At the sound of the clanging of car against car, the cat darted under a prickly holly. The train started to move but Henk would die rather than leave the cat. He called to it and pushed himself in under the bush, scratching his arms, which were still naked from his sunbathing. His bare toes were at least a help in being able to heave himself forward.

'Hurry!' Eleanor yelled frantically as he disappeared from her view; she had forgotten her intense dislike. Distraught, she grabbed her rucksack and her valise and was about to leap from the train when she saw him running after the train as he pushed the cat inside his shirt.

Eleanor dumped her things down on the floor, grabbed the rail next to the door and leant out so she might help him. But he was barefoot and though the train was still moving slowly, in moments it would be faster than he.

'Run, run,' she yelled, 'for God's sake!' She leant out as far as she could, reaching her arm out full stretch to clasp his hand, pulling him forward enough so that he could grab a metal rung under the car and pull himself up and in.

'You fool,' Eleanor shrieked at him. 'You idiot. That stupid cat,' she spat.

'Shut up, stupid woman,' he snapped as he soothed the cat inside his shirt. He hauled the door shut. His arms were covered in cuts from the holly bush, as were his feet from running along the rocky ground.

Eleanor's valise carried her first aid kit. She ordered him to sit, wetted a cloth and cleaned the wounds on his hands and arms and on the soles of his feet, soft and torn. Then she dabbed his wounds with iodine, which did not improve his mood. She handed him his socks to put on.

'Who is HvK?' she asked.

'Heinrich von Kleist,' he snapped, without a beat. 'German writer and dramatist. You have read *The Prince of Homburg*, perhaps? Or *Michael Kohlhaas*?'

She was forced to admire the challenge, his quick if caustic wit, especially in the fraught circumstances.

He reached around his neck. He looked as panicked as when the cat had jumped down onto the tracks. He felt inside his shirt; his eyes scoured the floor of the car. '*Scheiße, scheiße!*' he cried. '*Mein Medaillon.*'

His locket.

He looked back uselessly to where he'd almost lost his cat. All the low points on this journey, they were mostly physical, moments of danger. Danger he could deal with. But this? A lock of hair? So what! Yet its loss so dispirited him that he who never wept wanted to howl.

'This is your fault,' he cried. 'I blame you. You are the worst thing to happen to me in my life since the Nazis.' He dropped his face into the crook of his arm in despair.

Yes, it was the cry of a petulant boy, but Eleanor was still crushed by it. She looked around the floor of the car for the lost locket. It was gone. She felt the full burden of the blame with which he had cursed her. Without her, he would not have killed those two soldiers. She turned away and sat in the corner by herself, tending her own wounded psyche as he tended his physical wounds and the loss of the locket, which he used to clutch in his sleep. What had it really held? she wondered, remembering her sneer about the strand of Lenin's hair. A portrait of his mother? This made her feel even worse.

She wanted to hold him, some tender gesture to make up for it. Instead, they sat in stiff isolation as the next hour or so rolled by, he sleeping or at least keeping his eyes shut. She took out her compact, salve to her hurt, but the moment she looked at her face, she snapped the lid to the mirror tight. She tried to pray but nothing came, so she opened the Psalms at random, as was her practice.

'The Lord hear thee in the day of trouble,' she read. 'The name of the God of Jacob defend thee. Send thee help from the sanctuary.' How she loved the Psalms; something for every occasion and for every mood. She read on. Then she felt the train slow, and she stood and peered between the loose slats.

Lourdes.

In better circumstances she would have smiled at the medieval magic here, a superior if shallow Episcopalian smile, not too far from the atheist sneers of those raptors from the future whose views and company she so disdained. Her French pals all went to Mass regularly. Claude was devout and Madeleine, particularly devoted to the Virgin Mary, had been to Lourdes twice, once with her mother during her mother's last illness.

'The Virgin Mary didn't cure your mother,' Eleanor had objected, as much on behalf of her physician father and brothers as from any Episcopalian objection to papist nonsense.

'No,' Madeleine had replied patiently. 'But she gave Mama a happy death.'

As the train crawled along, Eleanor returned to the corner of the car and to the 20th Psalm, in whose words she found further comfort. Words. She was a writer, after all. But really, she knew words alone were not enough, that they did not explain her devotion. When she thought about it, she and those across the Tiber were exactly the same. She couldn't claim hers was based on experience and reason while theirs was not.

Her family had a summer house at Bar Harbor up in Maine, where she and her siblings had run wild during the long summer holidays. Yet every now and then, more often at dusk, something withdrew Eleanor from the play, and she would find a tree to climb, not to be by herself but to be with whatever it was that kept calling her. She saw nothing, but she felt it and she thought she heard it, not as words but, now and then, like a breeze played on a mysterious musical instrument. The experience was magical and drew her into its gentle cocoon.

That's how she got her family reputation as a daydreamer. It covered a multitude of sins at school and at home, and even to this day explained her going to France, becoming a writer, even sticking it out after the Nazis came. A prosaic answer for her family to behaviour that was flighty or, in staying after May 1940, simply nuts.

She thought of the house, her family, then and now. 'You'll be lonely, old and broke,' her mother had fretted after she agreed to the divorce from Fred. They were like a curse, her mother's words. 'I'll certainly be old, Mother,' she'd replied in defiance, 'but be damned if I'll be broke.' She'd omitted to address the most important of her mother's curses but then she'd been too young. Now, without Claude? She was alone and she was lonely. There were her friends, yes, Sylvia and Madeleine in particular. There were her brothers and sisters, dearly loved, but really, only Will, the youngest, was in any way a soul mate. Also still single, Will, the family darling, turned out to be the family warrior. Couldn't wait to get into West Point, just like she couldn't wait to get to France. Each had a calling. But as a young lieutenant colonel in the army, his calling was war and now it had come.

One day at Bar Harbor, away from the others, on the quiet, he said to her, 'You're talking to God up the tree.' He knew. He must have been about seven, she thirteen. He wanted to know what God told her.

'He doesn't tell me anything,' she replied. 'He doesn't need to. He's just there and everywhere. That's all you ever need to know.'

Will, who usually needed proof – preferably physical – of anything, had nodded his little head. 'I guess that's so, Elly,' he said.

Her eyes filled with tears and she prayed for him. Henk was curled up on the floor, vulnerable and small. She covered him with his coat. He did not stir.

9.30am, Friday, 12th December 1941

After their arrival, Bauer quickly reported to the German Armistice Commission, which had taken over the finest hotels along the grand boulevard with spectacular vistas south to the Pyrénées. As with the Loire chateaux, he was not interested in these sights – not for lack of appreciation but because their beauty mocked the plight of his son. They were also the barrier that stood between his quarries and their escape. How close to the city the mountains were quite shocked him. The killer or killers would have to get past him before they reached those mountain passes.

The senior officer, a general, seemed icy at first and preoccupied, but establishing their fellowship on the Russian front during the first war brought an immediate handshake and the offer of a cigarette.

'Egyptian,' said the general, who had a pal in the Afrika Korps, 'captured from the British.'

Bauer added to his esteem in the general's eyes by mentioning his Afrika Korps son, then they got down to business: the murders, which were news to him. Bauer would have his total support. As the French were interested only in catching smugglers and stopping the exit of recruits for the Free French, he would also immediately order army patrols along the border into Spain in this sector by troops at Orthez, on the other side of the demarcation line, in Occupied France.

'They're just sitting on their behinds getting fat,' he said.

They each smoked another cigarette and reminisced about the first war, forever having to save the Austrian neck on the Eastern Front, Lemberg, Gorlice – names now remembered only by old fellows like them who had been there.

The general told Bauer that diplomatic niceties meant he should report his mission to the German consul in Pau, an ancient Bavarian aristocrat who'd been shunted out of frontline diplomacy by the rise of Ribbentrop. Hitler wanting to treat the French with respect was all very well, but the farce they now had to go through to keep up the pretence that the French were in charge of France was a bureaucratic nightmare.

'Talk to our man at the consulate. Wolf,' he suggested. 'He's sound.'

Mid-morning, Friday, 12th December 1941

The consulate occupied what once had been a grand English club, when *les Anglais* from Edward VII down had turned Pau into a little England with its own golf club, even a fox hunt, all now much reduced or gone. Bauer and Kopitcke arrived to find it as quiet as a tomb.

'Maybe they've all gone native,' Bauer whispered, when suddenly, the door was opened to them and they entered what to the eye was still, outwardly at least, an English club. Yes, there was a photograph of Hitler but larger was a portrait of King George V and Queen Mary, another of Wellington and place mats with drawings of Windsor Castle. Bauer wondered if they'd also kept the whisky.

They were led to the consul's attaché, who to Bauer's surprise was a young Wehrmacht first lieutenant. But the fellow's uniform was just too smart and neat for Bauer, and while shaking his and Kopitcke's hands, the attaché kept his left hand in his pocket, which to Bauer was altogether too casual and disrespectful.

'Wolf,' the attaché gave his name.

Despite the general's recommendation, Bauer and Kopitcke took an instant dislike to this Wolf, reinforced by his lightly accented German – Bavarian or Austrian – which was as upper class as his manners. Too suave and good-looking for a man, Bauer thought, a typical effete southerner. If this lieutenant had ever been to the front, it was as an aide-de-camp to a backroom general. No wonder he'd weaseled himself into a cushy job here. Wolf absently removed his left hand from his pocket and then, as if embarrassed, immediately and self-consciously tucked it back out of sight.

In that brief movement, Bauer saw a curve in Wolf's palm where the index, middle and ring fingers had been, making a cruel-looking claw of the remaining thumb on one side and the little finger on the other. Bauer's face burnt with shame. 'You've seen plenty of action,' he said in an effort to clear his conscience.

'*Ratschbumm* at Smolensk,' Wolf answered in Landser slang. 'A Soviet weapon you hear only when it hits you,' he explained. 'Not enough to make me useless, but unfortunately, enough to make me useless at the front.'

'We didn't have that problem last time over there,' Bauer said with sympathy. 'Hearing them coming in was bad enough.'

'Oh, I think that's worse,' Wolf said with a grim smile. 'What you don't hear is only a problem if you survive.' He removed his ruined hand from his pocket now that he had inadvertently exposed it. 'I wear a glove but it gets in the way.'

Bauer's embarrassment intensified when Wolf said he had read the report on the murder of the two soldiers. He had also just put down the phone after speaking to the general, who had rung with orders to be passed to the Wehrmacht commander in Orthez to assist. Anything he could do personally, he would do. As for the consul, he added, he of course would also help, but Bauer got the strong impression that help was not what the old man did, and this confirmed his initial impression of the whole consulate. They'd just driven down from Paris, Wolf explained, where they had recently been for consultations, but this had taken it out of the old man.

'This must be boring after being in action,' Bauer said.

Wolf agreed but it was better than a staff job in Russia behind the lines with all those arse-licking officers who sent men to die but lived well themselves. 'I'd rather be back at the front as a cripple,' he said and his pale skin reddened with anger. 'I apologise,' he said immediately, 'I'm not much of a diplomat.'

Bauer wasn't shocked at all, only surprised to hear truth being spoken. He smiled.

'I'm the one to apologise, not you,' said Bauer.

Wolf explained he'd been posted initially to the German Armistice Commission because he spoke fluent French but then was seconded to the consulate to deal with the local French authorities concerning the region's contributions to the Reich's war needs. Wolf added that he was also the liaison between the Wehrmacht's occupation troops on the other side of the demarcation line nearby in Orthez and the German Armistice Commission, which in itself was time-consuming.

'Oh, there's the fedora gang over there,' he added with a wave of his arm out the window towards the Place Royale.

'What?' Bauer exclaimed in surprise.

'The Gestapo,' Wolf explained, misunderstanding Bauer's response.

'Yes,' Bauer replied. The euphemism was common enough. 'I'm just surprised they're operating here.'

'Officially, they're not,' Wolf replied. 'They're under the cover of the armistice commission. There,' he said, pointing out the window across the square to the Hôtel Majestic. 'Just ask for the Statistics Office.'

Bauer laughed. 'How appropriate,' he said.

'I hate to admit it, Kopitcke,' Bauer said once they came out onto the square, 'but my first impression there was entirely wrong, prejudice not the facts.'

Kopitcke's own prejudice remained alive and festering, much amplified by humiliation at the discovery of the young lieutenant's genuine war wound. He was sure the lieutenant was fishy. It was good to be out of there.

'We better get it out of the way,' Bauer muttered as he walked towards the Majestic and its Statistics Office.

HÔTEL MAJESTIC,
PLACE ROYALE, PAU

Late morning, Friday, 12th December 1941

Bauer wasn't looking forward to this, mostly because the Gestapo and his unit, the GFP, often covered the same turf. By default, the Gestapo, many with Nazi backgrounds, presented as the more politically reliable organisation, while the GFP were all ex-cops and had the copper's contempt for the amateur. To them, the Gestapo were just thugs with power, while they did the real work. But since they were here, they might even be useful.

He and Kopitcke were kept waiting when they didn't have the time to wait. Bauer was about to tell Kopitcke they were leaving when they heard someone coming, the sort of man who announced his arrival before he could be seen. So much for being secret, Bauer thought.

In through the door burst an agent in his forties whose girth overflowed his grey SS uniform. He gave his name as Pichler. Another southerner, from the Tirol with an awful accent, thought Bauer. Pichler was everything he despised in the Gestapo. By his gait and lack of manners, Bauer could have written the fellow's history with ease: no trade or qualifications except a veteran of the first war, drawn to any of the dozens of crazy militias that thrived afterwards, then the Nazis until the *Anschluss* elevated him from illegality to a uniform and its authority in a single day.

'What's this about?' Pichler demanded.

'What's this about, "sir",' Bauer barked, his military rank the equivalent of captain to Pichler's lieutenant.

'You're not in uniform,' Pichler answered without a hint of apology.

Bauer demanded to see his superior.

'He's based in Paris,' Pichler replied, sure of his ground. 'I apologise,' he added, backtracking some way.

Bauer explained his mission.

'That's your problem,' said Pichler. 'They were soldiers.' His job was to catch enemies of the Reich, Jews, especially the rich ones, English flyers, escaped prisoners of war, political criminals fleeing arrest from all over Europe. 'I got that red Hilferding,' he crowed, referring to one of the leading Austrian Social Democrats, now incarcerated in a concentration camp.

'Refugees who murder German soldiers seem to me to be enemies of the Reich,' Bauer said. 'I expect your cooperation when and if I need it,' he added briskly. They'd spent enough time here.

'You've been to the consulate,' Pichler said with a sneer. 'For all the help that lot will give you.'

That the Gestapo were spying on the consulate was no surprise, and hardly difficult from across the road. That's what they did. 'You must have time on your hands if you're spying on patriotic Germans,' Bauer said.

'Patriots, my arse,' said Pichler. 'That old fool's a Bavarian royalist, and the attaché is just another aristo pansy hiding from the front.'

'Lieutenant Wolf has an Iron Cross and an honourable war wound,' replied Bauer.

Pichler snorted in contempt. 'He also gets smashed and shoots his mouth off,' he said. 'If he does it in front of me, he'll end up in Mauthausen.'

'It's not your place to make threats against Wolf, a decorated veteran,' Bauer erupted. 'The Gestapo has no authority over any member of the Wehrmacht. How dare you impugn Wolf's honour!'

'Well then, sir,' Pichler came back at him, 'I expect you to exercise your authority. He's a defeatist and worse.'

Bauer stalked out in an unusually loud, bad mood, the likes of which Kopitcke had never seen. Without people turning snitch on their neighbours and enemies, the Gestapo would never know a thing, he said, and as for the Jews, why, the Gestapo couldn't catch a Jew in a revolving door. He was going to make a formal complaint about Pichler's insolence and insubordination. He was so angry, he forgot about his son. As they were driven off in a French police car they had been lent, he penned a quick note to warn Lieutenant Wolf. While he met the French inspector, he sent Kopitcke back to the consulate to deliver it in person.

COMMISSARIAT DE POLICE, PAU

Towards midday, Friday, 12th December 1941

His French counterpart was Inspector St Jean, appointed to the position directly from Vichy after the collapse, *pétainiste plus que Pétain*, as was said about him: more Pétainist than the marshal himself. A bald, tough, round-faced ex-Parisian *Sûreté* detective, he had been sent south with a new prefect because Vichy needed people tough enough to counter the German presence. Among other things, that meant tempering their rapacious reparation demands. His other, no lesser, task was to be the marshal's enforcer against communists and other antisocial infestations, including smugglers and black marketeers, who were thriving.

Given that the French were, in effect, powerless against the Germans, the first task required cunning and stealth. It needed someone who could present as strong and powerful – indeed, rather like his pet hate, de Gaulle in London – while having a pretty poor hand. Like de Gaulle, St Jean was a good hater, and hating Germans was the strongest card in a deck of many antagonisms. Also like de Gaulle, he was prickly and knew just how far to go, which was always one step further than the Germans or any of his other antagonists would expect. This required some quid pro quo, so St Jean was quite happy to hand over any prominent Jews, communists and socialists who fell into his hands. It was he who'd caught the Austrian socialist Hilferding, although the local Gestapo claimed the credit with their bosses in Berlin. They think he didn't know they were here and up to no good? They did nothing without him knowing, the fools. But the Germans knew who'd really done it. Annoying as he was to them, the Germans didn't want to run the show themselves, so it was better the devil they knew.

Presented by Bauer with a request for assistance – not a demand, St Jean noted, quite un-German – he sensed opportunity. He personally couldn't have cared less if someone knifed two German soldiers, as long as they didn't do it on his patch.

Bauer said he needed but one officer who could give him access to St Jean directly and to St Jean's network of informers.

And dogs.

There was no possibility St Jean would place an intermediary between him and these Germans or give them access to his network of informers, but he might spare a dog or two, just to keep them off his neck. He rang the relevant officer, discovered dogs were available, any number at the moment.

'Two are available,' he reported to Bauer, and only for today. The dogs would come from the Customs Department, which used them to hunt smugglers through the mountains. The French called these dogs *chiens de St Hubert*.

Bloodhounds.

Really, Bauer thought, all he needed was one terrier. Any dog could smell out a cat. But bloodhounds?

'Splendid,' said Bauer.

'You can have a car and a driver,' said St Jean, pleased by Bauer's attitude. He knew who was in charge. 'You can contact me on the car radio direct.' That would impress the German, he thought; he was equipping all his cars with two-way radios, saving on those inefficient police call boxes on each corner.

Bauer was impressed; he had what he wanted. In offering his hand to St Jean, who responded with a hand that deliberately crushed it, he understood he was to be kept under close supervision. More usefully, he also learnt who and what type of man he was dealing with. France's pride needed coddling. If that was the price of success, he would coddle for all he was worth.

St Jean kept up the bravado until he'd seen Bauer out the door. He was furious with himself for the bone-crushing handshake, an act of weakness. What had he been thinking? He returned to his office in a bad mood, grabbed up the next file so he could direct his fury with himself into whatever it demanded. Intelligence was reporting that more French POWs, having escaped German custody, were being passed down invisible lines to the Spanish border and thence on to London and that traitor de Gaulle.

'Like canapés at a society party,' St Jean grumbled. What exercised him were the lines, its members, they were here in Pau and in the towns south to the Somport. Yet he had no knowledge, not even a hint, of their existence. Such an affront to his authority could not continue. By snaring these men, he'd catch the *Gaullistes* and give them a choice of Gurs concentration camp or joining the Foreign Legion in North Africa, which was still loyal to the marshal.

Early afternoon, Friday, 12th December 1941

From Lourdes, the freight train meandered at a leisurely pace to the west along a river, which they would later know as the Gave de Pau. With their anticipation and anxiety coloured by the rawness of their quarrel, how far they were from their destination they did not know. It was hard enough sitting above the wheels as they ground on and on, seemingly forever. Then the brakes squealed and soon they stopped and each groaned, though inwardly, not keen to show any feeling to the other.

'Please, what is the time?' Henk asked as if it were the most urgent thing in the world.

Eleanor glanced at her watch. 'Two fifteen,' she answered.

His frustrated '*Scheiße*' was audible and, even to Eleanor with no German, quite clear in meaning. He had planned to arrive in Pau that morning; that's what the original *passeur* had promised. 'On the train arriving at eight-thirty from Toulouse,' he'd said. 'All things going well.'

What a fool he'd been to believe that. Even in Germany now, trains didn't leave or arrive on time. What chance in France? He wasn't forgetting he had killed two Nazis to get here. That hadn't been part of the plan. He hoped his late arrival wouldn't matter but he couldn't help worrying.

She saw his face. It wasn't hard to read the fretting knots across his brow, the sigh. How long, she thought, should she stick by him? At least until she'd found him a passage into Spain.

He peeked sullenly through the loose slats to make sure it was safe to open the door. Not that he would know where they were, but anything to be free of this car, this train, any train. He hauled back the door. Freezing air gusted in, swirling the dust on the floor. The afternoon light was pure and golden in a clear blue sky over rolling hills, brown with swathes of green from the fir trees. Then, beyond, to the south, above the surrounding landscape, rose jagged silhouettes whose glistening snowy peaks glowed golden and red on their steep western slopes.

'The Pyrénées!' both exclaimed. They laughed and they hugged each other, but the weight of their recent bitter quarrel and the recollection that they didn't like each other pushed them apart. Each gazed in silence, seemingly lost in their own thoughts of salvation. The peaks looked to Henk like he could step over them. His gloom about his locket lifted. He allowed himself to hope.

Eleanor tried not to look at him, tried to keep her eyes on the glistening peaks. She tried not to tremble. She had to light a cigarette. Her hands shook. Her face was flaming. So were her loins. Thank God he wasn't looking at her. She could hear the beating of her heart. It's a wonder he couldn't hear it too, she thought. Yes, it was fear, of course it was – fear that what had erupted in her from his touch might be more than a flash of desire; fear also that he might have caught her. She refused to countenance either possibility. She stole a glance, expecting, hoping to confirm that she had not fallen for this little pest who had been a burden to her from the moment he intruded into her life. Oh God, she almost said aloud. Don't do this. Was fate forcing her to be Selina from *The American Woman* to his Yann? Theirs was a noble love, driven by passion and the quest for grace. This had to be lust, a physical need fuelled by loneliness and circumstance. He mustn't know.

But he did. He'd felt her react to his touch, seen her face, and how quickly she'd withdrawn from him. He recognised desire. It was something he knew a lot about. It was a complication he did not need, especially from her.

TRAIN, OUTSKIRTS OF PAU

2.40pm, afternoon, Friday, 12th December 1941

Eventually, the train slowly rolled forward again, not a word between them as the chill wind whistled through the slats. They were cold and hungry. Eleanor had calmed down; what she'd feared was gone now. They finished the last of their water, an equal share from Henk's canteen: Eleanor, him, his cat. She focused on the rolling of the wheels, the clacking over each join, the monotony that had driven her insane. It was still torture but preferable to the alternative.

Then, dear God, she exclaimed, the train stopped yet again. Both looked out.

Houses.

This had to be the approach to Pau, although how far off, neither knew.

'You've been here before,' he said bluntly. 'Where do we go?'

'A long time ago. The station's down by the river, the town's up on the ramparts; you can see it clearly, a church and the chateau,' she said in as short a hand as possible.

But neither could see any town on any rampart, no church, chateau. Not yet.

'I can't remember anything else,' she said. 'I was preoccupied at the time.'

He stiffened, put his finger to his lips, peered anxiously through the slats. Voices, the crunching of boots along the side of the track, the sound of metal on metal, coming closer. He daren't open the door now. Whoever it was soon made it to the car behind theirs. Through the loose slats on both sides, they saw and heard the guard working the locks with another man. The bolt slid down on the door on the right side.

'This one's stuck,' Eleanor heard the guard on the left side say. 'You go on ahead.'

'Hurry,' said the other, and they heard the crunch of boots along the ground, and in moments, the lock on the right side of the car up ahead slid in.

The left door of their car opened about a foot.

'Get out now,' whispered the guard through the gap. 'We have to lock the cars. In Pau, the Germans have dogs.'

'Where are we?' Eleanor asked.

'Now,' repeated the guard frantically. 'Get out now.'

'My valise,' she cried.

'Fuck your valise,' he snapped. He pulled her out the door and she had time only to grab her rucksack. Henk, who needed no translation, had already grabbed his pack and the cat, which he tucked safely into his coat. He slipped down after her.

'Under the train,' said the guard, pushing them under. 'Till we go.' He hauled the door shut, locked it and went to the next car.

They huddled under the car between the rails, tight but enough room, just. Enough not to have his skin on hers. All they could see through the wheels toward the front of the locomotive were the legs of the guard and his colleague and the relentless locking of the cars until they heard only the chuffing of the locomotive as it waited.

Then, without warning, steam hissed as the drive wheels engaged.

'Now,' said Henk and he darted out from under the boxcar just as the locomotive strained forward and the tension rattled back through each car. But Eleanor was still underneath. The cars lurched forward.

Terror struck her.

'Move,' he growled from the evergreen undergrowth not two yards to the side of the tracks. In a 'what the hell?' blind rush, she scrambled between the wheels as they rolled into enough motion to do damage if she'd been caught, and crawled on all fours to the bushes, where he dragged her in. Heart still racing, she watched as the train rolled on and the guard jumped aboard the van at the end.

Her valise was gone.

She burst into tears.

'I have your book,' he said irritably, tapping his knapsack, whose bulk was now tripled. He'd slipped it into his bag when she wasn't looking, intending to read it as much to see if his English was up to it as from curiosity.

What book? She didn't know what he was talking about. 'All my cosmetics, a carton of cigarettes, fresh clothes,' she wailed. She saw the look of contempt on his face. 'You say one word about vanity, sonny,' she snapped as anger waylaid her tears, 'and you won't have a face to be vain about.' She had her small cosmetic pack in the breast pocket of Claude's coat at least. She wiped her face, took out her compact and tried to repair the damage. She looked dreadful.

The book he was talking about, she realised, was her own. Her instinct was to accuse him of theft, but that wasn't instinct, that was prejudice. He'd saved it, after all. If only he'd saved her cosmetics, whose loss was even worse than losing the cigarettes. Either would have been bad enough. To lose both was a catastrophe.

'I hope you enjoy it,' she said, forcing out the words, one by one. She thought she must have sounded false and, in a way, she was, but only partly so. The beginning of the sentence might have been completely false but, by the end, it was wholly true. Except this book was the last of hers she'd want him to read. She feared how he would surely misread Selina. She'd rather die than be exposed for what had been only a momentary lapse of taste.

A small skein of grey geese crossed the sky above, stragglers on the migration south whose calls woke Eleanor up to where she was.

She looked up to see the last of them fly towards the Pyrénées. Oh, to have wings. At least she knew which way was Spain and which way was Pau. She even heard ducks on the river.

'They wouldn't survive a minute on the Seine these days,' she mused grimly. He was quiet. Water flowed gently over rapids nearby. For a fleeting moment, as he listened, his jaw relaxed, his eyes seemed wide and blue and innocent – but then, as he struggled against the charms of the tranquil landscape, his eyes blinked, their colour clouded, as did his face, and his jaw tightened. Struggle over. He was still in enemy territory, after all.

'We must go in Pau,' he said abruptly, as if any delay might cause the outbreak of, if not friendly, at least 'fraternal' relations. They were of one mind on that, if only he'd realised. He set off.

'You're heading back the way you came,' she said drily. 'That way,' she said and pointed. 'How you survived in the army, I do not know.'

'My lieutenant always knows the way,' he said.

Then she remembered the dogs. What were they going to do about them?

What on earth was she talking about? 'What dogs?'

'The Germans have dogs. What if they walk the tracks and find where we got off the train? They'll follow us unless we get the hell out of this nasty little town as soon as possible.'

'First we must go in this nasty little town,' he replied, which she conceded, just as he conceded they had to deal with the possibility of the dogs.

'Come,' he said, 'bring your canteen.'

He slipped down the bank to the river's edge. She followed. They filled their canteens. He told her they would climb back up along the exact track they'd taken down. He splashed some of the water over the ground under the bushes, washing away their tracks and the marks they'd made.

'Now we walk back along the track,' he said. 'Quickly, before another train comes.' He beckoned her to walk along one rail, he on the other, their arms clasped to keep themselves balanced. He wasn't certain it would work, he said, but hoped just one train on the line after them would confuse any trail.

'I can balance myself,' she said, but when she tried to walk along the rail, she was off after two steps.

She steeled herself as she felt his hand and arm on hers, and she kept her head. She was astonished by his strength. He could have lifted her up and carried her – or just as easily hurled her away. In the firmness of his grip, she knew that, unlike her own feelings, she could trust him. She knew he didn't like her one bit, for which she was currently grateful, but here they were, thanks to the Nazis, stuck to each other for the time being.

After a short distance, they clambered up to the edge of a roadway. There was no house or farm they could see, no one to observe them. Where Eleanor found her own strength, she a light smoker who walked only to get to the Metro or from the entrance of the Louvre to whichever painting was taking her fancy, it had to be the luck of her genetic inheritance. The Gortons were a tough lot, after all, as was her mother's family, some of whom had survived the first winter of the Plymouth Plantation.

'Which way?' he asked.

She would go ahead on one side, he behind her on the other, she said. But first she asked him his name.

'What?' he said, irritation being his default reaction.

'Your French name.'

He hesitated. 'Roget,' he said, digging it out of his memory at last, but he couldn't remember his Christian name.

'Too late,' she said, not without a sense of superiority. 'You're under arrest.'

'Yes,' he confirmed, 'you are making a criminal very well.'

'Anton,' she told him. 'Anton Roget from Toulouse. Let's hope that's all they ask you if we're stopped.'

They came quickly to a road.

'No,' he said, 'not this one.'

'But it goes to the town,' she argued. 'Look, you can see it, up there.' She pointed.

'No, this road is not wise,' he said. It was a main road; the enemy would use this road. They had to find another way, a side road where they would not stand out. Eleanor thought it didn't matter which road they took. As she'd seen in the mirror of her compact, she looked much worse than any local. No one here would miss her, or him, for what they were. Refugees. She withdrew Mrs Teixeira's cross from inside her blouse so that it showed over the top of her coat.

Around 3pm, Friday, 12th December 1941

Bauer waited at the entrance to the marshalling yards near the main railway station close to the confluence of the Gave de Pau and a smaller river below the town. A cold wind was gusting. He had heard rain was forecast so was relieved to see French flags streaming against a blue sky from the chateau along the ramparts above. He heard the train approaching and soon the locomotive with its haul of boxcars behind crawled onto the track he'd reserved. No one could slip away, especially as each car had been locked a few kilometres down the line on his orders.

'That'll surprise them,' he'd told Kopitcke. They had only recently learnt that the cars were being kept unlocked as a help to escapees.

The train had passed through Toulouse and Tarbes and Lourdes under close observation without stopping. If they'd disembarked along the way, to what purpose when their goal had to be Spain, and Pau was the gateway? He'd soon have them, if not this train, the next, due in four hours, or the one after. The gendarmes were at the railway station, ready to check the papers of those on board the next passenger train, due in about twenty minutes. They too had dogs.

The freight locomotive released its steam and expired. The wind blew along the track and whistled through the nearby passenger shed. The guard stepped down nervously from his van to find Bauer and the dogs chafing to be let loose. While Kopitcke kept the locomotive crew back, Bauer had the guard unlock each boxcar, one by one, and pull back the door. The dogs sniffed everything, even running back to Bauer to sniff him. They kept doing it until the fourth car, where, even before the guard hauled back the door, they quivered with excitement and leapt up, barking.

Two young men stood at the door, downcast and defeated. All this way, their faces said, and right at the border we're caught. An older man and woman quailed in the corner. Bauer ordered them down and had the dogs inspect the males closely to find if they were carrying a cat. Fleas and lice probably, by the way they scratched themselves, but no cat. The four were taken to a nearby holding shed. Towards the guard's van, Bauer found another two men in a car and, dear God, with them, a small boy who had the most abusive mouth on a child he had ever encountered, a criminal in the making if ever he saw one. Neither of his companions had a cat. He ordered them all taken to the holding room.

'*Juifs?*' he asked once inside with the first captives. He demanded their identification papers, which had them all being as French as Marshal Pétain. '*Juden?*'

'*Français,*' the older man insisted. '*Français.*' So Bauer addressed him in French, which the fellow could not speak.

'*Sind Sie Juden?*' Bauer asked again but in a kind voice.

The older man and woman burst into tears. '*Bitte, bitte,*' they both begged him – please, please. They were Austrian.

'*Sie auch?*' Bauer asked of the two young men. You too? They nodded. He had them searched for knives, just in case, but both were clean. The fight in them was long gone. They weren't made for this: one minute leading a comfortable Viennese bourgeois life and the next day outcasts. Bauer could see they wouldn't make it, and that wouldn't be because of him. He wasn't the slightest bit interested in them. He was glad he'd detailed Kopitcke to make a proper search of each boxcar, otherwise he'd have had no end of trouble explaining why he wasn't going to waste time over a bunch of assimilated Jews caught on the wrong side of a frontier.

'*Los,*' he said. '*Los nach Spanien. Geh mal!*' Go on, go to Spain. Go.

They didn't believe he meant it, thinking they'd be shot if they took him at his word. He repeated himself, opened the door, and even then, they were too afraid.

'*Um Gottes Willen, los!*' he snapped, and they ran.

He turned to the two young men with the foul-mouthed child. They said they were brothers and French and had papers saying so, even the disgusting child. They were coming south to work on their uncle's farm, because they were too poor. And so on. They probably were brothers, all three, but the elder two were smugglers and their little brother, an apprentice in the trade, a useful decoy. He sent them to the gendarmes.

Watching them go, he was filled with a sudden and bitter resentment. Why were these two brothers here, petty criminals to boot, and his two sons were not? He'd heard nothing more about Georg. No news wasn't necessarily good news. The wind whistled through the gaps in the wooden walls of the shed.

Kopitcke burst in. '*Herr Kommissar,*' he called out excitedly. He was carrying a valise. 'The dogs found this in one of the cars, female clothing inside.' He placed it on the table and opened it.

'*En français,* Kopitcke, *français,*' Bauer said through gritted teeth as he pulled on his white gloves and started to go through the valise. Yes, woman's clothing – underwear, brassiere, damp socks – and good quality by the feel of the material. A dress whose lower parts were still damp. He smelt it. Unmistakeable. This wasn't water from a city or town tap with its chlorine. This was from a river or creek. Yes, a well was a possibility, but it was unlikely given the circumstances. With access to his crime-lab boys back home, he'd be able to prove it, probably even which river, given a little more time. Now his olfactories would have to do; they rarely failed him. Until proven otherwise, this dress had waded the Allier. A carton of cigarettes. Chesterfield. Here was further proof, but also temptation for Bauer. He allowed himself a moment to acknowledge the benefit of Kopitcke's Hitler Youth devotion to clean living, only to dismiss it: he'd take the cigarettes for his boys. They were a good omen that Georg was safe. Then he found a large bag tucked into the bottom of the valise. He opened it to find it packed with cosmetics: hand crème, face crème, two lipsticks – neither a colour a respectable woman like his wife would wear, he thought – and three bottles of scent. He looked at the makes. Corday, Patou, Schiaparelli. He had no idea but figured they were costly.

'There's so much,' said Kopitcke. 'Maybe she's smuggling.'

'Possibly,' Bauer replied absently. 'But vanity seems more likely as each has been used.' It was a wrench handing over the cosmetics to the police rather than his wife, but he had a higher purpose. 'Finger-prints please,' he said. 'Urgent.'

'So, Kopitcke,' he said. 'You're a rich woman who needs to get over the line for whatever reason. Why, once you're in Vichy, do you travel in a boxcar? What's your theory?'

Kopitcke hesitated; he always did. Just in case.

'Come on then,' Bauer encouraged.

'She's a foreign Jew,' he replied, 'not French.'

'Agreed,' Bauer said but diminished Kopitcke's pleasure by adding, 'except what is the evidence here to say she's a Jew?'

He followed Kopitcke to the boxcar.

'How did she get past us, eh?' he asked. Kopitcke knew the question was rhetorical. 'She was warned,' Bauer answered himself. 'Who warned her? Why, the guard warned her, because only the guard knew.'

'We'll arrest him,' said Kopitcke, 'and get it out of him.'

'We're in Vichy France, young man,' Bauer reminded him. 'But why warn the woman and not the Jews, eh? Or the French brothers?' he asked. He chuckled, warming to his subject. 'Because she paid him, that's why, and the others didn't.' Kopitcke could have told him that. You didn't need to be a genius to work that out. She was rich and, he was convinced, a Jewess.

'This it?' Bauer asked.

He hoisted himself up, not without a stretch: he was beginning to feel his age. Getting one-armed Kopitcke up was no effort at all. Losing one arm had put the strength of two into the one remaining.

'Let's have a look here,' said Bauer.

Kopitcke sneezed, his eyes watered, his nose streamed.

'It's only the dust,' Bauer said.

'No, sir,' said Kopitcke. 'Cats. They make me sneeze.'

Bauer snorted, in a mix of annoyance and elation. 'Why tell me that now?' he demanded. 'I needn't have organised those dogs if I'd known your nose would do it.' But he'd sniffed something else. 'Hah,' he said, pushing his face closer into one of the corners. 'My nose isn't too bad either. Look at that.'

Small lumps of cat shit, recently deposited.

'They're here in Pau,' Bauer said with a smile and clasped his hands. It gave him hope for his son, ridiculous as that might seem under the cold light of reason, and wholly without evidence − in great contrast to the cat shit and the valise they'd just found.

'You take the dogs to where the train was stopped. See if you can find a trail and report back.'

*

Kopitcke, the French handlers and their two dogs, went back along the railway line to where the train had been stopped, Kopitcke and the dogs with enthusiasm, the two handlers at a sullen trudge. The dogs quickly found their quarries had slipped away from the train and down to the river.

'How deep's the river?' Kopitcke asked and was directed to the rapids not far away. They could have walked along the edge in the water and crossed there.

Kopitcke agreed, but then they heard the approach of the next passenger train from Toulouse and watched from below the embankment as the overcrowded cars staggered past behind a locomotive that belched vast plumes of dirty brown smoke.

Driven by eyes and mouth, which were smarting from the smut filling the air, and with his sinuses overflowing, Kopitcke hurried to cross the river. But on the other bank, no matter that the dogs sniffed up and downstream for some hundreds of metres, they picked up no scent. Returning to the railway embankment, he had the dogs sniff up and down the line. At first they found what might be something, but soon lost it and then they dithered, awaiting direction. Moments later, one found the scent of a rabbit, which leapt from its hiding place with the two dogs in excited chase. The handlers, ignoring Kopitcke's shouts to return, followed with an enthusiasm previously entirely lacking, and though they came back empty-handed, they were still excited and began extolling the virtues of rabbit casserole to Kopitcke, for whom French cuisine was a torture of foreign tastes, textures and smells.

These French, he grumbled inwardly. He'd tell the boss exactly what he thought of them.

*

The guard who had locked the doors and the engineer who had helped him were outside, grumpy and aggrieved but also fearful. They figured, being German and in civilian clothes, Bauer had to be Gestapo. What had they done to be apprehended? they complained to Kopitcke as he came out of the boxcar. The engineer who'd been roped into this by the guard was particularly indignant. Bauer barked at them to be patient. He would see them one at a time.

Bauer's perfect French tempered the mood only momentarily after the guard was brought in, he who had indeed warned Eleanor and Henk to escape. He kept his cigarette and puffed furiously on it as he aggressively protested his innocence. Too much, thought Bauer.

He calmly assured the guard that he only wanted information about a young man and an older woman travelling together. The evidence indicated they'd been in that particular boxcar. He wasn't at all concerned whether the guard had warned them to escape or why. If he'd been in the same situation, he said, and money had been offered, well, he'd have taken it too. Times were tough. All he wanted was descriptions of the two, as detailed as possible.

'They – the young man, most probably – murdered two German soldiers in cold blood – not at the front, not as an act of warfare, which would have been entirely legitimate if committed by a soldier of the opposing forces. No,' Bauer explained, 'this was a cowardly ambush on two poor nineteen-year-old kids, barely out of their mothers' hands. The woman is his accomplice.'

The guard didn't trust the German, and he was putting an awful lot of trust in his colleague. 'Shut your gob about me saying the lock wasn't working,' he'd said the moment they knew they were to be questioned. 'This is half what they gave me,' he'd said and had handed over a third, which the engineer had taken, no questions. Not the cigarettes, however. They were secret gold. 'You betray me, everyone will know,' he'd added.

'You got any kids?' Bauer asked him now.

'Yes,' the guard replied, taking the cigarette offered by Bauer. 'A couple of girls and a boy.'

'How old's the boy?' Bauer asked. This terrified the guard.

'No, m'sieur,' he pleaded. 'He's only ten. You can't.'

Bauer kicked himself mentally, realising perfectly well the manner in which his words had been received. He apologised. He hadn't meant to threaten the man's kids.

'I was thinking only of when your boy goes into the army,' he explained. 'A fight fair and square between two opposing forces – we've lived through that and we know, you and I, that you'd want your boy to survive. But what if the fight's not fair? He'd have no chance. That's what we're dealing with here.'

The guard stood silent, pensive. He wasn't much mollified by the apology or explanation. He'd stand up to them if it was just him, but his little boy?

He told Bauer he hadn't seen the young man, only the woman. The young man was her son; he'd been down by the river filling their canteens. She was a lady; you could tell by the way she spoke, even though her clothes were dirty from the travel.

'No accent?' Bauer asked. 'Possibly American?'

'No,' replied the guard. 'She was from Paris and classy. She said her son was in trouble with your lot and they had to leave in a hurry. I'd asked her why they hadn't taken the train once they'd crossed the demarcation line.' He told Bauer what she looked like, but his description added little to the image Bauer had already created in his mind. 'Oh yes,' the guard added, 'she's taller than average.'

Bauer had already worked that out from the contents of the valise. Maybe they were mother and son after all, he mused. He pondered having the guard sit with a sketch artist, so he could get a drawing distributed, but there was no time. He didn't feel the need to speak to the engineer, who, the guard explained, hadn't seen the woman.

He went to his car and was impressed that the promised radio communication direct to Inspector St Jean really worked. He made do with a description – 'middle-aged woman, tall, brown hair and eyes, bourgeois, French-speaking, though possibly American, without a valise, although possibly with a rucksack' – to be sent to all hotels as soon as possible. St Jean agreed, but how actively he would execute the request Bauer could only hope.

He couldn't use emotional blackmail anymore. He had learnt that back in Nevers; even the Wehrmacht had seen no purpose in shooting the French hostages, and they had been quietly released. None of the foreign Jews had been shot, either. The army was apparently deep in a tussle with the SS over its powers in France, so the Jews were to be packed off to a camp in Compiègne while who could shoot whom, where and when was sorted out.

'You better catch the bastard who did this,' the *Kommandant* in Nevers had informed him by telegram, 'or you can go back home to Frankfurt and chase rats.'

He'd do anything to avoid that; being in the army was the only way he could keep in touch with his boys and abreast of what they were facing. Now that Georg was missing, it was even more vital.

Just then, the train from Toulouse staggered in under the awning over the passenger platform. While waiting for Kopitcke to return, Bauer joined the gendarmes, who, with their dogs, were stopping every young male.

BOULEVARD DES PYRÉNÉES, PAU

Around 4pm, Friday, 12th December 1941

'Where is Boulevard des Pyrénées?' Henk asked, once they'd reached the city.

'You're standing on it,' Eleanor replied. 'Why?'

'That is all I know about Pau,' he said.

'That's all one needs to know,' she muttered. What a cruel joke life was playing on her, she thought, acutely aware of her present emotional turmoil. She'd been in an emotional turmoil the last time she'd been here.

Then her blood froze. There, flapping in the breeze above the Hôtel de France, opposite the funicular station, was the invader's red flag with its crooked cross.

'What are they doing here?' she snapped. Closer, she saw the sign. German Armistice Commission. 'Did you know the Nazis were here?'

'Keep your voice down,' he said, moving away quickly. 'How do I know this?' he snapped back at her once they had retreated along the boulevard.

At least she couldn't see any of their uniforms about on foot, nor a bulging neck under a fedora. But they were here. 'What a stupid, stupid place to come to,' she muttered.

The hotels and the cafés were still here, she noted, now shabby and run-down. She told him she'd leave him in one of them while she found somewhere to stay. All were crowded, which surprised her, although instead of the wealthy English and Germans, whose outlandish fashions used to cause so much mirth among the locals back then, these people were unstylish from desperation and no one laughed.

Refugees.

They might have enough money for a cup of weak ersatz coffee, but they had nowhere else to while away the hours as they awaited visas that would probably never come. Their clothes were shabby because they were at the end of a tether leading back to Vienna, Prague, Berlin, Warsaw or Lvov that they could not finally cut. Their chatter was brittle and subdued, while some sat mute and alone, lost in their own tragedy.

Henk's clothes were of an even worse order of shabbiness, his coat smudged and dusty, his trousers torn; and his boots, tough as they were, looked as if he'd walked from Vienna. He couldn't help that, she conceded; she herself looked a fright if her reflection in the windows was any guide. She was changing her mind about leaving him here. Once inside, he'd let his damnation of a cat out, as sure as night followed day, and even if it charmed his fellow desperates, it would advertise his presence to the Germans. She was relieved that her annoyance with him could still flare. She conveniently forgot her own nationality and how her increasingly erratic Paris-pure accent might advertise her presence to the enemy just as effectively.

'Where are we going?' Henk demanded as he sensed her dithering. Impatient, he told her he would look after himself. In two hours, he would sit somewhere along the balustrade looking out at the view. If she didn't turn up, he would come back again every half hour until ten o'clock, when he would assume she'd been arrested and that would be that. To this unsentimental conclusion, Eleanor readily agreed. If she was arrested, too bad; she was hungry and dirty and fed up. With her next breath, she knew she didn't mean that and watched him as anxiously as any lover seeing her beloved walk off into possible danger. Realising what was going on, she snapped herself out of it.

She walked towards the part of the town she remembered, though it took her past the occupier. Lacking the fury that had carried her into the *Kommandantur* in Paris only days before, the sight of the guards outside the Armistice Commission in their sinister steel helmets was enough to turn her stomach.

As if she needed any reminding of her situation, she soon found she was passing the Spanish consulate, where the nationalist flag flapped from the staff and where Spanish civil guards in their black *tricornio* hats and warm capes held back a queue of stateless and listless misery pressed against doors that rarely opened. They had been there the day before, probably the night as well – you couldn't lose your position in the line. She with her American passport could easily have jumped the queue, but no longer. Though she still found it hard to believe, she was a wanted woman whose luck so far had held out. Her only protection now was her cash, her remaining stash of cigarettes and her wits.

To cap her travails, she soon found herself in front of the same hotel in which she'd spent her honeymoon with Roméo the louse. Here she'd lost the child that Hettie Rosen taunted her about so recently; here she'd discovered that he was a bigamist and had only married her because of the child, a sort of rogue's honour. The louse had at least paid the bill before decamping. Being here again, was it history as farce? This was not a memory she liked to revisit, particularly her obtuseness in the face of many warning signs, not least of which was that she, supposedly one of love's new storytellers, had not been in love with him. Yes, she'd tried to persuade herself that she was, but only a fool would have acted on such a quicksand of motivation. Why, then, had she been so foolish? Reaching thirty was a good candidate. And why did it still nag at her? Now she was forty-one – not a good age for a woman, even in France. And yes, she was alone again, and childless, thank you, Hettie; thank you, Mother. She might be terrified she'd fallen for, or was falling for, an unattainable louse, but at least she wasn't broke.

She kept walking, not knowing at all where she was heading or what she might do. Yes, a hotel, she was finding somewhere to stay the night. Tomorrow, she'd find passages into Spain if it took every dollar she had.

RUE HEDAS, PAU

Around 5pm, Friday, 12th December 1941

Eleanor went from one end of the town to the other without securing even a hint of a single bed, let alone two. She'd decided to forget the old fashionable hotels, which turned out to be wise as most had been snapped up by the Germans when the Armistice Commission and all their other commissions turned up after May 1940. The less fashionable were bulging with the less fashionable: refugees from the Nazis and just as many from Franco.

After returning to the street of her ancient unhappiness, she turned down another, which crossed a bridge. Her memory revived. Below was a sort of no-man's-land ravine that began behind the chateau and ran through the newer nineteenth-century town, a place where not long before, open sewers had run. A place to avoid, the hotel concierge had warned her then.

No PASARÁN! – They shall not pass – was freshly daubed in defiance on a wall. Here, the Spanish Civil War was not over.

She continued, with fading hope. Spanish voices echoed along the street, aggressive and loud. She could only smile, if grimly. Losing herself among a swarm of refugee Spanish republicans would be an ironic turn for a capital *R* republican of a Rhode Island variety. Came the tart thought too of what a home away from home this would be for Henk and his little darling. Why, she could hardly wait to tell him. But any amusing anticipation was tempered by the failing light.

As elsewhere in the town, just about every house advertised itself, officially or not, as a *pension de famille*, though the English translation 'boarding house' more accurately described them. Each was as un-inviting as the next. She knocked on the first door. Looking for a room?

Nothing here. Nothing in the next house, where Spanish was the only language on offer. Even the next, which had a sign saying ROOM FOR RENT. She was told to fuck off by another, who made Fagin sound like a country gentleman. This was getting her nowhere.

Returning, she noticed an alley through a doorway. Nothing ventured. She went through it and descended along a narrow, curved path lined by tiny houses stinking of unwashed bodies. Where the path gave out at the bottom were makeshift houses, some of canvass, some of tin, huddled against the foundations of the buildings that backed on to the ravine. Ashy smoke from chimneys that had the uncertain luxury of wood for making fires was filling the valley like a tubercular soup. She could taste it. And with no street lamps, the shadows from the walls along the winding path were turning sinister and threatening. This was just the place she could get herself robbed and her throat cut. She felt for the knife in her pocket, which provided some semblance of courage, although given her singular lack of experience, this was the courage of a fool. Possibly the sight of it would be intimidating if she got into trouble.

This was ridiculous. She'd find no hotel among this warren of unwanted humanity. Yet she did.

HÔTEL COSMOPOLITAN said the small sign, which, as Eleanor was to discover, was true, though in its own unique way. A rare electric light over the doorway was encouraging. Even more encouraging, it gave out real light. She saw this was not some death trap made of tin or wattle and daub and packed with detritus from the Spanish Civil War, but one of a set of real buildings fronting the laneway along the ravine. Here was the very frontier of respectability, desperate though it might be.

She went to the door under the sign and rang the bell. It tinkled so gently you'd think fairies might have lived within. After some short time, the door opened and rather than proud Titania, an aged woman presented herself, all skin and bone and a death's head skull capped by a bonnet. She kept dabbing her dripping red nose with a handkerchief that looked to Eleanor as if it could spread the plague.

'What do you want?' the woman demanded.

This was not encouraging, but Eleanor had run out of possibilities.

'A room for one,' she requested. Given the Germans were looking for an American woman and a young man with a cat, she thought it best to represent herself as a *femme seule* and as French as the Eiffel. Not that this helped her immediately.

'Nope,' said the concierge through her sniffle. 'You won't find a rathole in the whole town.'

Eleanor thought she was already in one, but instead of opening her mouth, she opened her wallet. In the blink of an eye, the mannerless slattern became a saint, crossed herself and said, 'Forgive me, madame, I have to be so careful these days. I run a respectable place, but look around you.' She drew Eleanor inside and quickly shut the door. 'I like to help people. You've no idea the types we see here now, criminals all of them,' she said, going around behind the counter, putting her glasses on and looking at the register. Her eyes barely glanced at the page before she closed it.

'You're a lady, I can see that,' said the woman. 'I might be able to offer you something suitable. I do like to help people, you know.'

She introduced herself as Madame Dumas and beckoned Eleanor to follow her up a narrow flight of stairs, which creaked as if each step rested on the back of a frog. Eleanor wondered how she was to spirit Henk up to the room later when every step was an alarm bell. Voices came from behind every door – French, German and possibly Polish or Czech, she couldn't tell. The place was bulging with people. They climbed another flight of stairs, which at least didn't creak. Behind one door on the next floor, someone was playing a violin. Could that really be Beethoven? Another door opened and two young women burst out, whispering excitedly in German, but the sight of the concierge stopped their chatter mid-word. Eleanor observed they looked frightened as they hurried past down the stairs on their way out.

'Jews,' said Madame Dumas. 'Poor things. I try to help them as best I can.'

They climbed the last set of stairs, which led to the attic level.

'Nice and quiet,' she said as she opened the door to the room, 'for someone refined like yourself.'

Two beds, thank God, the first thing Eleanor looked for. The roof was steep and so low that she had to stoop, but at least the room was serviceable – a wardrobe, a chair, a washstand with a basin – and it was clean. She felt the beds.

'No bed bugs,' said the concierge. 'Very nice and cosy.' The toilet was at the end of the hallway on the floor below. 'With hot running water,' she said proudly. 'You won't get that anywhere else here.'

A couple of long doghouse dormers with small windows let in some light.

'Best kept closed,' advised Madame Dumas, although how anyone above the age of three could manoeuvre themselves out to open or shut the windows seemed impossible to Eleanor. No matter.

She asked how much and was surprised the woman didn't try to cheat her by asking some exorbitant amount. For want of anything better, she agreed. Relieved, Eleanor sat on the bed and took out her cigarettes. She deserved one. She'd hardly savoured the first draught when the woman returned. She needed to see 'Madame's documents'. A concierge, she explained, had to register everyone with the prefecture as a matter of course. This was a respectable hotel.

Eleanor followed her back down the stairs.

'Toulouse?' said Madame Dumas, evoking doubt.

'Yes,' said Eleanor.

'A lovely city, Toulouse,' said Madame Dumas as she scratched the details into her register. 'I thought perhaps you might be American.'

'Oh?' said Eleanor, her heart sinking.

'You're smoking those expensive American cigarettes,' said Madame Dumas. 'Only Americans or black marketeers smoke American.'

'You've exposed me,' said Eleanor lightly.

'Hah,' Madame Dumas chuckled, dabbing her nose, 'I knew you were American. Your French is so good, though, one would never know.'

'Your second guess was correct,' said Eleanor, 'although "black marketeer" is such a coarse word, don't you think? I prefer "business-woman" myself.'

Before the concierge could respond, Eleanor opened her cigarette case. 'Would you like one?' she offered. Yes, Madame Dumas most certainly would, even with her chest, what's the harm in just one? As Eleanor lit the cigarette for her, she noticed the woman's pupils fix on the lighter, then back to the case. Lean and hungry as Cassius, she observed; she sensed the woman also had Cassius's itching palm.

'I'm sure we can come to some arrangement,' she said, opening her wallet. 'Such are the times, are they not?'

'Well,' said Madame Dumas, 'I can see you're really a lady. Yes, times are so difficult now. And I like to help people. Are you staying long?'

'Two days only,' said Eleanor, 'but I might have to extend.'

'You go up and make yourself comfortable, Madame Roget,' said Dumas. 'I'll send the boy up with a nice basin of hot water.'

As she went back up the stairs, she heard Madame Dumas's raised voice, berating and caustic in Creole, and then she heard a slap and a yelp. The concierge's kindness went in only one direction.

Soon came a knock on Eleanor's door, and there stood a boy of about twelve or thirteen, a basin of steaming water in his hands. '*Señora*,' he said shyly. The recent slap was still evident on his face.

She beckoned him in with a nice smile. He set the basin down. She told him to wait and felt in the pocket of her coat for some francs, but noticed his eyes on her cigarette case, so she asked if he would like one. The shy, sad little face broke into such a smile as he carefully removed one cigarette. '*Gracias, señora*,' he said and then he reached into his pocket and produced a cake of soap and handed it to her. Eleanor saw it was real. He put his finger to his lips, which formed a cheeky smile. Don't tell. She could have kissed him. Instead, she gave him the remaining two cigarettes in the case.

'You look after me, I'll look after you,' said Eleanor. 'Agreed?' He smiled.

Once he was gone, she liberated herself of her journey's grime and stink. Even the sight of her much-diminished supply of cosmetics, barely enough for a couple of days under normal circumstances, lifted her mood and her spirit. She was a black marketeer after all. Rain had been threatening, so she needed to find Henk. She departed down the creaking stairs, passing an older man trudging up. So many people came and went, she figured, the lower flight of stairs might not be the problem she had initially thought.

'Going out?' Madame Dumas enquired, poking her head over the counter.

'One must eat,' said Eleanor. If the steps were less of a problem, what about the concierge perched here all the time like Alberich guarding the treasure of the Nibelung?

'It'll rain later,' said Madame Dumas, 'it always does on that wind. Do you want an umbrella just in case?'

Eleanor was unsettled by Madame Dumas; an excess of kindness never came without a sting. An umbrella wouldn't be necessary, she replied, she wouldn't be out long.

ST MARTIN'S CHURCH AND HÔTEL DE FRANCE, BOULEVARD DES PYRÉNÉES, PAU

Around 5.30pm, Friday, 12th December 1941

The occasional wind gusts were strong enough to tear the remaining autumnal leaves from the trees and pull at Bauer's cap as he walked along the footpath away from the *commissariat de police*. He'd sent Kopitcke on to their temporary office in the Hôtel de France to sift through the information he'd requested from Germany, some of which had arrived. There had been nothing more he could do at the police station, short of going out himself to inspect each and every hostel and hovel in Pau for the killers. If he'd been able to keep the dogs, he might have done just that. A flyer had been prepared for printing and distribution the following morning, and St Jean had assured him his informers had been told and would, in turn, inform, if and when they learnt something. When St Jean decided to cooperate, he was quite Teutonically efficient.

The walk back to the office allowed Bauer to stretch his legs and be alone. Before continuing, he took a Pervitin tablet to keep himself going. After a slight rush, he suddenly felt sharp and alert, as if he'd drunk many cups of strong coffee, although without coffee's side effects. It really was a wonder pill. He'd received no news about Georg, not even that they were still looking for him and his platoon. If silence were a sign, then the Russian counteroffensive outside Moscow that the German public knew nothing about was succeeding. He wasn't ready to start grasping at the hope Georg and his men had been taken prisoner. He'd heard quite enough of what was taking place behind the lines in the east – the mass shootings of Jews, of captured Soviet officers, of civilians – to know that sort of hope was no hope. The Soviets wouldn't discriminate between the Wehrmacht and the SS special forces.

St Martin's Church, a little further on along the boulevard, had been his goal all along. He sat at the back, although hardly in contemplation, for his emotions were in turmoil. He tried prayer, but what was he to pray for? His son's soul? He wouldn't permit himself to think of such a thing. The boy was strong. He would survive, and his father would help him with all his might. A priest approached and asked if he would like to join him in prayer, and Bauer said he would, thank you. First he told the priest he was German and was worried sick about his soldier son over in Russia who was missing. God knew, so why not the priest? The priest was only fleetingly startled before he prayed for the hope of peace and reconciliation and for Georg and all soldiers to be returned safe and sound to their fathers and mothers. He also gave Bauer a blessing, and for a moment, no longer, Bauer felt an echo of the comfort he once took for granted. But he couldn't hang on to it. His boy might be lying in the snow. What was God doing to them all? What sort of God was He to allow all this to happen? His eyes flew open in anger. The priest was gone, leaving only a faint whiff of his physical presence in the stillness.

Bauer sensed him nearby, probably returned to the confessional whence he'd come to offer comfort. The priest had tried. The church felt as cold as a tomb. Even the weather outside was better than this. As he went out, he thought of the priest, who was about his age, old enough to have experienced the last war. He wondered if he'd been a priest then or even a soldier.

On return, he ordered dinner sent up to their office, which was in the Queens' Salon. There he found Kopitcke, innocent of any French history before May 1940, sitting at his improvised desk under bad portraits of Henry IV's queens, duplicitous Marguerite de Valois and ruthless Marie de' Medici, she who could have taught Machiavelli a thing or two about power.

'These just arrived, sir,' Kopitcke said, pointing to copies of files of known deserters since August, the who, the when and the where.

'About time,' Bauer muttered.

On the opinion of the French doctor who had performed the autopsy, Bauer had only the Wehrmacht knife to go on as possible murder weapon and had to take into account the possibility that whoever murdered those two soldiers might himself be from the Wehrmacht and thus a deserter.

Kopitcke was still shocked, he who idealised the Landser that he could never be. How could a German soldier kill men so recently his comrades?

'Deserters come in all sizes,' Bauer replied, 'from cowards to heroes.' In his experience, some were just fools, some obsessed by a slight or perceived wrong, some just wanted to sort out a girl who might've written a 'dear John' letter. They faced a grim future if caught, sent east to a punishment battalion at a minimum, which really meant certain death. 'Any, especially a coward,' he said, 'would kill to save his own neck, no question, as long as it was a knife in the back.'

Dinner arrived. To Bauer's dismay, it wasn't French, it was German. 'They're very good here,' said Kopitcke. 'They know what we like to eat.'

BOULEVARD DES PYRÉNÉES, PAU

Towards 6pm, Friday, 12th December 1941

Eleanor walked along the boulevard just on the hour. The breeze coming in from the west brought with it the salty tang of the sea. She did not quite believe it. Was the ocean not a hundred miles away? Her senses had not misled her, for this was indeed air carried in from the Atlantic, and with it came the memories of Bar Harbor holidays that this journey home seemed to be releasing so vividly. Those glorious long summer days; she could feel the sun and the salt on her skin. Fleetingly, she forgot the war, even her current plight, although her present bent for finding the dark cloud behind every silver lining brought some apprehension about going back. She was surplus to requirements, just an adornment, the bohemian aunt to nieces and nephews. That would soon wear off. And the only one she could talk to, Will, was off at the war.

She strolled as casually as she could. Few people were about. Henk was not among them. Where the hell was he? Her anxiety and irritation rose in equal measure.

The lights of a lone car poked out through the dark as it rolled slowly along the roadway, close to the footpath. Too slowly for Eleanor's liking, too close. She slid behind a statue and waited till its sinister and familiar form passed by. Only then did she continue her search. She came to the end of the boulevard, turned and retraced her steps back towards the chateau. Henk was still not in sight. What if he'd been picked up? Then, suddenly, there he was, barely inches away, as if he'd stepped out of a crack in the pavement.

'I was about to give you up,' she said in a snappish whisper. The fronds of the palms rustled against one another in the breeze. He shrugged his shoulders.

'Did you not see the Gestapo?' he replied.

'Of course I did.' Closer, she saw his brow glistened with sweat and his face was red.

'You're not well,' she said, unable to conceal her concern.

'Not at all,' he replied, as if she was being insulting.

He had thrown up not long before, but not from any sickness of the body. He was still shaken by what had happened. She'd be the last person he'd tell.

He'd been passing the Armistice Commission, where he'd seen the two German soldiers guarding the entrance. He'd stopped. Either of the Landsers standing there with his rifle on his shoulder could have been him. They could have been old pals. Why not go over? They'd happily greet him, even knowing he was a *Mischling*. He knew that didn't count with them; they didn't take him for one of those dirty Jews screwing Germany over. He was one of them; they'd have died for him, as he for them. He had a tin cravat around his neck to prove it, for God's sake. What the hell's the bloody army doing kicking out fellows like our Heiner with his Iron Cross? That's what they'd said.

Good to see you, pal, they'd say again, let's share a cigarette and a drink.

Oh God, yes, a drink with mates, belonging once again, knowing they cared for you and you for them.

Coming out of his reverie, God knows how, he'd caught himself barely metres away from them on the footpath opposite, about to cross over. The shock of what he'd been about to do froze him. He had willed his feet away from them and along the footpath, eyes front as if he'd been on parade. They must have been looking right at him, wondering what the hell he was doing. They might have put a bullet into him if he'd come any closer.

Once he'd retreated out of sight, he'd thrown up like some scared-to-death kid. But he had been scared. He'd scared the hell out of himself. Thank Christ it was so dark. What the hell had he been thinking? Was he going crazy? Hadn't he killed off that part of him when he'd knifed those two Landsers? He had to get a grip on himself.

'I'm all right,' he repeated impatiently when she kept looking at him.

'Follow me,' she said. He waited until she was ahead some distance, then followed along the opposite footpath, where through the windows of the cafés he saw the ghostly faces of the stranded. Gave him the creeps. They seemed to him to be waiting for death to come in and claim them.

After 7pm, Friday, 12th December 1941

They ate in a café that backed on to the ravine. The food available without coupons was Spanish and coarse, but after sausage and increasingly stale bread for a couple of days and latterly nothing but water, this could have been Maxim's. She'd reminded Henk of the French for stew before they'd entered. The less he said the better. She'd persuaded him also to keep the cat inside his coat, although that was easier said than done when it smelt food. He ate quickly and took himself and his darling away to a discreet place where he could feed it without attracting attention.

The cat was ravenous. 'Poor little cat,' he said in German. 'Soon we'll be in a place where the sun shines all the time and you won't be cold or hungry anymore.' When it had consumed every last drop of the stew, it quickly found a private spot for its ablutions. He liked its fussy ways. He'd be fussy too, come the day when they were safe and free. It returned to him, he picked it up, cuddled it under his chin and listened to its comforting purr.

After he went, Eleanor wasted no time trying the waiter to test her hunch that this was exactly the sort of place she might seek their passages into Spain. It took only a word and few francs to open a door, for this was still the time when, despite the constraints, French rather than German authority ruled, and the market for escapees with money was less clandestine than later.

She might have been entering an accountant's office with its desk and chair and the occupant poring over his ledgers and accounts. In place of an accountant's high collar and possible pince-nez was a rough open-necked shirt and dark eyes that needed neither magnifying glass to see nor a ledger to tote up figures. The man at the table in a fog of smoke from his constant cigarette was young and thickset, with beefy arms and hands. The lines on his face, Eleanor realised from his rough Spanish accent, were from the hard experience of escape and exile. With the memory of the Catalan nationalist back in Lyon and the minefield of Spanish exile politics, Eleanor got straight to the point. She wanted two passages into Spain as quickly as possible and as secretly as possible.

He laughed. 'You're American, aren't you? You got an American passport. All you need is a Spanish and a Portuguese visa. No problem. Just catch the train down to Canfranc.'

Eleanor was furious with herself for letting her accent slip. Worse, she hadn't noticed. She thought to deny it, but that would complicate her need. 'I can't go on a train. I need the utmost discretion,' she said. That's all she was going to say, otherwise the price would start going up.

'Jesus Maria, lady,' he replied in disbelief, 'you can't be a Jew.'

'No,' Eleanor confirmed.

'This for you?' he asked.

She nodded.

He shook his head. Did she have any idea what the mountains were like right now? he said. The high passes weren't passes at all, because of the weather, which, if she hadn't noticed, was getting worse. How was she, a woman, going to hike it into Spain?

She said that wasn't his concern; if she died in the attempt, so what to him?

'Yeah, but I'm not the one taking you to Spain,' he replied. 'The guides are fussy. They don't want to be held up by no lady thinking she's going for a stroll along the Champs-Élysées.'

Eleanor said she understood the seriousness of the situation all too well. She might not be able to claim she was fit, but she was tough.

'Look outside,' he said, 'you're one of thousands.'

'They're mostly Jews with no papers or an American passport,' Eleanor replied. She said she'd happily lie under a load of manure to get across the border. That's all she needed. Just across the border.

'Lady, that's all you're ever going to get,' he answered pointedly. 'Once you're past the high point, that's Spain, you're on your own. At least it's downhill.'

'I need two passages,' she said.

'The other party the same as you?' he asked.

Eleanor had to have known she'd be asked this. 'Does that matter?'

'Two ladies thinking they're strolling down the Champs-Élysées's double the trouble,' he said.

'He's young and he's fit,' Eleanor replied.

The man looked at her askance. 'Oh yeah?' Then he smiled.

'It's not like that,' she snapped. Whether she convinced him, she didn't know. She certainly hadn't convinced herself.

He lit another cigarette, took a few puffs to think it over, then told her to go to a café on Rue Bernadotte tomorrow at ten, the one that had a sign with two fishes over the entrance. He would send someone who would find her there.

'How can I trust you?' Eleanor asked. Anyone could come, and she'd end up in the hands of the invader.

'Lady,' he said, standing abruptly from the chair – this interview was over – 'I'd be sitting at home in Cartagena if it wasn't for the fucking Franco and the fucking Nazis, so if you want to insult me you can get your fat arse out of here right now. If I say I'll send someone, you can trust them, even if they say no.'

She took the reprimand. She was learning. Fight only when necessary.

'What the fuck have you done, eh?' he demanded. 'Cut off Hitler's balls?'

'How did you know?' she said, attempting a sly smile. He laughed, which relieved her. She was worried he might demand to know more.

'One thing,' she said. 'Do not say I am American.'

'Lady, your mouth says you are,' he replied, shaking his head.

'It won't tomorrow,' she replied.

He didn't believe her.

'Do I have your word?' she asked, favouring her request with a handful of francs. He said he wouldn't mention it, and she believed him.

RUE HEDAS, PAU

Towards 9pm, Friday, 12th December 1941

As she led Henk off the street down the alleyway, Eleanor told him they were about to enter a no-man's-land that spoke Spanish. 'You'll feel right at home,' she added. He grinned.

'What's so amusing?' she asked.

'You are,' he said. 'To survive, you should learn not to be so predictable.'

The wind with its Atlantic tang buffeted the ravine. They'd have rain before long, which, she figured, meant snow on the mountains. While he waited, she went inside, hoping the concierge would be asleep. But there she was, her beady eyes through the tiny opening in her door reflecting the light in the vestibule.

'Ah, Madame Roget,' she called as she shuffled out and smiled. 'You're back safe and sound.'

The front door opened and a middle-aged man entered, gaunt and sad.

'Good evening, m'sieur,' said Dumas with cheer.

The man nodded gruffly and went up the stairs.

'He's a Dutch Jew,' whispered Dumas, 'waiting for his wife and children to arrive. It's been two months, poor man. Have you heard him playing his violin? Such beautiful music.'

Eleanor smiled. The woman was a terrible liar.

*

Eleanor hurried up to the room. Getting herself to the window at the end of the dormer wasn't impossible, just ridiculously difficult, but she got there, opened the window and shook her head to warn off

Henk. God knows where he would go – back into that crack in the pavement? She hoped the rain would hold off. But better to be on the safe side about Madame Dumas.

While she waited for Madame Dumas to disappear, she took her basin down to the next floor, where she was able to find water that was blissfully hot. She took her fill and carried it back to the room. With the wind, she didn't take any notice of the window rattling, and only when she turned did she see a figure tumble in through the window. Thank God she'd already set the basin down, because her instinct was to hurl it at the intruder. It was him. He'd climbed the drain pipe to the roof and over to her window like a cat burglar.

'Unlocked,' he said, shutting the window behind him and snibbing the catch so it was as locked as it could be.

He removed cat and coat, pulled off his woollen jumper, shirt and undershirt, and immediately claimed her hot water and leftover soap as if she'd prepared it just for his arrival. Her dismay was actually disappointment. If only he'd waited a moment for her to offer it instead of just claiming it. Still, she thought, this was the first hot water he'd encountered at least since they'd crossed their Rubicon and probably well before that. She remembered the bruising and cuts on the pale soles of his feet. After he'd dried himself, she found her ointment, but he took it from her – no thank-you – and attended to his wounds himself.

'Fine,' she snapped, and he had to concentrate all the harder not to say something.

He couldn't stand it. Her need was oppressive. 'You speak too loudly,' he said, dropped his pants, crawled into the bed to escape, called the cat up from the floor, where it was washing itself, and closed his eyes.

Eleanor took up the basin. She was of a mind to tip it all over him and his wretched cat. She went back downstairs, tipped out the dirty water, washed and refilled it. At least the water was still hot. Back in the room, she took her time washing. He was asleep, although not untroubled as he tossed about, upending the cat, which decided her bed was more likely to provide a proper rest. She laughed, her mood always improved by hot water, soap and clean skin. Why hadn't she figured this out about him before? No wonder he preferred the company of a cat. He with his emotional detachment and complete sense of entitlement was a cat too. She was safe.

'What's mine is yours, is that it, pussy?' she said tartly as she manoeuvred herself between the sheets, upending the cat onto the floor. Though the cover was rough and scratchy, the sheets were clean. She had no need of James Joyce to send her into the arms of Morpheus; she said the Lord's Prayer and fell asleep. Whereupon the cat jumped back up and settled itself on the pillow beside her head.

Before 6am, Saturday, 13th December 1941

She felt Henk's presence, but what woke her was the cat's protesting meow. She opened her eyes in the clammy dark to see that it had spent the night on her pillow and was not keen to move. Henk gently retracted its tiny claws from the cover, lifted it up and tucked it inside his coat.

'I must go,' he whispered. The floor creaked as he stood.

'Wait,' she said as loudly as she dared. She got up and lit a candle. She peered at her watch, just after six am.

'Why so early?' she asked. She told him the concierge mightn't be a problem. 'You'll get drenched,' she said, indicating the obvious from the clatter on the roof.

'I will find shelter,' he replied.

'Why not stay here all day?' she said.

'No,' he said, 'I would feel trapped.' He was thinking not only of the concierge.

She offered him money. He declined. He still had the dollars she'd given him in Lyon. Enough if something should go wrong? she wondered, but damn it all, nothing would now go wrong. When he returned in the evening, she would have two passages into Spain.

She didn't know what to say, so she said, 'Don't forget when you order, say "*Je vais avoir le ragoût*", and for God's sake, don't feed the cat there.'

He went to the window much more gracefully than she had managed, looked back at her and held her gaze, as close as he'd ever come to exposing to her the human being inside the carapace that his stubborn will to live had moulded around him. Then in the blink of an eye, as if he had exposed too much of himself, he turned away and told her to put out the candle. She wetted her fingers and snipped out the flame. In an instant, he was gone.

Eleanor imagined she heard his footsteps on the slate roof. The room now felt empty and cold. It was as if he had left behind his loneliness and aloneness. He was so closed in, she wondered what he would do when escaping the Nazis was no longer his reason for being. Though she had retreated beneath the warmth of the sheets, she was too anxious to sleep further, especially as her anxieties were about him. She couldn't in good conscience stay warm and snug while he was out in the rain and cold.

*

Outside, he hurried away, an unseen wraith through the murk. Why hadn't he thanked her? he wondered. He'd intended to, but the words had failed. Words, his own, look what strife they'd got him into. Best to keep his trap shut.

COMMISSARIAT DE POLICE, PAU

Around 7am, Saturday, 13th December 1941

Kommissar Bauer had risen early. Even through the dark, he had seen from his hotel window that the skies were closed over Pau. The clouds seemed only head high. *Schadenfreude* was the appropriate word, that German word for pleasure in someone else's trouble.

'Look out the window, Kopitcke,' he'd said with relish once his assistant had joined him over breakfast. Something cheerful. During the night, the rain had woken him from a shallow sleep roiled by anxiety about his son. There had been no news.

'Wet down here,' he said, 'but higher up maybe there'll be enough snow to block Hannibal.'

He wasn't so foolish as to believe this would stop people trying to get away, especially if they were desperate and young. Now would be a good time, because you could expect the weather would keep the police indoors. You'd be right as far as the French police were concerned, but not for Kommissar Bauer or the German troops now fanning out along the border in patrols.

'Keep at it,' he'd told Kopitcke as he departed.

Kopitcke's job was to devote the morning under the sinister gazes of Marguerite de Valois and Marie de' Medici combing the recent Wehrmacht files on deserters for likely candidates for their killer. A perfect job for Kopitcke – methodical Kopitcke, that's what you could say about him – who seemed not at all deterred by the size of the job in front of him.

'At least you'll be out of the weather,' he'd said on Kopitcke's departure.

Bauer walked briskly into the *commissariat*, past a saluting officer. Contrary to his expectations, not only for a Saturday but also for the time of day, his French counterpart was already in his office. The details of the wanted woman had been distributed to all the hotels and, yes, reports had come in of women seeking rooms, but too many and too general to be of much use.

Then, as if in passing, St Jean said that one informant had reported a woman enquiring last night in a café about a passage into Spain. By the description, she sounded one and the same. 'A lady, that's what our man said,' he reported. 'Refined, not a Jew.'

'What about an American accent?' Bauer asked.

'No,' replied St Jean, 'from Paris, although she was smoking an American cigarette, so in that place she stood out like balls on a dog.'

'Aha, someone with money and connections to the black market,' said Bauer. 'Though,' he added, 'that description could also apply to an American, don't you think?'

Where was the café?

'Rue des Cordeliers,' St Jean said, which meant nothing to Bauer. 'The anarchists still hate the communists who still hate the socialists,' St Jean continued, sniffing with contempt. 'See what happens when people stop believing in Our Saviour?'

Bauer smiled politely. He agreed, but that horse had bolted when Galileo first raised his telescope to the sky and saw not heaven but Venus revolving around the Sun.

'What of the hotels here? Would they report anything to the police?' he asked.

'They didn't before I came here,' St Jean replied.

'The woman could be around there?' Bauer asked.

'Not in any of the reputable hotels without my knowing,' said St Jean. 'The disreputable ones I still have to bring under proper control.'

Bauer said he would visit these himself. All he needed was one or two constables to accompany him. He would also like to interview the informant himself as soon as possible.

'No, m'sieur,' said St Jean. He was obdurate. One of his telephones rang and he answered it.

Bauer wasn't sure if the refusal concerned talking to the police informant or included getting the assistance of the constables. He'd get some clarity once St Jean was off the telephone. But until proven otherwise, this woman was surely the American half of his quarry. He would go after her, alone if necessary.

'Absolutely not,' he heard St Jean snap into the telephone. 'Just where do they think they are? Berlin?'

That word alone was enough to interrupt Bauer's thoughts about catching the woman.

He watched as St Jean cupped his hand over the mouthpiece of the first telephone and picked up a second. 'Send two men to the Continental immediately,' he ordered. 'If the two German agents don't leave, arrest them and bring them here straightaway.' He replaced that telephone, took up the other to report the imminent arrival of the French police, then hung up.

'Two of your Gestapo agents have been demanding entry to a room in the Hôtel Continental,' he reported to Bauer heatedly. 'This is France, Herr Kommissar, not Germany.'

Much as he admired St Jean's firmness about French sovereignty, and much as he would by instinct find himself on the same side as the French concerning the Gestapo, he knew there was more to this than a matter of French pride.

'Duels!' exclaimed St Jean, whose outrage was feeding on itself. 'Who do your colleagues think they are, the three musketeers?'

Bauer heard the words, but really, duels? Musketeers? What on earth was St Jean foaming at the mouth about?

'What?' St Jean said, agape. 'You don't know?'

Bauer certainly did not.

'Late last night, the military attaché at your consulate severely wounded a Gestapo agent in a duel,' St Jean reported. 'If I find it happened on French soil, I'll have both arrested.'

Bauer certainly shared St Jean's astonishment. A duel? In this day and age? He had no need to ask who the Gestapo man was, but St Jean immediately confirmed his guess. Pichler. Now the Gestapo were trying to gain entry into Lieutenant Wolf's room at the Hôtel Continental, where the German consulate personnel were housed.

'Is the lieutenant there now?' Bauer asked.

'No, the Gestapo picked him up outside when he returned in the early hours of this morning,' said St Jean. 'Yet another outrage against French sovereignty.'

'Jesus Maria,' muttered Bauer. Of all things, and at the worst time. He had to see to this. Lieutenant Wolf was a serving Wehrmacht officer.

'Do you know where they've taken him?' he asked.

'I can guess,' St Jean replied. 'They've rented a villa on Avenue Trespoey. They think we don't know. They do nothing without my knowing.'

Armed with the exact location and name, Bauer ordered up his car.

'Please leave this to me, inspector,' Bauer said, promising to report back immediately, which suited St Jean perfectly. The moment he was free of Bauer, he would have the water to the Villa St Albert cut off. A difficult leak that would take as long to fix as the Gestapo were causing him grief.

From the car, Bauer ordered Kopitcke over to the *commissariat*. It would be a wasted effort sending his assistant into Hedas after the woman; he was just too damn German. But he was good at being a pest to the French.

'Bring those files with you,' he continued. 'You can keep working on them at the *commissariat*.'

RUE BERNADOTTE,
THE CAFÉ DES DEUX POISSONS, PAU

After 8am, Saturday, 13th December 1941

Eleanor descended the stairs as quietly as she could, hoping she mightn't alert Madame Dumas, but too bad, there was Dumas, bonjouring gaily, hoping Madame Roget had slept well, she was sure she had, but surely madame wasn't going out in this weather. Eleanor replied that she had no choice. Alas, said Dumas, she had already lent the umbrella to someone else, she was so sorry.

Outside, the rain was easing, but the pathway was waterlogged and muddy, so she had to pick her way carefully to get to the alleyway that led up to the street. The concierge's smiles and kindnesses were easier to take from afar. At the exit to the street, she realised she had no idea where to go. She'd omitted to ask the Spaniard the night before where Rue Bernadotte was, and the last person she was going to ask for directions was the concierge. Now, with the weather keeping everyone else indoors and Eleanor wary of asking around, she'd have to find it herself. Given Bernadotte had been one of Napoleon's generals, she assumed he hadn't started life in the medieval quarter but on its edge. Surely the town would celebrate one of their own becoming king of Sweden. After some traipsing up and down, she walked twice along one street, up to where it came to a large square, and voila, the Caserne Bernadotte. Then she saw the sign, Rue Bernadotte. She made her way back, though initially without seeing any sign for a café with the two fish.

'Oh for God's sake, Pisces!' she cried out in frustration. To her astonishment, her voice conjured the place up, just as if she were Ali Baba with his 'Open sesame'. There it was, staring at her, the Piscean symbol painted on the window, not hanging from a sign, and the café was right beside the house, well marked, where Napoleon's general-become-king-of-Sweden had been born. She was in a daze from hunger.

The windows were befogged, which at least indicated it was open and occupied. She pushed through the door into the now-familiar stench of cigarette smoke, bad breath, ersatz coffee and damp, unwashed clothes. She couldn't have been happier. Her hat and Claude's coat were hardly in any better condition than the clothes of her fellow rats. She found a place to hang them near the heater and sat at a table, where she ordered the breakfast stew everyone else was having, with or without coupons, it didn't seem to matter. Whatever it was, it was delicious. Sitting back with her fake coffee, she congratulated herself on how well she fitted in but wondered if her disguise might be too effective to attract the promised attention. She needn't have worried. A waiter approached and beckoned her to follow. She was, after all, just about the only woman, and the smoke from her morning Chesterfield was as outstanding as the finest Cuban cigar in a place where everyone else was smoking a mixture of cheap local tobacco cut with sunflower seeds and hay left over by the Germans.

With most of the army still in German prisoner-of-war camps, waiters were usually boys or over forty-five, but this waiter was slap bang in the ripest military age group, twenty-one or two, and looked strappingly fit. She wondered how he'd escaped, but only in passing. She had more urgent matters to deal with.

She expected him to lead her to someone else, like the Spaniard in the Hedas, as if every café in Pau were running a similar operation – and indeed, many were. But this time, once they were out of ear and eye, he himself was the one to talk to.

'Is this for you?' he asked abruptly.

'Yes,' she replied. 'And one other.'

'Another woman?'

'No, a young man.'

'Where is he?' he demanded.

'He's not here,' she replied.

'I can see that,' the young waiter said. 'Why not? We don't take people unseen.'

'I'll bring him later,' Eleanor offered.

'No need,' said her interlocutor. 'Nothing doing.'

'What?' she asked.

'You're an old woman,' he said.

Eleanor knew she had a short fuse. She had been trying to make it longer, but this young tough – for that's what he was, no wonder the army hadn't been able to nab him – she had a mind to whack his face.

'You'd take me if I were a man, is that it?' she said, sitting on the volcano inside her.

'Sure,' he replied, 'for the right price.'

'But I'm willing to pay,' Eleanor said with as much reasonableness as she could summon.

'Sorry, lady,' he replied, 'we like dough but our guides like their lives better.'

'I'm as strong as any man,' Eleanor argued.

'Lady, you got no idea,' he said. 'It's been raining here, not too badly. But up in the high passes? You figure it out. Besides, the Germans have started patrols up there now.'

'What?' she exclaimed. 'I thought – ' He cut her off.

'Don't matter what you thought,' he said. 'Even if you were a man, the price has doubled.'

'Then I'll find someone else whose courage matches mine,' she snapped, turned on her heels and stalked out, hat and coat in hand. Behind her, the waiter shrugged though gave her the finger.

Eleanor carried herself and her outrage out to the street. At least the rain had stopped. There was nothing for it but to keep on, although she did wonder about the trail she might be leaving behind. Was she blind in trusting to all these waiters? What, though, was the alternative? For *passeurs*, it was a seller's market, and she was a buyer.

She pushed herself on, glancing at her watch. Half the morning wasted.

VILLA ST ALBERT,
AVENUE TRESPOEY, PAU

Later that morning, Saturday, 13th December 1941

While Bauer had no idea what precisely had caused Lieutenant Wolf to fight a duel with Pichler, imagination was enough to know it had been Wolf the aristocrat who had challenged, and that he'd had good reason. From experience, he knew the Gestapo, made up of thugs with their gutter tactics, always played to win. The only way to deal with them was to treat them as they treated others, by feeding their fears. He had considered ordering a squad of soldiers from the German guard at the Armistice Commission to back him up but felt even this would have taken up time he did not have. He had to strike quickly. He would brazen this out alone. As he set out with his driver, he slipped another Pervitin pill into his mouth.

The house the Gestapo had taken was like many of its neighbours, a late-nineteenth-century mishmash of a villa, which, with its timbered upper story under a hipped roof and tower, might have been built by a German homesick for Rhenish castles. No guard nor any other sign indicated the Gestapo were in residence, and for a moment Bauer doubted St Jean's information.

When his car stopped at the front gate, a man appeared, and while he was not in uniform, everything about him, including his demand in bad French to piss off, wiped away Bauer's doubts.

He had already wound down the window. 'I am Kommissar Bauer of the Geheime Feldpolizei,' he snapped in German, showing his identification. 'Open up the gate now, or you'll be on the first transport to the Russian front.' That focused the man's attention. He jumped to open the gate, and even saluted as Bauer's car passed through.

From outside, one would think nothing was amiss. With its turrets and cornices washed clean, the place looked picturesque in a Grimms'-fairy-tale sort of way. Bauer jumped out of the car, swept up the steps and inside.

With his ID held open in his right hand, shoulder high, he went straight to the agent at the desk, a uniformed SS corporal. He'd take pleasure in informing St Jean of this insult to French sovereignty. 'Take me immediately to Lieutenant Wolf,' he ordered.

'B–b–but, sir,' the fellow stammered.

'Immediately,' Bauer snapped.

'I have to call the guard, sir,' he replied.

'Unlock the door or I'll see you're sent to Russia in the very next detachment,' Bauer ordered.

Chastened, the corporal jumped to it. Bauer followed. So far so good, Bauer thought. They passed through a doorway, along a short corridor and down stone steps to the floor below.

'Where is Lieutenant Wolf?' Bauer demanded of the guard, who looked to the corporal. 'I'm the one giving orders,' Bauer bellowed, which was enough for the guard to move at the double down another set of stone steps to an ordinary cellar, with Bauer on his heels.

The guard opened the wooden cellar door, and Bauer pushed him aside.

Wolf was sprawled on the cold stone floor. He instinctively covered his nakedness. Pathetically, he had only his hands, the left of which was clawed and covered nothing. His body was bruised all over.

'Get his clothes,' Bauer ordered the guard. 'Now.'

'Up,' he said firmly to Wolf, bending down to take hold of his arm and help him to his feet. Wolf stood, not without difficulty. Bauer heard no cry but saw the pain on Wolf's face, then the reason: a deep cut on his arm, doubtless from a knife. He apologised, but that's all he had time for. The guard returned with Wolf's uniform. Bauer noticed it had been folded oh so neat and tidy, not a mark on it, in great contrast to its owner. He helped Wolf draw on trousers and shirt. That would do for the moment.

'You have to walk,' he ordered Wolf. 'Move.'

Wolf nodded, held on to Bauer. They left the cellar, awkwardly made their way up, step by step, and then up the next set of steps to the first floor and out into the reception area.

Here, at last – Bauer had been expecting it – they were challenged by an officer whom the corporal had alerted. He burst through the front door in a fury.

'Halt,' the man shouted. 'Return this prisoner to the cell immediately. This is a Gestapo matter. The army has no right to interfere.'

The fellow was not in military uniform, but Bauer knew from the tirade and the leather coat that he was Gestapo. 'And who might you be?' he asked so dismissively that he thought the fellow might explode.

'I am Captain Leske of the Geheime Staatspolizei,' he shouted.

Same rank, Bauer noted. 'The army has every right to interfere, particularly the GFP,' he countered, firm in his knowledge of military law. 'Lieutenant Wolf is a serving Wehrmacht officer.'

'He's a traitor,' Leske shouted back.

Bauer crisply and coolly repeated chapter and verse of the regulations. 'Furthermore, captain,' he said, 'we are on French sovereign territory. What you have done and are doing is illegal under the terms of the armistice. I intend reporting the details to the highest authority.'

'Are you threatening a Gestapo officer in the course of his duty?' Leske demanded.

Bauer saw sweet reason was lost on this thug. 'If you don't get out of my way,' he said, drawing his pistol for the first time in anger since joining the GFP, 'I will arrest you. If you resist, I will shoot you, paragraph fourteen (a) if you care to look up the GFP regulations.' There was no such regulation but now wasn't the time to quibble about legality, especially with the Gestapo.

Leske's face went from red to purple to white.

'Russia or dead,' Bauer said, cocking his pistol. 'I can't tell you the pleasure it would give me to pull the trigger.'

'You will regret this, captain,' said the officer. 'The Reichsführer takes a dim view of his agents being attacked.'

Bauer couldn't be bothered arguing. He was sure the Reichsführer did take a dim view of a Wehrmacht officer felling one of his men, but the Reichsführer was in Berlin and they were in Pau. Leske glowered as he walked ahead of Bauer's pistol, out through the door and down the steps to Bauer's car.

'Start the engine,' Bauer ordered the French driver, a roly-poly middled-aged man whose name was Mascaro. 'Over there,' he motioned Leske away with his revolver as he pushed Wolf into the back seat of the car. 'Open the gate,' he ordered the guard at the entrance. As Bauer got into the back seat, Leske moved in front of the car. 'Go,' Bauer ordered Mascaro loud enough for Leske to hear over the sound of the engine. Mascaro hesitated. 'Run him down,' Bauer shouted.

'With pleasure,' Mascaro said under his breath, putting his foot down hard and releasing the clutch. The car leapt, Leske shrieked and jumped but the front mudguard collected him and sent him sprawling. The guard started to close the gate. Mascaro drove right through it. As they sped away, the car skidded dangerously on the slushy roadway. Mascaro quickly brought it under control. He grinned into the rear-view mirror at Bauer, who had not decided yet where to take Wolf.

'Drive around,' he said, 'in case our friends follow.'

Follow they did. Mascaro indicated to Bauer, who looked back to see another car like theirs leave the villa and try to tail them. In vain. Mascaro knew his town better than they did, and, with a cavalier attitude to speed, it pleased him immensely to give a finger to the Gestapo, even if it was in favour of another of the occupiers. All it took was one sharp strategic turn. Mascaro headed into the old town. The Gestapo nearly went over the cliff on a long detour down to the railway station.

'The Hôtel de France,' Bauer directed. Better there than the *commissariat de police*, where St Jean might arrest poor Wolf because of the duel, diplomatic immunity or no. At the Armistice Commission, Wolf would at least be under the direct protection of the Wehrmacht. He asked Mascaro to radio for a doctor to be called urgently.

'Thank you, sir,' Wolf murmured.

'Young man,' said Bauer, 'what on earth have you done?'

'Can you tell me the time, sir?' Wolf asked.

Bauer showed Wolf his watch. Well after eleven. Wolf nodded and slumped back.

'They took me from my hotel,' he said. 'I need to get into my room,' but he was shivering so much he stopped, and Bauer, foraging about in the back for something warm, told him he could talk later. His search was unsuccessful, so he removed his coat and covered Wolf with that, though his feet stuck out the bottom, bare and cold.

'God almighty,' Bauer muttered. Even his feet were bruised.

A BOOKSHOP,
RUE LAMOTHE, PAU

Early afternoon, Saturday, 13th December 1941

By early afternoon, Eleanor's optimism was fading. She had tried the low end of the town without success. Now she went to one of the cafés along the boulevard in which refugees, stateless and out of money, gazed out to a safety that was beyond their reach. Eleanor had a passport, the best passport of all, and she had dollars, which would stand for the Spanish visa she did not have. Henk's lack of papers — well, she thought, her dollars would solve that once they were across the border.

Determined, she placed some francs into the hand of the waiter and asked straight out. He laughed, said nothing, pointed to the weather, pocketed the money and returned to his routine. What was she going to do? Call the police? This put her off any of the other cafés along Boulevard des Pyrénées. Boulevard des Voleurs, she thought, boulevard of thieves. She couldn't just keep going from one café to the next, seeking passage into Spain. Their German pursuers were in Pau, after all. It would never have occurred to her their number was but two. In her imagination they were the Gestapo and they were many.

Soon she was sitting in the foyer of the hotel of her ill-fated honeymoon. Didn't the miserable place owe her? She'd been there hardly five minutes when a man tried to sell her coffee. Tempted as she sorely was, she replied she didn't need coffee, she needed to get to Spain. The fellow nodded. He might be able to help.

'How much?' she asked.

'It depends,' said the man, whose shifty smile confirmed her suspicions that she was talking to someone who could and might do a deal.

'On what?' she asked.

'Coffee and other goods one way,' he said airily, 'people the other, the risks are bigger.' He himself could, for a fee, take her to someone who might help. They haggled, but briefly. The desk manager behind his pince-nez was taking too close an interest in what might have been obvious to anyone running a hotel, even in normal times. Should she be flattered? she wondered, but decided the manager was being intolerably impertinent. She flashed him a waspish look as she tailed her gold-toothed rat out of the foyer and onto the street.

She followed him at a good ten yards' distance as he scurried along the street named for a famous French marshal. Just past the post office, he nipped down a side street – it was all she could do to keep up – and stopped outside a bookshop. Eleanor joined him and they both pretended to peruse the books displayed in the window.

'The woman,' he murmured, indicating the woman at the counter inside. 'Say M'sieur Edouard recommended you to her.' He strolled away, never to be seen again.

Eleanor easily kept her gaze on the books inside; she couldn't have moved if a truck had hit her. Among the volumes on the shelf, with its cover facing out, was her last book in its French translation, *La Femme Américaine*. Alongside was a small picture of her by a young photographer whose name she now forgot. She wasn't sure whether to feel proud or terrified. There was the life she was leaving, the life ruined by this race of barbarians. She thought of Sylvia and of Madeleine, and she missed them so much her heart hurt. Really, she wanted to cry, and she wanted a shoulder to cry on. But this descent into feeling sorry for herself wasn't getting her anywhere. Better to feel terrified. That at least was motivation.

The bell tinkled as she entered the bookstore. The woman behind the counter, of a similar age to Eleanor, said a bright 'Good day'. There was something attractive about her, beyond the obvious sympathy that an author might have for a bookseller, especially one who displayed her photograph and book in the front window. Eleanor wondered if the woman might recognise her, but managed for once to dismiss her vanity.

Eleanor responded and smiled, and then wandered the shelves. How was she going to raise the subject of a guide into Spain? she wondered. The smell of books, the warmth of the shop, so warm she removed her coat and put it over her arm – this was making her heart ache. Oh God, more photographs: Gide, Alain-Fournier, Breton, Aragon, even raptors like Hemingway. She would concede him a place. Just. Hah, no James Joyce, she noted. That made her feel better. All the bookseller needed to do was offer her a cup of tea. Eleanor found a book. Just the ticket. She went over and placed it on the counter, a Michelin guide to Spain, discreetly covering it with her coat.

'An excellent choice,' said the woman. 'Have you made your travel arrangements yet?'

'No,' Eleanor replied. 'A M'sieur Edouard recommended you most keenly.'

The woman looked about, and though no one else was in the shop, she lowered her voice. 'You are American, are you not?' she said in perfect English. 'Surely you can cross into Spain on the train to Canfranc without any difficulty.'

Why now? Eleanor cursed herself. It infuriated her.

'Believe me, madame,' Eleanor replied in English, for any further pretence would have been insulting, 'if we could cross legally, I wouldn't be here making a nuisance of myself.'

'We?' the woman asked.

'The other is my son,' Eleanor said. She saw the woman's face register the obvious. 'She's taking a child across the Pyrénées in winter?'

'He's twenty-one,' Eleanor hastily explained, only to realise she'd made things worse. The woman clearly didn't believe for one moment she had a twenty-one-year-old son, and while this was flattering, her flaming face told the truth, for any with the eyes to see.

'Oh, for God's sake,' Eleanor exclaimed, forgetting entirely her own imaginative skills, which were on display on a shelf only a few feet away, 'he's not my son but if I explained it, you wouldn't believe me in a month of Sundays, and it's best you don't know. Just believe me, we can't cross into Spain legally.'

She wasn't sure if this had broken the ice. The woman didn't reply immediately.

'Madame,' said the bookseller gravely, 'you have no idea how hard it is at this time of year. Even our guides find it difficult. You would probably die in the attempt.'

'I doubt it,' said Eleanor boldly. 'Our winters are much colder than these, and I am as strong as an ox. I take it from your answer, though, that you might be able to oblige?'

'You are in luck,' said the woman. 'We have room for only two more.'

'How much?' Eleanor asked urgently.

'Three thousand francs,' said the woman. 'Each.'

Eleanor blanched. 'At least we're dearer than butter,' she muttered; it was the current gold standard on the black market.

'Are people not worth more?' the woman said, undeniably correct.

At this price, Eleanor would use up just about all her remaining francs unless she was foolish enough to go to a bank. She quickly calculated. Three thousand was about 80 dollars at the current Vichy official rate, 50 at the black-market rate. What on earth was she complaining about?

'I'll give you fifty dollars US for each,' she said. 'One hundred for two.'

'In dollars, one hundred and sixty,' the woman said, quoting the official rate.

Eleanor protested. Dollars were dollars, after all. The black-market rate should apply.

The bookseller shrugged her shoulders. If it were up to her, she explained, it would be no problem, but the local police were cracking down hard on the black market. The new inspector from Vichy. If you were found with dollars, you went straight to Gurs as a black marketeer. Having dollars on you was proof of guilt.

It took all of Eleanor's self-control not to go to the display shelf at the window, take down a copy of *La Femme Américaine* and declare herself the author. Did not the seller of books have a moral duty to help authors, especially one whose book had sold well and, since it was on display, was still selling?

'Is this yours?' Eleanor heard the bookseller ask, and for a moment wondered if indeed she had worked out who she was. Then she saw in the woman's left hand *Finnegans Wake*, which had fallen from the pocket of her coat onto the counter. Her right hand, shaking, was fingering each page as if it were made of gold leaf. This brought Eleanor back to reality with a jolt.

'You could have your journey into Spain in return for this,' the woman offered.

There in front of her for the third time on this journey was Lucifer, Beelzebub, Satan, Old Nick himself, full of wisdom and perfect in beauty, God's favourite cherub. 'Accept,' he urged her. 'Who would know? Isn't your need greater at this moment?'

Eleanor gently but firmly took the book from the woman's hands. 'It's not mine to sell,' she said. This, her final rejection of temptation, was, like Jesus's, the hardest – but unlike Jesus's, it came through gritted teeth. She quickly took 160 dollars from her belt and handed them over.

The woman slipped them into her pocket. Eleanor was suddenly alarmed. What the hell had she done? No receipt, no evidence of her money or what it was supposed to buy.

'Please,' said the woman, putting her hand on Eleanor's. 'Trust me. I won't cheat you. Believe me. I just hope you know what you're doing.'

With no proof other than the sympathy she'd first felt, Eleanor did believe her.

She and her young friend, the woman explained, were to come to the shop tomorrow, Sunday, at 10.15 in the morning.

'That's it?' Eleanor asked.

'You don't need to know any more,' said the woman.

Eleanor nodded her agreement. 'Until tomorrow,' she said, and departed in as cheery a mood as the events of the past eight or so days allowed, the gaping hole in her stash of dollars notwithstanding. She had their passages, and how fitting that they were procured through a bookshop.

STUDIO COLOGNE, CORNER COURS
BOSQUET AND RUE SAMONZET, PAU

Around 2pm, Saturday, 13th December 1941

An even greater balm was to discover a *parfumerie* on the corner opposite the post office. As people who knew Eleanor well would have said, this was akin to a whisky bar for an alcoholic.

Worse, it was open.

She daren't go in the way she looked – she'd be like a visitation of the plague itself, she thought. She'd lost most of her cosmetics; her hair was a greasy rat's nest. And her face? She didn't have a face anymore, just a series of expressions, most of them sour. Madeleine would understand, if only she were here. But wouldn't Madeleine, following Wilde's dictum about dealing with temptation, barge right in? Why not, if you're on your last legs carrying the plague? She pushed open the door.

The aroma was intoxicating. The proprietress and her younger assistant, both elegant in black and with complexions a worthy advertisement for their trade, neither pushed her back out the door nor held crosses up against her. Instead, they smiled, wished her a good day and asked how they could be of service. How wonderful, Eleanor thought. She smiled with the pleasure of it.

The young assistant proceeded to suggest this and that. Eleanor was happy to smell each and every one she was offered from her favourite brands – Coty, Guerlain, Lelong. Top notes of citron, and could that be ginger? Rose in the middle note down to musk at the bottom. This was time out of time.

Eleanor decided she'd buy her favourite Schiaparelli to replace the full one she'd lost when she had to leave behind her valise. All she had left was the tiny bottle she was carrying in her travelling kit and it was almost empty. But the price was what she would pay on the black market back in Paris. Had paid – indeed, how else could she have procured it? Waltzed into Printemps with ration cards or on the arm of a handsome Fritz? She noticed the prices also marked, if discreetly, in Reichsmarks. But like Cortez in search of Montezuma's gold, why was she here? A philosophy discussion? She had none of the invader's foul lucre and she'd used up most of her remaining supply of francs. Why shouldn't she pay in dollars, as she had in the bookshop? This was an open black market in the guise of a *maison de parfum*.

Eleanor made the suggestion but the proprietress countered, not unreasonably, that she might like to change her dollars into francs at a bank. Eleanor couldn't do that. Too risky.

Not that she could explain her dilemma.

The *parfumier* explained hers. She would love to oblige, but if the police found her with dollars, they'd close her shop and lock her up in Gurs. 'Even respectable people,' she added, which certainly included herself.

After such wild expectations, Eleanor realised she'd have to adjust her ambitions in a southerly direction. She saw a Lancôme and its companion crème that she liked. Were they beyond her as well?

The proprietress named the price. Eleanor considered her situation. If she went ahead, she'd have about 500 francs left, when a miserable meal of *ragoût* of rat without ration tickets cost at least 50, and a cup of real coffee, if it were to be had, was almost the same.

To hell with it, she thought and handed over the francs. What use were they in Spain or Portugal, and if she was going to die, she'd do it as elegantly as possible.

Outside, the wind had turned even colder, for it was now whistling down from the north. She pulled her woollen hat tighter over her head and gathered up her scarf. Patches of blue began appearing across the sky, a good omen for tomorrow. If this continued, she and

Henk would be on their way at last. She could return now to the hotel, for what more had she to do?

Now that she smelt like a bunch of beautiful spring flowers, her mood was lighter, her thoughts gayer. She almost missed the *salon de beauté*, which was only metres from the *parfumerie* she'd just exited. Her hair would give Medusa a run for her money. She wondered if the prices would mock or beckon her. Clean, shiny hair, or her much diminished supply of francs? Caution to the wind, she went inside and almost kissed the coiffeuse when told the price. She'd be franc-broke, but damn it all, she wouldn't look broke.

COMMISSARIAT DE POLICE, PAU

After 2.30pm, Saturday, 13th December 1941

The duel and its consequences, still far from over, had frustratingly consumed Bauer's energies and time for the rest of the morning. He learnt the details, some of which he had expected: Pichler had impugned Wolf's honour. Wolf, who'd drunk too much, responded with a challenge, and on it went to an outcome that, at least to Pichler, had been unexpected. He had chosen fists as his weapon, knowing well that Wolf lacked a working hand, and had come off second best. That would have been a great surprise to Pichler had he been conscious, but in being felled, he'd hit his head on the stone paving and was now in a coma. It was best St Jean didn't find out that this had happened on *la terre sacrée et souverain de la France,* in the middle of the Place Royale, right in front of the Hôtel de Ville. The Gestapo might be on the warpath but Bauer had more important matters to follow. At least he'd rescued Wolf, who was now safe and recovering.

'You've got something?' Bauer asked after hurrying back in response to Kopitcke's urgent call. He was dog-tired so slipped another Pervitin into his mouth. That would keep him going.

Kopitcke most certainly did have something. Following the Herr Kommissar's dictum to discard most from the list of Wehrmact deserters they had received as fools, cowards or in girl trouble, he had eight possibles to show the boss. As he précised what he'd found, he handed each relevant file to his boss. Bauer saw they didn't contain much detail, but enough.

Two were soldiers with civilian backgrounds in petty crime, always in trouble for misdemeanours, the square pegs in a round hole that could be found in every regiment. Each had disappeared while on leave. Two others had absconded from labour battalions and four were *Mischlings* who'd been kicked out under the Führer's special order the year before. Having been recalled in late August this year in the face of the Soviet campaign, these four had done a bunk. One of them, from Vienna, had been able to stay in the army much longer than the others because of operational circumstances and, it was suspected, because he'd been protected by his unit, which was mostly Austrian. Then he'd been caught escaping into Switzerland and was sent to Mauthausen as a deserter, although, strictly, he'd already been kicked out of the army. He too had been recalled like the others to the Eastern Front, but to a probationary platoon.

'He was awarded an Iron Cross!' Kopitcke exclaimed with some heat. His sympathy for someone who had fought well and wanted to fight outweighed the unfortunate 50 percent of the fellow that was Jewish. 'I can imagine he'd be angry,' he added, as cover for his own anger.

Bauer perused the file. Father a member of the National Socialist Party, joined after the *Anschluss*, though he was a member of something called the Fatherland Front before that. 'Sounds patriotic at least,' he murmured. Mother, the Jew, was dead. The file did not explain when or where or how. The fellow had done time in an Austrian labour camp. No details apart from the dates. Bauer didn't need the details. Kids were given to being hotheads. In any case, going into the army really had been the making of this fellow, whatever he had done before. Look how well he'd fitted in and how well he'd fought.

'What of the other three?' Bauer asked.

One was an officer, a lieutenant with an impeccable record, Catholic until the Nuremberg laws, who'd never had any contact with Jewish culture and who had appealed all the way to the top. Mother a Catholic, the father was the problem. He'd even gotten his mother to testify that his birth was the result of her unfaithfulness with an Aryan man, but the blood test didn't back that up. The other two were ordinary Landsers, Christians for at least one generation, Nuremberg Jews. One had been a clerk, with no front-line experience; the other, as with the one sent to Mauthausen, was an experienced front-line soldier.

'They'd all be damn angry, don't you think?' Bauer said. He easily read poor Kopitcke's confusion: how stupid we are kicking out perfectly good soldiers versus how clever we are kicking out these pretend Aryans.

He immediately discounted the two petty criminals, both city boys. Rats back into a rat's nest. The imagination of a street gangster was so dim, it sent them back to Hamburg or Berlin instead of trying to make a complete break. Of the other six, the two from labour battalions also had neither the creativity to organise flight nor the need, he figured. Sooner or later they'd be found hiding out in some rural backwater. Which left the four *Mischlings*. He discarded the clerk and kept the other three, each of whom would at least be able to kill if necessary.

'What do you think about the one from Mauthausen?' he mused. 'The Aryan half earnt the Iron Cross while the Jewish half killed our soldiers?'

His joke failed because Kopitcke agreed. 'Herr Kommissar, that's it!' he cried and Bauer was yet again disconcerted by the way his assistant's intelligence had been so assaulted by his years in the Hitler Youth. His two boys couldn't avoid joining it, but Bauer had made sure they read widely and kept their Catholic faith as antidote. The thought of his sons spurred him. Activity would take his mind off their predicament, and there was still this notion in him that if he caught the killer, his Georg would be found safe and sound. Yes, it was a bargain with God, but had not saint after saint made such a bargain?

'We go with the three "maybes",' he said abruptly. 'Until otherwise proven.'

He sent Kopitcke to request that photostat copies of the official Wehrmacht photographs of the three be made and distributed. 'Request, Kopitcke,' he reminded his assistant, 'don't order.'

Then came Bauer's breakthrough.

GARE DE PAU

Around 3pm, Saturday, 13th December 1941

Bauer and Kopitcke hurried through the vestibule of the train station passenger hall. A gendarme was waiting and took them into the office.

'Good afternoon,' said Bauer affably to two youths sitting on a bench. He shook the hand of each in turn, which impressed them. Usually, an adult hand on them was for reproof. One was a spindly reed who had shot up and out along his limbs, with manhood sprouting on his upper lip. The other was still a boy.

'I hear you've got an interesting story to tell me,' said Bauer.

It was the boy who was the bolder, as if the other were muted by the awkward changes in his body. While the boy's patois, which was littered with Occitan, taxed Bauer's French, he thought it better to leave the youths with the impression he was M'sieur Le Commissar, as introduced, than to ask the gendarme to translate.

They were farm boys, cousins; their families' farms were across the Gave de Pau, beyond the spread of the town. In the hayloft of the barn in a far corner of the spindly lad's farm, not much used, they had chased a kitten, but then a young man had jumped down after them.

'He didn't have no shoes or socks,' said the boy.

'Did he catch you?' Bauer asked.

Yes, he did. One had been whacked on the head, the other pushed over, with a bruise on his knee to prove it.

'He was a Boche,' said the boy. 'He spoke Boche.'

'How did you know it was German?' Bauer asked.

'From the newsreels,' exclaimed the mute boy, suddenly unmuted.

They had run to the railway station, to the gendarmes – it wasn't far – and two gendarmes had gone with them to investigate, but the German was gone, a great disappointment to the boys.

The gendarme, now taking up the tale, said this had been reported to the police as a matter of course.

Bauer bade Kopitcke produce photographs of the three Wehrmacht *Mischlings*.

'Him!' cried the boy. The reed nodded his head vehemently. Hadn't he said he'd been *un vrai* Boche? A soldier!

Heinrich Pohl, lance corporal, the Iron Cross Landser from the Wehrmacht's Second Mountain Division, via Mauthausen.

Bauer radioed Inspector St Jean to expedite the distribution of Pohl's photograph, not only to his men but to the border post at Col de Somport. He himself would have the Spanish authorities in Canfranc and Jaca alerted.

'Add a reward,' he said. 'One thousand francs.'

St Jean almost choked. The amount was a considerable enticement, enough to buy five pairs of leather shoes on the black market, but his office couldn't possibly afford that. Assured by Bauer that this would be paid by the German authorities, St Jean hurried the printing of the photograph and reward on a wanted poster. The sooner he was rid of these damn Germans, the better.

BOULEVARD DES PYRÉNÉES, PAU

Around 3.30pm, Saturday, 13th December 1941

Standing in woods on a rise, Henk had observed the gendarmes cross the open field with the two little pests who'd disturbed his hiding place. Pau and the small towns and farms around were alive with refugees, like fleas on a dog. Yesterday afternoon, he'd been chased off by a group who'd taken over a disused shed where he had hoped to hide until evening. He thought himself in luck to have found the barn and had returned that morning. He'd been able to shelter from the rain and sleet, been able to dry his clothes, his boots and socks, air the wounds on his feet and stay warm. The building had no livestock, and the rain presumably acted as a further deterrent to any visitors. Yesterday, when he'd left, the sun was well gone. Only the farm dogs had detected him as he returned to the town along the lanes, which had been deserted. He'd made a mistake today expecting he would be safe. The appearance of those boys in the afternoon had reminded him it was a Saturday. No school. For want of anything better to do, he had started to read her book and had not noticed time pass, let alone the entrance of these two intruders.

They'd seen his kitten chasing mice across the floor and had tried to catch it, completely surprising him. Had this been war and they the enemy, he'd have been done for, caught reading a stupid book. Luckily for him, they were kids. Luckily for them, he hadn't killed both. But he'd snarled at them in German. Stupid, stupid. As soon as they'd run off, he slipped away over a stone fence behind which he crouched for cover. Then he ran into the evergreen wood, where he waited to see if they returned.

Which they had done, with two gendarmes. Better to know the authorities were on to him than not. Hopefully, they'd reckon on him heading south for the border. While the gendarmes inspected the barn, he doubled back, following a creek running through the evergreen wood towards the Gave de Pau; he eschewed the lanes he'd taken yesterday. The ground was slushy and frozen in parts. Few people were out braving the arctic wind at the spot where he emerged onto a path into the village and where he felt most exposed. Head down, beret pulled over his forehead, he trudged along the main street and across a stone bridge to the steep medieval streets below the chateau, expecting all the time to be picked up. His belief in himself was slipping.

His trail took him past the square where yesterday, in his crazy reverie, he'd almost handed himself in. The memory of what he'd nearly done made him tense. He clenched his jaw, hunched his shoulders and willed himself on, although his legs suddenly each weighed a ton and his feet were sore. Nazi flags above the building flapped wildly in the strong wind, whipping the air. In the blink of an eye, he was back in Mauthausen, same flags, same sound, except it was the sound of the whip on his face and on his back. His knees buckled and he stumbled.

'Young man, young man,' cried an old woman who was passing in the opposite direction towards the funicular. She grabbed his arm. Although old, she was peasant-strong, and he was able to right himself.

'Merci, madame,' he gasped, shaken. 'Merci.'

Thank God he remembered to speak French, but that was the extent of it. He could barely say anything else, and she was asking him if he was sick. He hoped '*non*' was the right answer. The old lady smiled.

Pointing up to the German flags, she muttered a harsh curse, and he nodded and managed a grin. Then his kitten started to complain, and he couldn't avoid showing the woman, who was even more charmed. She tore off a hunk of the bread she had in her basket and handed it to him, saying a few words which were as clear to him in their kindness as if she had spoken in perfect German. He knew what to say but was so touched, his lips moved but nothing came out. His eyes went moist. She saw and patted his arm and she spoke again.

What she said was that he should always remember that God loved him.

Again, words didn't really matter. Her meaning was clear. Even had he understood, he'd hardly been a good Catholic, the faith in which he'd been raised to cover his mother's Jewishness. After the fascist putsch in Austria in January 1934, when he was still at school, he'd discarded any semblance of religion to embrace the thrills of Marx. Discovering he was a Jew after the Nazis invaded in '38 had done nothing to propel him back to religion. Marx had been a Jew, after all. Clearly you didn't need to be religious to be a Jew.

All this notwithstanding, the woman's kindness was too much for him. His chest heaved as an involuntary sob tried to escape. He fought to suppress it, and he cursed as he ripped out his handkerchief to clean his face. What a mess he was, falling to pieces right on the lip of freedom. Look what had happened yesterday, right here, an act of insanity. Now this. He shouldn't have started reading her damned book. How weak he was to let a story rip away his defences, exposing needs he thought he had under control. What had come first, that book or just being at the end of his tether, he didn't know. What did it matter? Things were what they were. He had to focus. Yesterday had been a disappointment, but today, surely after all this, things would work out. His kitten purred under his chin. He tickled its neck.

'Fingers crossed, cat,' he murmured in German and gave the kitten a piece of the bread and tucked it back into his coat.

Towards 4pm, Saturday, 13th December 1941

'We're one step behind,' Bauer said as they walked back from the barn to the car, where Mascaro stood, smoking. 'We're always reacting, never getting ahead of the fellow. He's a soldier, a good one. Do you think he's headed for the Spanish border?'

'No,' Kopitcke replied. 'Eventually, yes, but why didn't he go yesterday? I would have.'

Bauer agreed.

'Why? What's holding him up? What's stopping him? The weather? No money to get a guide? He wouldn't be the only one stranded here. All those Jews sitting outside the Spanish and Portuguese consulates, they haven't killed two German soldiers.'

'He's not alone, sir,' Kopitcke reminded him. 'The woman. She can't be his mother, the mother's dead. It said so in the file. She was the Jew.'

'Which makes this woman?' Bauer asked. Poor Kopitcke reddened. 'Until otherwise proven?' Bauer added. Kopitcke couldn't quite bring himself to say it.

'Come now,' Bauer pressed. 'Haven't you seen an older woman you fancied?'

He had, but Kopitcke, raised a Protestant and now a Nazi, couldn't possibly admit such a thing. 'No, sir,' he lied with vehemence.

'The thing is, Kopitcke,' Bauer said, 'we know she's looking for *passeurs*. We know he can't speak French. We know she's got expensive tastes from the clothes and the cosmetics we found. She's the moneybags. That's why he's still here. Would a classy woman like that spend the night in a hayloft? She's not the Virgin Mary, that's for sure. No, she's in a hotel, but we've had no reports of any single woman of that description registering since yesterday. Yet she's here, and wherever she's staying, I bet she got him inside last night. Then he spent today hiding here while she's gone out and about trying to get them passages to Spain.'

Now they had identified Pohl, he and Kopitcke would go after him and the woman, with or without St Jean's help.

'I'd start with this place, *M'sieur le Commissar*,' said Mascaro. Bauer had asked his professional advice about a cosmetics shop, fashionable or not. The American woman had lost all her cosmetics on the freight train, and she had money. He was making a reasonable bet on her vanity. 'Between us, they also do business with the occupier,' Mascaro added, as if forgetting who Bauer and his offsider were.

They were outside the shop of a hundred fragrances on the corner where Eleanor had tended her vanity that very afternoon. Kopitcke in such a place would be the proverbial bull in a china shop, Bauer thought, so ordered him to stay in the car.

The bell announced his entry. The shop was as still and peaceful as a chapel. He was bonjoured with charm by the elegant proprietress and her young assistant. He bonjoured back just as charmingly. But charm, of course, strikes the sight only, and Bauer knew better than to pretend he was not a cop – the car alone was blindingly obvious – and a German one at that.

The proprietress gushed at his *merveilleux français*. 'A fragrance to take back to your wife?'

'No, alas, not right now,' said Bauer with genuine regret. He was here on official business. He went out of his way to explain that the case he was working on – the murder of two young men, just out of short pants, in an ambush by a German Jew – was entirely a German matter, with no implications for France or any French.

'But no one of that description ever comes into a shop like this,' replied the proprietress, puzzled.

'The young man has an accomplice,' Bauer explained and described an older, possibly American, woman with brown hair, a woman of taste and elegance. At that, he produced the bottle of Schiaparelli he had found inside the woman's valise and that he'd had the foresight to fetch on their way here. Eventually, he would give it to his wife.

The francs that Eleanor had so recently handed over to the proprietress were burning a hole in her pocket.

'No, m'sieur, no Americans have come in here for quite some time,' she replied as she casually moved to shield the bottles of perfume they hadn't yet returned to the display shelf. 'At least we can still rely on our German friends,' she added with an insincere smile.

She was too late. Bauer had already spotted the bottles, just as he had detected the faintest of warnings the woman's eyes had sent her assistant. The woman might deal with the occupier, he realised, but it was dealing of the double sort. No matter. His quarry had been here, most likely within the past hour or so. If only he'd had the nous to work this angle out earlier.

He kept up the façade of charm and gentility until, as he was about to leave, he picked up one of the stray bottles of scent, a Lancôme. Opened already, he noted. He put it to his nose.

'On second thoughts,' he said, thinking of his wife.

Standing outside the shop moments later with his wife's present tucked away in his pocket, he looked around at the pedestrians walking briskly by, their gazes fixed on the footpath. They saw the car by the kerb, he realised, and while Mascaro was in his French uniform, Kopitcke was in the back seat with his square German head. He could sense an invisible ring around him on the sidewalk, as if he were contagious.

Right across the street he saw the Hôtel Continental, the billet of Lieutenant Wolf. His cases were colliding. He wondered if the French police were still in the lobby defending French sovereignty against the Gestapo.

At this very moment, Eleanor walked out of the *salon de coiffure*, her spirit revived by the shine on her freshly washed hair and another application of her new Lancôme scent. She had shared some with the girl who'd washed and dried her hair, insisting despite the young lady's protest that such a fragrance was too expensive to waste on her. It was as if Eleanor had sprayed her with fairy dust, she was so happy. Her fiancé was about to arrive.

Eleanor, herself in a fairy-dust mood, ignored the cold wind to enjoy the luxury of her hair uncovered, like silk flowing freely over her ears and neck. She returned to the *parfumerie* on the corner, just to gaze again at the window display. Through the window she saw the proprietress and gave her a discreet wave, only to see a look of horror cross the woman's face and the strongest indication from her eyes to get the hell out of there. Then, reflected in the window, she saw behind her the car parked at the kerb, police or Gestapo. Unmistakeable. She was briefly frozen to the spot and had to force her feet to move, oh so slowly and casually, stopping fleetingly to glance into the window of another shop, although if you'd asked her what it displayed, she couldn't have told you.

Bauer was still staring at the Continental. Was there any need for him to go into the foyer? No Gestapo car was parked ostentatiously outside. They must have given up. Then his nose sensed the fragrance that wafted around him, the same fragrance, he recognised it. His eyes sought the source. That woman? Or that one over there? Neither fitted the description – an older, elegant brunette. Another was gazing casually into a shop window, a real beauty, but she was young, her hair a shining auburn. He looked in the other direction: a brunette under her hat, then another brunette, but they were together. Sisters? Then he saw a young woman, even younger, waiting by the kerb; she waved excitedly to an approaching boy.

He watched as the sweethearts kissed and the girl begged the boy to smell her neck, both sides, and both wrists. Touched as he was by young love prospering in these hard times, he couldn't help being disappointed. The black gloom was waiting over both shoulders. Was Georg dead? He shook the thought and the gloom away. This was getting him nowhere.

Back in the car, he noticed Kopitcke sniffing the air with distaste. The fragrance clung to his nostrils and seemed to fill the car. What a future awaited them, Bauer mused dismally, if the Kopitckes inherited the world.

Late afternoon to early evening, Saturday, 13th December 1941

Before they went searching the shady quarter around Rue des Cordeliers, Bauer told Kopitcke and Mascaro to go to the canteen in the *commissariat de police* to eat, and then return in half an hour.

Bauer had more important things to do than eat; he went to the communications room. The only cable addressed directly for him was from the *Ortskommandant* in Nevers, barking about his lack of progress in catching the killer, how it was now the third day since the murders and how long did Bauer think their patience would last and so on and so on. The threat of being dismissed was still there, except Frankfurt had been replaced with the Russian front. The German military was run on threats, direct or implied: do this or else. In Bauer's case, if only the *Ortskommandant* carried out his threat. Yes, sir, thank you very much, sir, the Moscow front, if you don't mind. On the spot, he would find his son.

He tucked the cable into his pocket. Then he ran his eyes over the available battle reports from Moscow. Any fool could see, reading between the spinning lines, that things were still going badly. There was no point in cabling his pals closer to the front who'd been helping. They had enough to do dealing with the Russian attacks. If there was any news about Georg, they'd let him know when they could.

'One of your boys is in Africa, isn't he, sir?' asked the communications clerk and handed him a sheaf of cables. 'Lots coming in.'

Bauer read, expecting something uplifting. This was Rommel, after all, the Afrika Korps. The news, however, was bad. The British had been attacking near Gazala since early morning. Tense, his mouth suddenly dry, he read down through what he was strictly not supposed to see. Indians had given a bloody nose to the panzers.

'Indians?' Bauer said out loud in astonishment. 'From India?'

The clerk shrugged his shoulders. 'That's what it says, sir.' Bauer went to the preliminary casualty list just as Kopitcke came to find him. He and Mascaro had eaten. They brought with them a copy of the 'wanted' poster.

'I've brought you a sausage too, sir,' said Kopitcke.

Bauer didn't look up, even when he'd passed the *B*s in the officers' list and there was no Karl-Friedrich Bauer, not until he reached the end. Then he took the sausage from Kopitcke, which was between two sodden pieces of bread.

'Thank you, Kopitcke,' he said. 'Very thoughtful of you.' He hadn't eaten but wasn't hungry. The Pervitin pills seemed to blunt his appetite, no bad thing when he was so busy. But since it was in his hand, he ate Kopitcke's kind offering.

'We'll go on foot,' he said as they came outside. Mascaro, with his French uniform, would be their cover and their guide.

HEDAS, PAU

Early evening, Saturday, 13th December 1941

Having drawn a series of blanks along the main streets in the area, they descended a rough pathway that curved down into the ravine, around the back wall of the chateau. The arctic wind was blowing hard from all directions, swirling leaves and paper every which way and keeping most people indoors, windows and doors firmly shut. To Bauer, the place looked more picturesque than he'd been led to believe by Inspector St Jean's sneering reference to a smoky rabbit warren of Spanish anarchists and communists. You could see stars across a clear, moonless night sky. Lanes normally clogged with muck, and walls and roofs covered in grime and slime, had been rain-swept clean. Even the Lord might see that it was good, but not Mascaro. The Spaniards were still there in their makeshift hovels and, worse, an infestation of refugees from all over Europe. Every inhabitant was either a smuggler or looking for someone to smuggle them across the frontier.

The sound of voices came and went with the gusts of wind. Lights were on in most windows, either from candles or paraffin lamps. These days, any dwelling with a secure roof, and sometimes not, was a boarding house, although few were registered as such. Boarding houses had concierges, although that wasn't the word Mascaro used: sometimes women operating on their own who collected the rent from their tenants, sometimes toughs who'd pushed in to run a protection racket, especially in the hovels packed with refugees from Central Europe, the Jews.

Threats and a little bit of bribery were the only way with any of them, according to Mascaro. Few here had proper resident permits; they could be kicked out over the border into Franco's welcoming arms just like that, and they knew it. Usually they tried to keep out of the way of the cops, but now, on foot, and in the dark, Mascaro caught them at home. It was dinner time, after all.

'This man, a Boche, doesn't speak French,' Mascaro barked his explanation at the residents of the first house after barging in. He handed over the 'wanted' poster. 'Arrived only yesterday,' he added and showed a few extra francs, to be handed over only on receipt of a useful answer.

'We only got yids here,' said the Spanish tough. 'You know that. You got their names.'

'There's a reward,' said Mascaro, stabbing at the figure on the poster.

'What about a middle-aged woman, classy, possibly American?' Bauer asked. 'Arrived yesterday.'

The tough cackled. 'Classy? She must be hard up.' He shook his head and laughed again. This place, the walls long stripped of paint and now stained and cracked, was a human dump.

In the next, a woman stood defiantly at the door, Spanish and tougher than an elephant. 'But yes' was her response, followed by 'possibly, maybe'. The more specific Bauer and Mascaro became, the less 'possibly', she became, the less 'maybe'. They realised all she cared about was the cash and she'd say anything to get it.

And so it went, door to frustrating door. Mascaro even pushed his way into some of the houses, room to room, kicking the doors open, startling the hell out of the occupants.

'You can tell the Jews, can't you?' Mascaro said. 'Frightened like rabbits.'

Kopitcke chafed under orders from Bauer to keep his mouth shut. What a haul they were passing up here.

'We're not after Jews,' Bauer had to remind him, 'we're after the murderers of two German soldiers.' Sometimes he wanted to send

Kopitcke right back to the Brownshirts, whence he'd come. Didn't he realise a lot of these Jews had been kicked out of Germany? What did Kopitcke want? To send them right back?

Then they came to the Hôtel Cosmopolitan, the second in the area claiming that status. The first, clinging to the passage that curved down from the street, had been almost respectable, the sort of place in which Bauer expected his '*madame américaine*', as he was now calling her, to hide. He had perused the register and gone with Mascaro room to room. Kopitcke, in tow, was their bloodhound, whose nose would detect the presence of the cat. Kopitcke's nose remained dry.

Bauer followed Mascaro in.

'Ah, it's you,' said Madame Dumas, matter-of-fact, when she saw Mascaro. He might have returned from a short errand. 'I haven't seen you around for a while.' Mascaro was acquainted with her – not as well as the local constables were, but he knew who she was. He'd told Bauer she'd been here since well before the arrival of the Spanish, a local fixture, one of the few remaining concierges who was French. 'Too grand for me now, are you?' she added.

'No, Madame Dumas,' Mascaro replied. 'Just don't get around these parts anymore.'

'Hah,' sniffed Dumas. 'The place is full of riff-raff these days.'

Mascaro slapped the 'wanted' poster on her counter.

'Who is it this time?' she asked and pushed her glasses up her nose so she could see the photograph clearly.

'A murderer,' Mascaro responded. 'If you'd seen him, it'd be in the last twenty-four hours.' She tut-tutted and said she didn't take in murderers and she'd know one if she saw one, yes indeed. She peered more closely at the photograph on the poster.

'No,' she said. 'But he's a Boche, isn't he? That's a Boche uniform. I wouldn't have a Boche here, you know that.'

'What about a middle-aged woman?' Bauer asked. 'A bourgeois. Would have checked in late yesterday. Brunette, could be American; she wears classy fragrances, smokes Chesterfields. A woman with your taste would certainly recognise her.'

Madame Dumas's sweet disposition suddenly went. 'How would I know classy fragrances or Chesterfields?' she complained, ignoring Bauer and addressing herself to Mascaro. 'Our conquerors take everything. Butter's not to be had, they take all our olives, they take all the good cuts of meat. Has your wife served you up any beef in the last year? Perfumes,' she grumbled. 'They probably spray it on their balls, they're so ignorant.'

Mascaro didn't know what to say. Or if Bauer would take offence. What the hell was she doing?

'Talk about a New Europe?' she persisted. 'Pétain, he's senile.'

'Steady on,' Mascaro intervened at last. 'You can't say that sort of thing.'

'I just did,' said Dumas defiantly. 'What are you going to do about it? Arrest me? I gave a husband and three boys to France in the last war. Husband and the eldest are in the ground. The remaining two couldn't care less about their old mother – that war did something to them.'

'Yes, madame,' said Bauer diplomatically. He understood her feelings. But since she had sons, she might think of the mothers of the two boys who had been murdered.

Dumas was having none of that. 'Boches killing Boches? They should do more of it.' She went to the doorway that led into her rooms. 'You should be looking after us, real French people, not helping the Boches,' she said and slammed the door, and suddenly the light in the vestibule went out.

Kopitcke was enraged. 'Arrest her,' he demanded of Mascaro.

'Pipe down,' said Bauer. 'It's all right, Mascaro.' The poor fellow had turned a terrible colour.

Bauer took the register nevertheless. It was still on the counter. He turned on his torch and perused it. There was no entry for yesterday or today. He pushed it back with a sigh. There wasn't much else he could achieve. That damn American woman was around; she'd bought herself enough protection. But she couldn't stay hidden. Nor could Lance Corporal Pohl.

*

They returned to the Armistice Commission. Bauer looked in on Lieutenant Wolf, who was still sleeping. He went to the communications room for further news from the Moscow front and from North Africa, and sent his boy outside Gazala one of his short 'from the old man' cables of encouragement. He still hadn't told his wife Georg was missing in Russia.

HÔTEL COSMOPOLITAN, PAU

After 10pm, Saturday, 13th December 1941

Eleanor had eaten in a café further away, where her now-fashionable and clean hair, not to forget her perfume, were less obvious. She hadn't been able to slip past Madame Dumas unnoticed on return. Oddly, she thought, Dumas said nothing about her hair, or her fragrance. Just a cheery good evening, hoping she would sleep well. She went up to her room to await Henk. She had no idea when he would arrive but hoped it would be after the concierge was asleep. If the wretch ever slept.

Reading was like breathing to Eleanor, something she did as second nature, but tonight she may as well have tried climbing Mount Everest. First she tried the Psalms. Then, failing to concentrate, she turned to the Books of Kings and their stories about Ahab and Jezebel, and though she read the words, they may as well have been in Swahili. She even tried *Finnegans Wake* but that still worked as a soporific when the last thing she wanted to do was sleep. She got up and, bending herself double, crawled out to the window. The light above the front door was off. She could see nothing.

Where the hell was he? What if he'd been caught, just when she'd procured passages into Spain for them both? She couldn't lose him now. She returned to the bed and took out her notebook and her pencil. How absurd, she muttered, and discarded them. Despite her determination to remain awake, she drifted away.

She was too anxious to sleep deeply and easily heard a noise at the window. She leapt up, manoeuvred herself along the doghouse dormer, and there he was, down in the laneway, about to throw another pebble. She beckoned him to come up. Leaving the window unlatched, she hurried down the darkened hallway and stairs to the floor below, filled the basin with hot water and returned. None of the other residents seemed awake or up and about. She had to be calm, to behave as if nothing had changed, yet her heart was beating furiously.

His footsteps were light across the roof. After falling in through the window, he slumped onto the bed, opened his coat and removed the kitten. It was as if he were removing a mere parcel. He dropped it on the bed to fend for itself without any of his usual reassuring pettings, which were just about the only sign he had a heart. He looked dreadful, as if the spark of life was draining from his eyes. His skin was pallid and frozen. He tried to speak.

'Shh,' she said gently. She knew misery when she saw it, and to hell with her fears. She brought the basin of hot water closer, wet a cloth and began to wipe his face and his neck. He was shivering and so tense she thought he would break under her touch. She told him she'd found passages for them into Spain, leaving the next morning. Whatever was ailing him, he didn't respond; his eyes had glazed over. Figuring he was ill, she drew off his woollen pullover and opened the buttons to expose his chest. He was sweating as if fevered. She wet the cloth again, pulled back his shirt and dabbed away the sweat. Still he shivered. She quickly pulled off his boots and his socks. His feet startled her: they looked like the feet on a Greek statue, so marble white and perfect, and to touch they were ice. She lifted each foot into the hot water – and, yes, she was acutely aware of Mary washing Christ's feet. Henk's were hard and they were heavy. She could feel the burden each had borne for so long. As she soaped away the grime and the cold, kneaded the tight sinews down to his toes, the muscles under his arches, they softened, and his skin and his flesh came to life and his shivering ceased. She lifted each foot from the water, pushed the basin away and began to dry them. Since Claude had been killed, she'd touched no man intimately, not like this. The longing to be Mary tending to the feet of Christ was overthrown by another longing as her loins surged with heat. Before he could see it too, she jerked her hands away, and her face bloomed to the colour of her now lustrous hair.

But he reached down, took both her hands in his, and drew her up so he could press his face into the warmth of her neck. She felt his fingers, hard and calloused. Yet his lips, with their erotic charge, were as soft as a maiden's. This was madness, yet she could not have pushed him away if he'd been the Devil himself. Which he probably was. His hands drew hers onto the buckle of his belt. 'Please,' he said and she lifted the clasp.

She pulled open his trousers yet hesitated to touch him in the way she had always taken Claude, but he took her hand to grip him as his lips found hers. The kitten scattered for safety as they fell upon each other, pulling away only enough clothing to allow him to enter her, both of them greedy and urgent, yet exquisitely tender.

Afterwards, as Eleanor found her wits again, she laughed and so did he, a sheepish sort of laughter. Only misery could acquaint one with such a strange bedfellow. She had never experienced a man like this, neither giver nor taker, but both. They lay in a tangle of clothes and bedclothes. She felt his backside bare to the cold air and drew the blanket over him but kept her hand on his skin to stroke him. He was smooth and muscled and masculine. Oh, how she'd missed this.

He asked for a cigarette.

'That's a change,' she laughed, reaching out from under him for her case. He took one, lit it and shared it with her.

He inhaled and his head swam; he was lightheaded enough as it was. He'd had plenty of fleeting sexual encounters in his time – this was just another; she'd wanted it to happen. He'd been in such a state when he'd come to the hotel, he'd doubted he would be able to climb up to her room. He was still a mess, but he managed a smile. How strange life was.

'You have a beautiful smile,' she remarked. 'You should smile more often.'

'Now I have something to smile about,' he said like a polite little boy. He asked details of the passages into Spain. She told all she knew, which was little. They'd be leaving tomorrow and, she assumed, they'd be doing it on foot through the passes.

'Are you sure?' he asked. He could do it, but could she? 'You have your American passport.'

'They're after me as well,' she reminded him.

'They can't know for sure who you are,' he said. 'You could be any American.'

'I don't think there's any competition around this town at the moment for being a middle-aged American woman. Give me liberty or give me death,' she said lightly, but she meant it. This bothered him. She could see his brow knit.

'The fault is mine,' he said.

'If you hadn't done what you did, I'd be sitting in a German internment camp being starved to death and you'd be back in whatever that camp was, or worse,' she said. She hadn't always believed that; now she was sure of it. But what was the point of discussing it? Done was done. You played the hand you were dealt.

His kitten intruded, looking to share the warmth and the affection, and snuggled in between them, purring. He stroked it.

'What do you think of my hair?' she asked. He hadn't said a thing. Had he noticed? He looked puzzled. He took a tuft in his hands and brought it to his nose.

'It smells nice,' he said.

'It didn't this morning, or yesterday,' she said.

'I didn't smell it this morning or yesterday,' he said. 'You would strike me.'

'I'll strike you now,' she responded.

'Ah,' he said 'Like I am your husband.'

'Not at all,' she said. 'They were much more observant than you.' Both Freddy and Claude, they noticed, they always told her how beautiful she looked.

'They? You have more than one?'

'Freddy was first but we divorced,' she explained. 'Then came the louse but that turned out to be illegal because he was married already. That rather put me off marriage.'

'And after that?'

She realised she hadn't thought much about Claude lately, if at all. Grief, or what she had thought was grief, her companion for so long, and the anger she had refused to recognise, were gone. When exactly, she had no idea. She was in a new world now.

'I was his mistress,' she explained. 'He was married, with children.'

'You shared him?' he asked, like some maiden aunt. 'How can you share someone's love?'

She thought a little. 'I shared his time, not his love,' she said. '"All love is sweet, given or returned, common as light is love, and its familiar voice wearies not ever." Shelley, one of the great poets.'

'You were not married to him,' said Henk. 'That means I can marry you.'

'Is that a formal offer?' she asked, amused.

'I would then be an American,' he said.

'You goose,' said Eleanor. 'That's not how the law works. You wouldn't be American, I'd be – ' She stopped. 'Where did you come from?' she asked. 'Vienna? I'd be Austrian. No, dear God, I'd be German. Frankly, sonny, you're not a good catch.'

'But I am your son,' he said. 'It says so on my French papers.'

'So it does,' she laughed. 'I go from scandal to scandal.' She touched his lips with her fingers. She felt him rise immediately, thrilling her. She sighed with sweet anticipation and moved to draw him in. This time, they went slower and more deliberate and sweeter and deeper.

After, when she opened her eyes, he was already asleep, his face nestled tenderly into her neck. She enveloped him with her body and drew the blanket over them both. Outside, the wind whistled and their enemies rested. They were safe. The kitten returned. She smiled as it crept between them. She was aware of how strongly he smelt – musky, unwashed, slightly sickly, a heady and dangerous draught for her, used to her fastidious Claude. This was how she imagined Yann from her novel would have smelt, if only she'd known it. Breathing him in, like smoke from an opium pipe, she was carried away to the deepest and most contented slumber she'd had since the outbreak of the war.

HÔTEL COSMOPOLITAN, PAU

After 9am, Sunday, 14th December 1941

When she awoke, he hadn't moved. She had gotten up only once during the night, to use the bathroom below, and had returned to where she'd lain beside him. Gazing at him now so minutely, she found that freed of its snarls and worries and with its golden bristles glinting in the morning sun, a face she'd first considered malevolently elfish was the face of a handsome Pan. Likewise, his ill-cut hair. She saw it was flecked with gold. In its disarray, it looked Arcadian. She ran her fingers through its wiry thickness.

When she looked back, his eyes were open, two intense shots of cobalt staring out from some other realm, of sadness and melancholy. The past, she inferred. The room was so still, you could see motes of dust hovering in the light of the sun streaming in through a gap in the curtains.

She had no idea what would happen if they made it into Spain. Was he really set on Jerusalem? Could she get him into the United States with her? Her mother, whose love and patience she had tried severely over the years, would have a heart attack. She blew this line of idle chatter away, content for the moment to enjoy having neither past nor future.

Then he came back to her, noticing her, and he managed a smile.

'Where have you been?' she asked.

He could not tell her that, his hold on the present was still too fragile.

'We're almost there,' she said to encourage him.

'The sun!' he exclaimed suddenly. And yes, that really was sunlight streaming in through the window, which faced south. What the hell was the time? They sprang out of bed. She grabbed her watch. After nine. They dressed hurriedly. She parted the curtains, opened the balcony door, and she gave a start.

'What?' he said and peeked through.

The town had been washed clean. Its prettiness held them only fleetingly. Should he escape across the roof in full daylight? Children put paid to that as they burst excitedly from a house nearby to play in the sun.

She gave him half her remaining francs. 'Don't forget to eat,' she reminded him and said she would walk past the statue of Henry IV on Place Royale at ten. She gave him the location of the bookshop, just in case. She didn't specify in case of what. In case he was late? Just in case, that was all; although how he, with his sense of direction, would find it, she left to the gods. He grabbed his kitten, his knapsack. She would descend, he would follow closely, enough sound on the stairs for one.

Before she opened the door, he kissed her chastely on one cheek, touching the other with his calloused fingers. 'Mama,' he said with a cheeky smile. She laughed, as much from the fun she was having as for the joy in her heart and the thrill of life coursing through her.

Other inhabitants were up, the violinist was playing, voices laughed. She had a strange sense of the day's ordinariness, a Sunday, a day of rest, no war, no Gestapo; slaughter and pursuit were to be given a rest. The sun was in the vestibule.

Eleanor saw the concierge's door was shut. She nodded. Henk slipped past her and out the door. Eleanor stood, pretending to look out at the morning as she savoured the smell of him hovering in the still air like the top note of a perfume, musky with a slightly sour flavour. Madame Dumas wasn't making an appearance.

Eleanor hurried back up to the room. She got hot water, freshened up, preened her hair, ministered to her skin with her cosmetics and sprayed on her Lancôme. There was no sense she was about to leave on a journey on which she might die. Nothing so grim crossed her mind. She was acting like a schoolgirl because that's exactly how she felt. What would Sylvia or Madeleine say? she wondered as she packed what little she had back into her rucksack and drew on her coat. She knew what Madeleine would say: 'Lucky you, darling.' Sylvia would be just a little bit Baltimore-Presbyterian shocked but pretend not to be.

A sharp knock at the door threw Eleanor out of her reveries and on her guard.

'Who is it?' she demanded.

The door opened; Eleanor had forgotten to turn the lock after returning. Madame Dumas pushed in.

'Did madame sleep well last night?' she asked with honeyed malice.

'Perfectly well, thank you,' Eleanor answered. 'Can I be of assistance?'

'How fortunate for madame to have found such a powerful sleeping draught,' Dumas said, 'and at such a late hour.'

She had seen Henk after all. How loud had they been?

'Yes,' she replied. 'Reading helps enormously.'

Dumas sneezed and then she produced the 'wanted' poster with Henk's photograph, clear and no mistaking him. 'HEINRICH POHL', it said. Eleanor knew his real name at last. 'WANTED FOR MURDER.'

'What is that to do with me?' Eleanor asked as lightly as she could.

'It has everything to do with you, madame,' said Dumas, as sweet as your grandmother. 'Your lover is wanted for murder and you are his accomplice. I can't have murderers in my hotel, you understand.'

'You are mistaken,' said Eleanor. 'I am about to leave. If you'll kindly get out of my way.'

Suddenly, Madame Dumas pushed Eleanor back with astonishing strength, slipped back out the door and locked it.

'You have a choice,' said Dumas from the other side of the door. 'Push that money belt of yours under the door and I'll unlock it and you can go. If you don't, I'll call the police. You have thirty seconds.'

Eleanor cursed herself and cursed the concierge, who told her not to waste time. She grabbed at the door and then she hurled herself against it. Maybe this would bring someone. Should she call for help? But that would be insane.

'Ten seconds,' said Madame Dumas.

Eleanor tore away the belt and pushed it partly under the door so it stuck halfway. 'Unlock the door first or you get nothing,' she said. Dumas pulled at her end of the belt. Eleanor wouldn't let go. Madame Dumas unlocked the door, Eleanor let go of the belt and pulled the door open at the same time. Madame Dumas sprang at Eleanor to push her back inside so she could grab the belt and lock her in again. Then she would call the police, keep Eleanor's money and get the reward.

Madame Dumas's leap was her last, for she had thrown herself onto the knife that Eleanor was holding at an angle, just as Henk had shown her, and it was now deep in Dumas's upper gut. Her eyes and face were astonished; she had no idea what had happened. She looked down, saw the protruding knife handle, saw blood spout in a single gush, went to cry out and slumped to the floor. Her chest rattled as she expelled her last breath.

Eleanor's hand flew to her mouth in horror. She started to shake uncontrollably. If she didn't contain herself, she'd be finished. She had the presence of mind at least to remember to breathe in deeply. That at least stopped her shaking. She was then able to drag Dumas by the legs into her room. She bent down and took hold of the knife but couldn't pull it out; it was stuck. The handle and her hand were covered in sticky blood. No time. She heard the residents one floor below, moving about, talking. The water from her morning toilet was still warm. She quickly washed and dried her hands. She bent down and grabbed her money belt, mercifully not bloodstained, and her rucksack, stepped over the body and shut the door behind her.

The landing was smeared with blood. Nothing she could do about that now. She forced herself to walk at a stately pace down the steps so as not to attract attention. Behind his door, the violinist was playing exercises. Behind other doors, women called out, children played. Down to the next floor, into the vestibule and out. She'd seen no one, and no one had seen her.

At the front door, she made sure she wasn't leaving a bloodied trail. The ground outside was still damp from the rain overnight. How long she had, she couldn't tell.

9.30am, Sunday, 14th December 1941

Eleanor kept having to tell herself, 'I've killed someone, I've killed someone,' lest she believe it were only a vivid nightmare. Soon the body would be found; soon the police would be all over the place. She had half an hour before she was to fetch Henk, three-quarters of an hour to the rendezvous at the bookshop. Nearby, the bells at St Martin's called people to Mass. She heard them all too clearly. Would she find comfort or condemnation? She called herself a Christian, and felt to the depths of her soul that she was. Yet she couldn't seek forgiveness. There was nothing to forgive. She was still too furious. Grief and regret might come later. That stupid, greedy woman had tried to rob her, had she not? And worse, shop her to the Gestapo. What else could or should she have done?

Her fury and self-justification gave her strength. Though she wasn't at all hungry, she knew she should eat and try to buy food for the journey. She forced herself into a café, one she'd not been in before, and for some of her remaining francs got yellow coffee and the stew, *ragoût* of rat doubtless. She couldn't taste a thing, but it would sustain her for a while. Surely the fortune she'd paid for the journey would include food.

By ten to ten, she was out of the café, ten minutes to the rendez-vous with Henk nearby on the boulevard. Suddenly she felt such nausea that she bent over from the pain of it and proceeded to retch up her breakfast onto the sidewalk in full view of any passers-by. She staggered a little and waited, still bent, to make sure the spasms had stopped. Someone did come up to her, a man whose assistance was gruff and practical, no hand-wringing. He said, 'There, there, lady, the food they serve in there'd make a dog throw up. Best get it out of you, and you'll be all right.' He offered his hand to help her stand up, and a dirty handkerchief should she need it. The sight of it almost had Eleanor retch again.

'Thank you,' she managed to say and produced her own hand-kerchief, wiping her face. 'I think I'm all right now.' If this had happened near any of her haunts in Paris, she who retained much of her American fastidiousness would have died of shame and had herself sent back to Providence in a box. The man looked at her; he understood. '*On vit mal*, eh?' he said. Life's hard.

She wobbled a few steps, but free of the noxious *ragoût*, she felt much better. Her body suddenly filled with energy and she arrived at the rendezvous spot across the Place Royale. Five minutes to spare. The Nazi flags, limp on their staffs above the Hôtel de France, filled her with even more determination.

She'd expected the town to swarm with police by now, to see cars rush past her like they did in the movies. Thus far, the place was Sunday-morning quiet, apart from the church bells. She'd been too self-absorbed to notice if the day was favourable for their escape. Now she saw the mountains snow-capped and registered the clear blue sky and, fleetingly, how beautiful the world was. But she was not someone given to omens.

Where was he?

She waited until nearly ten past ten, the longest minutes of her life. Had he been taken? She blew that terrible thought away. She couldn't countenance losing him, not now.

Then she saw two cars drive right past her, at speed, two of those cars whose profile and shape ever after would chill her to the marrow. They wouldn't have far to go if they were the police or the Gestapo, just down the hill. Where the hell was he? She was furious as well as worried sick. Five minutes to the rendezvous at the bookshop.

She wasn't ready for despair, on the contrary. Her old irritations and resentments rumbled to the surface like a volcano erupting and propelled her along the street. She was fearful of one of those cars pulling up sharply at the kerb, doors bursting open and those men in coats and hats racing out to grab her.

She took off.

By the post office, the *parfumerie* on the corner over the road, then down the next corner a matter of metres, the bookshop.

Five minutes late.

She entered, breathless. He wasn't there. She went to retrace her steps. The bookseller immediately beckoned Eleanor to follow her through a door into a storeroom at the back of the shop, where two young men waited. That's all Eleanor needed, more young men with their sullen silence.

'Where is he?' the bookseller asked the obvious.

'I don't know,' Eleanor confessed. She'd told him about the bookshop, given directions, but really, that was a waste of time.

'We cannot wait,' said the bookseller. 'Something's happened this morning. The police and the gendarmes are out. Are you coming or not?'

Eleanor dithered.

'Make up your mind,' she said.

'I'll go,' said Eleanor. Greater love hath no man, yes, but what could she do? She had given him francs and some dollars. She had no idea why he wasn't at the rendezvous. She didn't believe he'd been picked up; he was just too clever to be caught, and the police would be too busy attending to her recent handiwork. She was angry with him about everything and at herself for her infatuation. Her mood was so mercurial, her darling was again that little shit who had been nothing but trouble. What happened between them was just ships in the night, a look, a voice, then darkness and silence.

So she told herself, but she knew she was lying.

The bookseller pushed Eleanor out. Behind her, the door shut. The two young men were boarding a delivery van through the doors at the rear. The motor was already running; a driver sat at the wheel. Eleanor was the last to board. The bookseller herself went to shut the door.

'No!' Eleanor cried out. 'Please, can we drive along the boulevard, just in case?' she begged.

The woman gave Eleanor a hard, cold look and said, 'What we women do for love, eh?'

Eleanor heard her get into the front seat; the van moved along a laneway and onto the street. Inside was airless, though light came in through tiny round windows in the rear doors. She pressed herself to the glass but could not tell where the van was going until, yes, it turned and she saw the snowy peaks of the Pyrénées to the south. They were trawling slowly along the boulevard. If will had anything to do with it, she would have conjured him up out of that crack in the footpath he always seemed to hide in, but even her will wasn't strong enough.

'You must forget him, madame,' the bookseller said through the curtain separating the cabin from the rear of the van. It was sound advice, woman to woman, kind and practical. The bookseller understood, but really, Eleanor thought, she didn't understand at all.

The van turned down a street away from the boulevard. Eleanor sat back on the wooden bench. One of the men was sitting there now. Opposite her sat the other, and he grinned at her.

'What's so funny, fella?' she snapped. They looked away, leaving her to her unhappy thoughts.

HÔTEL COSMOPOLITAN, PAU

Towards 10am, Sunday, 14th December 1941

Bauer had been up early, going through reports in the communications room for possible news, but had found nothing detailed about the British attacks in North Africa or the troubles outside Moscow, no cable to him about his missing son. Since then he had been on the telephone, making sure the border around the Col de Somport was secure. The snow report was heavy on the peaks but only light on the passes. Still walkable for the sturdy if they had local guides. French Customs had the photograph of Pohl; the commandant of the German troops at Orthez had his men on patrols along the walking tracks and passes. The railway station in Pau was under close watch; the Spanish were watching at Canfranc.

He remembered Lieutenant Wolf, whose case he'd had to put to one side. The fellow was asleep in one of the hotel rooms.

Except he wasn't, as Kopitcke now informed him. He had left sometime in the early hours, telling the night watch he was returning to his own hotel.

'What the hell's the fellow thinking?' Bauer exclaimed in frustration. 'The Gestapo probably have him again.' He was about to call the hotel when came the thunderclap, in a call from Inspector St Jean.

The concierge at the hotel they'd visited the night before had been stabbed to death. St Jean ordered him to drop whatever he was doing and appear as soon as possible.

The time was ten to ten.

Bauer had a different driver, as Mascaro had more important duties to fulfil. His car stopped near the laneway that ran down to the hotel, where other police cars were parked outside. It was odd, Bauer remarked to Kopitcke, no crowd. A murder always attracted a crowd, but not here, not today.

St Jean was inside Eleanor's attic room. The body of the concierge lay on its back where Eleanor had dragged it, a knife thrust deep into her upper abdomen. Photographs had been taken, samples collected. He was highly exercised; his fury about a murder on his turf was narrowly focused.

'What do you think of that?' he said to Bauer. 'French, a good Catholic and a knife in her belly.'

'How long's she been dead?' Bauer asked as he bent closer to the corpse. 'This looks freshly done.'

'An hour or so,' St Jean confirmed.

'It's a Wehrmacht field knife,' Bauer said immediately, 'the same sort that killed our two soldiers.' He looked up at St Jean with a smile. 'Our murderer has left bloody fingerprints all over the hilt.'

He stood. 'Ah, look,' he said, pointing to the bloodied water in the basin. 'Pontius Pilate washes his hands.'

'Remove the knife,' St Jean ordered. 'Carefully now. I need those fingerprints as quickly as possible.'

Which was when Kopitcke's sudden sneezing and streaming nose uncovered the presence of a cat.

'Ach,' Bauer said. 'It is him. Pohl.' He'd expected it, given the knife. Now he had proof.

He said this with immense satisfaction, because now he would have the entire resources of the local police and gendarmerie to help him.

'The dogs are on their way,' St Jean said. 'He won't get far. I have ordered patrols out.'

The knife now safely removed and taken for examination, the ambulance porters were able to take the body. Bauer took one last look. Classic knife play, he could see, getting the victim to walk onto your knife.

Bauer looked around the room. He reported his and Mascaro's encounter with the woman the night before; how, when pressed, she'd started to abuse Marshal Pétain and the German occupation. Now, only now, he understood the canny old dame had been sending up smoke. Why exactly? he wondered.

St Jean told him the Spanish houseboy had turned up for work at around nine-thirty. His boss wasn't in her room. He went looking for her, eventually finding the fresh blood on the landing outside the attic room. He raised the alarm. Within fifteen to twenty minutes, the hotel was empty, every guest fled. Heavy belongings were left, doors remained open, soap on the table.

'The *Mary Celeste* again,' said Bauer, peering at the two beds. 'Only one slept in last night,' he noted.

'Let's talk to the boy,' said St Jean.

They went down to the vestibule, where he was waiting.

And so it came out. Dumas's guests were all Jewish refugees, each of whom she was blackmailing with threats of being given over to the Gestapo.

'How do you know this?' St Jean demanded. The kid was Spanish, parents communists, how could he trust him?

Unknown to the concierge, her Spanish boy, to whom she spoke in a childish creole as if he were a two-year-old and whom she paid meanly, spoke and understood French perfectly. He knew everything she did.

'She was running a protection racket, the old goat,' Bauer remarked, 'but she tried it on someone who had a knife and who used it.'

St Jean looked through the register. The boy showed him another register. She'd kept two.

'One false, which she showed you last night,' he explained to Bauer, 'and one true, which she used to threaten them. Pay up or the Gestapo will see this.'

Bauer looked closely at the real register. There was the name of the occupant of the attic room, arriving Friday evening, Madame Roget, Toulouse, and her identification card number. 'That'll be fake,' he said, 'but the other names all have the ring of truth, German and Austrian Jews, poor stupid mutts.'

The boy, whose powers of observation were quite nuanced, gave them a good description of the woman. Her hair was auburn, not brown, nor were her eyes, which were green.

'Like a cat's.'

Bauer looked at his watch. Ten-fifteen. The dogs had arrived and bounded excitedly up the stairs. Given the sheets on the rumpled bed for a scent, they went delirious with excitement. Bauer smiled.

'Exactly,' he said to Kopitcke's embarrassment. 'See, Kopitcke? Sex is indelible.'

Once outside on the street, however, the dogs fell into confusion. Three dogs pulled their handlers up the laneway and two others, just as determined, along the path that led to the chateau. The culprits had split up.

Bauer detailed Kopitcke to follow the chateau trail while he went up the laneway. St Jean was above such histrionics and returned to his office to direct his forces. He couldn't ignore this. Crooked she might have been, but a French citizen had been murdered, it seemed, by a German deserter who, worse, was a Jew.

10.45am, Sunday, 14th December 1941

Bauer's dog team and handlers took him along a direct course, first to the boulevard opposite the Hôtel de France, thence to a bookshop, which was closed.

The police forced it open. The dogs burst in, then through the open door to the storeroom, then to the back lane, where the trail went cold.

'They've driven from here,' said Bauer. It was ten-fifty, no more than two hours after the woman had been stabbed. How far could you get in two hours driving south? he asked the French dog handlers.

At best, they could be nearing the customs post at Col du Somport, he was told. 'Close it,' Bauer ordered only to be told that St Jean already had. The Aspe Valley was a funnel to the Somport pass; there wasn't any other way through to Spain unless you went into the higher passes, which was hardly likely, especially in winter, and not possible by car.

He needed to know how Kopitcke was faring. A radio call tracked him down to the boulevard, where the dogs had lost the trail, exhausted and confused.

Bauer assumed, unless otherwise proven, that she, the one with money, had gone to the bookshop and then to the boulevard by car, where they'd picked up Pohl. What explanation could there be for the other trail running out?

St Jean arrived at the bookshop within minutes.

'Hah,' he exclaimed to Bauer. What followed was a rant about the bookshop owner who was known to the police for selling a notorious board game that was won by the gangsters escaping the police. 'We got her into court, she batted her eyelashes and was so contrite, the judge almost apologised for inconveniencing her.' He wouldn't be surprised if the duplicitous minx wasn't selling depraved literature as well.

Then, grist to his mill, in came information, radioed to his car. She had a permit for a delivery van.

'In the name of the Father, how did she get the gasoline?' St Jean raged. 'She's using it to ferry escapees.' He sent out specific instructions to bring her in.

'Even if you have to drag her out of the confessional,' he added, highly unlikely for someone who had to be an atheist, but it sounded good. 'Your birds have gone to ground,' he said to Bauer. 'You should be after them.'

'They're your birds too, inspector,' Bauer said slyly.

'Indeed,' said St Jean. 'Let's go and flush them out, eh?'

A FARM,
FIVE KILOMETRES SOUTH OF PAU

Towards midday, Sunday, 14th December 1941

Eleanor and her two companions sat sullen and silent. The van was going south as fast as it could safely go along these back roads. She and the young man at her side were constantly thrown together as they followed a road that soon was as winding as it was hilly. She didn't look out through the portholes once. She had failed again, this second time much more painful than the first, and retreated into a passive indifference to her fate. If they were stopped and she was arrested, it would be a relief.

They left the roadway and bumped up a track to a farmhouse on a rise, which looked south to the snowy peaks. Above, the sky was vast and infinite and icily blue. It was the sort of day and view that in normal times always caused Eleanor to feel her humility before the Almighty and called to her spirit, but that now, in her misery, she ignored. She stared listlessly down at her shabby boots.

The bookseller emerged from the house with two young men. Eleanor imagined one to be Henk. Ridiculous, but she and logic were currently strangers. She ran across, only to see she'd deluded herself. They were as surprised to see her as she was disappointed that neither was Henk.

'Who's she?' one demanded.

'You know better than to ask questions,' said the bookseller brusquely. Plans had changed, she explained. She ordered the two young men she had driven from Pau to go inside and shave, and be quick about it. She'd explain why when they were done. They could use the farmer's shaving brush and blades.

'Listen carefully,' she said gravely on their return. The place was suddenly hot. She didn't know why, but the French police were setting up roadblocks around towns south to the Col de Somport.

'Looking for us?' one of the young men asked, which elicited almost a smack in the mouth from his companion. 'Can't you keep your bloody mouth shut?'

The bookseller said if he didn't, he'd be dead, by the hand of either the gendarmes, the Germans or his companions. 'Or mine,' she added. Something in her eye caught the cocky miscreant and he shrank before her.

They needed to detour. Their next stop would be on the Way of St James, the pilgrims' trail to Santiago in Spain from Arles via the Somport Pass. They would join it where it ran towards Oloron from Lourdes. Today being Gaudete Sunday, pilgrims were walking the Way, some having come from Lourdes the day before yesterday. There was to be a special Gaudete Mass in Oloron tonight.

'You will join them. The less you look like who you are, the better. You walk with them, you eat with them, you go to Mass with them later, and you spend the night with them at Oloron. Tomorrow you return to Lourdes by train, except you don't. Is that clear?'

No one dissented. Eleanor had picked up the gist and left it at that.

'You should know the "Lourdes Hymn" or at least the chorus. Pilgrims don't gossip or talk along the Way.'

'What happens after?' one asked.

'You'll be contacted in Oloron by someone.'

'What about her?' one of the young men asked, pointing rudely at Eleanor.

'She goes with you,' said the bookseller. 'Now get in. We'll be late.'

This produced an explosion of protest. She was a woman, how could she cross the passes, she'd endanger their whole escape, they'd tell de Gaulle about this if they ever reached London, and so it went, explaining to Eleanor exactly what was really going on. It dragged her out of her lethargy.

'I'm an American, buster,' she said defiantly. 'You pansies wouldn't know a real winter if it bit you. And just in case you don't know, it'll be America who'll save your sorry souls from Hitler. Understand?'

There was nothing like her dander to get Eleanor going. They'd no more get rid of her than they would their hands from their arms. She asked no favours of anyone, she told them. If she fell behind, which she wouldn't, she'd die, her funeral, but she would follow them to hell if she had to, and there was nothing they could do about it.

'Bravo, madame,' said the bookseller and Eleanor stepped triumphantly into the back of the van. She even beat them to a seat. She could hear the bookseller give the youngsters one last warning about shooting their mouths off before she got into the front passenger seat. Only the driver gunning the engine motivated the quarrelsome young men to follow, and they pushed each other in, the last swinging the door shut as the van moved off.

They drove away from the farmhouse along a track in another direction, again at uncomfortable speed and out onto a narrow road. No one said a thing. Eleanor wasn't sure if she'd won them over or not. She didn't care.

OGEU LES BAINS

Midday, Sunday, 14th December 1941

After a short drive, they turned in through the gates of a farm with high walls that ran along the main street into a village and parked outside a barn whose roof looked like a Dutch bonnet. The farmer, a large bear of a man, emerged from inside.

'Welcome,' he said gruffly and gave each of them a scallop shell threaded onto a string. 'You are now pilgrims along the Way of St James,' he informed them. 'God bless you and keep you.' Though the farmer was no priest, each of the young men crossed himself as he put the shell around his neck. Eleanor, the last to alight and be anointed, thought it wise she did the same. She reached inside her pullover and retrieved the cross Madame Teixeira had given her.

'Can we smoke?' one of the young men asked politely.

'Sure,' replied the farmer, 'wouldn't mind one m'self. But remember, pilgrims don't smoke along the Way.' The young men didn't care about the Way. They cared about the Chesterfield that Eleanor had already lit for herself.

'Always milder, Better tasting, Cooler smoking,' said the ads. ABC.

Throwing caution about conserving her supply of cigarettes to the wind, Eleanor offered her pack around, instantly turning the young men into friends, if not for life at least for the next stretch of her escape.

She gazed south as she smoked. Beyond the farmer's fields were the first folds of the Pyrénées, and just beyond them, steep slopes angled this way and that way at forty-five degrees, making daunting snow-dusted walls. Each angle was a turn in the Aspe Valley as it wound its way up to the passes that she could see under the snowy peaks. They'd be using these passes to reach Spain.

Could she really make it? Damn it all, look what she'd gone through to get this far. That Henk was not here suddenly filled her with terrible anguish.

Prayer, which had never come easily and had eluded her almost entirely since the terrible night, came to her now – not as a discreet Episcopalian retreat into some gentle mystical state of being with the sun and the sky as witnesses, but in a strong and fervent evangelical plea to save Henk and carry him to safety. Whether she'd cried out loud, she did not know. It was as if she'd been whacked on the back of her head. When she opened her eyes, she found she was on her back on the grass, with the young men by her side, cradling her head, her arms, calling to her. They were gallants, these boys. Was it a fit she'd had? The bookseller pushed them aside.

'Give her air,' she cried and lifted a small flask to her lips. 'Brandy, madame,' she said and Eleanor sipped and soon felt the warm liquid coursing through her. Revived, she apologised.

'Is there something I could eat?' she asked practically. She'd fainted. At least, they thought she'd fainted, which was fine by her. Fainting was better than the Damascene event it was – oh, she knew that. And, of all places, on the *camino* to Santiago de Compostela from Lourdes. She didn't want to be left behind as a lunatic or an epileptic, nor carried aloft in triumph for having had visions of Jesus or the Virgin. The farmer, not given to enthusiasms, quickly returned with bread and cheese, and she was able to eat.

'Keep up your strength, madame,' the bookseller encouraged as the sound of the Lourdes 'Ave Maria' chorus floated towards them. Soon, the promised pilgrims began turning in off the roadway on what was a slight detour from the Way. A mix of nuns, the elderly and schoolboys in oversize berets and suits, presumably a school uniform, and girls in shapeless smocks, they were led by a priest past the barn and out to the path across the farmer's field. By the time the stragglers passed by, each with the scallop shell around his or her neck, they numbered over a hundred.

The sight of Eleanor's young, male companions, a rare event with so many of France's young men still in German POW camps, dissolved any mood of piety and contemplation. This among the elderly no less than among the schoolboys in their teens, who intuited exactly who and what these tough young men probably were, figures to be admired, to be looked up to. The schoolgirls gushed and giggled so much the nuns scolded them, but that couldn't stop their shy glances at the young men, who reciprocated.

Eleanor joined at the end with her fellow travellers, each of whom, at least raised Catholic, took up the Lourdes 'Ave Maria' with varying degrees of conviction and accuracy. Oloron was a few hours' walk away along the ancient *camino*, which the group rejoined a little way past the farm, where it turned towards the river.

CHEMIN DES PIEMONTS, THE WAY OF ST JAMES, TOWARDS OLORON-SAINTE-MARIE

Around 1pm, Sunday, 14th December 1941

In Paris, Eleanor was always protecting herself and her church-going from the barbs and sneers of the raptors, who despised Christianity and all religion while being fervent followers of St Marx – people like Hettie Rosen, the true believer, or fellow-travellers like the odious Hemingway. Poor Christian that she'd turned out to be on this journey, or so she thought, what just happened had shaken her spirit out of its despair. Around her, the pilgrims were singing the 'Ave', whose rhythm and repetition were infectious. When the chorus came, she joined in, timidly at first, but soon as fervently as if she'd been born to it.

As she walked along, the ancient Way, now just a muddy cow track, her thoughts wandered back to the tree in the yard of their holiday home at Bar Harbor, a feeling so tangible and real that faith seemed entirely unnecessary – indeed, irrelevant. Jesus hadn't deserted her, she realised. She'd deserted Him, and as if to make the point, it was He who had given her the whack over the head, which still ached. Henk was safe and she would see him again, she was sure of it.

Soon the pilgrims were stretched out along the narrow path that followed the winding river. They had fallen silent, either in contemplation or, like Eleanor, withdrawn into their own thoughts and world. For company, they had the mumuring waters of the Gave d'Ossau and, now and then, small herds of cows and sheep, which eyed them with friendly curiosity. There were much straighter and quicker routes, but those were made for speed and efficiency, not for contemplation. This was the ancient way, the way of the pilgrims, no car or truck to disturb them – and no roadblocks.

They stopped by the river some time later, to rest, to collect water for their canteens and to eat a late lunch. The pilgrims shared with Eleanor and the young men the bread and hard cheese that was sustaining them on their journey. Fortified, Eleanor began to take in her surrounds. On the far side of the field on a rise was a farmhouse with smoke drifting from one of its chimneys. Vines grew in rows down the slope, the canes cut back for winter. A turquoise kingfisher sat on the stone fence looking for prey. She could hear the chirping of tiny finches somewhere nearby. Each sound, each sight, was as if in a halo. She imagined she could hear the crack of the ice on the mountains.

Suddenly, attention was on a figure emerging from the farmhouse. He came towards them at quite a pace, looking as if he might throw them all out. Instead, he spoke briefly and urgently to the priest, who nodded gravely. Eleanor tensed.

'The police have a roadblock outside the town where we meet the road,' the priest announced. 'We hope they do not stop us, but if they do, leave the talking to me.'

In normal times, this might have been cause for some excitement and gossip. Why, who, what? Now roadblocks were commonplace, an irritation to be borne like aches and pains in one's joints. But this one was more serious than that. Without a word, one of the schoolboys handed his beret to the nearest young man, indicating for him to wear it, which the fellow did. Once the lead was given, others offered their berets to the remaining young men, who now joined them in their schoolboy disguise, enhanced by their freshly shaven faces. Those who had donated their berets moved to the back of the group among the older people, to take an arm, like a grandson helping a grandparent.

'Not me,' said one of the ancients, pointing to a companion. 'He's much older than me. He can barely walk.' They all laughed and joked about who among the women was the eldest, but more important, who was single or a widow and needed a man.

'I'll have that one,' said a shawled old woman with wispy whiskers on her chin. She grabbed the boy as if she were the witch and he Hänsel.

'Watch out,' her friend cautioned. 'Marry her, you marry death.'

'She hasn't got a sou either,' quipped another, and everyone laughed, although the boy's laughter was nervous.

As the group set off, the mood tightened. The danger was not to the pilgrims, but they were certainly aware of the danger to their guests and possibly to the priest. Not far out of the town, they came to a narrow stone bridge, high over the river, whose waters now rushed through the gorge below. Eleanor noticed even the young men crossing themselves as each stepped onto its ancient stones.

'Pont du Diable,' explained Eleanor's neighbour. The devil's bridge. When in Rome, Eleanor thought, and crossed herself.

JUNCTION CHEMIN DES PIEMONTS AND
MAIN ROAD INTO OLORON-ST MARIE

Around 3pm, Sunday, 14th December 1941

Soon, through the trees, they could see the chimneys and steeples of the hilly town nestling in the valley where the two mountain rivers joined, one of which, the Aspe, led up to the frontier with Spain at the Col de Somport. Ahead, where the Way emerged from the woods to join a main road into the town, was the promised police roadblock. They were checking traffic into and out of the town. Given how few cars and trucks were supposed to be about in these times of rationing, the priest murmured his delight at the chaos.

'Ah, good,' he said. 'The Lord loves chaos.'

Without any bidding, the pilgrims took up the Lourdes 'Ave Maria'.

The old *chemin* hadn't been usurped completely by the modern road and continued alongside it, thus they could bypass the barriers set up across the bitumen. Unless stopped, the priest intended them to keep going.

Bauer stood by his car in his coat, observing two French police checking a driver and his truck. He could have stayed in Pau with Inspector St Jean but preferred being out in the field, leaving Kopitcke to maintain contact and to keep an eye on the problem of Lieutenant Wolf and the Gestapo. The police had put a block here only after he kicked up a fuss. All roads, he had insisted, not just the main one up the Aspe. Did they think the killers wouldn't try to avoid the main roads? To make his point, Bauer had himself driven to this very spot. See the number of vehicles heading out that had been stopped? he said. He'd been told hardly anyone used this route, apart from local farmers.

With him, he had his secret weapon, the Spanish boy from the hotel who knew exactly what the woman looked like. Persuading the boy to help had not been hard. Money plus the attention it would give him were enough. If he helped identify the killers, Bauer had promised him 500 francs, more than the penny-pinching Dumas had paid him in three months. This had opened up the possibility that the kid himself had done her in, but Bauer doubted it. Now he sat out of view in the front seat of the car, with instructions to give a prearranged signal if he saw the woman.

A policeman thrust the photograph of Pohl into the truck driver's face. Nah, never seen him. The police waved the fellow on and beckoned the next. By the muted and submissive reaction of many of the drivers, he knew they were not keen, any of them, to be so sprung. Some were caught red-handed with contraband. The police got excited about that. Not Bauer. He had bigger fish to fry.

The car radio crackled. Nothing had come through for the last hour, but there was something in the voice at the other end that had Bauer pay attention.

The bloody fingerprints on the handle of the knife exactly matched those on the valise found in the boxcar.

Bauer grabbed the microphone. 'No other prints?' he asked.

There were, but the bloody prints had almost wiped them out. Not usable.

The woman was the murderer? He had not expected that. His immediate concern was that the French would now go after her and ignore Pohl. His second: could she have killed the two soldiers as well? He couldn't dismiss the idea out of hand. Facts were facts. It certainly supported the notion that they were fleeing together.

He heard the pilgrims before he saw them. Catholic though he was – albeit a Catholic who attended Mass only at Easter and Christmas Eve – he had to ask one of the French police what was going on.

The Frenchman explained. Since the Spanish Civil War, he added, you didn't see many pilgrims going on the Way of St James into Spain. 'More in the opposite direction to Lourdes.'

'Where are you from?' the policeman called out as the pilgrims approached.

'From Lourdes,' replied the priest, 'going to Oloron for Gaudete Sunday.'

'Let's look at them,' said Bauer to his French offsider. 'Single file, one by one.'

'But they're pilgrims and they're from Lourdes,' the policeman protested. Hearing what was going on, the priest couldn't resist.

'This is the Way of Saint James,' he addressed Bauer. He knew his protest would be futile, but causing the man's conscience some grief would be worth it. Bauer did have a conscience but not one to be troubled by such a challenge.

'Forgive me, *père*, it is necessary,' Bauer said in a firm tone. We are looking for a murderer.'

'Among these?' said the priest, astonished.

Even Bauer could remember something in the Bible about Satan masquerading as an angel of light, but quoting the Bible to a priest was '*Eulen nach Athen tragen*', taking owls to Athens. Yet he didn't want to spend the rest of his life wondering if this was how he'd missed his quarries. The trouble with the French, they weren't thorough.

Eleanor was among the older people, well back in the group. With a large cross around her neck, her dark shapeless coat, her worn and now muddy boots, her mothy woollen cap, she figured she would pass the police muster. Then she felt something pressed to her hand and it was a large black scarf. The old lady behind her indicated she cover her head. Her lustrous auburn hair falling free from under her cap was far too bourgeois among these simple small-town grey heads, as red a rag to a bull as could be. With help from her companion, she quickly tucked her hair under the scarf, which she tied under her chin.

The singing died away as each passed before Bauer's eagle eyes, which moved from the Spanish boy in the car and back to the pilgrims.

Eleanor's fellow escapees looked young enough under their berets and among their peers. The bareheaded boys looked innocent as they helped their adopted grandparents, each of whom played up to their decrepit part, stuttering along, clinging to the young arm supporting them. Eleanor hoped she looked enough like a widow as she approached the eye of Bauer's needle, neither camel nor rich. As she came closer she caught a glimpse of Bauer, who, in his ancient tweed coat and his battered hat like some grandpa smoking a cigarette, stood out among the French uniforms.

There he was, she knew it, the face of the enemy, not in the grey uniform or the sinister leather coat and fedora she expected; she couldn't even claim he looked cruel. But in presenting so benignly, he looked the more chilling. She would remember this face, she thought, here was that whole damnable nation of sheep.

She had no need for prayer now, just a cool head. That notwithstanding, she imagined every police eye upon her, could feel them like tiny suns burning into her, little spots of prickly heat. Sweat seemed to be forming on her brow.

Unknown to her, the boy had seen her coming.

'You hear that, son?' Bauer said to him in case the boy had missed the radio conversation. 'The American woman is the murderer.'

Murder was a sin, Bauer had impressed upon him earlier. The young man she was in league with – another sin, by the way – was a German. Worse, he was a Jew and probably a communist. The boy did think of the money that M'sieur le Commissar was offering. But he knew who in the Hôtel Cosmopolitan was a Jew and who lived for money and who was kind and who was not kind, who had smiled at him and who had cursed him. So, she was old Dumas's killer, this woman with the beautiful auburn hair, now hidden under her scarf? If so, it couldn't have been murder. He knew that to point her out to the police would be wrong, so he sat mute and opaque to Bauer's desperate eyes.

Eleanor realised she was through the cordon only by the hand of her elderly companion drawing her close, and they rejoined the ranks of the pilgrims who were moving slowly into the town. They exchanged a furtive, reassuring smile.

*

With the last of the pilgrims gone, Bauer shrugged his shoulders. It had been worth a try. Police blocks were set up on other roads. The passes were secure. The queue of people lined up for questioning was still long. The day was far from done. The radio crackled again. It was Kopitcke, and Kopitcke was excited.

'Herr Kommissar, Herr Kommissar!' he cried.

Not given to elation without the facts to support it, Bauer waited. Of course, he hoped the reason for Kopitcke's excitement was that one or both of the killers had been found.

'Your son,' Kopitcke yelled, not quite trusting the radio set to communicate his voice at a level Bauer could hear. 'There's a cable from your wife for you.'

Bauer's blood froze. 'Well?' he snapped, at breaking point.

'It says: "Georg in hospital Smolensk. Stop. Recovering. Stop."'

'What else?' Bauer asked.

'Nothing, Herr Kommissar, just greetings from your wife. This is wonderful news, is it not?'

Bauer thanked Kopitcke and signed off. He couldn't stay here, so he excused himself and walked a short way along the road that led into the town. He came to an orchard whose trees were almost bare and let himself in. Sitting on the ground against one of the trees, he started to laugh. Then he fell back and looked up into the fathomless sky and he laughed and he laughed. If anyone saw him, what a sight. A madman? Sure, he was mad. Mad with joy. Mad with happiness. It was as if Georg was four and chuckling high in the air above him in his father's hands. Then Georg was twenty-one, in his uniform, about to set off, oh so proud, and his old dad had wanted to hold him tight, but that would have mortified the poor boy. So they just shook hands. He didn't know how badly wounded Georg was, but he was alive and he was recovering. This was as good an omen as he could get.

Impatient as he was for details about Georg, he stuck to his duty, and with the Spanish boy in tow, he had himself driven to the road-blocks on the other routes leading in and out of the town. He liked to show his face and share a few words, and if the friendliness he encountered was any sign, he had managed to blur the fact that he was really a German. They knew, of course.

Thence into the town. They were waved down near the railway station by a policeman. That got Bauer's hopes up – but no, a train with foreign Jews had arrived to be taken by road to the camp at Gurs. Some had just escaped and the police were trying to round them up.

'Like herding cats, sir,' said the policeman.

'Where do they make for?' Bauer asked.

'The nearest hole,' the fellow replied. 'But then they get hungry and hang around the cafés or the churches. Or if they've got any money or valuables, they get robbed. We usually pick them up after a few hours.'

Soon the driver was able to continue. At the local *commissariat de police*, Bauer looked over those picked up that day, Jews on the run, smugglers, petty crims – he knew by their faces. The boy shook his head.

Before he returned to Pau and the boy to his family, he quickly cabled his wife and then rang Kopitcke with detailed instructions to communicate directly with the Wehrmacht hospital in Smolensk: a message to Georg himself, requests for details about his condition from the doctor, and a message to his other boy, Karl, in North Africa.

'How is Lieutenant Wolf?' he asked.

'We can't find him,' Kopitcke replied. 'The Gestapo deny they've got him. They're still angry, Herr Kommissar. Pichler is still in a coma. And that old fox the consul, I don't know, he's up to something as well.'

'Up to something about what?' Bauer wanted to know. 'The lieutenant?'

'Of course,' said Kopitcke. 'I think he knows where he is.'

'A curse on the lot of them,' Bauer muttered. He was sick of the whole business and he was dog-tired. He took out another Pervitin pill. They didn't seem to be working as well. Maybe he needed to take them a little more frequently, at least until he had the killers hanging from the end of a rope.

Early evening, Sunday, 14th December 1941

Fortified against the cold by a plate of meaty stew, fresh bread and a beaker of wine in the refectory, Eleanor joined her fellow pilgrims as they walked across the square to the cathedral. She gazed up at its Romanesque curves and massive bell tower, and went in under the marble tympanum celebrating the defeat of the Saracens by the church's crusader benefactor. Inside, the spicy darkness enveloped her. She snuggled into a pew with her female companions of the Way. 'Rejoice in the Lord always,' the mixed choir sang in antiphon. Above the chancel and the altar, the vaulted arches of dark blue were dotted with golden stars, which glittered in the light of many candles. Purifying smoke billowed with each thrilling swing of the censer by the thurifer, who led the clergy down the nave in a train of carmine and sparkling gold. How she got herself up and down at the right moments was not of itself a mystery – the liturgy wasn't all that different from her own, after all. She wasn't drunk, at least not from the wine. The mystery was in how she didn't just sit there in a stupefied sense of well-being. Whether she survived her coming journey seemed not to matter.

The mood stayed with her as she returned with her companions across the dark square to the old monastery nearby, where she and the young men were being sheltered. Inside was a warren of tiny rooms, the cells of monks or nuns before the French Revolution. Now they were a refuge for those who had nowhere else to go. Only the large rooms had fireplaces, and here the walls rang with the laughter of the pilgrim boys and girls who had to be chased to bed by the priests. Eleanor and her companions for Spain were settled separately downstairs in the basement, where the rooms were few so only Eleanor had the luxury of a cell by herself, even if it was freezing. They had to be up in only a few hours, when they could eat with the nuns after lauds. Someone would collect them near dawn.

Eleanor's room was vaulted, not high enough for her to stand. The stone floor was bare of any matting. A single bed was against the wall on one side, with a tiny set of drawers as a bedside table, large enough for only a Bible and a breviary. A candle was in a sconce on the wall above the bedhead, and higher up, a crucifix. Below the arch of the vault was a tiny grated opening to let in the freezing air. She tried to fix her coat over it, but it hung too close to the candle, which she had lit. Monk's cell this might be, but being neither monk nor nun, she put the coat back on. The thought of her absent mink made even Claude's coat seem thin and cold, although waltzing south through France in a mink would have been something, especially in the boxcar. She sniffed the collar, wondering if she could still smell Claude, but could detect nothing. She tried to conjure up the smell of him but memory failed her. Or was it her imagination?

In preparation for her journey through the mountains, she went through her remaining clothing and the contents of her rucksack. Would her boots survive? They looked worse than they were; they would hold up. She still had her warm socks at least and her long fleecy underwear, which had not been in the valise she'd lost. She counted her remaining hoard of Chesterfields. She was down to her last carton. With her US passport and her dollars, these golden cigarettes should be enough to clear any obstacles she faced entering Spain without a visa. She thought of Henk and her heart ached.

She went outside for a cigarette. There, leaning against the galleted stone wall of the refectory facing the square, she found two of her fellow escapees stamping their feet now and then against the cold as they finished a shared cigarette. She couldn't very well smoke without offering her pack to them, though watched carefully that each took one only.

Had she seen all the yids inside? one asked. Infested, said the other.

Cold as it was, Eleanor felt her face flame. They saw her reaction, which was as much a surprise to her as to them.

'My family voted for Blum,' the first added quickly, a reference to the leader of the socialist Popular Front before the war, who happened to be Jewish.

'Mine too,' the other chimed in.

Had Eleanor been able to vote in France, she would most decidedly not have voted for any socialist. Now she was happy to leave the impression that she and Leon Blum were not only co-religionists but the Eleanor and Franklin of the French left. How the raptors would be dumbfounded.

The lights of a car caught them as it trawled slowly through the square and turned away. It was a police car. While her heart had missed a beat, she noticed neither of her companions seemed at all bothered.

'The priest says they know about the yids,' said the younger, forgetting he believed he was talking to one. 'They never come inside.'

'They've got enough to worry about,' said the other, although what that might be, he didn't need to say.

They weren't at all worried they'd be caught tomorrow. The police had been bribed; that was usually how it was done. They were young and scared of nothing. But what about the German troops up in the mountains? Eleanor asked. Yes, they'd heard about them too, but who knew the passes around the Somport better than the local guides?

The cold drove them inside. As they parted and wished one another a good night, the elder of the two cheekily offered to keep Eleanor warm. The other immediately upped his pal's offer on the grounds he was larger and therefore warmer.

She laughed. To these two, she might be old and she might be a Jew, but she was a woman. 'What is this,' she quipped, 'an auction?'

They went their way and she went hers.

On her way back inside, she encountered children playing on the stairs.

'You lost, lady?' one boy asked in accented but colloquial French.

'Ten francs,' said his offsider. Eleanor, who had thought the boy was being kind, realised this was a local extortion ring.

'That'll be the day,' she replied, but instinct had her give him 5 francs. She was conscious of how few francs she had left but needed all the protection she could get. 'I'm not here,' she added. 'Understand?' On that thought, she offered each of these little refugee Artful Dodgers one of her precious cigarettes. This had more effect than the cash, if their eyes were a sign. 'Don't smoke them all at once,' she added.

Bidding them all goodnight, she heard the mewling of a cat and looked down to see a kitten brushing itself against her boot. Instinctively, she kicked it away just as she realised with a jolt that she recognised it. 'Oh God,' she cried and ran after it as it fled. The senior Artful Dodger dashed past her and in moments returned with the biting snarling kitten in his hands.

'Show me,' Eleanor demanded. The Dodger hid the cat behind his back.

'How much?' It was his turn to demand.

'I just gave you two cigarettes,' Eleanor snapped. So much for rogue's honour. But it worked and the little Dodger thrust the cat into her hands.

The tiny creature liked her even less than the Dodger and chewed at her fingers in an effort to escape. She didn't care. It was black, it had a white tip on its tail, it had recognised her. He was here and she was so happy that she, who loathed cats, drew the little bundle of fury up and held it fondly to her face, whereupon it lashed out at her.

'You know who owns this?' she asked.

'Ten,' the Dodger demanded. Cigarettes or francs, he didn't specify.

Eleanor was so wound up by now, she'd have handed over the contents of Fort Knox. She slapped 10 francs into the greedy hand. The Dodger led her along the corridor.

'Where are you?' she called out. The corridor was now so dark she couldn't see the Dodger.

'This way,' came the voice out of the blackness ahead of her. 'There's steps,' the child added. She bumped into him. He'd been waiting for her. 'Here,' he said.

She followed him down. She had thought her cell was in the building's basement. Now she was descending to yet a lower level. With no railing to hang on to, just the cold bare stones, she stumbled but an unseen hand steadied her out of the darkness.

'Watch out, lady,' he muttered.

'Where are you taking me?' she said.

'Down here,' said the Dodger as they reached a corridor, where there was a faint light from some source up ahead.

'There,' the boy said, pointing, and hurried back up the steps. That bothered Eleanor. A little too quick to depart, she thought. She crept forward. As her eyes became accustomed to the darkness, she could see that the light was coming through the crack of a doorway. The kitten sprang from her arms, and just as it did, the door suddenly opened and the light shone into the corridor. A young man of slight build and dark hair appeared in a coat. He spoke German. '*Katz.*' Her heart leapt out of her chest. But that coat was a Wehrmacht coat and she had seen this young man before. Oh God, yes, he was the one in the German uniform she'd seen coming out of the lavatory on the train at the Gare de Lyon. She cried out. He saw her. That wretched Judas of a child had just shopped her. She ran back along the corridor into the darkness to spread the alarm. As she found the steps up, she glanced back to see if the German was chasing her.

He wasn't.

It was Henk.

'Eleanor,' he called out to her, the first time he'd called her by name. '*Warte, bitte.* Stop.'

She didn't stop, continued up the stairs, along a corridor and out through a door into the night, running she knew not where. She could hear his footsteps right behind her.

'Please,' he cried and grabbed at her arm. She pushed him away, flattening herself against the nearest wall, the base of the cathedral tower.

'You going to kill me too?' she challenged as he came to her.

'Don't be stupid,' he said.

'Who was that?' she demanded. 'I saw him on the train. Were you the one in the lavatory with him?'

He sighed. 'Oh Eleanor,' he said gently. 'Don't you see?'

If she wasn't stone cold sober already, she certainly became so. Even then, her intellect as sharp as ever, what on earth was he saying?

'We are – ' and he paused, looking for the best way to explain. 'David and Jonathan,' he said. 'He is my life.'

'Oh God,' she murmured as the truth hit her.

Suddenly he grabbed her, and he kissed her passionately. She struggled but he kept her tight; he was strong. After what seemed an eternity, he released her. She pushed him away, and she ran back inside. Where the greatcoated 'it' had gone, she neither knew nor cared.

Henk stood alone, caught in the lights of the police car that he had seen and Eleanor had not. Now the car was stopped, the window down, the policeman leaning out, laughing.

'Go after her, you dope,' he called out good-naturedly in Occitan.

Henk laughed, put on the best impersonation in his life, tapped his head in salute to the cop and to male fraternity, and slipped back inside. Cold as it was, he was in a great sweat as he hurried in through the door.

*

After failing to cross the Spanish frontier, they had no alternative but to drive back the way they'd come and decided to try their chances in Oloron. The towns higher up and closer to the frontier were too small. Oloron was large and packed with refugees, among whom they would not stand out. Their chances of finding a guide would be better. With Hugo's passable Spanish, they might even be able to hide among the Spanish pilgrims returning from Lourdes, for whom Franco had insisted the rail line south into Spain be kept open.

Once there, they needed a roof over their heads. For want of any alternative, Hugo had suggested a church, so before dumping the car, they found the old cathedral and its presbytery. The priest, a monsignor, was elderly and frail and frightened by the appearance on his doorstep not of a young German Jew − such were not unfamiliar around here − but of a German military officer looking worse for wear and whose only protection against the cold was his Wehrmacht greatcoat.

'Help us, father,' Hugo had said in perfect French. 'We're on the run from the Gestapo.'

He drew them inside. Then he cross-examined Hugo, who, while not lying, did not tell the whole story. Not understanding a word, Henk had sat anxiously through the conversation, only learning its details later.

'We were soldiers, father,' Hugo had explained. 'We were doing our duty.'

He then removed his shirt to show what the Gestapo had done to him.

'Oh, my son,' said the old man, who touched Hugo's skin in pity.

Strangely, the Monsignor had not asked how the two were bound to each other. He accepted that Hugo had gotten into trouble for the sake of his Jewish army comrade and friend who had escaped from Mauthausen. It offended the old man that the French authorities were assisting the Gestapo.

'You're safe here for the moment,' he said, then stated the obvious: 'But for the guides, you need money.' There were so many refugees, the church, alas, could provide only food and lodging. '*Hier* safe,' he said to Henk, thinking English and German close enough. Henk couldn't bring himself to believe the old man but Hugo was a Catholic, a real one, and he trusted the priest's word, as the priest had trusted his.

'I told him you'd been born and raised a Catholic,' Hugo said once they'd been given a room. Henk was past caring what he was; that mattered only to the Germans.

Now Eleanor was here too. Of course. Where else? He wasn't all that surprised. He had to find her. He had to make things right between them.

'Will she betray us?' Hugo asked, after Henk returned to their room.

'No,' Henk replied. He told Hugo the story. Everything.

'Is she in love with you?' Hugo asked.

'I don't know if it is love,' Henk replied. Even if this was just an infatuation, he had made her suffer. 'Give her a little while. I'll talk to her.' He reached for Hugo and found his injured hand with its hard scarring, and he drew it to his lips and kissed it. 'Don't worry.'

HOUSE OF RETREAT,
CATHÉDRALE SAINTE-MARIE, OLORON

Around 9pm, Sunday, 14th December 1941

Driven by fury, Eleanor had nowhere else to go than her cell. She needed to be alone. The moment she pulled the door shut, she burst into tears, which made her even angrier. How could she be so stupid, she berated herself, so superficial? Who was he, after all? A mere youth, not someone she'd look at in Paris – rude, ignorant, a miserable sad sack who'd tugged at her heartstrings when she and he were at their most vulnerable. Her ego was hurt. She lit a cigarette, blow the rules. By dawn, she'd be on her way to Spain. Out of sight, out of mind. Now she would try to sleep. To distract herself, she needed to read. The choice was her own novel, to remind her of the contrast between real love and her own ridiculous situation. Then she remembered, he had taken it. She tried her Bible, letting it take her where it fell open randomly. *As snow in summer, and as rain in harvest, so honour is not seemly for a fool.* She read on but couldn't really concentrate.

For all her misery, she had not forgotten that He had been right after all. She had the sore spot on the back of her head to remind her that she hadn't imagined the whole thing. Henk was alive and she had seen him again. He hadn't warned her was that their reunion would be so painful.

Same time, 9pm, Sunday, 14th December 1941

Bauer went to the communications room, where a swathe of cables awaited his return. He kept his composure as he opened the folder and read through them, starting with his wife's. How she'd managed to send it, he could only put down to her persistence. Even the wife of a police detective couldn't just blithely send a telegram these days. Everyone sent postcards instead. She would have played on Georg's survival in Russia for all it was worth, or, since women were doing those post office jobs now, the sympathy of one mother for another.

He who did have access to the system replied to praise her and provide the details, if in précis, to her and to Karl. Yes, Georg was in a military hospital in Smolensk with a bullet wound to his arm and some frostbite. He and his men had been cut off by the surprise Russian advance, presumed captured or dead, but he'd led them back to German lines in a forty-eight-hour struggle, during which they'd survived by audaciously stealing Russian rifles and ammunition. They had even outflanked a Soviet division headquarters and were mistaken for a major German counterattack instead of just the fourteen survivors of the initial rout. Georg had brought the whole fourteen back alive and was a great hero.

'Wonderful news, Herr Kommissar,' Kopitcke said quite genuinely. Gone, at least in this instance, was the resentment he usually felt towards those at the front.

'Yes,' Bauer agreed.

He was of a mind to trumpet it to the world as a proud father and a proud German.

He had served on the Russian front, the last generation to take on the Slavic hordes, and they'd had a magnificent victory. But that had been destroyed by the reds at home. Now they had to do it all over again, against the same Slavic enemy. Georg had said to him, 'Don't worry, Papa, we'll finish them this time, so my sons won't have to fight them when they grow up.' This was a boast, the son showing off to the father. Bauer didn't mind. In any case, it was true – but he, the father, knew how much harder it was now for his son and all the sons. The enemy was not the same. This war wasn't clean like the last time, because the Slavs were now infected by the Bolshevik virus. The army was fighting not only the Red Army but the entire civilian population, who were attacking the German boys from behind. At first he couldn't credit Georg's stories. Then there were the Jews. Bauer had not approved when the government started persecuting the Jews at home. He'd fought in Russia with Jews who were loyal and patriotic Germans. He still thought exceptions should have been made for Germany's Jews. Whether he liked it or not, it was too late now, because every Jew had been turned into a bitter enemy. The leading Bolsheviks were all Jews. Yes, they faced a poisonous cocktail of enemies, and if they lost, Christian and Catholic Germany would be completely destroyed. But Georg's survival and success against all odds now gave him fresh hope that both his boys might survive this war after all.

'We haven't got our criminals yet,' he said to Kopitcke. His quarries were still in hiding. The reports coming in had all turned out to be false alarms. Sooner rather than later, they would have to make a break for it, and then he would catch them. He had the patience of Job.

Then a commotion presented itself at the entrance. A car disgorged the Gestapo, who, in their singular way, barged right in. Leading them was Captain Leske, whom Bauer had held at gunpoint when he'd sprung Lieutenant Wolf from the cell at the Villa St Albert. He was in SS uniform, so Bauer did not at first recognise him.

Leske didn't bother greeting Bauer by name. He just threw a file on the table. 'Read it,' he demanded.

Bauer opened it. The first page was a précis of Lieutenant von Kaspar Wolf's military record: the Iron Cross; another citation; service in Poland, Denmark, Norway, then Russia; his hand wound; his withdrawal from front-line duty.

'Now this,' said Leske, pulling the page away to reveal Lance Corporal Pohl's military record. Leske's thick finger was on the relevant paragraph. Service in Poland, Denmark, Norway, Russia, Iron Cross.

'What's your point?' Bauer said irritably. Millions served in the same arenas.

'You blind?' Leske replied. 'Same platoon.'

Bauer quickly flipped back to Wolf's file. Yes, Wolf had been Pohl's platoon officer almost the whole time he'd been in the Wehrmacht, until his dismissal as a *Mischling*. He suddenly had a bad feeling, but Leske offered him neither time nor room to hide.

'Here,' said Leske, revealing a Gestapo report with two paragraphs outlined.

Bauer read the first:

The avoidance, then the outright refusal followed by a deliberate cover-up of the Führer's order to remove all Mischlings from the army is in the case of Lance Corporal Heinrich Pohl due directly to Lieutenant Hugo von Kaspar Wolf, with the connivance of the company commander.

Leske impatiently took back the letter. 'We'll be here all night at this rate,' he said and began to read the next paragraph: 'The formal complaint by Private Brandler of the same unit about a possible homosexual relationship between Lance Corporal Pohl and Lieutenant Hugo von Kaspar Wolf was investigated by the company commander and dismissed due to the lack of evidence. The complainant was disciplined for spreading false rumours and transferred.'

Leske put the letter down. 'Same company commander who protected the Jew Pohl,' he said as he threw a photograph onto the table. 'We found this in Wolf's hotel room.'

Bauer looked up sharply.

'Yes,' Leske confirmed with a leer, 'we got inside, despite your French pals.'

The photograph was of Pohl and Wolf, smiling and naked on some summery strand, arms around each other's shoulders. And yes, their penises were slightly engorged.

'That proves nothing,' Bauer countered. 'Soldiers always go naked at the beach.'

'They've got hard-ons for fuck's sake!' said Leske.

'That merely shows you've never been in the army, Leske,' Bauer retorted, although he knew by now he was in quicksand. 'I've seen sights like that on beaches with the men. Instead of accusing them of perversion, we had a good laugh about it.'

Leske turned the photograph over and read out loud the message written on the back: 'Remember? Blavand, summer '39. I ache for you to hold me tight while I fill your arse with my cock and its hot juice. Your Heiner.'

Bauer stared at the writing, only half listening to Leske, who was still going on, something about Wolf having returned to the German consulate after Bauer had liberated him.

'. . . papers . . . incriminating evidence . . . all the contents of his safe . . . Spanish currency missing . . .'

Bauer began to listen properly only when Leske told him that some passports and two or three pistols also seemed to be missing but that the records couldn't be checked properly until the next morning.

'One of the consulate's cars is gone, a Peugeot, as is Lieutenant Wolf,' he informed Bauer. 'No wonder you haven't caught Pohl.'

Leske paused, crossed his arms. Unfortunately for Bauer, he was not finished.

'At around half past eleven, quarter to twelve this morning,' he began his coup de grace, 'at the French checkpoint on the road up to the Spanish frontier at the Col du Somport, that same car was observed. Why among all the cars and trucks was it observed? Because the driver, wearing a Wehrmacht greatcoat, got out and spoke to one of the gendarmes.'

Bauer could guess what was coming but had to sit through the indignity of hearing it, word for painful word.

'He spoke perfect French and announced he was from the German consulate and needed to drive across the frontier urgently on diplomatic business. The French informed him the border was temporarily closed and that they would need in any case to inspect the officer's car; this was a joint Franco-German operation. They showed him the "wanted" poster as the reason. The German officer declined to allow a search, on the ground of diplomatic immunity, and returned to the car, which the gendarmes could see had someone in the front passenger seat. They turned around and drove back in the direction they had come. Have your French colleagues not reported this to you yet?'

No, they had not. Bauer had nothing to say. He recalled that his instinct about Wolf had been negative at first, but Wolf's wounded hand and record had completely banished his doubts. He'd also just come from the odious Pichler, whose sneers against Wolf had probably helped inoculate him against trusting instinct. What made this all the harder to cope with was that he had plenty of experience in Frankfurt weeding out perverts, closing down the bars, clearing the riverbank of their places of assignation. The coming of the Nazis had given the police much greater powers, which he had used to the full. Moreover, he knew that plenty of them had gotten themselves into the Wehrmacht because the Gestapo couldn't touch them there. And he, Bauer, had rescued one of them from the Gestapo, had covered up his nakedness, had got his wounds tended. Wolf had completely betrayed his trust and Bauer felt humiliated as never before – and worse, in front of Kopitcke, who had been right about Wolf all along.

'This is still an army responsibility,' he said, putting on as strong a face as he could. 'You can assure the Reichsmarschall that when we catch them, which we will, on my personal authority, these deceivers will be executed summarily.'

'That all you've got to say?' Leske said, taken aback by the gall of the man.

'Yes,' said Bauer.

'They don't deserve a simple bullet in the skull,' Leske said. The wind had gone out of his sails.

'What do you suggest?' Bauer barked angrily.

'You hand them over to us,' Leske replied. 'We need them to talk.'

'You can have Wolf,' said Bauer, 'but Pohl is mine. Understood?' He would make the evil little creep suffer before he personally dispatched him to hell.

Leske was surprised; he thought Bauer would resist on both counts. He agreed and then left with his gang.

Bauer had to sit down. 'Jesus Maria,' he muttered. He wasn't looking forward to informing the general. There would be no Honour Court the next morning to exonerate Wolf over the duel, which is what they'd planned. Nor, in the circumstances, would he need a field court to deal with Pohl.

'The consulate car,' he said to Kopitcke. 'Get the French to find it. Urgent.' At least this got Kopitcke and his 'I told you so' face out of sight.

Then he looked at the facts presented to him and their confusions, which he thought through carefully, one by one.

Where was the woman? With them?

He couldn't think to save himself. His hands were shaking as he took out the Pervitin and quickly swallowed another tablet. He ordered a cup of coffee and lit his pipe. The rush was taking longer to come and didn't seem as strong. The side effects were obvious but there was no time to worry about that right now.

Wolf and Pohl were still this side of the border. They had been intent on crossing legally, each with valid travel documents and a visa for Spain. This option was now gone.

He could assume, therefore, that they had not organised an illegal crossing. Now they had to. What were their choices? They could try to cross into Spain by themselves, but it would be certain death to traverse country of which they had no knowledge or understanding. They needed to find someone to take them across – they, a German officer and a German Jew, whose photograph as a wanted killer was everywhere. Where the American woman was he did not know. He would focus on the two men and worry about her later. Killer though she was, her only interest to him was if she could lead them to Pohl and Wolf. What she made of the truth about Pohl, if she knew, he could only guess.

In Lyon, the people smugglers had been quite happy to hand Pohl over in return for the release of their own from prison. The only reason it hadn't worked was that Pohl and the woman had got wind of it. He'd try it here with St Jean, whom he rang and dragged from his dinner table. Given that, St Jean was surprisingly agreeable. He would put the word out: a deal was on the table.

'Don't forget the reward,' Bauer added before hanging up.

What would he do in the same situation? Hide or dump the car? Dump. Its loss would be known by now. He would dump it in a way as to send the police in the wrong direction.

Where would I hide? he pondered.

Hotels? No, not now the French were all over them.

Then, he thought, a church or a monastery. Obvious for a Catholic like Wolf. It's what he himself would do in extremis, after all. Back in Frankfurt, the Church had sheltered Catholic politicians in trouble with the Nazis. It was all smoke and mirrors. If they wanted to hide someone, that someone stayed hidden and not even the Gestapo found them.

But where had the two ended up today? He couldn't just sit here waiting. He took up the telephone again and called St Jean, who this time was grumpy and short when asked if his men would search the churches and monasteries.

'Of course not,' St Jean snapped.

'What if the Church is protecting someone like Pohl?'

'We have an agreement,' St Jean replied. 'They wouldn't.'

'But how would they know Pohl was a killer? Do you regularly inform them?'

St Jean did no such thing and now resented Bauer's pestering. Naturally, the Church took in refugees and gave them food, but they didn't harbour them; they fed them and sent them on their way.

Bauer didn't like the answers he was getting, but at least he knew the lie of the land. He thanked St Jean. He had to do something, so he rang the duty officer in Pau first. A request to deliver the 'wanted' poster to each church and monastery as a matter of urgency.

'Now,' he said.

Then he rang the duty officers in each of the towns south to the Col du Somport and requested the same of them.

'Tonight,' he said. He hoped they would at least do it by early tomorrow morning.

He wasn't in a sleeping mood. The Pervitin was working at last. He intermittently turned to the cables about Georg to soothe the agitations caused by the Pohl case, with its frustrations and complexities. His professional humiliation at the hands of the Gestapo would last a long time. He set the cables aside. Something nagged him about the relationship between Pohl and Wolf.

He had never witnessed anything like that during the Great War. He hadn't been naïve, but it had never once intruded into his life as a soldier. Nor since had he heard of anything like that among the comrades of his unit. But if Pohl and Wolf were able to hide in full view, the army was in trouble precisely when the country was facing a terrible threat to its survival. He took a silent oath on the honour of his two heroic sons that their father would be as tough and uncompromising as they were. It was his duty to them both. As a Catholic, he had found the Nazis and their views uncomfortably pagan at times, but he did not believe that God wanted Germany destroyed, so this was his duty also to the Almighty. Tomorrow, he would get Pohl and Wolf.

HOUSE OF RETREAT,
CATHÉDRALE SAINTE-MARIE D'OLORON

Towards midnight, Sunday, 14th December 1941

Eleanor was woken by a knock on the door. She thought it was one of the young men come to waken her. Time to leave.

'One moment,' she called and slid herself out from the bed, keeping the blanket around her shoulders against the cold. She found her lighter and lit the candle on the wall. Whoever it was pushed the door open.

'Eleanor?'

Framed in the shadowy light of the little arched doorway was Henk. Behind him, one of the nuns, who had shown him where she was, flittered away.

'Please,' he said. 'May I speak with you?'

Dear God, no, she said to herself. What was the point?

'Of course,' she replied, immediately changing her mind and putting on a strong face. Why not? What had she to fear? She was over him, a momentary lapse. She sat on the bed, pulling the blanket tight around her.

He stepped inside but shivered. With the door open, the air from the passageway was drifting into the room, making it even colder. He wasn't sure if he should shut the door. He hovered.

'Do shut the door,' she said.

'I wish to explain why I had to leave this morning and not tell you,' he said.

'No need,' she replied. 'You had a better offer.' Immediately she regretted that, but it was out. Too late. Her and her stupid mouth.

'It was not like that,' he said, not rising to her bait as once he would have.

She said nothing. She wanted a cigarette but forced herself to resist.

'What happened last night,' he said, 'you and I – '

This is just what she didn't want to talk about. He saw the look on her face. He persisted.

'I must tell you I need you then more than I ever need anyone. Without you, I think I give cat away and jump off a cliff.'

Coming from such a paragon of self-containment and purpose, this shocked her.

'You gave me love. You ask nothing from me – how do you say?'

'Unconditional,' she said flatly.

'Unconditional,' he repeated. 'Like in your novel.' He saw her look sharply at him. 'You think I don't read it? I read it all yesterday and the day before.'

He paused.

'I disappear into it. You understand? I live in it. He is me. And she is – '

Again, he paused.

'She is his love; she is my love, who is Hugo.'

Praise like this came rarely to authors, she knew, sweet to their ears and to their professional egos. This came with an awful sting. He saw her flinch. Should he stop now? Was he doing any good?

'But I must explain,' he said. He couldn't bear for her to think worse of him than he deserved.

'You asked why I need to come here in Pau,' he said. 'After his wound, Hugo is posted in the Armistice Commission because of his French. He tries to get me out of Mauthausen. Then we have luck. Hitler wants me back in Russia, so opens the gates of Mauthausen himself. And the army place Hugo in the consulate here. He can get passports, visas, any document. This is our chance. He organises everything: the army pass and tickets to Paris, the passage from Paris to Pau. I will be able to cross the frontier with new passport and papers. We swap clothes on the train in Paris so I stop being in army uniform. While I am on the escape route, he drives back here from Paris with the consul to wait for me. But then we have that trouble and I am late by one day.'

Eleanor remembered all too clearly.

'Everything he does,' Henk continued, 'he does to save me from the Gestapo.' He sensed this might be painful for her, but he had to tell her. 'I know always that I am this way,' he explained. 'It's why I am in trouble at school, with police in Vienna, with my father, why I am sent to a labour camp. But Hugo, he knows but he hides from it until we meet in the army. You understand?'

Did he have to ask her that?

Because of their late arrival, he continued, he missed the initial rendezvous times with Hugo, but when he'd made it there at the right times on the second day, no Hugo. So last night, he'd gone to the consulate, which was closed, then to Hugo's hotel. He knew his room number. When he arrived, he encountered the Gestapo there and was nearly caught.

'I go to where the boulevard is very steep above the valley. If it is not for cat, I would jump. Instead, I come to you, and you take me in, and you love me. You think because of him, I don't feel love for you? Oh, my dear friend, you would be wrong.'

None of this helped Eleanor, but she felt she had to hear every last word and suffer for it like some masochist.

'This morning, I waited for you. A car stops. I think it's the Gestapo, but it is Hugo. He tells me what has happened. On Friday night, he fights a Gestapo officer and nearly kills him. They arrest him and torture him. The army police manage to release him from the Gestapo. We must leave immediately because the Gestapo, they have broken into his hotel room. We have no choice. I am sorry.'

'What do you want?' she said abruptly.

'I want you to know that I haven't betrayed you. I want you not to feel angry with me.'

Eleanor nodded. She knew what she felt but she wasn't about to tell him.

'How will you both get into Spain?' she asked, changing the subject.

'Now I do not know.' He explained how Hugo, working in the German consulate, had been able to get a Portuguese passport for him with a Spanish visa so he could cross legally into Spain. They might have gotten across legally early this morning, with Hugo on his German diplomatic passport and visas. 'But when we arrive, the frontier is closed and the French have my face on a poster as a killer. On our way back, we see police have set up roadblocks going to Spain.'

'I paid for two passages,' she reminded him. 'One passage is available. We leave in an hour,' she said, looking at her watch.

'Unless they take him too, I cannot,' Henk said.

How that cut into her. Brain understood. Heart refused.

'The priest told us why the police are everywhere,' he said. 'Someone stabbed the concierge in your hotel and killed her.'

'Oh God,' Eleanor muttered. 'Did they say who?'

Henk shook his head. 'But I know.'

'The rogue tried to take all my money and hand me over to the Gestapo,' Eleanor reported matter-of-factly. 'You were right,' she added as a concession. 'She walked right onto the knife.'

He nodded. 'Now you understand,' he said.

Hardly different from him having to kill the two German soldiers. She knew that, but it was a step too far to admit it.

A silence descended between them, all too open and raw. She didn't know what to say, except she wished he'd go.

'May I keep your book?' he asked.

She nodded. He stood for a moment, looked at her.

'Thank you,' he said. He smiled, opened the door and disappeared into the darkened maze, leaving behind only the terrible ache in Eleanor's heart. She pushed the door shut. She couldn't contain herself any longer, fell on her bed and sobbed.

How long she lay there she neither knew nor cared. The pillow was wet. She stopped only when she was exhausted. She turned over on her back and started to yawn, and this she couldn't stop either. It was as if some demon was inside her, seeking release and escaping bit by bit, until eventually she lay dazed and empty.

At the sight of him and his rough-hewn beauty in the doorway, like some angel in the niche of a cathedral, her heart had leapt. Her initial denials to herself vanished, and her hysteria too. She'd known in that moment just how much she loved him, in a way she'd never loved before. Not Claude, certainly not the louse, not even Fred. She had never been completely available to any of them, each of them the lover, she the beloved. Henk had unwittingly pointed out a terrible truth to her: until she met him, she had been unlike any of her female protagonists, all of whom loved completely and were prepared to pay any price for that love. She had lived her life as a taker, never having sacrificed herself for anyone or anything. Even her ambulance driving during the Great War had been an adventure that made life thrilling. Helping wounded soldiers was a corollary. To add to her self-torment, Hettie Rosen now came to her mind. That morning at the Parish Hall when Hettie had asked for money, whatever she had done or said to Hettie, it hadn't been enough. Her exasperation with Hettie had really been disapproval laced with distaste, which Hettie had understood all too well. She who called herself a Christian had offered charity without compassion, forgiveness or love, as cold-blooded a sounding brass or a tinkling cymbal as could be.

She knew all the precepts about love in the Gospels. She knew them all by heart, but they were not etched on her heart. The Lord had told her she'd see Henk again. Now she knew why.

The weight of her self-loathing pressed her into the bed. If she didn't get up, she never would. Even then, she slipped off the bed and onto the floor, the blanket having fallen away. On her bare knees, she knelt before the crucifix and she spoke the confession, 'Merciful God, our maker and our judge …' She said it again and again and again, until at last she was able to rip away the remains of that carapace of respectable civic duty to pour out the passions and aches of her heart, and she felt empty and as insignificant as a mote of dust. She glanced at her watch. Listlessly, she dressed and gathered her belongings and went out.

HOUSE OF RETREAT,
CATHÉDRALE SAINTE-MARIE, OLORON

3am, Monday, 15th December 1941

Eleanor found her four travelling companions eating with the priests and nuns in Trappist-like silence. Their guide was a young woman. Eleanor was quite taken aback. Hadn't she, a woman, been seen as a burden for male guides? How could a mere woman cross the mountain passes in summer, let alone winter? This girl was so very young and slight. Too late now for any qualms, and too bad if they'd been asked to eat in silence: she identified herself to the young woman and asked to speak to her privately, beckoning her to the corridor. The young woman joined her.

She had paid for two passages, Eleanor told her. Could they now add one more to the party? She would pay.

'No,' said the young woman. 'We take only six.' She was the guide for the first part of the journey, she explained. Because of the police everywhere, they could get out of the town only along the river, upstream, against the current, which was quite strong. The boats were light and had room only for six passengers and for her. They were leaving in twenty minutes.

Eleanor returned to the refectory, aware she was the sole disturber of the peace, yet again. She found the nun who had guided Henk to her.

Would she now take her to him? It was a matter of life and death. Without a word or a moment's delay, the nun set aside her food and quickly guided Eleanor down.

Eleanor thanked her, tapped on the door, opened it. 'Henk?' she called softly. There was no answer. She flicked her cigarette lighter and saw the room was empty. The nun had made a mistake. She went to the next door, hoping this was the right one, tapped and opened and called his name again.

'Yes?' she heard a voice say in French. She flicked her lighter on and there they were, having brought in the bed from the other room. She was no martyr: this was too much; she withdrew. She could hardly breathe.

'Eleanor?' she heard Henk call to her.

He appeared, curling the bed blanket around his nakedness.

'Get dressed,' she ordered. 'Both of you. Now. You're leaving.'

Henk dipped back inside. The candle was lit. She waited in the gloomy, dark corridor. In a short time, they appeared.

'You can't go in that,' she said, seeing Hugo in his Wehrmacht greatcoat.

'That is all I have,' he replied to her in French.

'Quickly,' she said. Without sentiment, she took off Claude's coat and handed it to Hugo. They were of similar stature, after all. When he removed his greatcoat in return, she saw he was only in a shirt.

'You'll still die,' she said.

'I survived Russia,' he replied.

'Quickly,' she said, as she peeled off her thick woollen pullover and handed it to him.

He resisted. 'This is too much, madame, what about you?'

'I have another,' she lied.

She had 200 US dollars, most in useful single dollar bills. She handed 100 dollars to Henk.

'You gave me twenty already,' he protested. She insisted. One hundred and twenty dollars for two to get from Spain to Palestine in such an uncertain climate didn't seem much to her. She really had no idea. Did anyone?

'Hurry,' she said, and they followed her back to the refectory, which she found without a mis-turn. She told them to eat as quickly as they could while she went to speak to the young woman.

'These two go,' Eleanor said in as soft an imperative voice as possible. 'I stay.'

This did not impress the young woman at all. Who were these two men? she demanded. Eleanor explained: one had been included in the original deal, the other was in greater need than she.

With French, Hugo understood what she was doing. 'No,' he said, 'I cannot allow this.'

'For God's sake, be quiet,' Eleanor snapped, and her voice echoed around the stone walls, roiling the peace. The clergy and nuns would have to be deaf not to hear, but you wouldn't know they'd heard a thing. They continued eating, their contemplations undisturbed by such worldly ructions. Eleanor made plain her feelings to the young guide. It was the woman's Christian duty to take these two men whose lives were in much greater danger than hers and who had done more than any of them here to prove their courage against the enemy. She left it at that, uneager to go into detail, for fear of ruining any chance they had. They were German soldiers, after all.

Her four companions came to her rescue. Her word was now law. If the two men weren't included, they wouldn't go either. The young woman was furious but relented, predicting disaster, don't blame her. She allowed them time to eat, though with bad grace, and then swept her charges out. The four Frenchmen quickly kissed Eleanor.

'Thank you for saving him,' Hugo said, 'and for this.' He turned and went.

Henk went to hug her, but she held him back. Then she grabbed him and held him, her nose and lips touching his neck, the smell and feel and the warmth of him, and she knew she'd never felt such love before.

'Go,' she whispered and unravelled herself from him. At the doorway, he turned back to look at her, he and his infernal cat, whose head was now poking out of the top of his coat. Then he was gone.

She ran to the door and saw only the turn of his coat as he disappeared up the corridor and away.

She stayed at the door long after they had gone, until she started to feel the cold. For warmth, she slipped her hands into the huge pockets of Hugo's coat. Her right hand found a pistol. *Finnegans Wake*, she realised, was in the chest pocket of Claude's coat, which Hugo was now wearing into Spain. She was aghast. How would she explain this to Sylvia? Sweet reason came to her rescue. Yes, it stabbed at her that she was letting Sylvia down, but she was equally struck by how justice might be at work here. Publishing Mr Joyce's *Ulysses* had made Sylvia's name, but she'd also made his, and then he betrayed her by selling the book to another publisher. She'd been loyal to him; the same could not be said of him to her. And as God was her witness, she, Eleanor, had carried his preposterous book since Paris, even going back when she'd left it behind, not forgetting an exchange that would have saved her a lot of money. She felt quite absolved of any responsibility for it, and what a load off her mind that was. The German pistol in exchange was dismaying. She looked it over carefully. A Mauser. She knew enough from growing up with her brothers and learning to shoot to see the safety catch was on. Caution had her return the beast into the pocket in which she'd found it. She couldn't leave it here, after all. She'd dump it along the way.

'Pockets!' she cried out, remembering with a terrible jolt that her small travelling cosmetics case was in the pocket with Mr Joyce's tome, because, oh God, worst of all, in the other breast pocket of Claude's coat, she had squirreled away her new Lancôme face crème and perfume. And yet she laughed rather than cry. God was clearly determined to cast her near-naked into the world again.

The nun who had guided her to Henk came over, put a kind hand to one of Eleanor's teary cheeks and handed her a napkin from the table. 'Poor madame,' she said. 'You come with me now.' She led

Eleanor back to the table and filled a plate with a wheaten porridge, which she sweetened with honey and with some pieces of dried fruit.

'Eat,' she said. Eleanor did as commanded. Her stomach was empty. She had to keep up her strength as she worked out what to do next.

HOUSE OF RETREAT,
CATHÉDRALE SAINTE-MARIE, OLORON

After prime, early morning, Monday, 15th December 1941

To avoid being alone, Eleanor attended the office of prime in a chapel of the cathedral. It allowed her time to reflect, to think, to work out what she had to do. Why not just give up now? she wondered, forget going home. But if she did that, where would she go? The only answer to that was ultimately prison – and worse, the guillotine. She had killed a Frenchwoman and was Henk's known accomplice. Her intellect rebelled intensely at such an unjust outcome. Her anger against the Nazis for Hettie flamed, and for Henk, even for Hugo. She had to find a way into Spain and she had to do it now. She slipped away before the service was over and returned to the refectory. The younger nuns were preparing breakfast for the Lourdes pilgrims, who were to return that morning on the train. She would ask straight out for help finding a guide. She couldn't imagine anyone here would have a direct line to the police or the Germans. If they said no, she would understand. She'd know where she stood. She made her initial plea to the one who had led Henk and who had fed her.

Supervising the preparations was the nun, who until now had been a nameless Good Samaritan. An ageless and generic face peering out from a black habit now took individual form. She was Sister Perpetua, she told Eleanor. She was older than she had initially looked, with fine, delicate lines around her eyes and her mouth. Her skin was like soft, aged silk. What now animated her so intensely was patriotism. She took Eleanor's hand firmly in hers. Her brother was a farmer in the foothills; this was where she had grown up, on the family farm. He and their shepherds knew the passes. She would find out what might be possible. Eleanor was not to despair.

'Come,' she commanded Eleanor, then led her along the corridor to another room and opened the door. She was not keen to light a candle, and looking through the doorway, Eleanor could see why. This was a repository for clothes left behind over the years by parishioners or deposited by novices when they first withdrew from the outside world. It was now much denuded by the refugees, but Eleanor should take what she needed. She couldn't cross into Spain at this time of year in no more than a coat. She told Eleanor she would come to her as soon as she had word from her brother.

Cheered as much as she might be in her present situation, Eleanor waded into the room, which was a jumble sale waiting to happen, except winter wear was already at a premium. What fun she and Madeleine would have had in this room. What on earth were chemises doing here? Some were so old-fashioned and worn they looked to have been left from the time of Henry IV. Layers, she said to herself, as she collected garments – layers, the more the better. She found no pullovers but found woollen socks, though not in pairs, and she found a scarf that was fur lined. Then, dear God, she found a fur. Smelling it gave her a possible reason for why it had been overlooked, but too bad, she thought. She'd smelt like a fox herself for most of this journey so far. This fur wouldn't make much difference. She took her haul back to her room, where she tried the items on, discarding hardly a stitch. The fur turned out to be a little more worn than she'd expected but better than nothing. Under her Wehrmacht coat, it fitted quite snugly. What she must look like, she thought, aware now that she didn't even have her compact mirror to see. A London pantomime dame, most likely, she thought.

She went back to her room. There on the little table with the crucifix Mrs Teixeira had given her and her cigarette case, was the bottle of Lancôme perfume that she'd already surrendered up to an unlikely fate with its companions. Somewhere, she thought, there's a moral in this.

Through the chilly vent in the wall, the new day was upon her already. She was ready to leave. All she needed was someone to guide her.

Around 3.45pm, Monday, 15th December 1941

The next Eleanor was conscious, she was looking up into the face of Sister Perpetua, who was shaking her awake.

'Madame,' she was saying, 'Madame.'

She'd slept more than nine hours, the sleep of the dead.

'My brother will take you,' said Perpetua.

'How much?' Eleanor asked, as her wits returned with zest.

'Six thousand francs,' said Perpetua.

Eleanor blanched.

Perpetua saw her reaction. 'It is very dangerous now,' she explained. 'Not only the weather but the police and the Germans are up there; they have seen them. He has a family. So do the shepherds. If anything bad should happen,' she added, explanation enough.

Eleanor thought: who am I to complain? She touched Perpetua's hands. 'I understand the risks,' she said. She would pay, but could she pay in dollars?

Perpetua shook her head. The familiar story. 'He cannot use them. They get sent to jail just for having them.'

Eleanor nodded her consent. Perpetua smiled. 'He will come for you at six tonight,' she said.

She departed, leaving Eleanor in a stew. Yes, she had the equivalent in dollars at the current black-market rate, but 6,000 francs in cash she did not have. What would Henk do if he were here? she wondered. He would steal it, no question, from the monastery if necessary. Even in her present desperate situation, this was an unthinkable proposition. The question remained. Where was she to find anyone willing to exchange her dollars? She could hardly go from café to café, especially when she'd noticed so few as she came through the town with the pilgrims. The police and the Gestapo were still looking for her. Then a thought occurred to her. Inspired, she rugged up in her mothy fur and went like a rocket to the only exchange in ready access. This took her outside into the thin daylight, across the yard to the cathedral.

CATHÉDRALE SAINTE-MARIE, OLORON

After 4pm, Monday, 15th December 1941

No one was there. Not a candle flickered from any altar. Vespers was some time away. She looked around to orient herself, and there it was, first noticed when she'd gone to the Gaudete Sunday Mass the night before.

A statue of the Virgin Mary robed in gold.

Luck was with Eleanor. The donations she'd noticed the pilgrims attach to the statue before their return home had not been collected. On close examination, this holy maid was well endowed. France may have been burdened by occupation and the crimes of the occupier, but innocence and trust still ruled in this small patch. Eleanor wondered if she could test this. Again, she asked, knowing the answer already. What would Henk do? Lest moral scruples intervene, she wasted not another second as she added Wells Fargo to the Virgin's many titles, stripping the statue of her hoard of francs as speedily as a gangster robbing a bank. Some of what she had thought was cash turned out to be messages written on small slips of paper, and these Eleanor returned. How much she'd gathered, she did not know until she returned to her niche and counted it.

Four thousand two hundred. Even with what she still had, she was short. That was that, she had to make do. The next question was the one that carried real moral weight: how many dollars should she offer in return? At the latest black-market rate, that would be 70 dollars, 113 at the official Vichy rate. She had 100.

This was no time to quibble. She peeled away 70. She added 5, as a guilt tax, which still left her with 25 dollars to get to Madrid. She hoped it would be enough. It would have to do.

In her pocket was the Mauser. She could hardly hand that over to the Virgin. She would offer it to the guide. Surely it was worth more than the amount she owed.

She looked up at the Virgin. No smile immediately formed on her face, no tears rolled down her alabaster cheeks, nothing to unsettle an Episcopalian. Yet the face was that of the young girl she'd been, her eyes downcast, a vision of humility. Whoever had created this figure had not made some mere store mannequin. The faith and love of all those who had knelt before her, who had stuffed their offerings and prayers into the folds of her veil and gown, gleamed out at Eleanor, making the gold of her robes even more golden.

She couldn't do it. She knew she shouldn't do it.

Quickly, she restored the money whence she'd lifted it, taking back her dollars though leaving the 5 dollar guilt tax, meagre in the great sum of things, but to Eleanor at this moment, as valuable as the widow's mite.

She returned to her cell. If Henk had been with her, he wouldn't have bothered one iota about taking the money and leaving nothing in exchange. In that case, lucky he was gone – but, oh, she missed him intensely and so fondly. Really, they hadn't been able to agree that grass was green, but she'd never felt so alive in all her life. What did she have of him to remember? Nothing. Not a keepsake of any kind, just memories. In her heart, she clung to him and she prayed for him to be safe.

What on earth would she tell the brother of Sister Perpetua when he came for her?

PRESBYTERY,
CATHÉDRALE SAINTE-MARIE, OLORON

Around 4.30pm, Monday, 15th December 1941

Bauer had spent the morning going from roadblock to roadblock. The only excitement was finding the missing German consulate car, discovered at the Gare d'Oloron, hardly surprising. It's where he, Bauer, would have left it. The police presence at the station would have stopped the two taking a train back up the line to Lourdes or up the Aspe Valley to the border at Canfranc. They weren't pilgrims going to Santiago. They needed help and would have to pay for it. So far, none of St Jean's informants, or claimed informants, had produced any hint of the two's whereabouts.

Acting on his hunch about the Catholic Wolf, he had himself driven to the cathedral's house of retreat, where, the police told him, refugees were always taken in. At the presbytery, the Monsignor gave no hint that he'd encountered the two men when shown the poster with Pohl's face.

'No, m'sieur,' he replied. 'We see many Jews, from everywhere these days. But Germans?' If his incredulity wasn't genuine, Bauer thought, he was an excellent liar.

'You might be harbouring murderers and perverts unwittingly, father,' Bauer pressed. He had made his faith clear on arrival – though, under the circumstances, he could only hope but not expect to be rewarded.

'Perverts?'

'Leviticus, father,' said Bauer, not having the precise wording nor chapter or verse at his beckoning.

'Which particular perversion?' the Monsignor asked. 'Leviticus claims so many.'

'Homosexuality,' said Bauer, sitting on his impatience. He had no idea Leviticus offered so large a menu, nor did he care.

'The Church does not approve of such things,' replied the Monsignor, 'but I'm afraid the French state is mute on the subject.'

'They are Germans,' Bauer countered. 'German law follows the Bible.'

'This is France,' said the Monsignor. 'You'll have to stick with plain old murder, I'm afraid. Names, a warrant, that sort of thing.'

The Monsignor smiled a cold smile. Touché.

'I've only ever had one confession of murder in my time,' he continued, detouring then derailing Bauer's train of thought. It was as if this were merely an afternoon chat over coffee. 'I told her' – he saw Bauer's reaction – 'yes, it was a woman. I told her she had to confess first to the police before I could give her any solace, which she did.' He paused to sip from a glass of water. 'Of course, in wartime, the difference between murder and killing is something that exercises jurists and philosophers,' he added.

'And theologians, father?'

'Well,' sniffed the Monsignor, 'Protestant theologians, perhaps. We don't approve of either murder or killing, but judgment is the Lord's.'

That smile again. Bauer knew as he knew his own name that his quarries were or had been here, but hell would freeze over before this old fox would admit it.

Once outside on the footpath, he paced back and forth in impotent fury. Afternoon already. He radioed St Jean, demanding again that he be allowed to search the entire place, 'from under the bishop's bed to the bell tower!'

'No, sir,' St Jean replied. 'I told you already. Besides, what proof do you have?'

'The Monsignor is not telling the truth,' Bauer barked back.

'If the Monsignor says no,' St Jean countered, 'who are you to say a son of the Church is lying? I cannot order for the monastery to be searched. We live here. We need the Church. Sooner than later, you will move on. The answer is no.'

Expecting this was the end of their communication, Bauer handed the receiver to the driver, but even Bauer could hear St Jean calling him back. The driver handed him the receiver again.

'There you are,' St Jean snapped. 'I suggest you return to the *commissariat* immediately. We have news.'

COMMISSARIAT DE POLICE,
OLORON-SAINTE-MARIE

Towards 5pm, Monday, 15th December 1941

Bauer arrived to be told St Jean had four trussed-up but truculent young Frenchmen in custody. Reliable information had come to the police during the morning about a small party of young men making its way into Spain, not up the Somport towards Canfranc, but up one of the other, more inaccessible passes. Thanks to the recent gift of warm air and rain from the Atlantic and the day's bright sun, there was an opportunity to flee, and they had grabbed it. Higher up, winter had descended, and, given the capriciousness of the mountain's gods, there'd been no guarantee they would get through. The same risk applied to St Jean and his men. But St Jean, with his detectives and a detachment of thirteen armed gendarmes as company, had gone up straightaway.

'Why didn't you call me?' Bauer said.

'No time,' St Jean replied.

This was a lie. Bauer understood he'd been kept in the dark so any glory would belong entirely to St Jean. 'How did they get past the police roadblocks?' he asked pointedly.

St Jean's Gallic shrug indicated to Bauer that they'd probably been bribed.

'I want to see the four young men,' he demanded. He had to make sure none was Pohl or Wolf.

The French gendarmes, weapons still in hand, still excited by their catch, and the detectives – success had many fathers – brought forward the four foul-tempered young men and their guide, a young shepherd who seemed entirely resigned to his immediate fate. The four *Gaullistes* kept taunting the police and gendarmes as collaborators and fools. One of the gendarmes had had enough and whacked the young fellow in the face, and he fell down. His pals helped him up.

'You like hitting French patriots, do you?' he retorted. His three pals took up the taunt.

Bauer could see Pohl and Wolf were not among the prisoners.

'This all of you?' Bauer demanded of one of the French boys. 'Two Germans, were they with you? And a woman?'

Now faced by a real German, none of the Frenchmen seemed keen to answer and their taunts against the gendarmes stopped. Bauer realised he would get more sense from the gendarmes.

*

What had happened up on the mountain pass was confusing at first hearing. Bauer couldn't make sense out of it. The gendarme sub-lieutenant explained that they had suddenly heard angry firing as they made their way up a track. Then a group of men had appeared; they were falling back, as if in retreat, and right into their arms. They captured the lot immediately. But the firing continued and was coming their way. They returned fire, even though they could see nothing through the mist, which was becoming thicker. Once they started shooting, the opposing fire stopped.

'Who was shooting?' Bauer asked. 'Partisans?'

'You better ask him, sir,' replied the gendarme and pointed to a youngster in a white German mountain troop uniform. He was a corporal, brought in by the French to have a flesh wound on his arm tended to by a police doctor. The story was starting to make sense to Bauer, but not in a good way.

The corporal was surprised but relieved to encounter Bauer. How was he to get back to his platoon? he asked. Bauer had more imme-diate concerns and, frankly, so did the corporal. That was more than a flesh wound, thought Bauer. The corporal reported that he and his patrol had been on an exercise, but then they'd been ordered to look out for two escapees instead. That afternoon, he was leading his patrol when a party had straggled along the track right in front of them. The corporal had called on them to halt and put their hands up. Most of the men started scrambling back the way they'd come. He ordered his patrol to fire. The mist was so thick, it was hard to see. Then the patrol came under sustained fire on their flank. He was absolutely certain the fire had come from Wehrmacht Mausers and that there'd been more than one.

'No doubt, sir,' he replied to Bauer's urgent request for confirmation.

He ordered his patrol to fire back and begin a flanking movement to get them. But then they came under fire from below. He figured that, in the confusion, they'd come upon French gendarmes, who were known to also be in the area. So he ordered his men to cease fire.

'How many did you see?' Bauer demanded.

'There were seven. We saw them clearly. Five fell back, but two of them flanked us, and they were the ones shooting at us. The froggies got the others.'

'What happened to the ones firing at you?' Bauer's head was bursting.

'We shot one for sure,' the corporal reported.

'How do you know? Did you find the body?'

'No, but we definitely saw him fall. He was firing at us from a ledge above. Novak got a good shot at him from the side and says he got him.'

'What about the other one?' Bauer pressed.

'He got away,' reported the corporal. 'We couldn't see him. The mist was too heavy. And we were being fired at by these froggies. Once we'd sorted that out, I sent my men to look, but I tell you, you couldn't see the hand in front of your face. I called them back. Then I discovered this.' He was furious as he pointed to the wound on his arm. 'How did they get Mausers, sir?' he wanted to know. 'Who are they?'

'Deserters,' Bauer replied. 'Ours.'

'Then they've found a hole to die in,' the corporal spat in disgust. 'Novak's certain he got that one.'

Bauer thanked the corporal, told him he'd arrange his return to Orthez as soon as his wound was fixed. He had the captured guide brought in and hauled him roughly forward by his lapels.

'How many in the party?' he demanded.

'Six,' replied the young man, who had taken over the party for the trek through the high passes. He removed Bauer's fingers from his clothes as if he'd been wearing a Windsor double-breasted blazer rather than a rough jacket spun at home from wool from the family sheep. In other circumstances, Bauer might have been amused by such insolence. Now it deserved a sharp whack, but he let it pass.

'Germans?' Bauer demanded. 'Were two of them German? Was there a woman?'

'They had the pistols,' the boy said. 'One couldn't speak French. The other had an accent. No woman – are you crazy? That's all I know. It doesn't pay to know too much.'

'Did you see one of them get hit?' Bauer persisted, but the boy – he was barely out of short pants – said he couldn't see anything. The two Germans disappeared up the slope, where they started firing back at the German patrol.

This was cold comfort to Bauer, who wanted them both alive. Revenge being a dish best served cold was for those who didn't have sons in the army. Pohl had eluded him yet again, even if it was an escape into certain death. And the woman? Maddened, he suddenly smashed his fist into the wall, something he'd never done in his life. The shock he felt was as acute as the humiliation that now followed because the witnesses, St Jean, even the *Gaullistes*, said nothing, whether from embarrassment or they were content silently to gloat, he didn't know. But humiliating it was. His knuckles bled; his whole arm was still juddering.

'Forgive me,' he muttered in the vague direction of St Jean.

'One was shot; neither will survive the night up there. They'll find the bodies come spring," said St Jean, calmly filling the silence as if nothing untoward had happened. He was not without sympathy for Bauer's evident frustration but what happened to the Germans was no longer of any concern to him. His men had captured the *Gaullistes* and he was delighted. The guide, the young fool, would be locked up and fined. He presented the four smart-mouth *Gaullistes* with two options: join the Foreign Legion immediately or go to the concentration camp at Gurs. They laughed at him.

'Gurs, m'sieur,' said one cockily. They'd easily escape from Gurs. But fighting for the Vichy swine in the middle of the Sahara Desert? *'Non, m'sieur, je vous remercie mais non.'*

St Jean wasn't going to tell them they'd be given no choice. Soon they would be sweating it out under Saharan skies at Tazzougerte, like it or not. Now he could get back to finding the murderess.

Bauer declined St Jean's offer of a lift back to Pau. He would remain in Oloron for the time being. He quickly washed his injured hand, which was starting to throb. He was angry with himself for losing control, especially in front of the French. They must think he was going crazy and maybe they were right. He inspected his face in the mirror and conceded he looked terrible. How long was it since he'd had a good night's sleep? This case was his toughest challenge and it was far from over. If he couldn't see the bloodied bodies of Pohl and his *Tunte*, he wanted to capture the American woman alive so he could personally execute her. He owed it to his sons, did he not?

COMMISSARIAT DE POLICE,
OLORON-SAINTE-MARIE

5.45pm, Monday, 15th December 1941

Bauer radioed Kopitcke in Pau to cable the *Kommandantur* in Nevers and their boss in Paris: '"Killer Pohl and accomplice Wolf believed shot by German patrol. Death probable but not yet confirmed because of weather conditions. American woman still at large." Tell them I'll report any further developments.'

He went to the canteen to gather his thoughts over some food. The place was crowded, legacy of the day's events; they still had the murderess to find. Not that Bauer observed any urgency. So far, luck had offered him meagre pickings in this case, just a couple of boys who had disturbed Pohl from his rathole. He wasn't one to go in for fickle superstitions. That was for crims, who always believed the lady was their companion, until she wasn't. That's why they were caught, they believed; nothing to do with police work. Preparation finally meets opportunity, as Seneca says of luck, the sort you make yourself.

Now, as Bauer made himself eat despite having no appetite and despite his right hand hurting like hell, preparation finally did meet opportunity through a voice that came to him above all the others in the room. His mind trimmed away the extraneous words, guided as if by instinct to fillet the man's story down to 'beautiful auburn hair' and 'older woman' and 'a real beauty' and 'steaming row', but best of all, 'they were speaking English' and 'sounded like Americans'.

'We thought she was going to smack him in the mouth,' said the only voice in the room Bauer was listening to, 'but he grabbed her and kissed her. You should've seen it, hot, hot, hot. First up, Maurice here reckoned they were mother and son, but if that was his ma, we should've arrested them both, eh?'

The group laughed. Bauer couldn't hear any more above the jumble of ribbings and wisecracks.

Where, dear God? When? As he was about to ask, two men stood up from the group. They were about to start their night's work.

'Heading for St Mary's to try your luck, are you, lads?' quipped a voice from one of the stayers.

'Sure she wasn't a nun?' said another.

Bauer had already set aside his knife and fork. Was she still there? He stood and left the room, unnoticed amid the ribaldry. He took out another Pervitin tablet and slipped it into his mouth to keep him going.

He called for his driver. He wasn't going to share this information with St Jean or the French. She was his. Shot while trying to escape. He wouldn't enjoy it, but the outcome would be entirely satisfying and appropriate. He'd be able to look his boys in the eye.

Just before 6pm, Monday, 15th December 1941

Eleanor was ready. Her rucksack was tight with her remaining cigarettes and what clothes she could fit in. With neither cleansers nor face crème for her face, she had to make do with freezing water and what passed for soap. At least she had her bottle of Lancôme. If and when Henk or Hugo discovered her other cosmetics in the breast pockets of Claude's coat, Henk, the Marxist fool, she thought, would probably throw them away as capitalist frippery, ignorant of their worth as bargaining chips.

She took the scent from her pocket, where she'd tucked it safely away, and sprayed herself liberally. If she was going to freeze to death or be shot by a German patrol, she wanted to smell as nice as she could. Given the clothes she was wearing, this was a tall order. She had ripped the shoulder epaulettes off her Wehrmacht greatcoat, although that would hardly make any difference to the silhouette she might present. The only thing that could be said was that it might give the Boches pause before they shot at her. Underneath she had on the fox, whose reek was another reason for her liberal application of scent, and three chemises she'd rummaged out of the lost-and-found cellar. Around her neck was a thick woollen scarf and over that the crucifix given her by Mrs Teixeira. If only Madeleine or Sylvia could see her now.

Like some incarcerated felon, she started to pace her cell. If her journey didn't start soon, she would go crazy. She looked at her watch. She lit a cigarette to calm her nerves. Moments later, the door was pushed open – no knocking – and there was Sister Perpetua. Like some schoolgirl caught red-handed by the principal, Eleanor hid the cigarette behind her back.

'Madame,' Perpetua tut-tutted.

Shamefaced, Eleanor stubbed out the offending cigarette. As Perpetua hurried her out, she let it drop inadvertently, a terrible waste. Too late.

*

The retreat's front door was open. No one sat at the reception desk. Bauer just walked in. He'd left his car some distance away, told the driver he would make his own way back. In his old coat and battered hat, he looked like any of the countless elderly refugees or pilgrims of the Way who passed through the doors. He shuffled along the corridor, passing the tiny rooms, some open, some closed, all occupied. No one stopped him. No one noticed him. But this was no way to find the American.

'Excuse me, youngsters,' he said in French to the children skylarking up and down the stairs. 'I'm looking for the lady with the lovely red hair, the American lady.'

His question drew silence and suspicion.

'Don't tell him,' warned the Artful Dodger in Viennese slang to his gang.

'I'm sorry, my boy, what was that?' Bauer replied. Viennese it might be, a dialect he found ugly and often incomprehensible, but this was simple enough.

'Who are you?' demanded the Dodger's offsider in French, as tough a little girl as Bauer had seen. A good question, Bauer thought. He hadn't prepared an answer. 'A friend' seemed inadequate.

'What did you do to your hand?' the voice of a younger child asked.

'I caught it in a door,' said Bauer absently. 'The lady is my wife,' he added, more to his immediate point.

'Why'd you do that?' the little voice kept on but Bauer's ears were tuned to the Dodger's.

'He don't sound like a Yank,' the kid said in Viennese to his offsider.

Bauer smiled. 'We've been travelling separately from Paris,' he said. 'We're trying to escape to America. My wife, you see, she is American.'

'You ain't American,' the Artful Dodger threw back at him in French.

'But of course not,' Bauer agreed, amiably. 'I am French. My wife is from New York. They told me she's here but I'm terrible with directions. I thought they said she was along here. Have you seen an American lady here?' He wasn't sure if his sad tone would affect this lot of hard-hearts, even if his acting skills seemed to be holding up.

'What'll you give us?' the Artful Dodger demanded.

'Yes, yes, of course,' Bauer replied, 'you deserve something.' He dug out notes from his pocket, where he kept enough French money for all immediate circumstances, and peeled off 50 francs in small denominations. He first handed 25 francs to the Dodger. It seemed a reasonable amount for a man to pay for the whereabouts of his wife. Eager hands took the rest of the money, and soon Bauer was down the stairs to the basement and outside a door.

'That's her room,' said the Dodger.

Bauer didn't need them to tell him what the Lancôme confirmed. He knocked.

'She's left you, mister,' said the Artful Dodger's offsider at the lack of a reply. 'She's got a boyfriend.'

'Yeah,' said another, with a spite that Bauer in a different setting would have enjoyed. 'They run off together.'

He smiled his thanks to get rid of them and pushed open the door, but they were too curious to leave. He shone his pocket torch around – not a good sign to the Artful Dodger, who cautioned the others to back off. In the air was her signature, the Lancôme, and on the floor was a cigarette, barely smoked. Bauer picked it up. Chesterfield. The blackened tip was still warm. He'd just missed her.

'You finish it, son,' he said, handing the cigarette to the Dodger, who slipped it behind his ear.

With the Lancôme as his compass, Bauer hurried back up the stairs and along the corridor, away from the entrance and eventually out a door at the far end of the building and across to the cathedral, where vespers would soon start.

CATHÉDRALE SAINTE-MARIE, OLORON

Around 6pm, Monday, 15th December 1941

Candles sparked on the altar and from the sconces along the walls of the nave. Some parishioners huddled in the front pews, elderly widows and spinsters who rarely missed a Mass, no matter the weather or time of day or night. The organ burst into life, heralding the approach of the clergy. Perpetua led Eleanor to the Mary chapel. Eleanor was glad she had resisted temptation. To wait under the gaze of the Virgin Mary covered in American dollars while her pockets were stuffed with the Virgin's francs was a test she was relieved she didn't have to undergo.

'*Deus, in adiutorium meum intende. Domine, ad adiuvandum me festina,*' chanted the priests as they processed down the nave with the Monsignor – O God, come to my assistance. O Lord, make haste to help me. An unseen choir of women's voices sang the antiphonal.

As the last of the procession passed, one of the monks peeled off and entered the Mary chapel. Perpetua smiled.

'Vidal,' she whispered to Eleanor. The monk removed the hood of the cowl he had worn to enter. He disrobed quickly and handed the cowl to Perpetua.

Eleanor was astonished. Perpetua was fifty-plus if she was a day. Vidal was young. Thirty? No more. This cheered Eleanor. He was sturdy, with big farmer's hands and arms, tall, a big man with a bashful smile on a round face, which was all the handsomer for three days or so of whiskers.

'You think we look alike?' Perpetua said whimsically. 'My baby brother. I can't believe he's got so big.' She took his arm fondly.

'Vidal, madame,' said the young man shyly and shook her hand.

'I'm sorry, but I can't pay you in francs,' Eleanor said immediately. 'I only have American dollars.'

Vidal frowned and he sighed. 'What to do?' he said. 'Didn't my sister tell you?'

'Yes, I tried,' Eleanor pleaded, 'but there is no one to change them.'

'I gotta pay off cops, I gotta pay for the horses,' he replied, annoyed. 'You reckon they'll take your dollars?'

Eleanor knew that, didn't she? Her escape looked to be over before it was beginning. Too late to regret her idiotic moral scruples. The statue of the Virgin Mary with its precious francs was barely feet away.

'Give them to me,' Perpetua said to Eleanor. 'I'll get the francs for you,' she told her brother.

'Where are you going to get that sort of cash from?' he demanded. 'Rob a bank?'

'That's my business,' she replied. 'Don't you trust your own sister?'

'Course I do,' he said gruffly. 'But when?'

'Now,' said Perpetua blithely. Whereupon she took Eleanor's dollars and proceeded to strip the statue of the Virgin Mary of all its francs. 'I've lost count, but I'm sure it's enough,' she said, returning. Eleanor knew exactly but wisely kept her mouth shut and her amusement hidden.

Vidal could never have believed his sister capable of such an act, and as for a bride of Christ? 'You'll go to hell,' he said.

'Look who's talking!' she retorted sharply. 'If Our Holy Mother doesn't worry, why should you? Cash is cash. Now go.'

Eleanor embraced Perpetua. 'Why?' she asked.

'You know why,' Perpetua replied. 'Our Holy Mother knows why.'

As she hurried after Vidal, Eleanor told herself that one day she'd return and confess to her little saviour.

They would have to go upriver first to avoid the roadblock on the Aspe Valley road out of town, Vidal explained. Beyond that, they would ride on his motorbike to his farm, where she would stay with him and his wife until the weather was clear. Either he or one of the shepherds would take her up through the pass to the Spanish border.

Eleanor happily agreed. She kissed Perpetua again, who gave her a blessing and a St Christopher medal.

'He will look after you,' she said.

With vespers continuing, Eleanor and Vidal departed through a door in the transept. The sky was moonless and thinly clouded, shading the starlight. The dark night swallowed them up.

BANKS OF THE RIVER ASPE, OLORON

Towards 7pm, Monday, 15th December 1941

Eleanor followed close on Vidal, who led her along a back laneway that paralleled the road, heading towards the river away from the cathedral. Soon, they crossed the main road and went down a rough track by some old houses to the bank of the Aspe, where the air was icy cold. At least she would not have to wade through it or cross it on stones. That terrible night she would never forget.

To avoid the roadblocks into and out of Oloron, Vidal had travelled down in a sturdy wooden canoe, which he'd hauled up onto the bank and left in the shadows. The flow of the river here was gentle and made little sound. They would have to paddle upstream, past the bridge. There, the rapids would muffle the little outboard motor they'd need to get them further upriver, to where he'd secreted his motorbike. Eleanor insisted she could paddle too, and he said he was glad because otherwise they wouldn't make it.

'Stop!' It was in perfect French and cut through the air like a shot from a gun but Eleanor didn't at first comprehend.

'Your hands up now.'

This Eleanor understood, all too clearly. Vidal had already raised his hands. She bolted like lightning behind the trunk of an old oak.

'Stop,' Bauer called as he revealed himself, his pistol raised. 'Stop or I shoot this man. You understand?'

At long last he had her. He was sure of it. Even in the dark, her auburn hair was shining. But hadn't he seen that face before? Yes, on the footpath outside the parfumerie in Pau. So damn close. This was vindication. She would pay for Pohl's murders and she would pay for the one she had committed herself. Justice at work. He pressed his advantage, even though his right hand, holding his pistol, was killing him.

'Do you not understand?' Bauer said, his voice tense, his anger rising. 'Come out, hands up, or I shoot your guide.'

Eleanor shook with fear. She was terrified. How brave one could be until one actually faced death.

'Our patrol killed your boyfriend and his wife last night,' Bauer called out.

'What did you say?' she spat as she burst out in fury from her shelter. Here was Eleanor's dander at work; her famously short fuse, with its own foolhardy will, rescuing her from possible disgrace. It was the sort of mind-snap that rewards some soldiers under fire with the highest medals of honour, if they survive.

'You foolish woman, you wasted your love and money on a Jew pervert,' Bauer sneered in triumph. 'I am glad this is the last thing you know before you die.'

'How dare you,' she retorted. She saw him warn Vidal to back away, then point his pistol at her.

Two shots rang out almost simultaneously, the sound ricocheting as one against the few houses that backed onto the river.

Eleanor felt the shot whizz past her. But it was Bauer who fell sideways to the ground, blood gushing from the wound in his neck.

'You devil,' she growled down at him, the Mauser she'd shot him with in her hand.

He didn't understand.

'Georg?' he asked, puzzled.

But it wasn't Georg he saw, it was his other boy, Karl, standing over him. He was in his Afrika Korps khakis, but they were covered in blood and part of his face was shot away.

'Papa?' the boy said in surprise.

'Karl?' Bauer cried out but then the boy was gone. His left hand scrabbled for his wallet inside his coat and he managed to pull it out, but he needed both hands to open it.

Eleanor was already bending down to do it for him.

'Photographs?' she asked, matter-of-fact. She wasn't ready to offer compassion; that would come much later. Bauer grunted.

She found pictures of two young men, soldiers in uniform. She held them close so he could see. He grabbed the one of Karl and gazed at it and then at her, trying to tell her something. In the next moment, his eyes glazed over. He was dead.

Vidal was trembling. He pulled urgently at Eleanor's arm. The boat was ready. If they didn't go now, they'd be done for. With the calm resolution of an Al Capone, Eleanor carefully wiped the fingerprints from the pistol she'd used, prised Bauer's pistol, another Mauser, from his right hand, pocketed it, and wrapped his fingers around the pistol she had used and which she dropped a short distance from his body. If the police didn't look too closely, they might reasonably assume the man had shot himself. One of his photographs lay on the ground, the other on his spread-eagled coat. His little bottle of Pervitin tablets had also fallen from his pocket. Ignoring Vidal's further plea to hurry up, she rifled through Bauer's pockets, where she found his thick cache of francs. How much, she did not know, and now wasn't the time to count it. She pocketed all of it.

Numb, her anger spent, she stumbled over to the boat and Vidal helped her in. He pushed them away from the shore, downstream at first. Then, after gaining enough momentum, he turned them back against the current.

'Paddle,' he urged. 'Hard.'

They had only a few hundred yards to paddle up to the rapids past a stone bridge, but the way was slow and arduous, the more so as they came against the faster flow.

'You saved my life,' said Vidal as they passed the body of their pursuer on the bank.

Yes, she thought, but she didn't deserve his thanks. The instant she'd heard the demand to stop, to put up her hands, she'd fled in panic, nothing heroic about it. She'd left Vidal, her saviour, to face the German alone. At heart, she believed, she was a coward. As she'd quaked behind the tree, at least she'd had the presence of mind to take the pistol from her pocket and release the safety catch. Though they were both alive as a result, she shot this man not to save Vidal's life nor really to save her own. Yes, she'd felt his shot miss her in the split second before she fired at him but she meant to kill him in revenge for Henk, and be hanged what St Paul said about vengeance being the Lord's. She would defend herself when her time came.

Suddenly, she stopped paddling. The full force of what the German had spat at her, signing his death warrant, now hit her. Those words, 'his wife' and 'Jew pervert'. If he knew the truth about Henk, he had to know he was dead.

'Paddle, for God's sake, paddle,' Vidal hissed.

She went through the motions. What was the point?

Henk had been painfully right about her believing she could sit out the war. Even the discomforts of daily life under the occupier she had enjoyed in a perverse way. She'd certainly enjoyed complaining about them. Her grief over Claude's death – even that had been fake. What she had done was wallow in her loss while her anger at what she took as Claude's betrayal festered away, repressed and unrecognised. Even then, had she not been the progenitor of her own misery?

If grief be the price of love, she certainly knew it now. Vidal could hear her weeping. Strange woman, he thought. Why would you cry at shooting a German?

'Paddle, madame, please,' he kept encouraging. 'One, two, one, two.'

Eleanor did as he asked, for his sake, not hers.

'One, two,' she said along with Vidal, even after they were a little more secure under the sound of the rapids and Vidal got the motor running. Still, they needed to paddle hard to keep up against the current.

VAL D'ASPE TO THE
VAL D'OSSAU

Between 8.30 and 9pm, Monday, 15th December 1941

Within an hour, she was on the back of Vidal's motorbike, her arms aching so much she barely had enough strength to place them tight around his waist. After only a few minutes, she was so cold that had her life depended upon it, she couldn't have let go. Soon even Vidal felt like a block of ice. For all she knew, he might have died and it was his ghost guiding the bike around the curves, on and on, ever higher, no headlight to guide their way. In her ears, the roar of the little motor as Vidal constantly changed gear seemed so loud, it astonished her they hadn't alerted every policeman between Oloron and the frontier, paid off or no.

How long they took to reach Vidal's farm, which was in another of the valleys heading into the mountains, she had no idea. They left the asphalt and rode along a gravel track up through a higher valley, a seemingly never-ending slip-slide affair through mud and mush, around the steep slopes, ever higher and higher. After they arrived, and for some time, she could hear nothing but the motor's high pitch. Nor could she move. Things did not much improve once she had been thawed before the fire. Her bones, her muscles and her limbs, unused to exertions beyond the demands of a shopping expedition, were stiff and painful. But she felt safe in the hands and hearth of this kindly, young Béarnaise farmer.

She counted the francs she'd removed from the dead German. Over 9,000, a fortune, 3,000 more than the cost of her trip.

'These are for you,' she said, leaving it to him and his conscience to return some of them to the statue. He nodded and took them. She also handed him the Mauser.

'Where and how the hell did you get it?' He'd been meaning to ask since it saved his life.

'A comedy of errors,' Eleanor replied, which made her even weepier.

'You might need it more than me,' he said.

She doubted that, she replied. To be found with a Mauser on the other side of the border seemed to her to be asking for trouble.

'I'll keep it for the journey,' he said in concession to her present emotional collapse. It might even come in handy if things went wrong.

Wednesday into Thursday, 16th and 17th December 1941

The weather worsened during the night of their escape, a blessing according to Vidal, who let Eleanor sleep inside his house, albeit in the attic. She did sleep, then she wept, then she made plans to write a novel of her love, this escape, something, anything. She was still angry, at the Germans, at herself. Most of all, she felt a simmering anger against God. They waited out the following day, not knowing when they might be able to move. Or if at all. She could see up the valley: the skies were clear cobalt blue. Why they couldn't go now, she didn't understand. She kept her impatience in check. Vidal said they would go when it was safe, which meant when the clouds were low and the mists heavy. Bad weather but not too bad. German patrols were still about in the high passes, so he'd heard.

'We leave in one hour,' Vidal said to her. They had just finished dinner. She was still sore from head to foot but strangely not at all weary. What was said about the hardiness of New Englanders was true, at least in her case. What she looked like was another matter. Since she'd lost her compact mirror, she couldn't check the damage. All she had was her reflection in the windows: an old hag with bags under her eyes from weeping.

They left before midnight on horseback. Eleanor was no novice when it came to horses, having ridden in Bar Harbor. That had been quite some time ago, but needs must. Vidal had to help her. 'You look after me, darling,' she said to the horse, 'and I'll look after you.' Quite how she might keep her end of the bargain, she did not know. She knew that you had to talk firmly but with respect to horses, and she hoped the animal would sense her need. As they set off along a track up to the pass, it seemed to Eleanor that it was doing no such thing. Every cell in her body juddered. She eyed the rifle Vidal had draped across his back. If only she hadn't given him the Mauser, she could put a bullet through the wretched beast's head. That this would also have ended her own flight didn't enter her thoughts. The revenge she'd wreak on this hack, if she could, helped not only to boost her spirits but also to keep her on its miserable back.

After an hour of this torture, they dismounted at a wooden barn, where Vidal watered and fed the horses and wiped them down.

'Thank God,' Eleanor said, looking spitefully at the horse which responded with what Eleanor took as a vicious smile and she snarled at it.

The rest of the route was to be on foot, taking them away from Vidal's family's land and up into the high pass, towards the frontier at the Col du Pourtalet.

'Are you up to it?' he asked.

'Vidal,' she said firmly, 'if I do drop, just leave me. On no account are you to risk yourself trying to save my sorry arse.'

He chuckled at her colloquial French, not taking her seriously. She made him promise. If there was to be any further death, it was to be hers only.

They spent the night in one of the huts used during the summer months by generations of shepherds who built them using the stones that lay so liberally about. But, as Vidal told her, despite Matthew's observation that the wise man built on the rock, the mountain gods often knocked the huts over if they were so minded. Repairs, especially to the roofs, were always necessary and were made during the summer months. Summertime was also when they were stocked with firewood, which had to be brought up on horseback from lower down. Eleanor did not mind sheltering there. It was better than any alternative currently on offer.

They ate some of the food Vidal's wife had prepared, and then they slept. When Eleanor woke, some time into the day, Vidal was gone. His rucksack was gone. She looked at her watch. Three in the afternoon. Outside, the sky was clear. In the strange stillness, she hoped she might hear him nearby. All she heard was her anxious and heavy heart. Perhaps she'd find kindling to help light a fire.

They were above the tree line. The succulent grasses that sprouted from the thin soil among the unforgiving granite and the rocky detritus of ancient glaciers were now burnt and brown. Yet their roots gave sustenance to the chamois, who were still poking around, although soon even they would leave for the lower slopes. Gnarled, woody bushes survived here and there in the shelter of rocky ledges, tiny miracles. No matter that Eleanor pulled and sawed at them with a sharp rock, they refused to give up a single fibre to her. The only piece of wood she found was a wispy stick. In the stillness, she heard the sound of running streams and the rattle of the pebbles and stones being washed down. She looked up. The sky was deep and empty, so blue and endless it was oppressive. Her ears, tuned to silence, heard the chirping of small birds. She could not see them, however she looked. Hearing a cry above, she looked up and saw a lone vulture passing overhead effortlessly, and then another, going south, late departures for warmer parts. Of all the ill omens to encounter, she thought, even for someone who didn't believe in them.

A failure as a collector of firewood, she found a rock to sit on. She was beyond caring. Her aches were now either gone or she was numb to them. Where was Vidal? What if he didn't come back? She was as alone as she'd ever been in her life. She'd not thought to ask him the direction – though, on reflection, hadn't the vultures shown her the way south? What then of the ill omen? She wasn't alone. She was back up that tree in the garden of their house at Bar Harbor. Her little brother Will was below, gazing up at her. 'You talking to God up there again, Elly?'

The fury that suddenly engulfed her had her up on her feet, her fists raised against the heavens, her voice screeching.

'*Menteur!*' she raged up at God – Liar! She continued in a mixture of profane English and French, spitting out words she never used in either language. He was '*une con, une* fucking *menteur, vous m'avez promis que vous le soignez.* I'll never forgive you.'

She was so caught up in her rage that she wasn't aware of the mist rolling down from the mountain until she could barely see further than a few feet. This shut her up. She fell back onto the rock she'd been sitting on, exhausted.

'Fuck you,' she muttered in English, spent. She decided to give up the ghost now. If only that Mauser was in her pocket instead of Vidal's. Instead, she would just lie here, go to sleep and be frozen to death.

Hardly seconds later, Vidal found her.

'What are you doing?' he spat under his breath, angrily hauling her up.

She said nothing, allowing him to lead her back to the hut, where he made a fire with logs from the wood pile and kindling he had found. If the Germans really wanted to put a spoke in their wheels, they'd simply visit the shepherds' huts and burn up all the wood gathered during the summer. It hadn't come to that yet. As he arranged the precious wood, he demanded to know why she'd been advertising her presence to every Boche and cop this side of the Spanish border? He didn't give her time to answer. He'd been searching frantically for her, he continued. He'd not been able to call out to her. 'For obvious reasons,' he added. 'Except you – ' He stopped and stoked the fire rather than his anger.

'I didn't bring you all this way for you to give up,' he said, once the flames had taken. His temper had subsided. 'You want those shits to win?' he asked.

It hadn't crossed her mind she might have been attracting a German bullet. She might have yelled louder. Yes, it had been the rage of a child, sore as her heart was – a tantrum. But hadn't she killed one of those shits, as Vidal called the Boches, three if she included the two killed by Henk, four if she added the grasping treacherous concierge? This made her feel a little better, although her anger at God had not abated. She wasn't going to apologise to Vidal for that. But he was right. Did she still not have a mighty score to settle with the whole benighted Germanic lot of them now?

'I'm sorry,' she murmured. 'It won't happen again.'

TOWARDS THE COL DU POURTALET, PYRÉNÉES

Afternoon, Friday, 18th December 1941

The clear skies kept them in the hut on Thursday night. The stars were so bright and momentous she could have reached out and touched the Milky Way. Their silhouettes against the rocky landscape would have been perfect targets. Armed with his rifle, Vidal kept watch from an eyrie above the hut with a view of the track. They couldn't afford a fire now. Eleanor insisted she swap places with him once she realised what he was doing for her. Besides, inside the hut without a fire was as cold as outside.

'I can shoot,' she told him. That he knew, so he relented. He was in need of sleep.

By Friday, Vidal was anxious to move. A new moon would rise tonight. They needed to get off the mountain before it waxed too much. Bad weather was coming. He could sense it before it arrived. No sixth sense, just his observations from a lifetime living here: the birds going to ground in advance of the snows. He hoped the weather would worsen but not too much.

They set out early on Friday afternoon. With luck, they'd be at the frontier before midnight. He told her he was making a detour to avoid the pass where, a couple of days earlier, the police, gendarmes and the Germans had run into each other and a tiny war had broken out. Everyone knew about it and had been delighted. Then he'd heard some French boys had been captured. Two had also been killed, so it was said. Eleanor bit her lip.

'We cross to Spain near the top of the same pass,' he explained, drawing in the dust with his finger before rubbing it all away. 'The frontier post is closed there now. It's still a dumb time of year to be doing this,' he muttered, as much to himself as to her.

Once outside, light sleet stung their faces. Their boots crunched all too loudly along the stony track through the intermittent mist. Vidal was carrying his rifle. He handed Eleanor the Mauser.

'Just in case the Boches make an appearance,' he told her. Did she know they came in from Orthez via the Spanish side of the frontier? 'Chauffeured up by Franco himself.'

They traipsed on for an hour. Light sleet continued to fall. Then, pebbles, followed by larger stones, started to fall around them and roll down the slopes. Vidal pushed Eleanor off the side of the track, where he crouched with her behind a large boulder. The stones kept falling around them.

'Chamois,' he whispered to her, 'heading to lower ground to get away from the weather.' He couldn't see them, but this was a sign the weather was worsening. They had to hurry if they were to make the hut at the frontier before the snows set in. He scanned the landscape up and around. There they were, the chamois. He pointed. Eleanor saw them, two females tripping with sure feet down the steep sides of a draw, followed by the buck. In other circumstances she would have been charmed.

A shot rang out, its sharp crack echoing around the rocky pass like the snap of a whip. Vidal pushed Eleanor's head back down.

Another shot.

One chamois fell. The others appeared, flying through the air, so it seemed to Eleanor, as further shots followed.

'German,' Vidal whispered to Eleanor. They were shooting at the chamois, merely because they could. He beckoned her to follow, as he crept further out of sight. Given her stiffening limbs, Eleanor surprised herself by scrabbling after him like a crab. How long it took before they heard the crunch of German boots along the scree, she did not know. It seemed like ages and their passing seemed to take an eternity. She even heard the Germans' voices, joking and cursing, until a sharp word from their leader shut them up. Vidal looked at Eleanor; his finger went to his lips. He wasn't confident that she might not leap out and start firing at them. There was no need for her to do so. The ribaldry of the Germans was a clear sign they'd stood themselves down from duty, at least in their own minds.

They waited for some time after the German patrol had passed. Night was already upon them. The sleet was turning to snow. Before they started out, Vidal handed her a flask of brandy mixed with milk. 'Drink,' he ordered. 'More,' he urged, after she had sipped daintily as if in a chic bar and not to keep herself alive. Now, so encouraged, she took a couple more generous draughts, fuelling her spirit as much as it moved her limbs.

After midnight, Saturday, 19th December 1941

Eleanor stuck to Vidal like glue for the hours it took them to struggle through the falling snow up what was no more than a summer cow path to a track leading to the top of the pass. How he knew where to go was a miracle to her. Snow a foot deep had covered everything. Inside Eleanor's layers of refugee chic was a sauna. Vidal had them stop every hour to drink water. Eleanor asked for brandy.

'No,' he said. 'Only when we arrive.'

She was numb to anything except the movement of her legs, when suddenly, she bumped into him. He'd stopped.

'We're here, madame, thanks be to Our Holy Mother,' he told her. 'You're in Spain.'

She didn't quite believe him. At the beginning of her journey, she'd fancied her escape into freedom in quite a different way – a blue Mediterranean sky, a clear view of France behind her and a warm Spanish welcome before her, and in the distance, Madrid, a warm bath, bed and a branch of Wells Fargo. Now she could barely see the hand she held up in front of her. Although Vidal was with her, although he had carried her through, grief at Henk's death gripped her heart. He had been dealt such a lousy hand. She was still too furious with God, her mouth too full of ashes, to exalt at her escape.

UNION STATION, PROVIDENCE, RHODE ISLAND

11am, Thursday, 15th April 1943

Eleanor's two sisters, Constance and Muriel, stood either side of their mother on the concourse, as much to shield her from the cold, which had returned the day before, as to provide support for her against what they already knew but she did not. Nor, indeed, did Constance's and Muriel's own families know. Nosy as they were about the return of their gorgeous and scandalous aunt, today their young ones were all at school or in the services. Their husbands had come, however, including Joe, Muriel's husband, who was home on leave from the navy. They weren't going to miss this special occasion and stood in a male huddle with Eleanor's older brothers, Charles and Jim, all physicians, like Eleanor's father. You could hold a meeting of the AMA at a family dinner.

The senior Dr Gorton, grey-haired and erect, usually the epitome of a rock-faced New Englander, was like an excited child. He pressed against the gate to the platform. While he didn't play favourites, he'd always had a soft spot for dreamy Eleanor. She could do no wrong, which in her case over the years had certainly covered a lot of the waterfront.

Only Will was missing, the hole in the family fabric, killed in action with the 43rd Infantry Division on Guadalcanal the previous October, which made the return of the prodigal daughter and sister the more poignant.

'Where is she?' Dr Gorton fretted. The expected train from New York, already announced, was failing to appear. He hadn't seen her since the summer of 1939, her last trip home for the publication of one of those books of hers. He was proud of her success – less of the books themselves, which didn't appeal to him at all, than of the money she made. Why, she was rolling in it – thank God, given she had no husband to support her. He merely repeated what Constance and Muriel said about the books, which, coming from a man sounded hilarious and exposed the extent of his reading. He was a practical man – history, facts, that sort of thing. Eleanor knew that.

He turned back to see his wife with their daughters. 'Don't you excite yourself, Mother,' he cautioned.

Then the locomotive appeared, slowly drew in and stopped at the buffer, where it expelled clouds of steam and smoke, obscuring the cars behind. Passengers began to alight. He jumped up and down.

'Where is she?' he cried, unable to see through the crowds, mostly servicemen, racing for the exit. 'Is she coming?'

'Your father's behaving like a child,' Mrs Gorton observed severely.

Eleanor walked along the platform. She was about to reach her goal, except now it seemed a thoroughly bad idea. What on earth was she doing? She couldn't see her mother yet, but knew she was waiting on the concourse, doubtless her lips thinning. They would thin even more in a moment. She quailed. Worse would be the pained silence. Really, she could turn around now and get back on the train before they saw her. But since it had taken her sixteen long months to get from Paris to Providence, and she had only just managed to beg, borrow and steal a passage from Lisbon at the last moment, the thought of a return to Europe was more daunting than facing the disapproval of her mother. What she'd gone through to get here! After her escape from France, she'd languished for two weeks in a Spanish jail, from which she'd been freed only by her remaining stash of dollars. Penniless and over one hundred miles from Madrid, she expended her remaining Chesterfields to reach there. Then she'd been stranded a further fourteen months in Lisbon.

So she had told her mother and father. The Spanish part of her story was true. Over the Portuguese chapter, she'd dropped a veil of mystery, as she had done over the details of her escape from France. Now she had to face the music.

Eleanor and her family appeared to one another through the thinning crowds and the vanishing steam from the locomotive.

'What's that Eleanor's carrying?' her mother said instantly.

'Calm yourself, Mother,' said Muriel.

'Father,' said Eleanor as she came past the ticket barrier. She kissed him, and to save herself from falling into an unseemly heap of tears on his shoulder, she gently removed the shawl that was shielding her baby's face from the cold.

'What do you think of your new grandson?' she said.

'Why, Eleanor!' her father exclaimed in genuine but delighted astonishment. 'Oh my goodness,' he kept saying, darting his eyes from his favourite daughter to this startling revelation.

Mrs Gorton saw quite plainly what was in the bundle in Eleanor's arms.

'Calm yourself, Mother,' Constance echoed her sister.

'Stop saying that,' she said curtly. 'I am calm. Very calm.'

Eleanor's sisters and brothers enveloped her. Constance lifted the baby from Eleanor's arms with gushes and kisses. What her brothers were thinking, Eleanor had no idea. She had to confront her mother.

'Well, Mother,' she said, leaning in to kiss her on the cheek, 'it took a little while longer to get here than I expected.' Barely holding up, she dabbed tears from her eyes.

'Does the child's father come attached to you as a husband, by chance?' Mrs Gorton asked, pained.

'No, Mother,' Eleanor replied, starting to laugh. Her mother was so her mother. This started off her sisters. 'Oh, come on, Mother, you can't say you're entirely surprised,' she said at the thin lips pursing in front of her. 'Aren't you happy? I am.'

'But what are we going to say?' Mrs Gorton said.

'Whatever you want to say, dear,' said Eleanor.

'Yes, Eleanor, but what's the truth?' Mrs Gorton asked. 'Surely we're entitled to that?'

Her mother was quite right. 'Yes, Mother, you are.' The advent of this baby had lifted her from a dark place in her heart, restoring her will to live and her joy. She'd tell them the truth, but not right now.

Mrs Gorton's travails about social death vanished as the absence of Will was suddenly so painful that they all cried in an atypical public display of grief.

'I thought it was going to be another one of those novels of yours,' said Mrs Gorton eventually, trying without much success to be stern again. She was still wiping her eyes. A new novel, something to be borne rather than enjoyed, would have been a relief compared to this.

Eleanor didn't have the heart to confess she had the manuscript of *Three Women* with her, the novel she'd written in Lisbon during her confinement and her baby's first months. At last she had found a way to write about Claude by writing about the women in his life. That and the baby, and the job she'd held until the week before the child came, had occupied all those Lisbon months.

Soon after her arrival in Lisbon, even though she was pregnant, her fluency in French and things Parisian and the experience of her recent escape had opened doors to a job with a shady crew of young men, rather like her brothers, who worked out of the American embassy. 'I was a spy,' she'd tell her family later, somewhat embroidering her role, though the same crew were keen to see her in Washington as soon as she was able.

As a civilian, she really was at the bottom of the list for a seat on one of the Pan Am Clipper flying boats that took off daily from the Tagus river in Lisbon for the United States on a long and dangerous trek via South America. Motherhood hadn't offered any advantage either. She'd have to be Eleanor Roosevelt and not Eleanor Gorton-Clarke to get a seat. She'd had the added difficulty of her new baby's nationality. Yes, he was eligible for American citizenship, thanks to her, but they could apply only after returning to the US. What he was in the meantime, and what papers he could travel on, seemed a lawyers' picnic. Was he stateless or Portuguese or, grimly, a subject of the *Deutsches Reich*? And did having an alien as a father matter if father and mother were not married – or, worse, that the father was a subject of the Third Reich? Or, more likely, thanks to Hitler, stateless?

Her colleagues with their influence, plus the whoppers she had unashamedly spun got the baby a US passport. It had been only slightly unorthodox. They'd known she was telling fibs, but they were gentlemen and they were gallants. With the last impediment to her return removed, save getting an actual seat on the Clipper, she waited. That had taken a month and another whopper from her gallants about her importance to the war effort back home.

'What's his name?' She heard a sudden demand. It was her father, bringing them back to present joy.

'William-Henry,' she replied, 'for Will and for – ' She stopped.

'His father?' Dr Gorton asked, coming to her aid without the slightest guile.

'I call him Henk,' she said, holding up.

'Well,' said her mother as she joined her husband to gaze at the child, 'he is certainly a pretty fellow. What gorgeous blue eyes he has, Father.'

Eleanor exchanged a look with Constance and Muriel. This, indeed, was a welcome if surprising turn.

Her brothers began to shepherd the family towards the exit. They could do the rest of their talking at home. Eleanor turned to see her father gazing down at the baby in his arms, love at first sight.

'Oh,' said Muriel, as they started walking to the cars, 'I nearly forgot. This arrived for you from your publisher. About four months ago. We thought of sending it to Lisbon, but it seemed safer to keep it here until you arrived.' She handed over a parcel in brown paper tied up securely with string.

Curious, Eleanor loosened the paper and what if *Finnegans Wake* didn't slip out. She had to grab it to stop it falling to the concourse floor. She gave a startled cry, more like a shriek, loud enough to attract attention. How, dear God, had this curse of a book followed her? The last she'd seen it, it was in the left breast pocket of the coat she'd handed over to Henk's lover. Was this some last cruel thrust into her heart?

She was so confused she didn't at first see what had happened to the book's cover. Was that a great hole in it? She looked closer. It was a gaping hole, and in the middle, something metallic. She tried opening the book but could not. It smelt of something familiar. Lancôme but wasn't that a top note of Schiaparelli as well?

'Oh my God,' she exclaimed.

These were the precious dregs of the perfume in her travelling cosmetics case fatefully pocketed with Mr Joyce in Claude's coat and the crème she'd bought in Pau in the other. How and why did the book smell better than she did?

Her brothers were hurrying her, but she was not for hurrying.

She turned to the back cover, which was undamaged. She opened it. On the inside was a message, printed in blue ink in spidery letters, rather like a child's.

We are sorry your book is wounded by a German bullet but if this book and your cosmetics are not in the pockets of your coat, Hugo would be dead so they save his life high in the Pyrénées. So, one more thing I thank you from my heart. We are come in Brasil and try one day to go in Palestine if they do not intern us, with love from Henk and Hugo and Kätzchen.

Only her brother's arms stopped Eleanor falling to the pavement. Doctors though they all were, her brothers and her father squabbled about what to do. Her sisters pushed them away.

'She's fainted, you idiots,' said Muriel, who ordered them to carry her to the nearby bench, where she revived Eleanor with a draught of whisky from a flask she carried in her purse for just such an occasion.

Eleanor slugged back more whisky, then grabbed the brown paper wrapping she'd absently let drop in her confusion and shock, and which Muriel had picked up. Her eyes scoured it urgently for a sender's address but there was none. She flipped the back pages to see if Henk had written more, but no, that was it, the past, the present and the future in one pithy message. She gazed at the damaged front cover of *Finnegans Wake*, at the flattened German bullet lodged through page after page. This surely was an act worthy of God's cry at the fall of man on page one of Mr Joyce's delirious prose, which only Sylvia, the agnostic, could pronounce. There was no retrieving it now. All Eleanor could remember was the beginning. *Baba-* something or other.

She hugged the book and she started to laugh and she couldn't stop laughing. She couldn't explain why she was laughing, except to say she was so happy, then she burst into tears. If the gift of William-Henry was the unexpected blessing and joy of life from a journey of death and loss and love, here, she realised, was the alpha and the omega of that journey, this ridiculous book that at last in its turbulent life had done something practical. Rescued from the grasping hands of the Gestapo, it had saved the life of one of the Gestapo's enemies. It was glorious proof that Henk was alive and had escaped Europe. Until her Muses got to work again, it was a perfect family tree for their tiny son. It was certainly more truthful than the story she'd concocted back in Lisbon.

Sylvia would understand her keeping it.

Eleanor knew that her war was over, at least for the time being. She knew also that she had a bit of making-up to do with God. He, whom she had turned on, had certainly not turned on her. The dust and ashes she'd tasted on the border with Spain were now those of repentance.

She heard the little boy cry. 'Hurry up, Elly,' her father called. 'He needs you.'

The
WOMAN FROM
SAINT GERMAIN

AUTHOR'S NOTE

This is a work of the imagination but grounded in a real world of time and place as much as I have been able. One starting point was the predicament of a young man like Henk. Another was literary Paris and Shakespeare & Company. Eventually, they joined up.

Immediate questions were: I already knew a bit about Henk's particular situation, but what happened to the 50% *Mischling* German-Jewish men in the Wehrmacht in 1940? If you were so categorised, was there any way to avoid being dismissed? If not, then what? Hide? Some did. Escape? Yes, but where and how? Through Vichy France to Spain was possible. How then did one find a passage across the demarcation line into Vichy France in late 1941? Where did one cross, and how?

Most illegal journeys followed a similar course; a rendezvous in a café with a local *passeur*, joining a disparate collection of people, locals merely avoiding the delays at the legal crossing points and black marketeers as well as the desperate fleeing the Nazis. Then followed an often perilous river crossing at night under the noses of German patrols. For those bent on escape, Lyon was then the most important way station in Vichy France between the demarcation line and the Spanish frontier. Until November 1942 when the Germans occupied all of France, the next hazard was the hardest of all if you didn't have a Spanish visa – which most did not – actually crossing the Spanish frontier.

What if you were Henk, bent on the same journey? I knew others fleeing Germany and Austria had done it but finding the location of the German Armistice Commission in Pau really fired my imagination.

All writers know half the fun of research comes from such seren-
dipitous discoveries, as long as research is not an end in itself. In these
days when the internet is under attack and subject to widespread
misuse, I want to make special acknowledgement of Wikipedia,
which is always my first port of call and always delivers me something
and somewhere useful on my writer's journey. The State Library of
Queensland is another; it still amazes me that I can access books and
articles from home via the SLQ. These are just two examples of the
fulfilment of the internet's early promise.

On Wehrmacht deserters, academic history journals in English
and German were useful sources, as much indirectly as directly – the
small detail hidden away in a footnote, for example. Also useful were
the many websites dedicated to the armies of the Second World War
run by enthusiastic amateur historians, who deserve special tribute.
YouTube was also a source of obscure and not-so-obscure documentaries and interviews, mostly in German.

Books and memoirs and documentaries about escaping Nazi-occupied Europe are legion, including many about the freedom
trails, which later in the conflict rescued so many downed Allied
airmen. People like the American diplomat Varian Fry loom large
in many of the stories from the early years of the war. Fritz Werfel
and Alma Mahler are but two of the more famous refugees who
succeeded in escaping. Many did not. The books *Love and War in the
Pyrenees* by Rosemary Bailey, *Through the Valley of the Shadow of Death*
by Gerda Bikales and *Cruel Crossing: Escaping Hitler Across the Pyrenees*
by Edward Stourton were useful to me.

Janet Flanner's wartime reports from Europe in the *New Yorker*
are compelling reading. Most useful for my story was 'The Escape
of Mrs. Jeffries', Flanner's report about an American woman who
remains in Paris until 1942 before escaping via Pau over the Pyrénées
and on to Madrid and Lisbon in 1943. From such precise reporting,

one gains priceless detail and flavour, for example, how bookshops played a vital role for people seeking passages to safety.

The subject of Americans in Paris is an industry in itself. Charles Glass's book *Americans in Paris* was a good source. The website of the American Cathedral in Paris offered up gems from its past through its magazine, available online, which I was able to use for flavour. Very useful for life in Paris under the occupation were the books *When Paris Went Dark* by Ronald Rosbottom and *Paris in the Third Reich* by David Pryce-Jones, the latter in particular for its evocative photographs.

Photographs from that time and place, now easily accessible on the net, are a source of wonder and inspiration. To see these faces looking out at you from this other country called the past is quite moving. Who are they? What are they telling us? Again, they fire up one's imagination.

I want to single out *The German War* by Nicholas Stargardt for helping me understand the motives, thoughts and actions of Bauer, the German detective.

Lastly, this story owes much to the remarkable Sylvia Beach, whose memoir *Shakespeare and Company* gave me the *Finnegans Wake* event, out of which I admit I have made a meal and for which I may not be thanked by Joyce purists. In a way, she stands as the story's *Ur-Mutter* and of the main character, Eleanor.

ACKNOWLEDGEMENTS

My thanks go to my dear partner, Alex, for his love and support; to my dear pal Blanche for the same, and for reading the MS and offering suggestions; to my film and TV colleague Catherine Millar also for reading and commenting; to my Sydney pals Paul and Chee Wee, who read the MS and told me they loved it – sweet words to a writer who at that point had heard only silence – and who helped Alex and me explore Pau and the Pyrénées; to my agents at Cameron's, Anthony Blair, who has stuck with me through more thin than thick, and Jeanne Ryckmans, who got the MS over the final hurdle. I am grateful to Fiona Henderson and all at Simon & Schuster for their great enthusiasm and efforts, and to editor Vanessa Mickan for her generous support and wonderful attention to detail. Finally, to the tiny abandoned cat that Vanessa found on one of her walks while editing the MS and which she took in and of course called 'Henk's Cat'. A photograph of it sat before me as I went through all the corrections.

Love it or your money back
Guaranteed
★★★★★
Read

At Simon & Schuster we know there is nothing quite like discovering a really special book. Those books that make thinking a pleasure; put a smile on your face (or tears in your eyes); reignite your daydreams; and transport you to somewhere entirely new. This is exactly what we want to give you with our **Guaranteed Five Star Read** selection.

However if you're not completely satisfied with one of our books which features the Guaranteed Five Star Read sticker on the cover, simply complete this form and return it to us with your copy of the book and your original receipt:

Name: ....

Address: ....

....

Email address: ....

Phone number: ....

Please post to
Simon & Schuster Australia Guaranteed Five Star Read
PO Box 448 Cammeray NSW 2062 Australia

This offer expires 29 February 2020.
For full terms and conditions please visit www.GuaranteedRead.com

Visit **www.simonandschuster.com.au** or follow us online for great book recommendations, free chapters, author interviews and competitions.

SIMON & SCHUSTER
AUSTRALIA
A CBS COMPANY